MINIONS.

Garrett Addison

ISBN-10: 0987509136:

ISBN-13: 978-0-9875091-3-0

ACKNOWLEDGMENTS

Many thanks to my friends who gave me the encouragement to keep writing, and those who didn't which only made me more determined.

This is a work of fiction. All characters appearing in this work are fictitious. Any resemblance to real persons, living or dead, is purely coincidental.

'Do not fear the devil and all his minions'
- Anonymous

Chapter - 1.

Devlin Bennett rifled through his backpack with each person who strode past as he sat in a small, mid-Melbourne park. He wasn't really looking for anything, but what was important in his ruse was that his eyes were cast downward in an effort to prolong his anonymity.

No matter how he looked at it, his day had not gone as he'd hoped. While he wasn't so naïve as to expect his life would return to normal immediately, he expected at least something from people he knew. A long time ago he could have described them as friends, but now apparently they were no more than acquaintances. Of the five people he'd planned to meet today, two wouldn't even speak with him, two met him only to say they couldn't, and perhaps more correctly *wouldn't* help, and the last wanted to add a little physical assault to the rejection.

For now though, sitting on a small grassed area in a mid-city park allowed him to participate in the world without being noticed. It was just what he needed. His scan of the newspaper didn't feature his photograph, which was both a blessing and a curse, but his notoriety would mean he was sure to be recognised eventually. Moving interstate and staying overnight in some suburban rat-hole might have bought him a day's grace, but he couldn't escape from the inevitable. He was sure to be identified sooner or later and his bruised ribs were too sore to face any confrontation that would require him to thrust his chest out to demonstrate whatever self-assurance remained.

It didn't take him long to summarise his situation; it was mid-afternoon, he was out of people he knew to try for a job, and he was down to small change in his pocket. His predicament wasn't ideal but he tried to keep positive. If nothing else he was well dressed in his court-room suit and he had his iPod. At least his attitude was far from beaten.

He recalled the simplicity of his hope to make a clean start, quietly confident that a job wasn't going to be too hard to find. He remembered actually stressing over whether to be picky, aim high and accept low, or take anything. If only he could get that chance. He hoped he wouldn't need to relocate again, but perhaps this too was unavoidable.

He looked at his phone willing it to ring, but he'd not had the chance to pass on the number to anyone so the odds if it ringing were decidedly remote. Then again, that it might ring was arguably more stressful. It almost warranted turning the phone off, but he couldn't bring himself to do it.

Amid his current stresses there remained something therapeutic about the dappled sunlight through the trees with a slight breeze. Eyes closed, relaxed and distracted, he failed to notice the approach of a hooded individual behind him.

It only took a second, but in one movement the previously unseen youth closed the last few steps, grabbed his phone and sprinted away. Instinctively, Devlin leapt to his feet in an effort to give chase, but he quickly appreciated the futility of any pursuit. He also accepted it was just a phone and not a particularly good one, and that doing anything would only draw attention to himself. He gave up before he began.

Devlin swore out of frustration and anger. Now devoid of any means of being contacted, there was little point in even reporting the incident when he didn't even have a contact address. He felt the heavy blow to his morale; his glass previously half full was now decidedly empty.

Desperate for options, he flitted through his wallet, naively hopeful of unearthing a previously hidden cash reserve but all he found was an otherwise forgotten business card. He picked up the card and fumbled it between his fingers, the action prompting him to remember its source. Glen. He thought of the man he'd met earlier on the train and his offer, even if it was invariably only made to be polite. *"Let me know how you get on,"* he'd said. He had nothing to lose. At worst, the guy could only hang up, but then again, there was even a possibility that the guy would give him a break.

He considered making a nervous call when it struck him that Glen's address was also on his business card and within walking distance. Sure, a call might save him another assault but it wouldn't allow him to assert his innocence in person, if it came to that. The fact that coinage for the call was going to bite deeply into his remaining cash was the clincher. He grabbed his backpack and set off.

Chapter - 2.

Nebojsa Kendic made no effort to hide what he thought of all those around him in the conference room. He wasn't there to be nice to these people, these insects, that was why his employer had asked him to be present. Internally described as their 'big gun' and externally as the 'attack dog', everyone knew he was there to push his cause over the line, whatever the cost. The net effect was the same; he would have *his* effect on people. It suited him perfectly.

He smiled at the very thought that he was now in demand. The contrast with before he'd come to this country justified his lapse into recollection. He missed the old days, not so much the people, but definitely the opportunities where under the pretence of ethnicity he could do many things. For this very reason, he enjoyed his time during the war immensely. He didn't need to pretend to have any social conscience, just as he didn't need to hide what drove him. He didn't need to consider the enemy people, though none of his peers did either, and through this common interest it was possibly the first time that he ever really mixed well with others. The truth, however, was that what he was, what he did, was not the result of some nationalistic fervour or pack mentality. Nebojsa was born the way he was, and he was simply fortunate to be born in a place and a time when his particular qualities would be well regarded.

That all good things come to an end was a problem. As the end of the war approached, there was a time when he actually worried for the future. He wasn't important enough to be indictable for any *alleged* war crimes, and a distinct lack of witnesses alive and so able to come forward was in his favour. It also helped that his efforts were typically on a smaller scale than the incidents that seemed to attract wider attention.

His time waiting for asylum to be processed was very trying. Forced into close co-habitation with others he was perpetually on edge. Worse still were the stories that others incarcerated with him felt necessary to share. He shelved his want to kill them like the scum that they were and focussed on using the time to his advantage. He listened intently, said nothing, and even taught himself to shed a tear at will. His efforts were noticed, just as he'd planned. That he kept to himself and was seen to cry regularly spoke volumes to the staff watching over them in their caged confines. They bandied terms like 'Post Traumatic Stress' and by simple analysis of geography managed to glean that he was simply too scarred. The fact that his home town was currently being investigated as the site of a massed cleansing helped him no end. There was no-one alive to challenge him, so who would argue at his assertion that he was alive only for the fact that he'd left the village days before the arrival of the squads. There was some truth in this in that he'd visited his family there, sure. But his family couldn't believe that their son was an active participant in the madness of the war. In that sense, he was, and wasn't, in equal measure. That his parents' bodies were found in their home, rather than needing to be identified from limited dental records after exhumation was testimony to the real fortunes of war.

Fortune continued to favour Nebojsa. Queued for psychoanalysis by the woman they variously called the 'pijan', the drunk, one day she called in sick. The following day, probably with only a marginally lower blood alcohol level, her records incorrectly noted that he had been processed without raising any red flags. The final hurdle in his migration was easier than he expected.

Now surrounded by natives of his new home, he remembered the anxiety he felt at the prospect of becoming like those around him. He didn't want his relocation to be the start of his demise, such that in years to come he'd look back and wonder what he'd become. Far from his homeland, he made a decision that his new setting would be the making of him, and that he would better himself thereafter. As a new migrant, he appreciated that he was expected to take one of two paths; assimilate, implicitly turning his back on his past, or join the sub-cultural enclaves of his homeland. Nebojsa chose neither. He didn't align himself to those with whom he shared a common language, because they were never '*his*' people and they meant nothing to him. He wasn't prepared to deny his history either; his history helped make him who he was. Who he is.

Chapter - 3.

When Devlin got to the address on the card his first reaction was to stress that he'd been misled by the corner store owner he'd asked for directions en-route. Simple logic however calmed him; he had the right street and the right suburb; he had the right address.

Glen's office was a pair of non-descript, single-fronted, double storied, Victorian shopfronts. On either side was a brothel, or Devlin assumed they were brothels on account of the large recessed entrances covered by closed circuit security cameras. Of course the business names were dead giveaways. The brothels and Glen's office, intentionally or otherwise, appeared to be the centrepiece of the street, like two feature clocks on a mantelpiece with a small, plain knick-knack between them.

On closer examination, Devlin thought the building could just as likely have been a private residence or a business. There was no signage to indicate it was a professional venue and the more Devlin looked, the more feasible it seemed that it could be part of the brothel complexes. He suddenly felt as if he'd just been let in on a joke. *Surely, Glen was all above board.* He might have been down, but he certainly wasn't out and while he'd convinced himself that he would probably take any job, he didn't want to have to confront *that* kind of job. He knew he could always walk away, but hoped that it wouldn't come to that.

He strode the final few steps to Glen's door and knocked a confident knuckle based rap, ignoring the adjacent buzzer. Devlin felt his heart race waiting for Glen to answer. He tried to calm himself, remembering he had nothing to lose.

Glen opened the door and immediately started talking. "You aren't late, but we don't have much time. Come on in. Let me sort you out a job." He turned and gestured for Devlin to follow. "Close the door and come this way."

Devlin almost baulked at the invitation and considered challenging Glen's assertion that he would need a job, but what was the point? The assumption was right on the money and didn't warrant any feigned attempt to convince anyone otherwise. He allowed himself to be led down a long corridor and into a sitting room with a semi-circle of large leather high-backed armchairs facing a wall of televisions. He sat adjacent to Glen in one of the central chairs. He scanned the screens before him, only then noticing that the right most screens appeared to display closed circuit vision of other rooms, presumably in the same building, before Glen blanked the screens *en-masse.*

"I know who you are. I know who your family is, who your father is and who he could, might have been," Glen began. "But that doesn't matter."

Devlin slid his hands under his thighs. "Not that it's a big deal or anything, but why didn't you tell me you knew who I was?" he asked. It was a big deal.

"You and your family have had more than your share of media coverage."

"So how much do you know?"

"What I know about you isn't really important. What *is* important, however, is getting you started."

Devlin struggled a gesture between incalculable gratitude and cautious apprehension. He made to say something but no words seemed fitting.

"Welcome to I.M.A. Independent Media Analysis." Glen smiled briefly. "We started doing media analysis, but we evolved with technology until I inherited some money from my uncle. Actually, he was particularly wealthy and left me a lot of money. Everything really."

"Sorry to hear that. Were you close?"

"My uncle was a bastard," Glen said, pausing only to drink from his bottle of water. "Let's just say that he owed me an apology and my family disowned me for my very accusations. My hope he would apologise died with him."

Glen was quiet, distracted. Sensing an uncomfortable pause, Devlin waited for him to continue.

"Anyway," Glen re-focussed. "I was checking my email one day while watching an old movie with a guy on his death bed when it came to me. What if I could extract one last message from my bastard uncle? It made me think. I figured, what if someone could store an email to be sent when they die? *'LastGaspStore'* was born."

Devlin couldn't help a look of shock. "YOU started LastGasp'?"

Glen smiled. "Everyone's reaction is the same. Everyone's heard *of* LastGaspStore, or *LastGasp'*, but no-one *really* knows much about it. That's what's so surprising given that about 50% of the population are active users."

"Where's the surprise? Maybe your numbers are wrong."

"Until now it's been a private company, and so I don't *need* to advertise my numbers to keep the share price inflated. More important though is that I need that secrecy, for both the good of my members and to prevent the competitors and hackers. There are actually many more users, but not all of them are active."

"Why the big deal about wanting to prevent hackers?"

"Perhaps this would be clearer if you understood more." Glen took a breath and started what seemed a well-practised summary. "A LastGaspStore user gets to write a message which will be delivered after their death to a number of people that they identify. User accounts are free for a nominal number of addressees. Additional addressees or additional messages, each with their own distribution list can be purchased." Glen paused, as if no matter how many times he'd given his summary it never failed to yield the same questions. Now he just waited.

"Who would pay for an email after you die?"

"Not everyone is thirty-something and single like you, Devlin. Some people like to have their house in order, and as for your question about paying, most users just use the free account. It gives them the means to say things that perhaps they never got to say, or wanted to say, or maybe they just want to make sure that a secret doesn't die with them. The catch is that they can't edit their message. For that, they need to pay."

"So if most users don't pay a cent, who makes the money?"

"One of the interesting elements of the system is how *active* users are identified. Periodically, users are sent confirmatory emails or are required to touch base to ensure they are kept active. In much the same way, all message addressees are emailed. This provides the means to ensure the addressee can be contacted in the event of a user's death. All of these emails represent focussed contact with a particular demographic. Various parties are only too keen to pay for the opportunity to be mentioned or advertised in our periodic contact. Life insurance companies, for example, are always on the lookout for people doing wills and starting to think about their own mortality. I might add that LastGaspStore secrets are not for sale.

"There's no competition. Small players periodically come and go, lured by the niche and advertising revenue. But this isn't like your average *dot-com*. They always underestimate the many pitfalls in what they are trying to achieve, and there are more than you'd believe. I know mainly because I've had to overcome them all, some before and some after someone found them. For example …" Glen stopped and checked his watch. "Actually, hang on a minute. We need to watch this," he announced before turning his attention to one of the televisions. He reached for his remote control and operated it to re-activate the bank of screens, increasing the volume of one and muting all others. "Top row, second from the left" he said, directing Devlin to the correct screen.

Glen's timing in tuning into the television was not perfect. They'd missed the first part of the featured business news report, but Devlin picked up on the nature of the item immediately. Glen smiled a proud, confident smile, while Devlin took a little more time to absorb the news. LastGaspStore was to be purchased by the largest internet company of them all. The price was not disclosed but rumours abounded.

Glen silenced the television on the completion of the report. "I took the liberty to include you in my staff lists prior to the sale."

"Thanks," Devlin said cautiously.

"The big upside is that all of my staff have just obtained a sizeable chunk of stock. You included."

Devlin's appreciation settled in and overpowered his inherent scepticism. "Holy crap! Thank-you!"

"Anyway," Glen continued, ignoring Devlin's fervour. "It's easier to buy than to develop from startup and attract adverse publicity and associated hits on your share price when you get it wrong. Thus the sale."

"But why would they bother to buy into the niche? Websites are a dime a dozen."

"LastGaspStore is not a website," Glen paused. "It's a service, and frankly it doesn't worry me if it goes out of vogue. Perhaps you might appreciate things more if you understood the nature of our members' messages. It's about time for a staff meeting anyway."

Chapter - 4.

The new day hit Malcolm Venn hard. He woke restrained in what could only have been a hospital bed. He hated restraints, and this was not the first time.

He looked around the room keen for any cue to aid his orientation, but all he saw was the solitary, empty seat beside his bed. The room was small with little space beyond the clinical stainless steel bed with dropdown rails, and the obligatory locker for whatever personal effects he'd managed to keep hold of. At least it was a single room so the sounds and smells were his own; something which could not be said in a room shared with others.

He did his best to recall what he could of the night before. He remembered enough to understand what had happened even though he lacked the details. More important, however, was his recollection of the plan. His plan extended beyond some gaping holes in his short term memory, and he remembered it with perfect clarity.

With little else to do, he took stock on what he could gauge of his health. His forearms and hands were heavily bandaged, but there was no pain despite the bandaging, until he tried to clench his fists. He felt fine. Better than fine really, but over the years he'd learnt to not offer superlatives, good or bad. He resented that others could describe themselves as feeling 'great', or 'really bad' and it would be treated as just part of the ebb and flow of life, but anyone with bipolar disorder knew to keep these thoughts to themselves. Experience had taught him that any hint of honesty on his part would always come back to haunt him, and he'd regret it.

Wriggling in the bed, he was alerted to the presence of a catheter. He closed his eyes to remind himself that being bed-bound for longer than just overnight was just part of the plan. He called out to anyone within earshot, "I'm awake now!" There was little more to do but manage his concern and wait.

The door to his room opened before too long and a cute woman entered sporting a non-committal smile. "Morning, sweetheart. I'm Mary and I'll be your nurse for a while." She sat next to the bed after struggling to adjust the pillow under Malcolm's immobile shoulder.

The opaque glass in the solitary window beside his bed hinted no more than the fact that it was daylight outside. "I'd say good-morning, Mary, but sadly I'm not sure if that would be accurate."

"Well, it isn't morning. I'm on the afternoon shift." Mary was relaxed as she spoke, but seemed more fixated on the door than Malcolm. "You've got a visitor outside who wants to speak to you."

"Police?" he asked, though in reality he expected this the moment that he woke and became aware of his surroundings.

Mary nodded. "Are you ready for visitors?"

"You tell me."

"You have the right to keep them waiting …"

"That's not what I meant," said Malcolm. The nurse had obviously presumed guilt based on the presence of police at the door. That he was in trouble for something wasn't an extraordinary leap of faith, considering. "What am I on?"

"You're not on *truth serum* if that's what you're asking!" she said with a laboured laugh. Malcolm sensed the tone in the nurse's voice as she looked to gauge whether he was being unduly and unreasonably paranoid. "You've been asleep for a few days. There was too much of everything else in your bloodstream for us to give you anything! So no meds."

Not perfect, but acceptable, Malcolm thought. "So my thoughts are my own?"

"I'm not the doctor, but you've had nothing since your admission."

Malcolm believed the nurse. No doctor would have prescribed anything for him once the results of his blood tests were available. He'd made sure that as many drugs as possible were represented in his cocktail, though it did require a little research to concoct something that wasn't lethal.

"And your visitor?"

"Just tell me what you know about me first."

"Alright," she began; a little hesitant. "You were admitted after having been singled out for erratic, but not violent behaviour. You had no identification on you."

"So you don't know who I am?"

"No, which is possibly at least part of the reason why the police are here. Then there's the matter of the blood on you when you were admitted. Quite a lot of blood really, and while you had suffered some injuries," she said, pointing to his bandages, "not all of it was yours."

"Anything else?"

"No. And you haven't had any medication."

Perfect. Malcolm wriggled in his bed to get comfortable. "Of course, now that I'm awake there's no legal reason why I should be restrained, right?"

"Unless there's concern that the patient poses a threat to themselves, staff or anyone else."

"Well, I'm not harming you or others, and I want them off. And we can lose the tubes too."

Mary shrugged cautiously and set about removing the Velcro straps that were securing Malcolm's chest, shoulders and forearms. "This isn't your first hospital visit, is it?"

"I don't think that's significant in my immediate care," Malcolm replied arrogantly. He watched as each of his bindings was loosened and then removed. "And I want to see the doctor before I see them," he said, pointing toward the door with his newly freed arm.

The nurse nodded. "I'll be back for the catheter." She left the room carrying the restraints. She locked the door as soon as she was outside and Malcolm pictured her briefing the police with what she had learnt since he'd woken.

So far, so good.

Chapter - 5.

Glen led Devlin past the kitchen heading for the only door leading off a short corridor. "Look up and smile," Glen said, pointing to the series of video cameras along the length of the hall.

They stopped at the door and Glen entered a code into a keypad while he used his body to obscure what he was doing. Devlin stood, fixated on the heavily reinforced door frame; the polished steel standing out clearly adjacent to the painted walls of the corridor. The door opened and with it came a wall of loud music.

Glen invited Devlin to enter. "We call this room the 'bunker', for obvious reasons," he said at a shout above the noise.

Devlin nodded a greeting to two men and a woman, standing around a long hardwood polished table covered with five laptops, while waiting to be introduced. He surveyed the room, bathed in bright artificial light, noting the single door at one end and another bank of televisions on the opposite wall. The door sealed home behind them with a low vibration.

One of the three responded to a gesture by Glen and silenced the music. He was tall, wearing just jeans and an old t-shirt and young; Devlin guessed about twenty or so years old.

"This is Ikel," Glen started the introductions. "Clearly, my staff have all heard the news. Though I would have thought that they were paid enough to not worry about such trivial matters?"

"I know, but it's just so cool," Ikel replied. "Actually, my name is Michael, but you might as well call me Ikel. I had a cold when Glen and I met, and he thought I said 'Ikel'. I guess you had to be there, but the name stuck."

Glen introduced the remaining pair. "And this is David and Lori."

The woman smiled openly. She was probably average height, Devlin thought, with short cropped auburn hair, and wore torn, designer denim jeans and a t-shirt a size too small with 'Get I.T. here!' boldly written on the front. The t-shirt was marketing at its best as only on a second glance did Devlin even notice the corporate logo to the outside of each of her breasts. He tried his best not to stare, but the shirt was intended to be worn by women only and larger breasted women at that. "I'm Lori. It's short for Loretta, which I hate, so I'd prefer 'Lori'."

David was the last to meet Devlin. "So you're the fresh meat?" he mused. "I'm just kidding, it isn't bad here," he added, rubbing his eyes beneath his sun-glasses which made perfect sense in the glare of the room.

"You are on a plane that has just been taken over by terrorists," Glen began after coaxing everyone to take a seat. "For arguments sake, these are decidedly nice terrorists who give all passengers a sheet of paper and a pencil. What do you write?"

Devlin resented being put on the spot. "I'm not the best person to ask. I guess others …"

"I'm not asking other people. I'm asking you," Glen insisted.

"Do I know if the terrorists will deliver my message?"

"A great question, but you're stalling. Assume 'yes', just answer."

"OK," Devlin conceded. "There's nothing I'd want to say."

"Not a note to your mother?" Glen said with raised eyebrows. He turned his attention to his remaining staff. "What *would* others write? More to the point, what *do* others write?"

Ikel spoke first. "Regrets."

"Love notes and things left unsaid," added Lori solemnly.

"Confessions. Pleas for absolution. Desperate attempts to make peace," David contributed in turn.

Devlin wasn't convinced. "OK. I'd still probably just enjoy the view from the plane," he offered defiantly.

All eyes centred on Glen. "Lori, David, Ikel, I'd like you to meet Devlin Bennett. Facing death, he is possibly the only one in the world with nothing to say. He is also the same Devlin Bennett, recently released from remand, all but convicted of manslaughter, but acquitted, or really had the conviction effectively overturned on a technicality. All fairly remarkable notoriety of his own doing despite a famed family pedigree, but incarceration has, apparently, neither humbled nor hardened him."

Devlin was still not used to being outed and feared the reaction of others, but the outing could have been worse. There were no gasps, sighs of recognition or looks of disapproval.

Glen took a deep but quiet breath. "Devlin, you're welcome here and you are among people you can trust. Everyone has a past. Everyone *here* has a past. Lori was a prostitute, Ikel is a drug dealer and user, and David here used to be a Catholic priest. But that's not why you're each here."

Glen settled himself. "It struck me once, some time ago as I sat late one night having a coffee on a warm summers' night. Across the road, there was a woman having an argument with some man, presumably her boyfriend. As it grew heated, the woman became more and more scared. Eventually, he all but threw her into a taxi and off they went. Everyone returned to their mundane chatter and the night went on. She was later found, beaten to death.

"And this affects me, how?" Devlin asked.

"It doesn't. My point is that I knew *my* life would have been a whole lot different had I spoken one timely word in that poor woman's defence. I didn't need to be a hero, and I didn't need to make a difference to others. I only needed to make a difference for myself. I'm offering you the same opportunity."

"I'm too cynical to want to make a difference," said Devlin. "Sorry to disappoint."

"Cynics and sceptics make better readers," said Glen.

"What's a reader?"

"It's just a nickname for your role, the others here will explain." Glen nodded to each of his charges and turned for the door. He left the room being sure to secure the door behind himself.

Chapter - 6.

As soon as Glen left the room, Ikel restored the stereo, but not to the same excessive volume as before. It was only then that Devlin became aware of the effect that Glen being in the room had on the others. "Do you always shrink into the background when Glen's around and then burst to life when he's gone?"

"He's a good man," Lori began. "I've been here for about six weeks, a little less than Ikel, and we're still largely in awe. David's been here for longer, but he's only marginally more comfortable with him. Anyway, it's time you got started." She invited Devlin to sit beside her at one of the otherwise idle computers. "Formally, your role is *'Media Analyst'*, but we prefer the name *reader*. Glen's a decidedly clever guy, and we figure he chose the title because it looks better on a résumé when we eventually move on."

"Does it work? Has anyone who left actually kept in touch?" Devlin asked.

"Not to my knowledge," replied Lori. "It's a great job though and staff turnover is fairly low."

"Turnover isn't low, it's just periodic. You just haven't experienced anyone leaving yet," David corrected, while remaining fixated on his computer screen. "People leave just as in any job, and no, I didn't keep in touch with them."

"So what do I do?" Devlin asked.

"Can you read?" David muttered.

"We do mainly read," said Lori. "But there *is* a little more. Technically, no reading or manual intervention is really necessary because it's all automated, but there's a need for some degree of *quality control.*"

"You proof read people's letters?"

"No, we don't proof read, and legally we couldn't make changes anyway. Especially since September 11, Glen was keen that LastGasp' didn't become the last bastion of fanatics and martyrs."

"That's very noble of him. Was this for Western sensibilities or to protect his brand?" Devlin offered, immediately appreciating that his comment was not well received.

"You haven't known Glen for very long but I'm more than confident that you'll come to like and admire him as we do." David spoke maturely, drawing approving smiles from Lori and Ikel. "Until then, keep your bullshit thoughts on him to yourself."

"Sorry to offend," Devlin said unconvincingly.

Lori picked up from where she'd left off. "Anyway. Readers read the messages. We just read them. If something isn't right we flag it and the system handles it. Nothing to it really."

"So what stops us changing them?"

"There's no means for us to edit them. The entire system really dances on a legal tightrope. If we could edit messages then we could conceivably be exposed to scrutiny about who actually composed the messages. Do you know anything about 'libel'?" Lori asked, not waiting for an answer. "The messages can't be sent until the user is confirmed to be dead, otherwise imagine what would happen with a message revealing a sordid past or some other secret that was too juicy to live with, but too good to die with. That's why controls are in place to ensure they aren't sent prematurely. Glen's a genius really, in more ways than one."

"So readers read *every* message?" Devlin asked. He struggled a little mental arithmetic before adding, "Just how many messages are there?"

"We *can* read all of them, but we generally don't. The system automatically flags the ones which need a little human filtering and then a percentage for quality control. God only knows how many there are, but logically we only need to read them when they are added or changed. So volume varies; sometimes we're pretty busy and sometimes substantially less so. We all read a lot more than we need to. Glen reads too."

"I still think that Glen reads every message," Ikel commented.

Lori smiled and explained. "Ikel has a theory that Glen reads every single message. We know he reads a lot, but we don't think he'd do 100%."

"He knows about every single one I've flagged and he doesn't sleep so that would have to free up some time," Ikel continued his case.

"So all you do is read?" Devlin asked, not interested in the distraction of Ikel's theory.

"Yes, and no," said Lori. "Yes, we mainly read messages and related research, unless there's an issue making contact."

"Make contact? Why?"

"Remember what LastGasp' is all about. People write messages to be sent, typically as email, after they die, but sometimes it's up to us to hand-deliver them. The purist might argue that there's no point in going to that much effort, to send a message which is only effectively obligated to be sent by a, now, dead person.

But Glen is a big believer in his obligations. Anyway, here's how it all works."

Devlin positioned himself so he could see Lori's screen as she clicked and typed. It looked simple enough; select something, read it, then attribute it with a big green 'tick' icon, or any or many of a series of red 'flags'. Clearly Lori held Glen in high regard and as far as she was concerned, Glen had thought of everything. She digressed into lengthy technical explanations until she saw his eyes glaze over and this forced her to rein in her language.

"The system isn't airtight," Lori pointed out. "To be airtight, you'd have to lock everyone out, but the reality is that anyone who wants to get in will get in if they are determined enough. Meanwhile, any and all access is logged. What you read, how long it took you to read it, what you rubber-stamp or vet, and you absolutely can't change anything."

"Maybe I'm missing something, but I don't get why this bunker is really necessary."

"The security is just something that we all accept. It isn't something to be challenged. On top of that, the most brilliant thing is that all users are basically anonymous, even to us readers, right up until we need to hand deliver a message, if hand delivery is absolutely necessary."

"Why the big deal in anonymity?" Devlin insisted.

"How's he coming along, Lori?" Glen enquired as he re-entered the room.

"I think he's just keen to get into it. He's critical enough."

"I'm not critical, just naïvely sceptical," Devlin sniped defensively. "And frankly I still don't really know what goes on here."

Glen smiled. "Perfect. Thanks guys, I'll take it from here."

Chapter - 7.

Malcolm understood that to even appear to be in a hurry to be released from hospital would not be in his best interests. Such behaviour would only be interpreted as guilt. Even outside of his current environs, it would not take a large stretch to deduce that someone covered in blood was guilty of something.

He knew he couldn't present himself as angry, confused, aggressive, moody, depressed, elated or any one of the myriad of other emotional adjectives that would potentially be interpreted as markers of mental health issues. The system was nothing if it wasn't predictable and this was, after all, in his favour. Provided he didn't pose an immediate threat, there would be no reason for him to remain at the hospital long. All he had to do was wait, behave reasonably and he'd be able to return to his projects.

The nurse returned to the room, this time accompanying a recently post pubescent male with the obligatory stethoscope draped around his neck. Malcolm figured that the guy had to be a doctor, and it took all of his control to resist a quip with references to *'Doogie Howser, M.D.'*. The nurse handed the doctor the patient file, and he read with a concentration that defied his adolescent appearance.

"Hi, I'm Doctor Nick Turner. I'm the resident. How are you feeling?" Satisfied that he understood enough of the patient history, the Doctor began before he'd actually finished reading.

"Fine. I got carried away, that's all."

The doctor finally gave his patient his undivided attention. "What's your name?"

"That's not why I'm here."

"I'm trying to help. What harm would it be to tell me your name?"

"No harm, but it also wouldn't help me or you. So earn your pay and tell me how you plan to '*help*'?" Malcolm didn't need to be difficult, but there was also no necessity for him to be excessively *compliant* either. "I'll bet I'm one of what, fifty, maybe more, who've crossed your books recently."

"OK, so …" the doctor tried to talk.

"I'm not finished. My blood-work would have ruled out an attempted overdose, so you don't have any grounds for any psych intervention, so don't waste my time. I've got things to do."

The doctor thought for a moment. "Eighty one fellow revellers were admitted in the forty eight hours following the festival. Of those, only nine, including you, are still with us. And yes, none of them are demonstrating the same clarity and mental state without paranoia as you."

"So, *Doogie*, can I go?" Malcolm couldn't help himself.

"There are police outside who want a chat. I'm fine for you to go if they give the nod," the doctor conceded, ignoring the 'Doogie' tag.

"Send them in, but you'll need to stick around. I won't speak to them without an impartial witness, and you two at least have a mandate to advocate for me."

"Sorry, but I don't have time for that," the Doctor replied returning his attention to the patient file. "I'm sure they'll co-ordinate a lawyer for you at your request."

"We're all busy, Doctor.   A lawyer imply guilt, so I don't need one. I just need a witness to listen to what I have to say."

"The Doctor can go, but I'll stay," Nurse Mary offered some middle ground to appease the request.

"If you want your bed back, you'll both need to stay when I speak to the Police." Malcolm noted that his comment restored the Doctor's attention and knew he retained substantial bargaining power.

"I can stay for ten minutes, no more," the doctor said with more than a little reluctance.

The nurse allowed a solitary, thickset, older man in a cheap suit to enter. "My name is Detective Alan Reymond and I'd like to ask you a few questions."

"Can I call you Alan?" The guy looked older than Malcolm expected.

The Detective sighed indignantly. "No, but if you'd like to be informal, then perhaps if you tell me your name, then you can call me *'Detective'.*"

"Can I first confirm that I have been advised by Nurse Mary and Doctor *Doogie* here that I'm not currently medicated." He paused, allowing the Detective to exchange confirmatory glances with the Doctor and the Nurse. "My name is Malcolm Venn." He liked the way the name rolled off his tongue and it was sad that he'd have to come up with an alternative.

"Where do you live?"

"N.F.I."

"Do you mean N.F.*A.*, 'no fixed address'?"

"No, I mean N.F.I, *No Fucking Idea.*"

"Was your ID stolen?"

"No, I just don't need it."

"You'll need some identification before we can confirm your identity."

"No. *You* need some ID.to confirm my identity. I know who I am."

"Alright," Detective Reymond sighed. "I *need* to confirm who you are."

"Confirmed identity is ordinarily a requirement before your discharge can be processed," Doctor Turner added while checking his watch.

"Ordinarily so, yes, but you and I both know that it is *not* mandatory," Malcolm derided the doctor's comment.

"Well, it's necessary for billing, and …" the Doctor started before being cut off.

"The care I've been afforded is publically funded. Whether it was provided under the pretence of 'care' or protecting the community at large, it's still free."

"Thanks Doctor. I'll take it from here," the Detective nodded to the Doctor before returning his attention to Malcolm. "I understand that you're keen to be discharged, but until I'm satisfied as to your identity, you aren't going anywhere." He spoke in a calm, age mellowed tone. "And there's the matter of the other party's blood. Hospital policy notwithstanding, I'm primarily interested in the origins of the blood."

Malcolm was surprised that it had taken the Detective so long to broach this point. He settled in to give his account of the blood's source. He told of where he'd been living and of Angie. He said enough to get the Detective interested but no more. Such was his plan.

Chapter - 8.

Glen escorted Devlin back out to the lounge room with the comfortable chairs. "What do you think so far?"

"It's difficult to say," replied Devlin. "I still don't know what the hell it is that I'll be doing. All I really know is that you're clearly a clever guy who's carved quite a lucrative niche, you've got a system for which security seems a near paranoid concern, and you've got a handful of staff who admire you as a demi-god."

"Well, so far you're pretty right, though I'll have to speak to the others that I'm only revered as a *demi*-god," Glen said dryly, adding, "I'm joking, Devlin."

"How long have you known about my history?" Devlin asked.

"Your history is not particularly different to a number of my employees, past and present, but that's not what's important." Glen juggled a small white box between his hands. "What *is* actually important is whether you choose to stay or leave."

"I'm staying," Devlin announced without hesitation.

Glen smiled and offered a congratulatory handshake. "I'd hoped as much." He tossed the little box onto Devlin's lap, "otherwise that box of business cards would be a waste." He handed Devlin a bulky envelope. "Here are your system login details, a security pass for the building, some starter cash and a phone."

"My phone got stolen today, so that's a real bonus."

Glen raised his eyebrows at the comment and sighed, but moved on immediately. "You'll need to change the password and PIN when you first use them. It's most important that you, and only you, use your login and know your access details. Incidentally, the phone number isn't listed. The rest of our numbers are already programmed into the phone. The rest of the security arrangements will be explained by the others."

Only when Glen stopped talking did Devlin peak inside the envelope. On seeing a mass of cash, he quickly flitted through the wad of notes looking to approximate the value, but stopped his count at $2000. "How much money is here?"

"There's ten thousand there. I'm not paying in advance, it's just that if I'd needed to use someone to find you, they'd try and charge me. As our meeting earlier saved me their finder's fee that I would have happily paid, then you might as well have it. In any case, I figured that you'd appreciate a little financial assistance."

"Thank-you!" Devlin struggled to focus amid his turn of fortune.

"If I may continue?" Glen looked to calm Devlin's fervour. "I pay cash, so up to you as to what you tell the tax-man. Mention my name at the bank up the street and they'll look after you. The establishments next door will look after you too if you tell them where you work."

"Brothels aren't my thing, but thanks anyway."

"Moral high ground isn't my thing either. What else?" said Glen, moving on immediately. "You can decide when you work. Most readers end up working long hours. I don't make them, but of course I don't mind. Bear in mind that I want only that they do it for themselves, not me."

"I'll work hard!" Devlin declared.

Glen was more serious than Devlin expected. "The money you are paid is not to buy your trust, nor do I think this money buys your allegiance. You do what's right. That said, I hope you're happy here and stay for a while."

"I may never leave," said Devlin, keen to arouse a smile in Glen, but without success.

"Everyone leaves for a reason. Sooner or later everyone tires of just being a reader," Glen said sincerely. "Everyone goes when they are ready, as will you.

"Anyway, join the others and they'll teach you the rest. I have other things to do."

Glen walked towards the front door, and Devlin watched him leave the building on the closed circuit televisions. His euphoric mood was interrupted by a tone from an unfamiliar phone indicating that a new text message had arrived. It took a moment for him to realise that the source was his new phone. After fumbling through the phone menu, he read the message.

```
Casey Lawrence is now
dead.
```

Devlin was initially puzzled before appreciating that the message had been sent to a phone number, not specifically to him. Even though Glen described the number as unlisted, it was not unreasonable that the number had previously belonged to someone else. He wrote off the call as misdirected and headed for the bunker.

Chapter - 9.

Ikel beamed a welcoming smile as soon as he saw Devlin enter the bunker. "We all knew you'd stay!." Lori and David were less animated in their welcome, but still they looked happy that there was a newcomer to the fold.

"Was the admiring staff exhibition purely for my benefit?" Devlin asked. "I have to know."

"I'll speak for myself," Ikel started. "I like him. He's a good guy. You'll like him."

"We'll have to see," Devlin said, inviting discord.

"He's forthright typically because he *is* right. He speaks his mind and will always tell the truth," David spoke defensively. "What you do thereafter is your problem, not his. It's the same with this work."

"Point taken," Devlin shrugged. "Perhaps I'll understand your devotion when I understand what I really have to do."

"Hey, I'm unskilled, doing a worthwhile job that I enjoy and to cap it all off, the money is good!" Ikel contributed with a smile to lighten the mood. "Had it not been for him, I'd be in a gutter or ditch somewhere by now for sure."

"Think what you like Devlin. It's your life," David said abruptly, voiding Ikel's attempt.

"Care for a snack?" Lori piped in. She stood from her seat and coaxed Devlin and Ikel to the door.

Clear of the work room, Lori headed for the kitchen. "When David gets like this, we normally give him a little space. David's right of course, and you'll learn this for yourself in good time, but stress gets at him just as it will get to you."

"I'll bear that in mind." Devlin was momentarily distracted by a tone from his phone. It took some time of fumbling with the new device before he understood that another text message had been received. He resisted the urge to view the message while Lori was talking.

"You don't *need* to agree with David to work here, but you'll want to stop being so provocative, at least until you get to know the ropes. Perhaps then you might see things differently." Lori spoke confidently, more to defend David than to put Devlin at ease.

Ikel led the way to the armchairs. "You'll like it here," he said warmly.

"Are you a reader too?" Devlin asked. "You don't strike me as having the same background as Lori."

"I'm a reader, just like you. And no, I 'spose I prove you don't need heaps of school to work here because it's not just reading." Ikel drank from a can he'd grabbed in the kitchen. "Ready to know what we do? "

"Now's as good a time as any," said Lori. "The system essentially looks after itself, so we really just do the bits that Glen doesn't want automated. The truth is that our reading doesn't just identify the martyrs, and then it depends on how we flag and the associated 'protocol'."

"Protocols?"

"Relax," said Ikel. "It's just how Glen describes what happens with each flag. He won't say more."

"OK, so what happens with the messages?" asked Devlin

"That depends on what you read, but it's not that simple," answered Lori. "You have to remember that what you can glean from the messages couldn't be used directly, if only to protect the source."

"So people are stupid enough to confess to a life of guilt and then we tell the police?"

"Tell me, Devlin, how did you first hear of LastGasp'?" asked Lori.

"I saw it mentioned in a newspaper years ago."

"That hardly narrows it down. We rarely make the news now because it's the same old story. The case that you refer to was probably the result of our delivery of a message implicating someone in some illegality. This would have resulted in a volley of questions about the legal side. 'Should the government or police have the right to access private data?' and 'Does LastGasp' have a legal or moral obligation to pass on information'."

"Does LastGasp'? Do we?" Devlin asked still unclear as to where the revelations were heading.

"No, the government can't *legally* get access to our data, and we don't need to pass on information," Lori sub-consciously emphasised the legal word. "Glen has made being a step ahead of the law a way of life. Privacy laws, for starters, couldn't and still can't touch us. Such is the benefit of a paper legal system in a digital age."

Devlin paused to consider what he'd been told. "I don't believe that people would implicate themselves and I don't believe that the police couldn't get at the data."

"People really are *all* too willing to implicate themselves. Guilt is a terrible thing and it makes people do things that you wouldn't predict. And trust me, LastGasp' is secure. I know this because if people were to get into LastGasp', LastGasp' simply wouldn't exist. It would be drowned under an endless stream of lawsuits from breaches of privacy and resultant defamation and libel issues. Then would come the second tier of lawsuits after LastGasp' hit the front pages, lawsuits for breaches of privacy just because privacy couldn't be assured."

"Surely there are hackers who could get in."

"Possibly, and but purely on account of the fact that I'm not being issued with a new summons every minute, I'm confident that the system *is* secure."

Devlin was not convinced. "Government agencies must be able to get in and you'd never know it."

"If the Government got in then they'd just make the information public but the protocols seem to spread the information to the right parties."

"So the police *do* get the information?"

Glen interrupted on his return, surprising everyone. "Thanks Lori, Ikel. Leave us."

Devlin let himself be coaxed back to the comfortable armchairs as Lori and Ikel moved away. "It's a little odd that no-one knows about your protocols, Glen."

"Yes, I heard what you said and how ably Lori was explaining things.   To answer your question, protocols are in place for everything we can glean from messages."

"So what happens to the information?"

"When you're ready I'll explain."

"What about privacy? Surely there must be laws against this."

"Privacy is a funny thing, Devlin. For so long as the system is secure then everyone's privacy is assured. Amongst other things, for privacy to be legally breached, it must be proven that information was actually passed on. But privacy also works for us. Privacy is why the protocols are secret. Privacy absolves you from responsibility if LastGaspStore was ever breached because you are not privy to the protocols." Glen smiled smugly.

"So who gets the information?"

"Never you mind. I'll ask you what you think in a few days. For now, I'll write off your concerns as a naïve lack of understanding." Glen turned to Lori and Ikel who had remained distant but within earshot. "Let him in."

Chapter - 10.

Where previously Devlin had been merely shown the system, now he was allowed free reign to actually *use* it, drawing on Lori and Ikel for assistance where necessary. David passively observed the tutelage, seemingly ready to intercede should his greater experience be warranted.

The first message Devlin read was benign and sentimental, just as he'd expected. The text was a series of words from a married family man to his wife and family. As he read, he was more than aware of his own cynicism. The guy had taken up the free package; a simple means to ensure that his family knew he loved them. Words left either unsaid, or unproven, or perhaps words that needed to be reiterated.

Message after message followed with nothing that sparked any interest. Devlin could feel his enthusiasm starting to wane; a well-paying job was nothing if it meant a life of tedium, but it was a start, perhaps until the heat died off.

"Here's one!" announced Ikel. "Have a read when it comes your way."

The screen before Devlin alerted him to a new message, lacking in any identification just like the rest, other than an icon indicating that it had been marked for peer review. He started to read and immediately came to the realisation that this was not a message of love. Nor was it a message of regret. Instead, Devlin read a sad tale of a lonely man and his rave-like justification for his personality and his many failings. This was someone writing his own epitaph for anyone who might be interested, but Devlin felt that few would cry for the passing of this man primarily on account of the thinly veiled references to his penchant for young boys. The paedophilic references turned his impression of member #1009345 from worthy of passing disinterest, to one of disgust. "You're kidding me!" he announced to the others.

"We don't get many of them, but we do get them," Lori sighed.

"What now?" Devlin asked.

"Flag it, and move on. Yours is not to judge any further," David said authoritatively. Lori and Ikel nodded their concurrence.

"It could have been worse. The last one like that I read was more masochistic and graphic. At least this one demonstrated some decorum," said Lori.

"Oh yeah. He was a real sick fucker!" Ikel said, determined to say something.

"Ikel, quiet," David started calmly, pausing only to find the right words. "In another life at a time such as this, I would have espoused the virtues of forgiveness and love, and for my own benefit, sought solace in the Judgement. I turned my back on that life because I learned to understand that Judgement takes too long. Now, you need to learn to be comfortable that flagging the message is all the judgement that's needed from you."

Devlin was nowhere near as collected in reply. "The guy's a paedophile! I'm glad he's dead! There's my judgement!"

"First things first. These messages haven't been sent yet. This guy is still alive, he's just getting his house in order," said David.

"It might be a *ghost* anyway," Ikel added.

"A ghost is a bogus or dummy member, created by persons unknown," David pre-empted Devlin's next logical question while reaching for his drink. "They keep us on our toes."

"Why would someone create a ghost?"

"Remember that LastGasp' is a miracle of legal loopholes," Lori answered while David drank from his mug. "All it needs is one security breach to bring it unstuck. A ghost message could be just a setup. Some information planted to see if anything happens."

"Except this one isn't a ghost," David added. "There's no definitive identification of anyone, perpetrator, friends, or victims. This one's just a *paed'*. Rack it up and move on."

"So we do nothing?" Devlin asked in disbelief.

"You've done enough already. You've flagged it. Move on," said David.

Devlin sensed he was about to upset David again, when Lori began. "What could you do? There's nothing that you can do in this case.

"Think about it. No-one can access the message text except for us, and there's nothing identifying in it. This one's a lost cause. We don't, and can't, know who sent it. And this guy hasn't left any clues to help us track him down, directly or indirectly."

"But surely the police could…" Devlin thought out loud.

"The police can't do anything. They aren't allowed to access a private database because of privacy, and even if they *could*, which they can't, what could they do with it? Little more than us," Lori spoke understandingly.

"But they aren't all like this," David said optimistically.

"So I've seen," Devlin said. "So I put up with the crap to be periodically distracted with paedophilic epitaphs. Great! And for the record, Glen and you all sold this job as a means of making a difference. I don't see this as making *any* difference."

"You miss my point. I said the messages lack identifying header type information, like the member name and their contact details. But they're often not totally anonymous."

"So you *can* identify people?"

"Of course. Some people with nothing to hide mention names, including their own, often writing about themselves in the third person like an obituary. Others who actually do have something to hide also name people or themselves. Directly, or indirectly we can often identify people."

"Glen is the best at it. Identifying people that is," added Ikel. "I'm OK, but David is bloody hopeless."

David took the light-hearted criticism well. "And because I'm so bad at it, there's a whole Research Interface to help. Lori will show you that I'm sure."

"Lori?" asked Devlin.

"I'll show you it later. Let it run, and it comes back with masses of information which you can use to help identify the message sender. It's much like an Internet search, but this will give you more. Lots more!"

"God knows where it all comes from, but it's not perfect," said David. "Glen's algorithm doesn't seem to be as good as Google's, so you just get masses of information. It's really just a tool to enable you to qualify a protocol."

"It's only when you can identify people that you understand the breadth of the LastGasp' member base," Lori added excitedly. "Politicians, rock-stars, sports-men and women."

"None of this explains what happens to the information,"

Lori, Ikel and David looked at each other, albeit fleetingly, before David answered. "We think that all of the protocols basically mean that Glen gets notified, thereafter, we each have our theories or suspicions for what happens next. It's fair to say that none of us think that the police formally receive the information."

"Why?"

"Don't you think that the police would have a mandate to do something with the information? Or they'd drive constitutional changes so that they could, legally, get the information for themselves. We'd hear about it if they got the information one way or another." A smile appeared on David's face, adding, "But I never said nothing happens. Ikel calls it 'Karma'. I prefer 'Divine intervention'."

"Like what kind of Karma?"

"We read things and routinely what we've read come to light in other ways. You'll see for yourself soon enough. For example, recently I read a message from a woman mentioning, amongst other things, regret for a love tryst with her husband's friend. We flagged it. Not long after you might have seen in the news a guy being charged with a near fatal beating of his friend."

"Hardly definitive," challenged Devlin.

"Perhaps, but the devil's in the detail. There was explicit information in the message that matched the defendant's justification.

Our means of identification might not be an exact science, but at least in this case there was no mistake."

"That's hardly proof that Glen or LastGasp' information was involved. It sounds more like a co-incidence."

"And so LastGasp' remains safe from litigation," David replied in a matter of fact manner. "That's the point. Even we couldn't swear to Glen's or LastGasp' involvement. We experience a lot of coincidences!"

"Right," said Devlin, beginning to understand. "Paedophiles go free, but Glen makes sure that adulterers get some justice. So did he contact this guy directly?"

"Maybe, but you'd never know. Cases like this happen all of the time, but you'd never know if you didn't know what to look for. Thus the TVs and if the truth be known, most of our reading is of newspapers rather than messages."

"Most of us virtually live here so that we don't miss stuff," Ikel added.

"So do the paedophiles get theirs?"

"Stop being fixated on paedophiles! Just focus on the messages," David insisted. "The Research Interface is there to help us identify people, but you'll discover after you use it that it's next to useless in its current form. Glen will get his algorithm right sooner or later."

"OK. So what gets flagged?" Devlin realised that there were things that, for now at least, he needed to accept.

"I'll explain it as it was explained to me; to each of us. Flag what would make your ears prick up and take notice if you overheard it."

"Got any other examples?"

"Come on!   Think about it," David made Devlin think. "What would make you listen harder if you heard it?"

"Anything sounding like a confession? Murder? Rape?"

"Yes, and no," said Lori. "You're right, but you needn't *just* think of the sinister side. There is an upside of human nature you know."

"What about someone who's looking to take their own life?" David complimented Lori's approach. "What about someone writing of their ongoing search for a person that could be someone you know? Would this attract your attention?"

"And all this gets flagged?"

"'*Flag it*' is as much as you need to understand."

"Of course, we can use our own discretion too," said Lori. "We call that a personal protocol."

"That sounds more promising."

"Glen calls it 'doing what you think is right'. *Promising* it may be, but there's a rule. It mustn't get back to LastGasp."

"*That*'s it?"

"Yes. *That* is it," said David. "But it isn't as simple as your naivety would have you believe. All you need to do is identify someone, without any identifying information, and then do what you think is right. But what would you do? If you just confront the person, on the assumption that you *can* identify someone, a complete stranger, then they'll know the source, and *that* can't happen."

"What if …"

David stopped Devlin before he could complete his point. "Whatever you're suggesting, a re-think is in order. Violence won't get you anywhere, and it only takes for you to be implicated in any capacity for LastGasp' to come unstuck."

"I could go to the media. An anonymous tip?"

"Same deal. The media are as dumb as they are ruled by the dollar," David challenged. "Technically, the media are even worse than you confronting someone personally. Not only would your target person be able to identify where the information actually came from, but the media would, sooner or later reveal their source. Both of which are bad.

"Making a difference here is simpler and more productive than you'd think. Just flag it and move on."

"That's not making a difference!" announced Devlin. Incensed, he looked to enlist some support. "Lori, Ikel, help me out here. I feel like I've entered this under false pretences. Make a difference, my ass!"

Lori and Ikel did not rally to Devlin's call. They looked to David, demonstrating their allegiance accordingly. "Ikel. Take him out for a bit of headspace," said David. Ikel stood obligingly, and ushered Devlin to the door.

Chapter - 11.

Ikel led Devlin outside without a word being spoken. Clear of the building, Ikel began to speak casually as he directed Devlin along the footpath in what appeared to be a random direction away from the office. "You've got the wrong idea about LastGasp', and us."

"Bullshit!" Devlin replied abruptly.

"Hear me out. We all want to make a difference, and we do. It might not be as glamorous as being a whistle-blower, or as overt as getting your hands bloody, but it helps."

"Helps who, Ikel? Who does this really help?" Devlin asked angrily, as if he was not to be so easily placated.

"I'll do better than that. How about I 'ken show you." Ikel removed some keys from his pocket and unlocked an adjacent B.M.W. by remote. "Get in. We're going for a drive."

Devlin got into the car, as instructed. The car was clearly new, but there was a smell that Devlin could not place and he pondered its source for a moment. It was a bodily odour of some description that made him suddenly self-conscious that perhaps he was the source.

Ikel drove with the exuberance of his youth, aggressively accelerating and braking, and continually searching for spaces in the traffic. Despite this, Devlin was surprised to feel relatively safe, albeit with his seat-belt securely fastened.

"I 'ken love this car. I've only had it for a few weeks, but I still get a buzz every time I get behind the wheel!" Ikel spoke without taking his eyes off the road. "Paid cash of course, and the money was all clean."

"Where are we going?" Devlin enquired; the distraction of the drive having a calming effect.

"Not long after I joined, I read a message. I knew who it was straight away. It was from a dealer I knew from my past life. I hated him, but that's a different story," Ikel said with a calmness at odds with his driving. "As it panned out, he figured that sooner or later he'd get his, but he wanted to leave some cash to his surviving family and friends, if any."

"So you flagged it and then what?"

"Let me finish. The dumb prick figured he could use LastGasp' to detail where he'd hidden five hundred thou', cash. And why wouldn't he? LastGasp' is secure, and the messages won't get sent until after he's dead. What a great use for LastGasp'!" Ikel braked abruptly and pulled over to the kerb outside a suburban train-station and pointed to a bank of lockers. "24. Locker 24. That's where the money is."

"You stole it?"

"I'm a lot of things, and in my past I've been even more, or perhaps less, but now at least, I'm not a thief," Ikel replied. "There was nothing special about the message itself, so it didn't raise the usual red flags. Lori and David didn't flag it, but I knew who it was. I didn't flag it either."

"So the money's still there?"

"It could be. All I know is I didn't touch it."

"Why not?"

"Of course I could, but why?" Ikel looked at Devlin philosophically. "It's only money. I could steal it probably, and possibly get away with it, for a while, or forever. But what if I got caught? With my history, I'd get jail time for sure. More importantly, there's more at stake if LastGasp' got involved, and it would. Why else would I travel across town to break into *that* particular locker? Any half competent investigation would eventually implicate LastGasp', thanks to me. That's worse, and sooner or later you'll understand this. Respect for the *'greater good'* says I leave it alone. Meanwhile, I'm getting paid 'ken good money."

"Look me in the face and tell me that all that cash is nothing, irrespective of what you earn now!"

"What I get out of LastGasp' is more than money. Understand this, and you'll understand LastGasp'."

"Ikel, the only thing that I really understand is that you all appear to be fanatical in your support of Glen. And for all of his alleged vision and what LastGasp' appears to offer, your idea of making a difference makes little difference to anything except your wallet … but hey, apparently this is not about money!"

Ikel was quiet for a moment, giving Devlin an opportunity to calm down. "Would you be happy if the money was handed in? Or if Glen had it?"

"At least that might explain things more than this bullshit ambivalence to money." Devlin thought for a moment before asking a logical question. "Did Glen take it?"

"God knows. Glen keeps pretty well to himself and we rarely see him. But I did see him here one time. I come here every now and then to focus."

"You saw him at the locker? And how does coming here enable you to focus?"

"To be honest, I think that Glen was watching me, and he just wanted me to see him. He never said anything to me afterwards. And for your other question, you haven't really experienced it yet, but it can be a little stressful. Coming here lets me think a bit."

"Can we head back now?"

"Not just yet. I want to make one more stop, but great to hear that you want to get into it." Ikel pulled out into the traffic and returned to his previous driving style.

Devlin used the opportunity to think. Cynicism aside, amid the blur of cars and the erratic driving, he couldn't help but consider Ikel's take on matters. He lost track of where they were heading.

"Last stop, then we'll head back." Ikel broke his silence as the car stopped outside a well-kept cemetery. He slumped forward, draping his shoulders over the steering wheel. "I would be here by now if it wasn't for Glen."

"I get it! You'd be dead. Glen is a saint. All praise to Glen."

"That's him, my uncle, over there," Ikel said, pointing to a grey haired man tending gardens in what appeared to be the better end of the cemetery. "I just wanted and needed to be more.

"Glen's no saint. He just understands people better than most. He understands what people need, not what they want."

Devlin ignored the philosophy of Ikel's comment. "Can we go now?"

"OK. It's time we headed back anyway." Ikel restarted the car and raced off into the traffic.

Both Devlin and Ikel were silent for some time. While the silence was not uncomfortable, Devlin started to see that there was potential for this time in the car as an opportunity for good or bad. He knew that his provocative attitude would not cast him well to his new work peers and he accepted that ultimately he'd need to start to foster a friendship of some kind.

"Sorry to be a prick," Devlin started. "I never used to be so negative. I guess I've just got a lot to take in. And despite how great Glen's been, this really is a bit odd."

"It's OK. I thought it was all weird too when I started. Meet a guy who offers you a job, and a fat wad of cash and it's all legal. I was suspicious too, but gradually I realised that it was OK. I'm just trying to save you some time before you come to the same realisation. Meanwhile, here's a tip."

"What?" replied Devlin humbly.

"Try and get on with people. It's easier that way," Ikel smiled, even momentarily taking his eyes off the road.

"Ikel, can I ask you a question?"

"Go nuts."

"Why haven't you asked about my past?"

"Your past makes you who you are. Glen taught me that. Why do you want to know?"

"Does it matter? Why didn't you ask?"

"OK. Maybe because it's none of my business or because we'll get to talk about it eventually at work. Happy yet?"

"Not really. Don't you care about what I almost went to jail for?"

"Nope. I could just as easily have said that I don't give a shit, but that isn't entirely true. I'd be interested in your take."

"What do you mean '*my* take'? I've been acquitted!" Devlin said, trying not to take offence.

"Yes, you've been acquitted, but someone is still dead. The rest is just gravy." Ikel lacked subtlety.

Devlin thought about what Ikel had said and how he'd summed it up perfectly, particularly for as much as the world cared. "Mind if I get it off my chest then?"

"Sure. Traffic's bad anyway."

Devlin accepted that sooner or later he'd need to talk about this. "He ruined my life."

"And you ended his."

Devlin didn't bite back. His anxiety was growing and suddenly his disclosure was overwhelming. He writhed in his seat, straining against his seatbelt. "Ikel. Sorry, but I don't think I'm right to continue."

"That's OK," Ikel said with a shrug.

Chapter - 12.

Detective Alan Reymond arrived at the address described by the person at the hospital. He knew the visit was to be of dubious worth, but what else could he do? The young doctor was unwilling to release him into custody, even just for formal questioning, based on the farcical story that Venn had described in an attempt to have someone verify his identity. Presumption of innocence aside, he'd still made sure that the guy was securely locked in his room with a uniformed officer posted on the door.

Gut-feel told Reymond that he'd be back at the hospital before too long, lobbying another doctor after shift change that the patient was a crank not deserving of a hospital bed out of the public purse. Still, he knew he needed to do a little homework before he could justify any case against, or theoretically *for* the guy.

Performance artist indeed, Detective Reymond thought to himself. Venn had suggested that the only way for his identity to be confirmed was by way of a woman named 'Angie', the performance artist no –less. He'd provided no surname for her, and only a house description, street name and suburb, which had thus far proven accurate in that there was no mistaking 'the worst house on the street' in this instance. On a street of old-money, bluestone residences, there was only one decrepit, single storey wood and weatherboard. As Reymond looked over the house from his car, he reminded himself that the fact the house even existed proved nothing, much less the identity of Malcolm Venn. All it really proved was that Venn had ventured to this part of town.

Now for the fun part, Detective Reymond sniggered to himself. While Venn had not provided a full name for the person who'd be able to shed light on his identity, he had provided a description of her. 'Angie with big tits'. He re-read his notes purely out of habit, but there was no way he'd have forgotten *that* description. He left the comfort of his car, forgoing his jacket despite the late afternoon chill and headed for the front door.

Near on fifty years of Policing had given Detective Alan Reymond a certain insight. He could tell when someone was lying just by looking at him. It was this particular skill that had made him not write off Venn's story. This time his experience told him that all was not well at Angie's house. He felt it as he approached.

There was nothing he could describe, but Reymond could still feel something out of place. Looking through the window into the lounge room, he could see that the house appeared comfortably lived-in and he could feel a draft of warm air from under the front door. He could hear music, smell food cooking in the kitchen and it smelled good enough to remind him of his missed meals. But there was something else.

Reymond knocked on the front door and as there was no reply or sound of any movement from inside his first reaction was of annoyance. As much as he doubted he'd gain anything worthwhile from any meeting with 'Angie', if she even existed, he couldn't rightly justify leaving such a loose end. He didn't want to have to come back later. He knocked again, this time a little louder and called out, "Angie? It's the police, and I'd love a quick word if I could."

There was still no discernable noise or movement from inside the house, but as he moved towards the lounge room window for a closer look, he heard a rolling sound. It sounded like a bowling ball rolling towards pins, but softer and slightly less determined. Through the window he was finally able to confirm what was making the noise as he watched a tall drinking glass roll along the corridor outside the lounge room. He marvelled at his hearing and wondered if he'd have heard anything if it was his right ear close to the window, largely deaf thanks to years of fruitless practice at the shooting range without ear plugs. His insight had been proven right yet again.

Reymond was thankful that he didn't have to contain an over-zealous young partner determined to produce his weapon and force open the door. Older and wiser, he knew that such a reaction was unlikely to produce any better result than more reasonable behaviour. He called out again as he tried the front door. Finding it unlocked, he cautiously opened it, announced himself once more and entered.

Angie was not in good shape when Reymond found her; seated on the floor with her legs splayed wide, propped into a moderately upright position against her bed with her head hanging forward. She wore only underwear and a partially unbuttoned cream coloured silk top. Her bruising was obvious, and Reymond had seen enough domestic violence in his day to understand that the beatings that she'd suffered had been inflicted over a protracted period. Admittedly, had she not been partially undressed, her bruising would have gone un-noticed. Whoever had done it to Angie, his first thoughts were of Venn, had taken care so as to allow her to still exist in public without drawing attention. Of immediate concern however, was her apparent overdose. There were several medicine bottles open on her bed and bedside table, pills scattered on the floor and she appeared to be teetering on the verge of unconsciousness.

Reymond called for an ambulance as he more closely examined her condition, passing on whatever information he could. He noted her shallow breathing, feint pulse and dilated pupils while taking inventory of the medications that she'd potentially taken. He'd made this type of call before and he knew the drill. He put the woman into the recovery position, rolling the unconscious patient onto her side and began the wait for the ambulance which he'd hoped would not be too long.

Venn had been right when he described Angie as having big tits. Reymond knew that it was unprofessional, particularly in her current state, but he couldn't help himself. He might have been old, but testosterone still featured in his bloodstream. He admired her breasts, from a distance, marvelling at how they, in a small way, were possibly helping to keep her alive as they propped her head off the floor.

His daydreaming over, Detective Reymond alternated between checking her vital signs and snooping around the room, all the time listening for the ambulance. He found the woman's handbag and purse, and matching the photo on her drivers' licence, he was able to confirm the woman's identity, Angela Clarke. Now he was getting somewhere.

As the wait dragged on, Reymond examined the medicine bottles. In his haste to get the ambulance on their way he'd reported it to the emergency services operator as a probable suicide attempt, but the more he looked, the less likely that seemed. He'd learnt a lot about various pharmaceuticals over the years and he recognised most of Angie's medicines as being anti-depressants and mood stabilisers of various grades. He didn't profess to be an expert on the matter, but it seemed an odd choice of drug for a suicide. Reymond took a closer look at each of the tiny medicine bottles spread over Angie's bed noted that each had been prescribed, but clearly not consumed, over a period of years.

He opened the top drawer of Angie's bedside table in search of the obligatory address book. He didn't find what he was looking for, but the base of the drawer was awash with pills of various sizes and colours, much the same as those now scattered across the floor. It didn't take much deduction on his part to query why Angie would scatter medicine bottles across her room when there was an ample supply of the tablets readily accessible loose in the drawer. "What was in the containers, Angie?" he said to himself as he looked over at her lying prostrate on the floor.

It was then that Detective Reymond saw it, a tiny dot of blood on the back of Angie's blouse. The blood was like a magnet for his attention, and he started to examine the lie of her clothing. Oddly, despite the way she was lying, her clothing failed to adhere to her body's shape. Reymond could see the outline of her bra strap raising the material of her top, otherwise pulled taught by the way that she was lying, but her clothing was still being forcibly kept from her skin. Reymond was curious as to why. He knelt beside the woman and started to slide her blouse up her back. "Excuse me, Angie" he said respectfully, mindful that she was oblivious in her current state. Inch by inch he revealed more bruising, until the fabric failed to be pushed upwards any further, caught by something unseen adjacent to Angie's bra strap. Reymond lifted the blouse over the obstruction, exposing a syringe needle, without syringe, still embedded to the hilt between the woman's shoulder blades.

"How did you do yourself there?" Reymond asked rhetorically.

Chapter - 13.

It was early evening and the area around LastGasp' was undergoing its daily transformation from daytime coffee district to night-time entertainment precinct. The municipal council's recent investment in gentrification, including lighting and security had attracted the businesses and the people. The brothels, like the cafés and the restaurants, were doing a roaring trade.

Ikel turned down the laneway behind LastGasp'. "Glen's got a few car-parks under cover. First in, best dressed. It's really no safer than the street, for you or your car, but it's well lit and I feel better with my wheels under cover. Still, some pricks have got at my car a few times," Ikel explained. "There's a kind of security system there too," Ikel smiled, clearly a party to some joke.

The car pulled into a small carpark underneath a building that was lit like the nativity. On opening the door, Devlin understood Ikel's joke. The smell of spent urine was overwhelming. It seemed that the council's financial injection into the area had not extended to the provision of adequate public toilets. Puddles were on the ground everywhere, and urine stains, old and new, marked the walls around the five parking spaces.

The odour bit hard into the back of Devlin's nose and throat. "This place reeks!" Devlin said, almost gagging. "So the security system is purely olfactory?" Devlin had at last placed the strange smell in Ikel's car.

Ikel looked puzzled, not exactly understanding what Devlin had said. "It's not a factory security, it's stinky security! And Albert is the night watchman!" he said, pointing to a stationary mass at the front of the car. "ALBERT! Wake up you lazy bugger!"

Roused by Ikel, Albert stood slowly. He wasn't very old, Devlin figured, guessing about fifty, but the years had not been kind. Alberts face was sullen and weathered. He wore tracksuit pants, a t-shirt and an oversized coat that would have been more fitting on a polar expedition. He started to stare at Devlin. "Who's this then?"

"This is Devlin. He's new. He's alright. Be nice!" Ikel replied, tilting his head and raising an eyebrow to Devlin in suggestion that he take up the social exchange.

"Hi," said Devlin, still reeling with the smell. He looked over Albert again, this time noticing his lack of appropriate footwear. It had been a mild day, mid-autumn, and the evening chill was settling in, but Albert was wearing cheap rubber sandals exposing browned toenails that curled over the end of his toes. Devlin was fixated in revulsion at the combination of the smell and Albert's feet.

"I don't bite!" replied Albert gruffly, stepping forward to offer his hand. "I can tell a lot about a man from a handshake."

"So what can you tell about me?" Devlin asked, only half interested in the reply. In close proximity to Albert he noticed the overpowering ambient smell of urine was magically fused with a mixture of sweat and alcohol and he figured that any reply wouldn't warrant much consideration.

"What can you tell me about mine?" asked Albert.

"Maybe later. We gotta' get upstairs," said Ikel, much to Devlin's relief. Ikel led Devlin from the carpark into the darkness of the laneway.

"I'll be here," said Albert with a look of lonely sadness as he was left on his own again.

The fresh air of the night was utterly fragrant compared to the carpark. Devlin sucked in deep breaths as they walked. "Is Albert on the LastGasp' payroll?" he asked, half in jest.

"Albert's alright," Ikel explained. "The downside of being undercover is that the carpark never gets rain to wash away the smell. Glen slips him some cash every week to splash the hose around, otherwise this place *really* stinks!"

"He either isn't getting paid enough, or he's not doing a good enough job. Why doesn't Glen give him a real job?"

"I think Albert used to work with Glen. Ask him yourself one day. He's really good for a chat. He's there most days and he enjoys the company."

"I might do that. I might get him in for a shower and a change of clothes too!"

Ikel stopped in his tracks and grabbed Devlin on the shoulder forcefully. "No-one comes inside except us, or someone that Glen gives the nod to. And even then, outsiders aren't allowed anywhere near the bunker. Remember that," Ikel said aggressively. "Albert might be a special case, but he's not allowed in either."

"OK. I forgot!" insisted Devlin, still a little taken aback at being apprehended.

"Don't *forget*. Don't ever forget." Satisfied, Ikel released his grip on Devlin and continued walking.

"I still don't get the fixation on security," said Devlin. "Why?"

"Glen will explain why. I'll just tell you to accept it." He kept walking. "Come on. It's 'ken cold and I want to get back."

Chapter - 14.

Detective Reymond briefed the paramedics on their arrival, pointing out the syringe and his belief that this was not a run of the mill overdose. They'd reacted assuming some opiate derivative had been used, based on a simple swab test, and the *Narcan* they administered made Angie alert almost immediately. Still, she was slow to respond to a volley of well-intentioned questions from the paramedics. She settled her gaze on her attendants and began to answer their questions cautiously.

Reymond stayed silent in the background, watching with interest as the paramedics tended to their patient. He'd seen them in operation on overdose cases before, but he noticed a difference in their behaviour on this occasion. This time at least it was unlikely that they'd be met with an expletive ridden tirade about their role in wasting their patient's score, or interfering with their patient's suicide. Instead, they expected to be thanked, even if not verbally, and there was a noticeable zeal in their work as a result.

As soon as he was given the nod, Reymond stepped in to ask his own questions. Her punctured lung mandated further hospital based care, but he would be OK to ask a few questions, and more importantly, *she* should be OK to answer them. Of course anything she said in her pharmaceutical grade state of alertness would be inadmissible, but it would surely point him in the right direction.

"Hi Angie. My name is Detective Alan Reymond. I actually came here to ask you about Malcolm Venn but ..."

"Is he alright?" Angie interrupted, coherent but incapable of maintaining her focus. She laboured shallow breaths, erratically scanning her surroundings like a pet rabbit in the presence of a large dog.

"Yes, *he's* fine. I guess that answers my original question in that you do actually know him," Reymond said in a fatherly tone. When Angie nodded he continued. "Angie. I'm assuming I may call you 'Angie', I'd actually like to talk about you, and who did this to you, but I am somewhat curious as to why you would ask *that* about him?"

Angie shrugged. "I've been worried for him. Is he in trouble?"

"I'm not sure really. He's currently in hospital," the Detective said, watching Angie's increasing lucidity.

"But you said he was, *is*, alright!"

"And he is, it's just that …"

"So why are you here and not him then?" Angie enquired edgily.

"Well, he's looking at getting discharged now, but we just needed to check some things before he does."

"Like what?"

"Like who he actually is, and like why he was admitted covered in blood?"

Angie sighed. "He is who he says he is, as much as I know anyway. I've only known him for a few weeks but he's been special to me."

"'*Special*' people don't beat people they love." Reymond was not going to let the woman's bruising go un-noticed. "Are you as special to him as he is to you?"

"Malcolm didn't do this to me!" said Angie, picking up on the manner with which the comment had been made.

Detective Reymond heard the reply and almost scoffed at his feeling of *déjà-vu*; familiar words he'd heard many times before, spoken by different damaged women doing their best to sound convincing. The truth remained, however, that Malcolm was out of the frame for her immediate assault if not for the domestic abuse. "So who assaulted you?"

"No-one I know."

"Angie, whoever it was would have killed you had I not been visiting at the time," Reymond insisted.

"And it wouldn't have happened had Malcolm been here, so don't go giving yourself commendations just yet," Angie said forthrightly. "Yes, *someone* did it, but no-one that you or anyone else will do anything about."

"Whoever it is, we can help," Reymond said, determined to salvage some confidence in his profession. "It would help Malcolm if you could account for the blood on his clothing."

"It's not what you think. The blood is an important part of my shows."

"Go on…" Reymond braced himself for what Venn had eluded to.

"I'm a performance artist, and I use blood in my shows."

"The blood was human."

"Yes, and all legally sourced as out of date blood product. Not fit for medical use, in this country at least, but quite good enough for what I use it for."

"And what do you need it for in your show?"

"*Shows!*" Angie emphasised the plural. "I do a variety of acts, all featuring blood. Birth, death, war, health, female circumcision, menstruation, domestic abuse."

"A bit close to home?"

"Possibly, but it's a living, and I'm not in any great rush to be out of work."

"You're in demand?" asked Reymond with some disbelief.

"Yes, mainly on the alternative circuit. I'm a little too *avant-garde* for the mainstream theatre generally. I do overseas as well, but only if I'm really strapped for cash as the bureaucracy on international transportation of bodily fluids is a pain."

"But why *human* blood?"

"Nothing feels or tastes or *smells* like human blood. It complements my theatre as a total sensory thing."

"And how does this involve Malcolm Venn?"

"It doesn't really. We were mixing a batch when he got a call and rushed out. The mixing can get a little messy, but he left just the same." Angie didn't wait to be asked to explain. She laboured a deep breath and continued. "I get a number of bags of blood product, expose it to air for a while, mixing constantly and just as it starts to congeal, I add a little sodium citrate to stop the clot and then re-bottle it. Genuine stage blood."

"Can I take a sample? Just in case," Detective Reymond asked. It took him a moment to remember that Angie was not in need of an alibi. Weighed against what the hospital had reported when Venn was admitted, Angie's story was undeniably plausible, but it wasn't what he'd expected.

"I've done nothing wrong, and I'm not even a suspect in any crime, so why would you need a sample?" replied Angie defensively.

Reymond changed direction, not wanting to labour the point. "I'll do my part for his discharge. I'll pop in for a chat while you're in hospital."

"Do we have anything to talk about?" Angie asked.

"My job is hospital liaison, and there's no way that any medical practitioner will ignore your current state without getting me involved."

"Just tell Malcolm where I am," Angie said.

"*That*, I will do, Angie."

Chapter - 15.

There was no work being done when Ikel and Devlin returned to the building. The mood was decidedly casual as Lori, David and Glen all shared a drink, sharing a joke and laughing in the kitchen. Ikel helped himself to a beer from the fridge and another for Devlin.   Lori and David gave sincere welcoming gestures before continuing their conversation.

"Calmed down a bit?" Glen enquired. "I'm not a complete charity, you know. I pay well because this is a stressful job, but I guess you'd never have guessed would you?

"We all get stressed at times. It's just something that you accept. You also need to understand that it will get worse, not better. You'll read worse than you read today, and you'll feel just as helpless, if not more so."

"I don't believe that no-one takes matters into their own hands."

"Just accept that there's a greater good," Glen replied. "How you believe this greater good comes into being is much less important."

"But …" Devlin persisted before being interrupted.

"Relax and don't worry about it." Glen had a way of talking that Devlin was beginning to understand. There was something amazing in his tone that conveyed what he was thinking. It was clarity of communication at its best. Devlin understood that it was time to leave it alone, and Ikel and the others knew that it was now time to change the subject.

"I have a confession to make," Lori took command of the conversation. "I'm terminally curious and I looked in your backpack while you and Ikel were gone." Smiling, her confession was not one of regret, but more of a statement of fact.

"You're unbelievable!" Ikel laughed. "I should have known you wouldn't be able to help yourself. Sorry Devlin. I should have expected it and warned you. Maybe I was expecting David to keep her honest."

"You know how devious women are!" said David as he wandered off towards the bunker.

"It's all right. There's nothing in there anyway."

"I'm curious, sure, but I'm not a thief. Your pictures, change of underwear and a t-shirt are still there," said Lori a little defensively. "Do you know where you're sleeping tonight? And no, I'm not offering."

"It's not a problem. Really," Devlin replied, genuinely not fishing for offers, but receptive to any raised. "My plan for the day just didn't extend to the need to find a home."

"Glen?" Ikel questioned.

"I couldn't let my latest employee sleep in a park or something, not that you would with cash in your pocket," Glen said. "The hotel is just around the corner."

"I'm capable of sorting myself out. I'll be OK."

"Yes, you are capable, but it's part of the deal. Lori or Ikel will show you the way."

Devlin didn't put up much of a fight. "But I can find my own way there I'm sure."

"Suit yourself," said Glen, turning to Ikel and Lori. "Make sure you let Devlin here find his own way to the same hotel that you stay at."

Devlin rolled his eyes for his arrogance.

"Anyway. I'm out of here," Glen announced. "Get some rest, clear your head. Work starts tomorrow. Ikel and Lori will fill you in. You good?"

"You bet I'm good!" Devlin replied, a little deflated when he saw Glen shrug, turn and head for the door. He followed not out of obligation, but out of appreciation, desperate to convey his sincerest thanks away from the others. Judging by the effort he was making to leave, it seemed that Glen was equally keen to shun the appreciation. "Thank you. For everything," he said after almost needing to hold the door closed to prevent Glen's escape.

Glen looked at Devlin with some annoyance. "When, or if, I do something for you, then, and only then, will I accept, but not expect, a thank-you. So far, I've done nothing."

"But …"

"So far, I've done nothing. Trust me," Glen continued. "*When* you learn about yourself and your life, *that* will be something. And you will."

Devlin felt like a child. "Thanks for the beer then."

"Go and have another, but not too many and I'll see you tomorrow." Glen left without waiting for any acknowledgment.

"Care for another?" asked Ikel on Devlin's return, pointing to an unopened bottle of beer in his hand.

"Ikel! I want to go," complained Lori as she put on a jacket in preparation to leave.

"I'm just being social. One more won't take long," replied Ikel. "You could always go yourself."

"You know I hate being on the street on my own," Lori whinged like a child. "One more then," she huffed, walking off. "Men!"

Ikel and Devlin shared a jovial drink, but they both felt a certain obligation to finish quickly. Theirs was a pyrrhic victory. Lori returned soon after and started hinting heavily to leave.

"Let's go," said Ikel.

"Finally!" said Lori, marching for the front door expecting the others to follow. Devlin and Ikel obliged. "Bye David! Wave guys!" she said, directing Devlin's attention to a camera above the door.

"Dave's got the night shift!" said Ikel. "You'll get to enjoy the night-shift too, once you're settled in." Ikel ushered Devlin outside to join Lori before securing the door shut.

"Nobody said anything about shift-work!" said Devlin. "What other nasties are involved in this job? And why is a night shift necessary?" he asked as they walked along the street.

"It's not a big deal," replied Ikel. "We all take turns, even Glen. Actually, it's pretty cool with the place to yourself. You should hear that sound system when it's arc'd up!"

"But why?"

"Most of the time you'll just end up watching TV or movies," Ikel replied.

"Actually, it's mainly for security," Lori corrected. "Glen insists that the building is almost permanently occupied."

"More security!" laughed Devlin mockingly. "I just don't see the big deal. If he's, sorry, *you're* all that fanatical about security surely a lone person won't do much. I couldn't offer that much to secure the premises and a little old building between a few brothels doesn't seem to provide that much security anyway!"

Lori sighed. "The building is secure. Very secure. There's only one point of entry and all access via that door requires an access code. Any breach, or attempted breach, of the building will result in specialist attention within a few minutes apparently, but I've never seen it. Apparently attempts do happen. Irregularly, but they happen from time to time. And Glen also performs drills."

"I'll bet it looks pretty cool when it happens. Did you see the movie 'SWAT'?" Ikel added.

"Anyway," Lori continued, clearly not appreciating Ikel's interruption. "There's automated facial recognition software controlling access to the building. There's touch sensors on all the door handles for fingerprint cross referencing to your image for the other software. All Glen's design and implementation. Of course, this can be over-ridden if someone is in the building to buzz you in."

"You're crapping me!"

"Not at all. We should have checked it on the way out, but Glen obviously thinks it can wait until morning."

Devlin was still incredulous. "I haven't had a photo taken yet."

"You've already touched the main door and the bunker door and your photo would have been taken from the building security system. Glen would've checked that it was all in order while he left us for a time in the bunker."

"The work room is a different matter. We call it a bunker for good reason. Nobody's getting in there, except us. Without sanctioned access, there isn't even any mains power to the entire building, until it's reset. The building itself is locked down with its own independent power."

"If people were that desperate to get in, surely they'd, I dunno, blow up the entrance, or the whole building for that matter." Devlin looked for a flaw in the rampant paranoia evident in what he was being told.

"Ever heard of a brothel being destroyed?" Lori asked.

"Not lately," said Devlin thinking hard, still somewhat distracted by the revelations of security.

"Not lately. Not ever. Not anywhere," Lori made her point. "I'll bet that George W. Bush himself could visit the 'Baghdad Bordello' confident he'd be safe inside!"

"Of course, as soon as he left there would be crowds waiting to off him, but that's another matter," Ikel added.

"Anyway," Lori continued. "Glen chose his location with care. He's smarter than anyone could give him credit for, except perhaps us. Now come on, I'm cold and I want to get home." She broke into a brisker walk expecting the others to follow.

"Lori. Why are brothels *secure*?" Devlin asked after jogging a few steps to walk next to her.

"Ikel invariably knows better than me. Just because Glen outed me as a former prostitute doesn't mean that I know everything about the subject."

"Sorry, I didn't mean to offend. I'm just curious."

"I'm not offended. My past makes me who I am and in this case it funded my education. I don't know the business, only the trade. I do know that when I started, they took the time to tell me how safe I was and how my safety was paramount. In retrospect, I can see that my safety and customer security and discretion all amounted to good business."

"And customer satisfaction!" added Ikel.

"Thanks Ikel," Lori said cynically. "To answer your question, I think you have to think a little of who is inside. Any violent attack on a brothel is just as likely to endanger a single mum making ends meet, or a politician, an underworld figure, the coach of the local football team, a parish priest. Anyone."

"Collateral damage is one thing, but there would be consequences," Ikel said, finally being constructive.

"Ikel's right. Brothels give exposure, excuse the pun. With exposure, the potential for justice goes up substantially. Someone will pay. Glen's just using this simple fact of life.

"I might add that we readers are only effectively quality control and there's no physical data storage at LastGasp' that I know of. All of that is surely stored in some thermo-nuclear, war-proof data repository. The legal face of the business is some other entity entirely, but they have no idea what goes on, intentionally. And the monkeys who look after customer interaction and support are elsewhere too, god knows where. They only have access to billing information, which is a single payment up-front, with no means of relating payment to messages. Glen's probably the only one who knows anything about how it's put together. Trust me. If you aren't supposed to have access, you don't have access."

"We can continue this at dinner if you like." Ikel brought attention to the fact that they'd arrived at the hotel.

Lori waved to the staff at the front desk as she passed heading for the lifts at the far end of the lobby. Ikel ushered Devlin to the desk where the staff were waiting attentively. "Hi Morris. This is Devlin. Glen's sorted out the booking."

Morris was seasoned in his role. He had the look of a hotel manager who'd been in the hospitality industry for a long time, but the perpetual niceness had not taken its toll. His greeting and demeanour seemed genuine as he handed Devlin a card key and beckoned for an attendant. "Nigel will show you the way, unless you'd prefer for your friend Mr Donovan to direct you?"

"I'll sort him out. His room is with Lori and me anyway." Ikel assumed the role of escort. "Come on."

"This place isn't bad," Ikel started to explain in the lift. "Actually, it's pretty good! The food is excellent, the rooms are nice and big and they're quiet. So you won't hear the street below. We've ordinarily got the entire floor to ourselves so you can just sing out if you need us."

"Sounds fine. For at least a little while."

Ikel laughed. "I thought the same thing at first, but I'm more than comfortable here now, especially while Glen pays! You could settle in, but as that won't take you long, we might as well just have a drink.

They headed to the bar adjacent to the hotel restaurant as they waited for a table. Ikel ordered the beers and they sat in an unobtrusive area hidden from the greater restaurant. Initially both Ikel and Devlin were silent; Ikel because he was parched from the volume of talking he'd done escorting Devlin on his brief tour of the hotel facilities, and Devlin just digesting everything.

Devlin sat with a contented smile enjoying the beer and the moment. His day had come full circle. From waking almost destitute, being assaulted by 'friends' and being robbed, he was now employed, well paid and the guest at a nice hotel.

"What do you think so far?" Ikel asked after watching Devlin as he sat with an almost blank, vacant expression but a relaxed smile.

"About what? I like the hotel, and the beer is good." Devlin replied cautiously.

"And LastGasp'?"

"Do you want me to be honest?"

"I like honest. Save your subtlety for someone else. It's wasted on me!"

"OK. LastGasp' seems good. It seems like a good job, for at least a little while."

"That's honest?" commented Ikel disappointedly. "I thought you were going to say something interesting."

"Alright. Honesty," Devlin took a deep breath. "LastGasp' seems like a crock of shit, but hey, I can do anything if I'm getting paid for it. You seem like a nice guy and I can see that we'll get on OK. Lori seems nice, but I'm interested as to why she'd look in my bag. Women would chuck the shits if they knew a guy went snooping in their handbag, so yes, I'm a little put out by that. David strikes me as a bit of a prick, but perhaps we'll get used to each other. As for Glen? I'm appreciative for him giving me a job." Devlin waited for Ikel's reaction.

"Great," replied Ikel simply.

"Is that all you're going to say?"

"You want *my* opinion on *your* opinion?" Ikel teased, taking another drink of his beer. "LastGasp' is alright, so you're wrong, but maybe this is something that you need to discover for yourself. David is a bit odd, but he's OK once you get to know him. He has trust issues too, so you should understand him better than most."

Ikel writhed in his seat, standing to remove a vibrating phone from his jeans pocket. He checked the caller I.D. on the display and answered. "We're in the bar." He ended the call and looked to Devlin. "Lori's going to join us."

"Did you and Lori join LastGasp' together?" Devlin asked, looking to learn more about her.

"No, Lori met Glen through me a bit after I joined. I knew her from years back and we bumped into each other in the street. Then Glen recruited her. That's mainly what he does."

"I thought I was just filling a recent vacancy, or that Glen was just doing me a favour."

"People come and go, so he just keeps bringing newcomers on board."

"I'm just thinking," Devlin hesitated. "I was just thinking about everything I know about LastGasp' which, admittedly, isn't much. I'm interested in why people wouldn't stay. Doesn't that interest you?"

"Not really."

"Pay is good. Conditions are good. I've known people to stay in crappy jobs for ages, so I just find it interesting that there are no staff who've been around for longer than a few months."

"I asked Glen about Derrell, and why he quit," replied Ikel. "Derrell was another reader who left before my time. But Glen used to talk about him often.

"I thought you said you weren't interested!" sniped Devlin.

"Well yes. But anyway, Glen just said everyone leaves for a reason and when they're ready. Clearly I'm not ready and so I'm staying."

"Have you ever heard the expression 'if something's too good to be true then it probably is'?"

"Yes. So?"

"So I'm looking for a catch."

"There's no catch," Ikel replied succinctly.

"Given my recent history, I'm very mindful of keeping my nose clean."

"LastGasp' isn't illegal. Even Lori told you that?"

"That wasn't what I asked."

"LastGasp' doesn't demand anything illegal, and neither does Glen for that matter. You have my word on this. Happy?"

"I guess." Devlin allowed his concerns to be placated for a while. "Time will tell."

"Time will tell what?" asked Lori on her arrival, keen to catch up with the current conversation. She had changed her clothes and looked substantially fresher than when they left LastGasp'. Now she was wearing an open necked blouse that revealed more skin and bust, and it had the desired effect. Both Ikel and Devlin were fixated on her.

"I'm hungry. Let's eat!" Lori all but demanded. She headed away from the bar to the tables. Ikel and Devlin took the hint and quickly finished their drinks in order to follow.

Chapter - 16.

Malcolm waited restlessly for Detective Reymond to return; he knew it was only a matter of time. With the restraints removed, he could move about his bed and the room, but there was no escaping the fact he was idle when he had things to do; his projects were waiting. His scan of the papers however told him that the wait on one such project was nearly at an end. His timing had been almost perfect.

Reymond returned to Malcolm's room not long after dark. "We need to talk about Angie," he announced as he slumped himself on the bed-side chair.

"So you met her then?" Malcolm said, reclining on his bed, surfing through the channels on the ceiling mounted television. He regretted not giving the Detective any eye contact, but his plan was not about making friends. In the greater scheme of things, Reymond was little more than a spectator, an important spectator admittedly, but really just a bit player without whom his discharge would be delayed.

"Met her. Saved her." Malcolm felt Reymond watching him closely. "We need to talk."

"What happened?"

"Aside from the beatings?"

"Fresh ones?" Malcolm asked curiously but not really surprised.

"Not that I saw, but I'll be checking with the doctor after her admission. It's interesting that there didn't appear to be any bruising less than about a week old, and you've been here in hospital for a few days. Wouldn't you say?"

"What's he done this time?"

"Thanks for sparing me the denials, but talking in the third person doesn't convince me."

"Detective, I don't need to convince you of anything. Angie is a friend, and while I can't vouch for how *you* treat *your* friends, I sure don't treat them that way. Where is she?"

"You do at least *sound* concerned," Detective Reymond persisted.

Malcolm didn't need to feign concern. The more that Reymond delayed answering the question, the more he feared for the flaws in his plan. Leaving Angie alone was not ideal, but it was necessary. "Just answer the question. Where is she?"

"She's still in emergency, but she's sure to be admitted. When I got to the address you described, she was not in a good way. Initially I thought it was an overdose. There were pills everywhere, and I called it in like a suicide, until I saw the syringe."

"Angie isn't a junkie."

"I never said she was." Detective Reymond drank from a disposable cup he'd brought in with him. He continued only after unconvincingly staging the savour of a second mouthful. "There was a syringe embedded between her shoulder blades. Thereafter, I considered the overdose to be an assault."

As focussed as Malcolm was on his plan, he was not above reflection as to how protecting her could have been managed. Any purist privy to his plan would consider Angie to be inconsequential, but Malcolm wasn't a purist. After closing his eyes and breathing deeply for several moments, he resigned himself to the greater good of his plan. "How is she?"

"She'll live. We're still waiting for test results to confirm what else was in the syringe, and the actual needle. Blood-work is pending. Of course, the HIV tests will take a while for a conclusive result. She asked after you as soon as she came around."

"She *was* clean, at least."

"She was reserved about your relationship too," the Detective said. "I've always been amazed that battered women always slipped back into being half of a relationship, a dysfunctional relationship admittedly, but a relationship nonetheless. You're only out of the picture for the attack with the syringe. The puncture mark around the needle was clearly very recent, even if there was evidence of some rust at the wound, and the makings of a bruise was not visible until she'd arrived here."

Malcolm didn't say anything. He had a good idea who would have been responsible and what the guy was capable of, but this was not the deal. Clearly the bastard had no intention of letting Angie get away lightly, but obviously he had a soft spot for her. Malcolm could imagine the bastard trying something new, forcibly giving her something to take the edge off her fear. He could picture their confrontation as clearly as if he'd actually been there himself. Angie cowering in the corner, the guy yelling himself into a frenzy before he started to sink the boot in, over and over. Then Angie would do what she always did, offer sexual servitude in order to placate the man. Periodic rape didn't solve her problem, but it made her immediate concern that this time he might go too far, even for his standards, dissipate somewhat. Malcolm knew that just being with Angie had given her not only physical security, but also a little self-confidence, and he wouldn't have liked it. Poor Angie. At least in hospital she'd be safe for now, and thereafter his plan would see to her continued safety, or at least get her off the hook for her to chart her own path.

"You know who did it, don't you?" Reymond asked. "Is *he* the same guy who's responsible for her other injuries?"

Malcolm considered telling the Detective what he knew, but this information was not part of the plan. He hoped he'd convinced Angie to remain strong for a little while longer.

It was now time to leave. He knew he wouldn't see Reymond again, but it was nice to meet him just the same.

"If it's not too much trouble, and unless you've got something else to talk about Detective, I'd like to get out of here."

Chapter - 17.

Angie was under close observation in the ward. She soon came to realise that this meant that she was to be periodically disturbed by a zealous nurse checking her vitals before leaving to wake another patient. This was different to all of her previous hospital stays where she'd invariably been admitted while unconscious or near comatose. She reasoned that this particular nurse's routine was no different to those of her past admissions, but being awake, the near continual disruption was annoying. She was exhausted but had been unable, or possibly unwilling, to really sleep, choosing instead to doze with Malcolm sitting at her bedside. She must have fallen asleep more deeply than just a simple doze, and now she was awake only to discover that he was gone. Again.

A strangely familiar face entered the room. He identified Angie, obviously recognising her, and walked slowly towards her, waving to the nurse scurrying around the room tending to each of the patients in turn.

"Not too long, Ghoul," the nurse said softly so as to not wake anyone not already awake. "She needs some rest or I'll need to sedate her." She shamelessly spoke about her patient as if Angie wasn't in the room.

The guy shrugged off the comment, pulling up a seat at Angie's bedside. "Hi Angie, do you remember me?"

"You were the one who called the ambulance. I can't recall if I thanked you earlier." Angie rested a moment, labouring to breathe with one less than perfect lung. "I can't remember your name but I know it wasn't what that nurse just called you."

"Fair enough. My name is Detective Alan Reymond. All of the nurses call me 'Ghoul' and I've long since given up caring enough to try to stop them!"

"Why?"

"Why do they call me 'Ghoul', or why haven't I stopped them?" Reymond replied playfully. "I've given up trying to stop them because I'm old and I'm more interested in the fact that they know me well enough to consider me as regular as a piece of furniture here. As for why they actually gave me the name. My primary role is 'hospital liaison' and I also have the dubious honour of being the name at the bottom of many of the city's police reports of suicides. Some comedian considered it downright ghoulish that I was routinely involved in so many suicides, apparently, and the name has remained with me." Reymond yawned, hiding his gaping mouth behind a manila folder. "We really need to talk Angie."

"There's not much to talk about."

"He'll do it again," Reymond said, ambiguous as to whom he was referring to. "I can protect you." Angie only shrugged. "Malcolm's not the good guy here."

"I sincerely doubt that. But you go ahead and think what you like."

"You know you're not the first victim of domestic violence who's shunned Police involvement. Will you be so *lucky* next time?"

Angie had heard all of this before.

Chapter - 18.

Devlin woke not to an alarm, daylight streaming through the glass wall, or a wakeup call from Ikel as planned, but to the unfamiliar sound of his phone indicating the receipt of a message. It was a little after 4am and he considered ignoring it until at least daylight but curiosity got the better of him. It was close to a full moon outside and the moonlight was more than adequate for him to find his phone in his trousers on the floor without having to turn on a light. He grabbed the phone and returned to bed. His new phone was substantially better than the cheap one that had been stolen and it took him a moment to familiarise himself with its menu system until he worked out how to access the new message. Same brand, same menu structure, but just the buttons were different. He read the message.

```
Leon Newman is as
good as dead.
```

This was not what he expected or wanted to read as he woke. He hoped that the dyslexia of his youth had returned or that he'd otherwise misread it, but there was no mistake. He racked his brain to recall if Leon Newman registered any memory. He could not recall anyone by that name and comforted himself that he'd received someone else's message. Rubbing the sleep from his eyes, he remembered the message that he'd received the previous day but all but forgotten it amid the enthusiasm of getting started. Now he quickly navigated the menu of the phone to re-read yesterday's message a second time.

Casey Lawrence is now
dead.

Devlin suddenly felt the need to be more awake and turned on the bedside light. Again, he couldn't think of anyone he knew by that name, no matter how distantly, but now he also felt that it was unlikely the messages had been misdirected. They were clearly similar and clearly intended for him. That they were sent to his phone number and not technically to him was a moot point.

He also discovered that each message had been sent from the same number; his own stolen phone. The likelihood that he'd received these messages by accident or coincidence was suddenly decidedly remote, particularly as he expected only a few people would know his new, unlisted, number.

Devlin rang his old number, figuring he'd be able to quickly separate truth from conjecture by just speaking to the guy who'd stolen his phone. As he listened to the ringing tone, he thought of what to say, but he never got the chance as his call went unanswered to voicemail. He listened to his own voicemail recording but opted to hang-up rather than leave a message. As soon as he ended the call, he received another message.

Carson Sullivan is
now dead.

Devlin settled himself and composed a message in reply. He wasn't concerned about tone or how his question would be received, only that it would be received.

Who are they?

Devlin sent his message and waited. A reply came almost immediately.

`Readers.`

Devlin was shaken. An odd thought then struck him and he fumbled for the contacts list in his phone. His was the first name in the list and from this he gathered that each of the numbers were in a formal, 'Surname, First Name' format. He scrolled through the names recognising Ikel and Lori only because their particular entries appeared to be in a 'Surname, First Name (Nickname)' format. But these were not the names he was looking for.

When Devlin reached 'Kendrick, Derrell' he paused, if only to recall his alphabet. 'Kopac, Morris (Hotel Manager)' followed, teasing Devlin and making him wonder how many names there could possibly be between 'Kendrick' and 'Lawrence'. He needn't have worried; the next name in the list was 'Lawrence, Casey'. He expected the name, but it still came as a shock. He continued scrolling through the names, passing 'Newman, Leon' and inevitably, 'Sullivan, Carson'.

Devlin put down the phone and thought a thousand thoughts, but he only said one word. "Fuck." With his head in his hands, he considered his options. He needed to talk them through, but it was still a few hours until dawn. Initially he thought he'd be able to wait to speak to someone, but even a few restless minutes alone proved difficult. He tried watching television and doing push-ups, but nothing was an adequate distraction. There was nothing on TV and his personal fitness was inadequate to sustain more than a minute of exercise. He considered a shower that he knew would clear his head, until he heard the now familiar sound of the receipt of another message.

<pre>
Don't join them. Be
sure you understand
the greater good.
</pre>

Devlin abandoned social niceties. He quickly dressed and headed for Ikel's room.

Ikel was slow to answer the door, but Devlin was persistent. Banging on his door, he eventually convinced Ikel that he really needed to talk, and no, it couldn't wait until morning. Ikel reluctantly opened his door before returning to bed. Devlin made himself at home in Ikel's room, turning on lights before sitting on the foot of his bed.

"Ikel. Who's Casey Sullivan?" Devlin opened with the first of at least three pressing questions. On seeing that Ikel had fallen asleep again with his head under a pillow, Devlin looked around for his phone. "I just want to check your phone," he announced as a matter of courtesy, irrespective of whether Ikel was coherent enough to listen. Subconsciously, Devlin wasn't sure whether he wanted Ikel's phone purely to verify that it contained the same numbers as his own, or to deny Ikel the ability to claim that he never knew Casey.

Devlin searched Ikel's room for his phone without regard to the obvious breach of privacy of a person he'd only just met. Ikel's room was a mirror image of his own, otherwise it was identical except that it had a definite 'lived in' feel. The room was full of clothing and personal effects, but it felt more like an adolescent's room than a bachelor pad. He found the phone still in Ikel's discarded jeans from the day before.

Devlin braced himself for the worst and took a long breath as he prepared for what might be revealed with Ikel's phone, but it had been turned off for the evening. He switched on the phone and immediately navigated to the contacts list, finding what appeared to be the same list of names and numbers as his own.

Still in Devlin's hands, Ikel's phone then vibrated to indicate the receipt of three messages in rapid succession. Devlin's first reaction was to read the messages, but even in his stressed state he accepted that reading Ikel's messages would be, without question, a breach of privacy. While there were some social conventions that were still reasonable and binding, Devlin decided that others were decidedly less applicable under the circumstances. By comparison, the unwritten rule about not waking a new acquaintance, come friend, pre-dawn was more of a guideline.

"Ikel. Wake up!" Devlin removed Ikel's bedclothes and pillow and shook him ruthlessly. "You've just got a few messages and I need you to compare them to mine."

"Fuck off!" Ikel replied eloquently, clearly reluctant to waking. He rolled over, dragging his bottom sheet over himself.

"Please. I've got some messages that have me a little spooked," Devlin pleaded as he considered emptying a glass of water over Ikel's head. He then suggested a path of least resistance, "or can I read your messages?"

"Casey, Carson and Leon. Dead or not, there's nothing you can do for them. Now turn the 'ken phone off and let me get back to sleep!"

"So you've read the messages already? What about *these* messages? Wake up!" There was no chance that Ikel was going to be allowed to go back to sleep now. With persistence, Devlin *encouraged* Ikel to sit up.

"We all used to get the same messages," Ikel began, yawning. "Sometimes the message text was different, but generally the same. Leon, Carson, Casey. Sometimes others. Generally they come at night, but that might be more because the phones don't work in the bunker. That's why I switch off mine at night." Rubbing his eyes, he added, "I'm assuming that you've got some messages too."

"Yep, I've got them," Devlin sighed. "Actually, I got the first one not long after I agreed to come on board."

"Yup," said Ikel.

"You don't think it's a little odd that the messages start when I joined you and Glen and co?"

"Not really. If I remember correctly it was the same with me."

"What about the fact that the guy that nicked my phone yesterday, *before* I joined LastGasp', is the one who's sending them?" Devlin said, certain that this would be of interest.

"Are you sure?"

"My phone got stolen. I'm sure of that. And now I'm getting messages from the stolen phone's number," Devlin replied cynically.

"It's easy to send a text message setting any sender number you like, if you know how," Ikel replied. "It doesn't mean the guy that took your phone is the one sending them."

Devlin understood what Ikel was saying and he felt his anxiety subside a little, but it didn't answer all of his questions. "So who's sending them? Who sends your messages, or who *allegedly* sends them?"

"Who's to say it's not different people? I've got my theories."

"You're not interested in finding out? You're not curious?"

"Curious? Yes. But I'm also tired," Ikel yawned.

"I don't mean *now*! But haven't you checked?"

"Yes and no. I don't really care."

"But why me? Why do *you* receive them? And incidentally, who are they, Leon, Carson and Casey?"

"Dunno. Don't care. Ask Glen if you like," Ikel replied with disinterest. "I asked him ages ago, but he wasn't worried. He said they used to work with him, but they moved on. Maybe he'll give you a better answer."

"You could've told me!" Devlin sniped. He considered that there was little else to be done at this hour, and the thought had a calming effect. "Ok then. Go back to sleep and we'll hook up later for breakfast."

"I'm awake now, so we might as well have an early one," Ikel reluctantly suggested. "I'll even lend you some clothes. Lori said you didn't have any more."

Chapter - 19.

Angie was happy to see Malcolm when he visited her in the hospital ward. She felt terrible as a result of the anti-retroviral medication that she'd been given following what had been written up as just a 'regular' needle-stick assault, but seeing him grounded her and made her smile just the same. He obviously didn't come to talk, or stay, but the fact that he even came at all meant a lot. It was just like him really, she reasoned. Malcolm had appeared in her life not long ago, and she'd become used to the way that he seemed to just want to co-exist. More than once, he'd been in the right place at the right time when Nebojsa had made another of his visits, and just Malcolm being there seemed to prevent the guy from inflicting his usual sordid misery.

Nebojsa had gradually scared off all of her friends and potential mates. However, Malcolm was not so easily perturbed, even though he lacked the physical presence that would be necessary if he ever came face to face with Nebojsa when he was in one of his moods. Angie felt that this day would come, but she selfishly resisted the urge to warn Malcolm away, opting instead to offer *anything* to encourage him to stay. Malcolm wasn't interested in any kind of relationship, or even a physical friendship, but he liked having a room to call his own when he needed it.

"Feeling better?" Malcolm asked as he sat himself by her bedside.

"He sends his best wishes. He asked after you by name." Angie tried a little dark humour, but then regretted it. She knew that Malcolm would understand but she was in no mood for his preaching. He meant well, but he seemed to be incapable of believing her when she'd said she'd tried everything. She'd moved countless times, even interstate, but Nebojsa had enough contacts to track her down, and his 'business interests' seemed to give him the ways and means to travel to *visit* her wherever she'd attempted to put down some roots. She'd gone to the Police as a matter of routine, but their interest had waned considerably after she'd retracted her complaints the first dozen or so times. Of course the fact that Nebojsa was so well connected and Angie wasn't, made the accusations appear all the more vexatious.

Malcolm reached for her hand. "Just a little longer, Angie."

Chapter - 20.

Devlin was well into his second plate of food before Ikel joined him. They both ate socially but quietly, not unlike a couple comfortable enough with each other to not *need* to talk. He was beginning to relax, and he no longer felt the compulsion to be guarded in everything that he said.

"So what's on today?" Devlin asked.

"We'll go to work, and we'll take it from there," Ikel replied. "We'll read a lot of messages, sure, but no two days are the same. Hopefully we'll get a chance to get out of the office for a bit. Glen will probably want you to stay with me."

Devlin received another text message on his phone. Ikel had explained away his immediate concerns but still he couldn't bring himself to read the message. Noting Devlin's apprehension, Ikel grabbed Devlin's phone and read it for him.

"Relax. It's from Glen. He wants you there by seven."

"Are we going to chase up Lori?" Devlin asked.

"No point. She's less of a morning person than I am, so you're best to steer clear of her until lunchtime if you can. She won't even answer her door most nights and mornings, so much so that I've wondered if she's even in her room."

*   *   *

Judging by the volume of coffee on offer and being consumed on their arrival at LastGasp', Devlin was sure that falling asleep would not be a problem. David was still in yesterday's clothes but was wired and Glen was shamelessly pushing double shot lattés.

After checking his watch, Glen impatiently ushered his staff to the bunker, but he held Devlin back. "You'll have a visitor soon."

"Who?" asked Devlin, a little surprised to be separated from the others

The buzzer sounded and Glen checked his CCTV monitors. He smiled, "Right on cue." He headed for the front door, returning a moment later with the new arrival, a middle aged Asian man, and flippantly started some introductions. "Devlin, this is Conrad."

Devlin offered his hand, but the newcomer kept his hands in his pockets.

"Don't let Glen make you think this is social. My name is Conrad Tran, I'm with the Federal Police." He spoke with a thick local accent that belied his Vietnamese ancestry.

The mood in the room was very weird, the sum of obvious hostility from the newly arrived Conrad, Glen seemingly very deliberately trying to bait him and Devlin just feeling uncomfortable. Glen delighted in breaking the silence. "You're welcome to do your thing here. Your call, but I'll just leave you to it."

"You're a comedian, Glen. We'll go elsewhere of course," Conrad replied. Devlin sensed the history between the two of them, and none of it seemed friendly.

Devlin looked to Glen for his concurrence or approval. "Don't look at me!" Glen mocked. "Head off with Conrad here. He's not bad, even if what he wants is, strictly speaking, outside of his area of responsibility."

Devlin sensed Conrad's rising frustration amid Glen's continued antagonism. "Should I have lawyer join me?"

"Relax. You haven't done anything wrong, and you don't need any lawyer," Glen calmly answered, ushering Devlin and Conrad out of the building before closing the door behind them.

"I hate that guy," Conrad began as soon as they were outside, continuing into utterances progressively less coherent until Devlin struggled to understand anything he said. He waited for Conrad to get what he had to say off his chest, enjoying the spectacle of a middle aged, lean and well-dressed guy standing kerbside outside a brothel venting with a passion.

Conrad composed himself and pointed to a small café across the road and started walking, clearly expecting Devlin to follow. They dodged the early morning traffic heading for the coffee shop that was doing a roaring trade in takeaways. Only after brushing past the crowds at the front counter did Devlin realise that the rest of the café was essentially empty and not that noisy either. Conrad held up two fingers to the barista at the counter and took his seat at a corner table, presumably *his* table.

Now settled, Conrad began. "Sorry about that. I appreciate that you haven't known him long, but he really gets on my wick!"

Devlin was cautious and careful not to demonstrate any indication, either to confirm or confront Conrad's opinion. "So what's this all about?"

"*This* is all about coffee. I've ordered you a latté which I guarantee will be the best that you've ever tasted." Conrad smiled, well aware he was not answering the question.

"You know what I mean."

"Yes. Moira will be along in a sec' with your coffee. I'll explain my side then. Why don't you tell me a little about yourself while we wait?"

Devlin shrugged, uncomfortable about offering anything to anyone, particularly the police. To him, it was oddly reminiscent of being forced to sit next to his school principal on a high school excursion many years ago. To the best of his recollection, he was reluctant to say anything to anyone in authority then, and the same applied now.

"Enjoy your job?" Conrad offered another means of seeding a conversation.

Devlin decided that this question at least was benign. "Yes." Benign or not, he was not prepared to give too much away too easily.

"I know of several others who used to work with Glen, *for* Glen. I'm pretty sure they enjoyed their job too."

"Your point being what? I wouldn't have thought job satisfaction was a significant concern for the police."

A waitress, presumably Moira, returned with two steaming coffees. Conrad, pushed one cup towards Devlin and immediately started to enjoy the other. He sat back, as if confidently expecting accolades to flow. "Ahhh, the life of a reader. Pay and perks. Wanna' know how I know so much about your role?"

"Not really," Devlin replied honestly, if not a little distracted by his coffee. Conrad's prediction was correct.

"Casey told me. Well actually, Casey told me about the pay, but I didn't believe him until Carson confirmed it. Leon told me about the other aspects of your package."

"So we agree that it's a good job. Anything else?" Devlin tried his best poker face but he doubted whether he was convincing. He figured it was unlikely that anyone would reveal details of their package, but then again this information was surely accessible to the police. He wondered if mention of Leon, Casey and Carson constituted confirmation of anything, or anything significant.

The two men sat in silence, absorbed in the background hum of the café counter and the taste of their lattés. Devlin didn't give any suggestion that he was going start communicating freely.

On finishing his coffee, Devlin figured that their casual meeting was soon to be at a close. "If you like the sound of working with Glen so much, why don't you ask him for a job?" Devlin asked, half in jest.

Conrad looked up, alert. "The job would be great, and pay substantially more than I get now." He stared at Devlin, adding, "but it's not worth dying over."

Devlin was no poker player and he knew that his eyes would have betrayed him. There was no point in claiming ignorance. "What did you say?"

"It's just an expression," Conrad replied confidently. "No job is worth dying over, especially a job with Glen and not just because the guy's an asshole."

"How so?" Devlin replied, knowing that his question could be misinterpreted as divided loyalty.

"Leon and the rest. How much do you know about them?"

Devlin shrugged. "Not a lot."

"You might like to ask Glen. I don't want to be the bearer of bad news." Conrad gave Devlin a knowing look. "I've gotta' get to work."

"Why don't you tell me now?"

"Ask Glen. I've got to go."

"Doesn't *this* count as work?" Devlin recalled what Glen had said when he'd introduced Conrad. "Come to think of it, what was it that Glen said about your job and your area of interest?"

"Glen!" Conrad closed his eyes in an effort to calm himself. "Not technically. But …"

Devlin interrupted him, incensed. "Conrad, what exactly is your job?"

"Technically, I'm a researcher."

"Are you even with the Federal Police?"

"Yes, and I have contracted to state and overseas Police forces too."

"Are you actually a Police officer, or not?"

"Not technically, but…"

"And Glen knows, right?"

"Yes, *he* knows. He baits me about it as a matter of routine."

"Routine? What kind of an idiot are you? Why see him at all, particularly if you have issues."

Conrad composed himself. "I'm trying to help."

"Me or you?" Devlin replied aggressively, suddenly aware of why Glen had been so un-concerned about Conrad. "Even I understand how attractive LastGasp' would be to a researcher!" He figured it was time to leave.

"Me *and* you. You're in trouble!" he said, grabbing Devlin's arm as he brushed past. "Take my card. Call me any time."

Devlin accepted the card more out of reflex than deliberate action. "Thanks for your concern," he said cynically. Conrad's innuendo about Leon and the others was all but an acceptance of responsibility for sending the messages. He angrily pushed his way past the crowd.

"Please! I can help!" Conrad called out. Devlin was already out of the café, but not out of earshot.

Chapter - 21.

Devlin returned to LastGasp' and was buzzed in. He headed for the kitchen and only after pouring himself a coffee did he notice Glen waiting for him in the adjacent lounge.

"Was Conrad good to you?" Glen asked with a smirk on his face, offering Devlin a seat.

"You might have told me he wasn't *really* Police," Devlin said taking his seat next to Glen. "He nearly had me!"

"It's ok," Glen replied, unfazed. "Now's as good a time as any to be reminded that there are people who want in."

"I'm starting to understand the fascination with security. I figure it's to keep people like Conrad out, but I still don't get why he's so keen to get in. I know you told me yesterday that it wasn't about money, but I didn't and still don't really believe you."

"Newcomers always think LastGaspStore is about money. But money isn't everything."

"I still don't see the big deal."

"The problem lies in what they want to use LastGasp for. Personal gain, or the greater good."

"How?"

"Have a think about it. Now go and get some work done."

Chapter - 22.

Tania Wilson was slowly getting her life back in order. The time since the death of her brother had been a blur of emotions and even a few well-meaning *friends*. Long forgotten people had come from nowhere to help in any way that they could and it had been greatly, but not graciously appreciated. But gradually these people were giving her more and more space to process her grief, surely the first stage in leaving her alone. Who was she kidding? These people were abandoning her again. The reality was that they were more than likely friends of her brother rather than hers. He was the good one, she wasn't.

She was finding the going difficult, particularly of late. No stranger to abandonment, to have a glimpse of positive attention only to have it dissipate just as quickly left her all the more raw. Her well-meaning therapist had naïvely suggested that she was still too angry. Tania was persistently keen to point out that the woman was clearly only focussing on her most recent past.

The funeral over, her brother's limited estate settled, there was now no *real* impediment to her returning to whatever kind of normality her grief would allow. The reality of the matter was of course very different, and she knew she would never approach normal. It was this that her therapist seemed unable to understand.

It was time to start to get on with her life though. Tim would not have wanted her to dwell on things outside of her control. The big brother had always been philosophically smart about such things. Inspired by the memory of his strength and understanding, she decided it was time to pick herself up. She took a long shower, dressed casually for the day and did her makeup for the first time in days. She drew the curtains in every room and opened every window, much to the appreciation of her scattered indoor plants who'd suffered for a lack of sunlight as a consequence of her despondency.

Tania was not fastidious. Had it not been for an older woman she'd met at a group session, she hated the term 'sponsor', she knew that she'd be deep in accumulated mess and washing by now. She noticed the woman's perpetually close pet cat of course, but not that the woman had kept on top of her domesticity. Now she felt a little guilty, particularly when she only knew her as 'Cat'. She knew a brief thank-you note would go a long way to show her appreciation and offset her guilt. A handwritten note would be best and more personal, she reasoned, but this upside was balanced by the fact that she did have the worst handwriting of anyone that she knew. The ability for the recipient to read the message was surely more important than the sincerity implicit in a handwritten note. *No time like the present*, she moved to her computer desk, amazed at her sober initiative.

For reasons which now seemed irrelevant, Tania had named her computer 'Simon'. As Simon started, she smiled with a tear in her eye at *his* nametag which had been a gift from her brother. Even something as innocuous as using the computer was not going to be without memories.

Eventually Simon indicated he was ready. It had been weeks since she'd accessed her email and she braced herself for the prospect of many messages. Slowly her email in-box filled. She expected nothing from friends or family of course, but a plethora of spam emails advising of lottery wins and bargains for Viagra and penile enlargements. Simon laboured away during the download. She'd resisted all efforts to upgrade her computer and as such her relationship with Simon had been a long one. The reality of it was that had Simon actually been worth anything, she would have sold 'him' long before now. As he chugged along with effort, she considered whether their relationship had run its course. *Poor Simon*, she mused.

Simon sat on a large desk overlooking the park on the other side of the street. With the window open, the morning sun was glorious and Tania allowed herself to be distracted until she noticed that Simon was no-longer making sounds of hyperactivity. There was nowhere near as much new email as she expected and it didn't take long to work out what had happened. It seemed that she'd received so much spam that she'd exceeded some limit imposed by her service provider. The result was that in the last ten days, all she'd received was daily reminders that her mailbox was full. *Dammit.* She wondered what the senders of those emails would think when they received the obligatory bounce message as if she'd disappeared off the face of the earth. She wondered if anyone would care.

The more she thought about it, the more she accepted that few of them, if any, would change the way she felt. Notwithstanding the fact that it would have been nice to see who had emailed her, the fact remained that they would invariably have contained the same general thing. 'Sorry to hear of your loss', 'he was a lovely man', 'a kind friend'. All about him, not about her. Even dead, Tim was the good one, and she wasn't.

In this train of thought it made perfect sense that a standard universal reply would be more than appropriate. She quickly typed a message and addressed it to everyone she knew, thanking them for their support and kind words. She wondered for a time if Tim himself would have done a better job, drawing on some government standard template. She then added a post-script that her email server had been overwhelmed and hit the 'Send' button before her usual tendency to proof-read set in. Simon obliged and she returned to the more taxing task of preparing a more personal thank-you note for 'Cat'.

Chapter - 23.

Technically hospital wasn't really a holiday, but the Malcolm it served the same purpose. It allowed him to rest and in doing so he might just avert an episode. No matter how committed he was, he did not want to live with the implications of failing health. Not again.

The use of the hospital was a risk, and a risk that was not taken lightly. It violated each of his simple rules. *Don't draw attention. Don't go on record. Avoid the police.* Instead, he'd made a spectacle of himself, was now on file in the public health system and indeed the public *mental* health system, and on this occasion had actually invited specific Police involvement. It was not ideal by any means, but it was necessary. Malcolm didn't dare dwell on what might have happened. Instead, he concentrated on the upside of his gamble. He'd effectively hidden in plain view, implicitly acquired a watertight alibi, *and* got some chemically induced rest. He would have liked to gloat.

Now though, he was out of hospital, rested, grounded and ready to resume his work. He picked up from where he left off.

Chapter - 24.

Ikel intercepted Devlin mid corridor en-route to the bunker. "Come on. We're going on a field trip!" he said exuberantly. Devlin followed Ikel out of the building.

"Care to tell me where we're heading?" asked Devlin as he walked beside Ikel along the footpath.

"Hang on," Ikel replied, nodding to Conrad as they passed him, leaning against a car, presumably his own. "I'll tell you when we get to my car," Ikel said softly, glancing back over his shoulder at Conrad.

Albert was asleep in front of Ikel's car, oblivious to the heavy smell of ammonia that permeated everything. As soon as Ikel laid a single step in the vicinity of his car, Albert appeared aggressively, but he quickly relaxed as soon as he recognised a familiar face. "Anyone we know?"

"Just one drop off today. We won't be long." Ikel unlocked his car and got into his seat, clearly not wanting to mislead Albert that he was interested in any conversation.

Albert understood. "Maybe later then," he said, resuming his rest position between puddles after nodding to Devlin.

"So where are we going?" Devlin asked as soon as they were inside the car and mobile.

"LastGasp' is pretty much automated," Ikel began. "But if contact is lost, then we need to manually drop off messages. And that's what we're doing now. I didn't want to say anything before with that idiot Conrad sniffing around."

"Do we know who the member is, or just who we are visiting? Or is this how we get a definitive identification, only when we ask the recipient?"

"I see your point, but it's not like that. Once the member is dead, we can identify them without too much guesswork on our part. LastGasp' is technically like a bank, and so we get notified as soon as someone dies so that their assets and accounts can be frozen."

"So who died?"

Ikel wriggled forward in his seat and reached inside the back of his jacket, removing a large envelope. "Everything I know is in this. I remember the address and the woman's name, but nothin' else. You'll have to read it yourself."

Devlin examined the contents of the envelope immediately, curious as he was. He found a single page describing the message recipient's contact details, and what invariably represented the message itself, formatted simply as text but on LastGasp' letterhead. After the first few paragraphs, he found himself skim reading. He returned the pages to the envelope and restored his attention to the traffic as it flashed past. "How often do you do this anyway?"

"It depends really. I might get out of the office every day for a week and then I'll have a week when I'm like a rat in a cage and stuck in the office."

"What's so good about doing this? Other than giving you the opportunity to play race car driver in your toy here."

Ikel smiled at Devlin directly. "That. And the sympathy fucks."

"You're kidding?"

"It's another undocumented perk of LastGasp'. In fact, because I'm such a great guy, I'll let you *have* this one, or *do* this one." No matter how he phrased it, the innuendo remained. "I'm not promising anything of course, but if you're there when she needs someone to hold, then who are we to stand in the way!"

"Thanks. But I'm sure that nothing will happen."

"Suit yourself. I know you're not gay based on the way that you looked at Lori last night, so don't be too quick to rule it out. Just in case, I'll drop you off and leave you to it for a while."

Devlin was starting to feel a little pressure, irrespective of whether he felt that anything sexual would come of the task of delivering a message. "Keep the motor running Ikel. I don't think that hand delivering a letter will take too long!"

"It's *never* as simple as handing over a piece of paper. They'll need to talk about it."

"Fine," Devlin said with a measure of reluctance. "What do I say?"

"Just read the message for background. You'll be fine."

Devlin re-read the message, this time a little slower. He quickly gathered what were perhaps the important aspects of the message content to allow him to meet the recipient, a woman, Tania Wilson, who was obviously someone's much loved little sister. There was nothing particularly confessional, or even interesting other than a series of recollections and memories which might strike a chord with someone with a shared interest. Lacking that background, Devlin felt like someone sitting in on the eulogy at a stranger's funeral.

The end of their journey was marked with Ikel's tyres screeching to a halt. "I'll give you an hour, but ring me if you need longer… Stud!"

Devlin raised his eyebrows to Ikel. He returned the papers to the envelope and got out of the car leaving Ikel to speed off immediately. He sauntered to the subject address, looking to waste a few minutes here and there if at all possible, certain that nothing would eventuate in spite of Ikel's best wishes. He looked at his watch and given that he could hear movement from inside the home, he figured that he'd wasted enough time. He rang the door-bell and waited.

Chapter - 25.

Tania Wilson was surprised to hear the bell ring. She'd never been a morning person and everyone knew to give her a wide berth, typically until well after lunch. Everyone except her brother. He'd described it as 'poking the bear' and he'd revelled in tormenting his sister with early morning wake-up calls for as long as either of them could remember. The door chime initially made her think of a new means of retaliation, until it struck her that it couldn't possibly be Tim. A shadow was re-cast on her temporarily heightened mood. She opened the door and did her best to greet her visitor simply but nicely and with a manner that did not reflect her disappointment. "Hello."

"Good morning," the visitor began, looking her over as subtly and best he could through the security screen. "My name is Devlin Bennett. You don't know me, but I work for an organisation known as 'LastGasp'. Our recent emails to you have bounced."

"So?" Tania couldn't help herself. It was not her time of the day, and rapidly approaching her time of the month, and she was in no mood to be annoyed with something inconsequential. She remembered periodically receiving an email from some organisation calling itself LastGasp', but she'd habitually deleted it as *spam* given that she didn't know the sender.

"Well yes. I appreciate that you've recently lost someone special. LastGasp' provides a service whereby people can create messages to be sent posthumously, and I have one such message for you."

"You're not a Jehovah's witness are you?"

"No, I'm not." The guy smiled, clearly not offended at the accusation. "Can I come in to explain further?"

"Just give me the message," Tania ordered on seeing the envelope in the man's hand.

"Of course." The guy fumbled before removing some papers from the envelope, wincing briefly as he gave himself a small paper-cut in the process.

Tania opened the screen door a little and accepted the papers cautiously. "Anything else?" she asked, looking at the man sucking his finger.

"No, that's all." He reached inside his jacket and presented a business card, "In case you need anything else, here's my card."

Tania accepted the card but was more interested in returning to her solitude. The man had been polite enough, but she didn't feel up to extending any great effort of hospitality to a stranger. She closed the door and watched the guy wander off looking at his watch.

Privacy restored, Tania returned to her lounge room. She watched her visitor through her window and saw him pause kerbside before heading to the coffee-shop. The guy didn't look like a stalker, though perhaps it might be possible to watch her from there. She knew how bad the coffee was and thought he would only be there a little while, unless he was decidedly committed.

Tania sat on her old couch, took a deep breath and began to read the papers that she'd been given by the guy from LastGasp'. Her suspicion as to the authenticity of the message was put to rest immediately. There was no doubt it was a letter from Tim. She soon found herself alternating between many emotions simultaneously. Above all else, she enjoyed the joy of his presence, coupled with the disappointment that this letter would be as close as she'd ever get to time with him.

She also felt more than a tinge of guilt at her treatment of the visitor. The least she could have done was offer a half decent cup of coffee. There was still time for her to demonstrate a little social conscience. She quickly grabbed her phone and called the guy's number from his business card. She kept it brief, opting to say her apology in person, but in any case she wanted him to stay where he was.

*   *   *

The phone-call from Tania surprised Devlin no end. He'd been hopeful only that the remainder of the hour until he'd be picked up wouldn't drag on. Waiting in the suburban café his hopes had largely been dashed by cheap coffee and the omnipresent stench of a smoker who'd casually decided to hover around him. Only after the first taste of did he notice and understand why he was the only one drinking coffee. He'd suffered through four mouthfuls and was on the cusp of either leaving or ordering a canned drink of some description; something sweet to offset the residual bitterness in his mouth. Tania's call removed his indecision.

Unlike the café suggested by Conrad, this one was not attracting the 'on-the-way-to-work' set of people, or the coffee gourmands either for that matter. There were several other patrons seated in the shaded courtyard overlooking the park facing Tania's home. There was a guy sitting on his own in the corner who shamelessly enjoyed the expression of distaste that Devlin demonstrated with his beverage, but the others were more reserved, or at least more subdued in their reaction. The only upside of this particular café was its proximity to the park. He savoured the fresh smells of the gardens that returned after the departure of the smoker.

Devlin watched Tania cross the road towards him and then into the café and he stood as she approached his table. She waved to the woman at the counter and made some gesture which appeared to be known between them before she joined him at his table. He could see the residual redness around her eyes, but also that there was a brightness about her face he had not seen when they'd spoken at her door. He knew the letter had been the cause of both the tears barely masked in her eyes, and the happiness that now radiated from her. In delivering the message, Devlin was oddly proud for the minor role he'd played in the transformation of this woman. Only now did he notice how pretty she was. Devlin was daydreaming while looking at her until she spoke.

"Thanks for seeing me again, Devlin. I just wanted to say 'Thank-you'." She dabbed her eyes with a tissue before continuing. "My brother, Tim, and I were close, and I've been a bit of a wreck lately without him. Only after I read Tim's letter did I realise that you were doing me, and Tim, a service. And for the record, it's a service for which I'm inordinately appreciative."

Devlin sat quietly while Tania shared everything that she'd managed to glean from the letter. Most of what she described was just recapping on what he himself had read, but Tania also managed to extract subtleties that he had overlooked. He felt the joy that he'd help deliver until he waved to Ikel when he saw his car pull up. He said his farewells to Tania, and set off.

*   *   *

Malcolm Venn was not a coffee drinker, not now anyway. A long time ago he was a habitual espresso man, but as his consumption gradually increased, so did his periods of being what his mother described innocently as being 'unwell'. His appearance of psychological stability was every bit as important as it was with other sufferers of mental illness. Caffeine in the volumes that he once consumed had influenced his behaviour, only marginally, but more than enough to alter other people's perceptions of him from being a 'happy eccentric' to 'erratically unstable'. Had his medical history not been a factor, of course, the caffeine would just as easily have seen him be described as *particularly* eccentric', but once mental illness is a consideration, it has a nasty habit of forever tainting perceptions.

His serious coffee drinking days were behind him, but Malcolm still enjoyed caffeine in moderation, typically by way of a daily can of Coke. He also appreciated the look of satisfaction on the face of a coffee drinker when they partook of their regular hit, particularly their first for the day. This time, however, there was no militant reaction to bad coffee in the park-side café. This was no surprise to Malcolm as he'd seen others, even that very same morning, refuse to pay for their cups. The way that they'd screwed up their faces in revulsion spoke volumes of the inadequacy of the bean blend, the hygiene of the machine, or the incompetency of the coffee maker herself. It all just added to the entertainment as he sat watching Tania's home, waiting for when she'd finally make an appearance after hiding herself away. He couldn't believe his luck when not only did he see her, but she even sat at the table right beside him, close enough for him to hear everything she said as she spoke to someone, clearly one of Glen's new monkeys.

It was nice for Tim to lift Tania's spirits temporarily. She was going to need it.

Chapter - 26.

Devlin was contentedly silent in the car on the way back to the office. His expectations of *'making a difference'* had been far more grandiose, but oddly there was something amazing about how Glen's prediction had played out. He felt he had indeed made a difference, but in fact he'd done almost nothing. He was just the messenger, but he felt accomplishment just the same.

"Too bad. Maybe with your next one!" Ikel commented. "I can tell a freshly fucked glow when I see one, and I can see that you didn't get any!"

Devlin smiled. "I still feel good though. Are they all like this?"

"What? Pretty? No, most of the people we hand deliver to are old or ugly, or both. Old people crack me up. They join LastGasp' knowing full well that their wife or husband couldn't even turn on a computer, let alone access email, so how is it that they are supposed to get a message? Lori could impress you with the numbers on the proportion of the population that are old and also LastGasp' members."

"Actually, I was referring to whether every message gave you a warm and fuzzy feeling."

"Fuck knows," Ikel replied. "I don't even read them now. I just get the address, look at the name and fantasise about whether I'm going to get some. It's not often though, but only because David gets most of the good ones!"

"How does that work?"

"He's a bit of a dark horse. I think he uses the Research Interface to track down pictures to improve his odds. He takes the best ones and leaves me the rest."

"You said David was crap with the Research Interface."

"Actually, I said David was crap at identifying people. But there's no other explanation for the volume of nice ones he gets. Maybe he's good when he's got an incentive."

Relative quiet returned to the car, periodically interspersed with almost comical outbursts from Ikel directed at other drivers. Devlin was oddly calm. Not only was he getting used to Ikel's driving, but he was also feeling remarkably comfortable with Ikel as a person and a friend. "I think I'm ready to tell you why I killed him."

"OK then."

"I didn't mean to," Devlin began, planning his words carefully.

"Dev', I'm not a jury. Say what you want."

"OK. I didn't mean to kill the guy, at least not initially. I'd known the guy since school and when he made a flippant comment, initially I just wanted to confront him, but then I lost my cool. There was a struggle and before I knew it we were throwing each other up against a fence. I didn't even notice the thunderstorm until WHAM! I felt like I'd been hit by a truck.

"He happened to be touching the fence at the time of the strike. His convulsion bounced him off the fence and threw him backwards quite a way, and I was knocked out for a while just from the proximity of the strike. Somewhere in all of this, presumably in his convulsion with the shock, the knife, his knife, must have been thrown into the air, only to hit him when it landed. What are the odds of that happening, let alone the odds of it piercing his heart?

"When I came to, I saw he was dead and I was shaken up obviously, and not really happy, but not disappointed either. I would have been content to close the page on that chapter of my life, and I did. Until the police did some fishing around and came up with what they described as a 'body of evidence' that I wanted him dead."

"Did you?" Ikel asked.

"Yep, and even now I'm glad he's dead. In retrospect, things might have been different had I lied, but I didn't. I was honest and naive and I told them as much. This really just set the ball rolling, and I was going to be held responsible for his death."

"But you said you blacked out?"

"I did. But with a finger print or two on the knife, and my admission, they had enough, particularly with nothing conclusive that I was *actually* knocked out."

"Then what?"

"They called it manslaughter, and the only reason that they didn't try for murder, particularly with my intent, was that the knife wasn't mine. It went to trial. I had some piss-ant, freshly graduated lawyer on my side, courtesy of the state, against an admittedly pretty reasonable case. I was gone even before the media got on board."

"How's that?"

"It made for good copy. 'Nice guy killed by bitter and twisted long-time friend'. The guy was played up as a saint. Father of two, his kids now father-less. Once happy wife, now a widow. And I was played as the quintessential bastard. And my family being who they are, or were, you can't imagine what that caused. Until then, my father was the poster-boy for family values, out-spoken social reformer, being groomed for all manner of politics, state and federal. There was even talk of interest from overseas, like the U.N.. My predicament forced him to pick a side, which was pointless really because there was no future for him whichever way he swung. But he chose. Cut me adrift for the abomination that I am. So there I was. I've got no family and no friends able and willing to contradict anything being said about me."

"So what happened?"

"I was about to be hung out to dry. And then it just stopped. My snot-faced little lawyer noticed something in the medical examiners' report. Yes, there was a knife in the guy's heart, but that isn't what killed him. It seems that a second lightning strike got him, possibly at the exact moment that the knife was set to pierce his skin, straight into his heart. Despite calls of irrelevance, it was brought to the attention of the court and the jury found me not guilty. That's the short version anyway.

"It's funny how media hype of a killer is page one stuff, but an acquittal of someone who is technically innocent until proven guilty is relegated to page seven."

"And then what?"

"Then I was released, theoretically with a clean record. I moved interstate immediately, met Glen on a train and the rest you know. Somewhere in the detail is the fact that the few friends I thought I had aren't there for me now, and I remain an outcast from my family."

"But why?"

"Stuff came up in the Police investigation and then the media got on board. It changed everything." Devlin went quiet, drifting away into his thoughts.

"What came up? Why'd you need to speak to the guy in the first place?"

Devlin thought long and hard about whether to say any more. So far he'd explained more to Ikel about that entire episode of his life than he had to anyone else since it all began. But what he'd covered so far was the easy stuff, but to say more would be to potentially re-open a very recent and deep wound. He considered whether he was strong enough to say more. More importantly, he needed to assess whether Ikel was capable of hearing it.

"The guy called me a paedophile," Devlin said at last. To him, this would explain many things, but he'd since learnt that the rest of the world would require further explanation. He waited for the volley of questions in reply.

"That explains your outburst at that message yesterday," Ikel commented, adding, "but it doesn't explain why you killed him."

"I didn't intend to kill him."

"So, if I called you a *paed*, would you assault me, kill me?" Ikel teased, only half in jest.

"Fuck off, Ikel!"

"*Sticks and stones*, Dev'. What's the problem?"

Devlin expected questions, but answering meant raking over warm coals. He breathed deeply, composed himself and began. "It changed everything, Ikel. Get called a murderer, and there's an expectation that you can do the time in jail for it, get out and then resume a normal kind of life. Admittedly as an ex-con, but still a relatively normal life. True, ex-cons might never really get a truly 'fair go', but the point is that you can get on with your life.

"Get called a paedophile though, and nothing is the same. There's no such thing as an assumption of innocence, and the entire legal system will be corrupted just to appropriately *deal* with you. The greater community at large wants you dead, and castrated, but they'll invariably settle with you just being dead. Friends don't exist, and opportunities don't exist. Who cares that there were no grounds for the accusation in the first place. If I say anything in my defence, then I attract a wider audience. Say nothing and the silence says it all. *Where there's smoke there's fire.*"

"So why'd he say it then?"

"I don't know. The fact that he's dead hurt me more than anyone else. If I knew where he got the thought in his head, then I might have some recourse, or maybe even get to the root of it all. That's what I went to talk to him about. But once the Police did their investigation, they learnt about his accusation, and from there it was very easy to make a case for revenge. And the media? My favourite headline was 'Paedophile's revenge kills family man'. There's no future after that."

"You still glad he's dead?"

"Close. I don't care he's dead. As unfortunate as it is that he's left behind a widow and kids, I didn't mean to kill him. That's been proven. Whether or not his family or the world at large actually believe it is another matter. I'd still love to know where it all started, but as I'm *persona non grata*, the chances of me ever finding out are virtually zero anyway. Who would care if the truth actually did come out?"

It occurred to Devlin that Ikel hadn't exactly supported his quest for the truth. He couldn't let the thought rest. "Do you believe me?"

"What's to believe? And what do you care if I believe you or not?"

Devlin considered whether he'd be reduced to convincing the world one person at a time. "Do you believe what I'm saying is the truth?"

"For what it's worth, yes. But the truth doesn't prove or accomplish anything. I've seen a thousand messages of secrets that would have been better left to die with the sender. I always wonder what good those messages will do when they are received. You'll see this soon enough."

"Perhaps, Ikel. Perhaps." Devlin drifted into deep, silent thought. He thought about what Ikel had said, but also about how his little outburst must have appeared. He didn't want to appear obsessed, but the fact was that he held only a thin veneer of calm to suppress his anger about *that* entire episode. He knew that this would be something he'd learn to live with, but in the meantime, he'd have to get a better grip on his emotions. As he calmed, the more he focussed on Ikel's last comment and immediately his curiosity about LastGasp' returned with a vengeance.

Ikel broke the silence. "See how you feel about truth in a week's time."

Chapter - 27.

Nebojsa Kendic was anxious. He always called this time of waiting, 'lay' time, and no matter how many times he'd waited through a lay period, it never got any easier. If he made it through the first day, lay time would be over, but that still meant a long wait until this evening. He couldn't help but mull over the root of his concern. That whore, Angie, was currently off-limits and in hospital, and god knows what she'd say to people without his *calming* influence. He wasn't really concerned for what she'd say, but rather for how it would be heard. He knew he was untouchable, but Police interest, if it came, was an annoyance and a distraction in what was sure to be a busy day.

Every other time there had been Police involvement it had cost him time he could ill afford. Conceivably, his ability to come away cleanly as he'd done in the past would be compromised if any amount of background checking had been done. He thought for a moment how much of his *'lay time stress'* was not attributed to actual Police involvement, but rather concern that the *seeds* he'd planted to provide for his continued security would be adequate, or whether he'd need to sow more widely. Nebojsa likened his contacts, or more specifically those indebted to him, to seeds from which something beneficial would grow. His seeds had variously afforded him whatever he'd required for as long as he could remember, but he was mindful that there would always be new people worthy of knowing, new seeds. Different people could serve him in their own special ways, beit exoneration from guilt, the timely provision of information, anonymity from most media, and importantly what amounted to 'untouchability'. Ultimately he knew that this time would be no different, but it did make him think what new contacts were worth discovering. He sighed deeply and poured himself another shot of Vodka and drank.

There was no point worrying right now anyway, it wouldn't help, but he hated being so reactive as to wait for what might happen. He wouldn't tolerate anything but pro-activity in his professional life, and it was frustrating that his personal life could be so different. At work, he had an uncanny ability to anticipate people's reactions, and combined with his domineering personality, he'd been on the corporate fast-track, despite a distinct lack of qualifications. As his realm of responsibility increased, so too did the number of staff at his disposal, each dedicated solely to turning his intent into a reality. Often his minions would struggle between themselves in an effort to impress him, and the result of this was that every conceivable detail would be dealt with. His private life was a different matter. He knew that all he'd need to do was mention a personal distraction and a well-meaning but essentially self-serving subordinate would take matters into their own hands, all in the name of demonstrating devotion or something equally nauseating. But he wasn't interested in their assistance, in just the same way that he wasn't interested in their sycophancy. Instead, he liked to deal with his personal matters by himself. As frustrating as the duality between his personal and professional life was, the fact remained that he enjoyed dealing with personal matters. Corporate power could not compare with the power he could wield in his private life.

Angie was Nebojsa's latest experiment and it was through Angie and her predecessors that he'd learnt a lot about himself, and about others. He'd learnt that he had a way over people, a way that drew them in to do his bidding, no matter what it was, and largely for essentially nothing in return. He'd learnt that in dealing with all people, the key was to find what drove them, and when this was found, they would invariably fall into line. To some, all it took was a glimmer of respect, or emotional attachment, or even banal friendship before they were but putty in his hands. To others, perhaps they needed just a little more *physical* encouragement.

Nebojsa hated the word '*threat*' on principle. 'Threat' implied that he'd state his request at least twice; before expecting it to be carried out. 'Do this or I will ...' was invariably followed by 'do this now!'. Nebojsa never asked twice. Nor did he need to. He found that his actions spoke more forcibly than he could ever shout. Rape with a promise of a return visit would encourage compliance far more simply than anything he could say prefixed with 'do this or I will...'. As much as Nebojsa could have enlisted a staff, he kept focused on his actions as being primarily for his personal development. As such, delegation to a subordinate would deny him an opportunity to learn, just as much as it would deny him some enjoyment.

Nebojsa had experienced a number of side effects from his self-education. Aside from considerable pleasure and the obvious professional upside of his burgeoning self-confidence, he'd also amassed a sizeable fortune. But above all else, he'd fostered a remarkable understanding of many things, some tangible, others less so. He understood the true value of money from what people would give him, and he only ever needed to ask once. He understood a virtual sliding scale of the concept of value in general. People would value pain, or more importantly, a lack thereof, higher than any possession or chattel that was theirs to give. People would value their own pain, or lack thereof, below a promise of pain for a loved one, particularly children or spouse. He understood that people would *always* believe that things would return to normal after any hint of short term pain or emotional anguish.

By far the most important thing that Nebojsa Kendic had learnt was that everyone had something to give. The rich could give him riches. The powerful could give him power. Those in the know could give him information. Even people with what others might describe as having 'nothing to give' could in fact give him something, even if it was as simple as a boost in his esteem after an otherwise uneventful day. In return, Kendic would always give something in return, some kind of reasonable exchange for what he himself had been given: something to share his understanding. To the wealthy, he would give them an understanding of poverty. To the powerful, he would return an understanding of humility. To the wise, he would teach them how little they understood of themselves. To those with less to give, he would grant them the opportunity to learn from his experience, as well as reward them with a sizeable portion of his wealth. As a result he'd found a certain equilibrium in his net worth. His wealth would come and go in ebbs and flows, but his understanding would always grow.

Angie though was somewhat of an anomaly. She had nothing except spirit, and Kendic found this more intoxicating than even his continual pursuit of understanding. She'd shunned his gifts and rejected all of the wisdom that he'd been willing to share. And she had neither shared nor parted with her spirit, despite his best efforts, and this is what interested him the most in her. Where others might, initially at least, resist, enlist assistance from friends or authorities, or even fight back, Angie would calmly accept the inevitability of the immediate situation. But she would not concede. As he yelled, so would Angie respond with promises of vengeance. As he beat her, so would Angie try to fight back with all of the physicality of her diminutive frame.   As he tried to impose his will with merely his presence, so too would Angie stand, a defiant spark in her eyes indicative of a fire in her belly.

For the time being however, all Nebojsa could do was wait.

Chapter - 28.

"Is that it?" Devlin asked the others after an hour of reading messages in the bunker. He'd been content to listen to the banter among the other readers sparked by the various messages that each read. Sometimes it was a message that struck a particular personal chord. Perhaps the sender seemed to be identifiable, the text comical and worthy of sharing, or sometimes it was a matter of which of Glen's protocols were in order.

"Pretty much," Ikel replied. "Why? What's the problem?"

"No problem, I guess. It's just that there's been amazingly few confessionals from sexual predators, rapists and murderers. I'm wondering if the others left out of boredom."

"Surely you've seen other confessions though," Lori contributed. "And remember that these messages would be sure to go unsaid if not for LastGasp'."

"Yes, but personal failures and sob stories aren't anywhere near as interesting."

"If it gets too much, you can always head outside for a chat with Albert," said Lori. "It's not exactly 'fresh air', but you'll get used to the smell. He's removed just enough from LastGasp' to understand."

"It's not too much, I just figured there'd be more. The vast majority of what I've read I've just rubber stamped."

"And you didn't find it interesting?" asked David.

"Well yes. Just because they're inconsequential to LastGasp' doesn't mean completely un-interesting. I just feel like I'm sharing in the highs or lows of total strangers."

"That shouldn't be too surprising. That's exactly what they are," David said dryly. "This job is not for everyone. Some find it hard to read personal details, and others find a lack of identifying information in the messages frustrating."

"It can get a little monotonous too," said Lori. "It's hard to not be affected by the message content, particularly for the imbalance between the good and the bad. You'll learn that uplifting recollections are so much harder to convey unspoken with a stranger than painful memories."

"What's that supposed to mean?"

"Pain, anger, regret and sorrow aren't more powerful than joy, pride and happiness, but shared in print, it's easier to feel for anguish," said David. "You'll see."

"Just keep your abstraction, said Lori. "Keep distant from what you're reading."

"It's harder than you'd think when you know so much about people you've never met," David commented, rubbing his brow above his sunglasses. "I'm getting out of here." He rolled his seat forcefully away from the table until the wheels crunched into the wall, then stood for the door.

"Does this make it any more interesting?" Ikel pushed an envelope across the table as soon as David closed the door behind himself. "It's today's pay."

Devlin cautiously reached for the envelope and flitted through its' contents using the table to hide his actions. He kept composed as his quick count of the cash inside passed into the thousands. "How often is payday?"

"Most days we get ten or twenty thousand," said Ikel. "Today there's *only* fifteen."

"You're kidding?" questioned Devlin. "And it's all above board?"

"Of course," said Lori, as if there was no doubt. "It's all fine."

"Forgive the suspicion, but it doesn't seem reasonable for the work."

"Stressful work always pays well," said Lori. "I'd recommend using the Research Interface to break up your reading. Have you even tried it?"

"I did. I researched myself, and that only compounded my concern that this mightn't be entirely legal."

"What's wrong?" said Lori. "All that information's available somewhere. This just brings it all together."

"But financial records and conversation transcripts? Come on."

"It's all legal, end of story," said Lori. "Perhaps one day I'll help you prove it."

Devlin accepted the rebuke and settled in for more reading, but the next message was from a man who'd lost his family to a drunk driver. The man held no regrets and he was confident that his wife and young children knew he loved them, but how he longed for another hour, another day, another family embrace. Devlin entered this man's sorrow and noted a distinct air of finality in the message.

After discussing it with Lori, he flagged the message with a suicide protocol. While Lori didn't even reach for another tissue, Devlin temporarily found himself lost in this man's sadness and decided a little fresh air might help.

What began as a short stroll on the street became a lap of the block after deliberately changing direction to avoid Conrad, hovering outside LastGasp'. Curious about Albert, he decided to pay him a quick visit.

It had been a warm sunny day and evaporation had removed the puddles of urine, but the smell remained just as strong as ever. Albert sat on a milk crate looking as if tranced by an afternoon sunbeam and he stood as he heard Devlin approach. "I hope you brought the coffee."

"Hi Albert, remember me?" Despite what Ikel had said, he couldn't help but speak in a slightly condescending manner. He couldn't shift his belief that the old man could not possibly be sober and tolerate the smell.

"Of course I remember. The new guy's come to chat with Albert," he said mockingly. "What do you want?"

Both Lori and Ikel had painted Albert as a 'salt of the earth', but likeable, if not aromatic, old guy. Devlin had assumed that *friendliness* would be part of the package, but immediately he felt he'd made a bad assumption. He floundered to recover ground. "Sorry. I didn't mean it like that! I just thought…"

"Don't worry about it. I'm just fucking with you," Albert snickered to himself. "Ikel's already told me all about you. So is this a social call, or do you want something?"

"Well actually I just came out for some fresh air and to say hello. Ikel and Lori said you were good for a chat, so I guess I came to see for myself."

Albert nodded before breaking into a deep, chesty cough. He held up his hand as if to indicate that the interruption was nothing out of the ordinary and that it would pass. Devlin took the opportunity to look around the car-park, the heavy smell of ammonia biting into the back of his throat. He naturally attributed Albert's coughing episode to the smell, and sub-consciously at first, then physically began to cough himself, though not to the convulsive degree that Albert was experiencing.

Finally, Albert composed himself and returned to a normal breathing pattern. With bloodshot eyes, he started talking once more. "Tell me the truth. Was it a rapist, a sinner's rant or someone who should be on a suicide watch?"

Devlin was initially puzzled at the question before he twigged at what Albert was asking. "The latter. Poor guy lost his family to some drunk."

Albert nodded. "Don't worry, I won't write you off as the sentimental type just yet." He sat himself back down on his crate and picked at something between his toes. "How are you settling in? They're a good crowd up there."

"I'm getting there, just getting to know the ropes at the moment. Ikel and Lori are certainly nice. And David, well he's a bit moody for my liking."

Albert nodded knowingly, fidgeting and looking around the car-park. "I'd offer you a seat, but I've only got one crate."

"That's OK. I've got to get back anyway," Devlin figured that his visit had come to a natural conclusion. "Can I bring you anything when next I visit?"

"I'm not a charity. Just your company and a chat would be nice." Albert smiled deeply, adding, "Though feel free to bring a snack if you like." He started to laugh, but the laugh quickly degraded into another coughing episode. He waved Devlin off, indicating that he needn't wait around to close out their conversation.

As Devlin returned to the office, Conrad was brazen in his effort to engage him, waiting on the footpath directly in front of LastGasp', but Devlin just ignored him and pushed past. He almost felt obliged to buy the guy a coffee, if only for his persistence.

It was apparent as soon as Devlin entered the building that the mood was different, but it took some time to identify exactly what was wrong. Instead of what had previously been a casual work environment, he was met with a decidedly hostile atmosphere. Initially, it seemed that he'd interrupted some heated debate between Glen and David, but not a word was spoken between them as soon as they had company. Whatever the cause, the mood did not improve with Devlin's entry, or even the subsequent arrival of Ikel and Lori from the bunker. David soon stormed from the building, leaving Glen to make light of the situation.

Despite his best efforts, Glen could not mask a tension that remained long afterwards. Everyone else had adjourned to the bunker, but not a word was spoken among them. There was no idle banter, no passionate discussion about a message flagging, or even subjective conversation about a potential sender identification.

Glen made an appearance in the bunker and made an announcement. "David is leaving." He silenced the volley of questions that ensued, particularly from Lori and Ikel, and continued. "He's got his reasons, but it's his call and that's OK." He left the bunker immediately.

Devlin was slow to embrace complete deference to Glen. He was beginning to understand why Ikel and the others thought so highly of him, but he was not so easily silenced. He followed Glen from the bunker intent on finding out more and intercepted him in the kitchen. "Can I talk to you about David and why he's going?"

"I've already said all that needs to be said on the matter. David's history." There was nothing sinister about the way it was said, but it was said with an air of finality. Devlin considered pressing the point, but he left it at that.

Devlin was in no mood to return to the bunker. It felt like when he'd survived a round of redundancies at work many years earlier; most of the people remained, and effectively nothing else had changed, but a gloom was present. Whether David had left of his own volition or was pushed or sacked, the work group dynamic would be changed regardless. He opted to head back to his room at the hotel.

Chapter - 29.

Having left work early, this was the first time that Devlin had spent any time in his room during daylight. It occurred to him that at least one down-side of living at a hotel was that his room was never really '*his*' room. He knew that even after weeks *in-situ*, if he lasted that long, his room would look no different to how it looked now. Perhaps there would be several days' worth of casual clothes all cleaned and pressed and hanging in the wardrobe whereas now the wardrobe was empty, but the room would never be home. While his first impression of the room was that it was spacious and luxurious, he now saw it for what it was, just a room.

Devlin was surprised at his reaction to David's departure because he knew he'd miss the perpetual 'stick in the mud' attitude. Particularly in comparison with easy-going Ikel and friendly Lori, time with David was almost a chore, but it was tolerable. Glen was sure to recruit someone to take David's place and Devlin couldn't help some apprehension that any newcomer might well be worse.

Whether he liked the guy or not, he felt like he needed to find out more about why David was leaving, and it occurred to him that David may well still be in his own room in the Hotel. With this in mind, he grabbed one of the obscenely overpriced bottles of Shiraz from his in-room bar and headed for David's room which he knew to be only five doors along the corridor.

David was not very friendly as he greeted Devlin at his door, but he did invite him in after Devlin held up the bottle of wine. "Come for the news?" David asked cynically. He poured two glasses after removing and savouring the smell of the cork.

Devlin drank from his glass, enjoying the taste but nothing more. "Glen spun me the line of people leaving when they are ready. I guess I want to know whether you are in fact *ready?*"

"Ready. Not ready. It doesn't really matter. I'm leaving."

"But why?"

"I didn't play by the rules."

"Does that mean that you can't play by the rules, or you were busted for not playing?" Devlin asked earnestly as he watched David nervously pacing in his room. David had obviously consumed quite a quantity of alcohol since leaving the office; with several spirit bottles on the bar were uncapped and somewhat depleted. He gathered that David wasn't entirely comfortable in his departure.

"Caught with my hand in the cookie jar, does it matter that I was eating the cookies or that I was caught? I'm fucked in any case," David replied, slurring the occasional word.

"So did you choose to leave?"

"LastGasp' is all about trust. If Glen doesn't trust me, or I guess I don't trust him, it doesn't matter. Without trust, LastGasp' is nothing. Without trust, I can't work there."

"That doesn't actually answer my question."

"I don't frankly give a fuck as to whether I've answered your question?" David sculled the last of the wine in his glass and immediately poured himself a refill.

"What does a *Media Analyst* do when he leaves LastGasp'?" Devlin asked, looking to start some conversation as a distraction to the drinking. "I think I asked more or less the same question when I started."

"My answer then was a little naïve, though I can't remember even the gist of what I said."

"I think you said ex-employees typically don't keep in touch."

"Something like that." David sighed and then drank the last of his wine straight from the bottle. "Actually, can you please take Lori a message?" He scribbled a brief note on the hotel stationery and sealed it inside an envelope. "Of course, I'd take it myself, but …you know the deal." He handed the envelope to Devlin and then ungraciously coaxed him to the door.

Devlin took the hint and proceeded on his errand with only a simple goodbye.

Chapter - 30.

Devlin took his time in delivering David's message. He figured he was under no obligation to deliver the message *immediately*, only to deliver it, and as such he allowed himself to be distracted. He headed to the car-park to discuss matters with Albert, taking a roundabout route and enjoying the mid-afternoon sunshine on the way.

As well lit as the car-park was, it was still substantially less bright than the sunshine outside. Combined with the ammonia fumes, Devlin's eyesight was struggling to adapt to the changing light to see if Albert was even there. "Albert?" he called out.

"I've heard," Albert announced before he was even visible, slipping into view only after Devlin was almost on top of him. "No great loss. Maybe his replacement will be better."

"So no deep seated compassion for the man from you then," Devlin quipped. He'd anticipated Albert's almost obnoxious forthrightness, but still his comments seemed more than a little harsh.

"Don't sound surprised. You've bitched to me about him. I thought you'd be happy."

"Well yes. He wasn't a favourite of mine, but still, I didn't want him to leave under a cloud," Devlin conceded. "It's just changed the mood in the bunker, that's all."

"That will pass. It always does." Albert fumbled in the pocket of his excessively out-of-season coat, and only after extracting a phone did Devlin understand why. He answered the phone looking at Devlin, nodding but without saying a word. "Glen wants you upstairs." He waved Devlin off before starting another chesty cough.

Chapter - 31.

By the time that Devlin joined the remaining staff in the lounge room, LastGasp' had almost an air of sedition about it. He could tell just by looking at Ikel and Lori that they were in a confrontational mood, and it appeared that Glen was going to keep them waiting until he was ready. Revolution or not, Glen was still in charge but his forever loyal employees were looking for an explanation. No-one looked particularly happy, and Devlin's arrival seemed to only add an urgency to the room.

With his staff assembled, Glen took control. "Sit down and listen in. I'd like to explain some things about David." As ever, he was calm and collected, and in just a few words Devlin could feel the ambient tension reduce. "I'd like to explain David's departure as clearly as I can, knowing full well that you'll want to get his side of the story, if you haven't done so already." Devlin felt himself lower his eyes like a teenager being confronted for some regrettable misdemeanour.

"I'll miss David as much as any of you, arguably more so. He's been a good friend, and he's worked well. It's sad he's gone, but we'll all move on." Glen sighed non-committally looking at everyone, but no-one. "It's funny, you know. Had it been anyone else, David would have been a voice of experience, because he'd already experienced losing someone. But alas, you're all going to have to trust me and learn from it. Actually, it's this that LastGasp' will miss the most, because David had a sense of maturity about him that will be missing in the short term, until at least one of you step up. And I know you will. Until then, we'll cope."

Devlin thought Glen's speech was nothing extraordinary, but it served its purpose. His assembled audience was silenced, temporarily at least, and their attention was distracted from their concern for the departure of a peer, a friend. However, it did not satisfy Devlin's curiosity but Glen silenced him with a gesture of his hand before Devlin could utter a syllable.

"I'd like to leave you with a quick video, and I'd like to re-iterate my security concerns." Glen stood and pointed his remote control at the bank of televisions. He left the building leaving Devlin, Lori and Ikel fixated on the preliminary static of a video.

It didn't take long for Devlin to work out he was watching security video of LastGasp', semi-professionally collated into a multi-scened movie. The quality of the imagery and associated sound was excellent. High resolution and in full colour, it was more than adequate to identify people right down to skin blemishes and the subtleties of breathing patterns. Since his first day, Devlin had been well aware he was under surveillance in the building, but he was taken aback at the extent of the surveillance evidenced in the video. He'd naïvely assumed that there would be some dead-zones in the building, invisible to the cameras, but clearly he'd been mistaken.

It was apparent that the subject of the video was David Yeardley, the latest now *ex*-employee of LastGasp'. Initially everyone watching assumed that the purpose of the video was to allow some degree of sentimentality, in much the same way that home movies had become routine at twenty first birthday parties. There was nothing amusing in the watching, other than sly nose-picking caught on camera as clearly as the subsequent expression of relief on David's face. Clearly, he was happy to remove the nasal obstruction.

Devlin also watched the evolution of David. Vision of the bunker and David with unfamiliar faces, presumably other past employees, gradually progressed, presumably chronologically, to include Lori, then Ikel, and finally Devlin himself featured. It was also easy to see David's confidence decrease and stress increase as time, and the video, continued. Smiles became fewer, and increasingly erratic outbursts featured more and more prominently. David was burning out, slowly but surely.

After several minutes, Devlin and the others naturally came to wonder about the purpose of the video. Glen didn't seem the sentimental type, and this was clearly apparent in the movie and Devlin began to look for Glen's intent or hidden agenda. It was reasonable that security was relevant to the movie, based on his preamble and his incessant pre-occupation with the subject. Gradually, Lori and Ikel both started looking at each other and to Devlin, which served to confirm that Devlin was not the only one struggling to understand why Glen considered it so important that they all watch.

Suddenly, it all became apparent when an unknown face appeared on the video, re-focussing everyone's attention. It was a woman, tall and leggy, and suggestively dressed. The video, clear as ever, showed David greet the woman at the door, escort her to the kitchen and then proceed to the lounge. David had broken Glen's golden rule, inviting a stranger into the building.

"Fuck!" Ikel said what everyone was thinking. "No wonder he left!"

"No. Glen would have sacked him on the spot for this," Lori added, not prepared to miss a second of the video.

Of course the point was moot. Whether David left of his own accord when confronted with the video, or Glen summarily terminated his employment was irrelevant. There was no way he could remain part of LastGasp', that much at least Devlin now understood.

The next question raised in watching the video was the identity and the purpose of the woman, and why David would breach security so blatantly. It didn't take long for this question to be answered. Soon the small-talk between David and the woman progressed to what was clearly foreplay, but only after cash was exchanged. Only the ceiling based or similarly high mounted camera position and the lack of a musical soundtrack separated the vision of David from amateur pornography. Ikel laughed inappropriately, but unavoidably, testament to his youth and immaturity. Lori and Devlin were silent.

Then the scene in the video changed. Clearly another night, clearly another woman, clearly the same David. And another. And another. Commitment to LastGasp' was not the only reason why David was so routinely on the night-shift.

Glen timed his return perfectly. No sooner had the video stopped, that he appeared on one of the CCTV screens, waiting outside the building, buzzing to be allowed in. "No-one is allowed in here except us, or people explicitly sanctioned by me," he re-iterated as soon as he reached the sitting room. "I want you all to go, now, and I'll see you tomorrow."

Chapter - 32.

The walk back to the hotel was quiet. There was no light hearted conversation or venting of pent-up frustration or even disappointment at David. They just walked, fixated on the journey. When they reached the hotel, Lori broke the silence only to suggest that tonight she'd opt for room service, forgoing the nightly dinner and drinks ritual. The suggestion was accepted by Devlin as a great idea, but Ikel protested that he'd adhere to his routine regardless of whether or not he had company.

Just as Lori turned her back for the stairs, Devlin remembered the note that David asked him to deliver. He hadn't forgotten his errand, at least initially, and not surprisingly it had felt inappropriate to raise the matter after watching David's first foray into video pornography. "Wait!" he called after her. "David asked me to give you this."

On receipt of the message, Lori read it and thought for a moment. "Did you read this?" she asked, holding up the note.

"No. Why?"

"When did he give it to you? What state was he in?"

"He was getting pissed. I wanted to talk to him, but by the time I got to his room he was already draining his bar. He cut short our chat and told me to deliver the note."

Lori checked her watch and did a little mental arithmetic. "So, what, you last saw him about an hour or so ago?"

"Thereabouts. Maybe a little more. What's the problem?"

"Fuck!" Lori exclaimed. "We need to get to him now!" She removed her low heeled court shoes and started to run for the lifts. Devlin followed, inspired by the urgency that warranted her use of an expletive.

The speed of the lifts had not been an issue before, but now Lori was impatiently shouting in the vain hope that it might make them go faster. "Come on!" She watched the above door display indicating the current floor as it progressed slowly to their floor.

Devlin remained distant from Lori's urgency for a while, but the entry of other hotel guests to the lift slowed the lift even more and threatened to force her over the edge. He considered it high time to find out what was happening, as much to appease his curiosity as to prevent Lori from openly abusing the new lift occupants for their role in slowing the lift. "What was on the note?"

Lori looked at Devlin, suddenly appreciating that he was oblivious to what was so clear to her. "All the note said was that 'Derrell had it right'. Of course, that means nothing to you, but Derrell was a reader like us. He left before even David joined LastGasp'." Lori paused to allow the other lift passengers to alight at their floor. As soon as she and Devlin were alone again she continued. "I never knew him, but I remember the day he died. I'd not long joined, and one day Glen was emotional. You've known Glen for a little while now, so you can appreciate how out of character that was. David and I asked him what the matter was, and he told us."

"Told you what?"

"That Derrell was dead and that he was a reader, but more than just any reader, apparently, his words. Glen also told us that Derrell had committed suicide. And that's what I'm worried about."

On cue, the lift doors began to open and Lori forced them open still further and faster, desperate to resume her race to check on David.

David was not answering his door or his phone and Lori's concern was obvious. She rang the hotel manager, Morris, requesting that he arrange for the room to be unlocked. She was sparing with the details, but keen to impress him with the urgency.

Morris arrived almost immediately with an aide and tried to open David's door with a master-key, but failed on account of the internal latch. This at least seemed to confirm that David was in his room, but did little to quell Lori's concern. Morris resigned himself to the necessity to break in the door, and nodded his approval to his offsider who braced himself, and shoulder charged the door.

Chapter - 33.

As a child, Devlin had visited a working whaling station in the days before public pressure or a change in economics saw it become a whaling museum cum tourist attraction. He remembered the sights and smells of that experience vividly. He remembered the smell of the blubber being rendered, and the resultant stench that seemed to remain with them long after leaving the site and even persisted after several changes of clothes. He also remembered the sight of the butchery, and the lifeless masses of the queued whales awaiting their turn for processing. But most of all, Devlin remembered the blood. Pooled blood on the ground, blood stained equipment, and rivers of blood draining away into the adjacent ocean.

As soon as Devlin entered David's room, his first thoughts were childhood memories of the whaling station.

Devlin was no expert, but first impressions suggested that David had committed suicide. Not content to just slash his wrists and sit in a nice warm bath, David appeared to have also hung himself naked from the ceiling fan. At the speed he was spinning, it was difficult to identify the exact source of his bleeding. Perhaps there was more than one source, Devlin couldn't rightly tell. The fact that the fan was spinning on a fast cycle while David bled out had meant that centrifugal force had played a pivotal role in spreading his fluids widely. A substantial proportion of the flooring, furniture and much of the walls were splattered liberally. Morris would need to fund substantially more than just a new door frame.

Devlin didn't bother entering the room as there was clearly nothing that could be done. He simply closed the door behind Morris and his assistant and started to comfort Lori.

Chapter - 34.

As ever, Detective Reymond hadn't waited to be formally assigned to the suicide call. In truth, he wasn't in the mood, but he knew there was little point in denying the inevitable. Suicides were 'dead' jobs as far as any police were concerned, with no upside. There was no chance of a happy ending, no positive interaction with people, and nothing that might make a career. As such, anyone with an interest in professional advancement would always avoid anything resembling a suicide.

Reymond had long since lost interest in the pursuit of greatness, and by pure virtue of his age, was beyond his prime and he knew it. Old or not, he'd found a comfortable niche which had allowed him to remain with the only job he'd known, short of parenting, long beyond what would be considered typical. The deal was simple; he'd pick up the slack that detracted from the work of 'real' Police officers, and in return he'd be able to continue in his role for so long as he was able, legally and physically. This left him all of the un-glamorous jobs but not the mundane administration which would continue to be done by a civilian, proving that he was still off the bottom peg in the office hierarchy. Theoretically this meant a variety of work, but seasonally, particularly at Christmas, he was almost full time dealing with suicides. The rest of the time he 'wasted' at the hospitals and a miscellany of other tasks, none of them prestigious, none of them career building, but all of them necessary from the perspective of the mandate of the Police force in general.

Reymond was in familiar territory when he paced across the parquet flooring of the hotel foyer. He'd been there before, though the details of his past visit were somewhat blurred with those of what amounted to hundreds of similar cases and surrounds. If this was another suicide, as the hotel manager who'd called had insisted, then it would not be the first where a poor soul had decided to take his own life in the relatively modest surrounds of a mid-range hotel. Nor was it likely to be the last. He met the hotel manager who escorted him to the incident location.

"Did you make the discovery?" Reymond asked.

"Yes. With my assistant and another two hotel guests. They are both workmates of the … deceased. Is *'deceased'* the right word?"

"If he is, then *deceased* is fine," Reymond laboured a smile. He appreciated that this was invariably not a pleasant experience, despite its almost banality to him, but it was important to keep the dialog open. "I'll need to meet with them later, of course. No real rush."

"Of course." The hotel manager opened the door to David Yeardley's floor from the stairwell and drew Detective Reymond's attention to the only room in the corridor with a uniformed staff member loitering at the door.

"I cut him down from the fan and checked for a pulse. To do this I had to turn off the fan at the wall and I used the sharpest knife that was at hand. It was most likely the same blade that he'd used. Other than that, I've done nothing else except post my assistant at the door to keep other guests away."

"Thanks Morris. You've done this before, haven't you?"

"Yes, some time ago," Morris sighed. "It's one of the joys of the hospitality industry. There was another incident here some months back, but I was at head-office, and so the police would have spoken to the duty manager."

"Security?" Reymond nodded and raised his eyebrow towards the domed security camera mounted unobtrusively on the ceiling as he caught his breath after the near sprint up the stairs. He fought the thought of being too old to take stairs when there were invariably perfectly operational lifts available for use. If he was truly too old to take the stairs, then surely he was too old to be on the job. "Video?"

"Generally yes, but this floor is for less transient, longer term guests. So we afford them a little more privacy," Morris answered the question in a matter-of-fact fashion. "In any case, the only door to the room was secured from the inside. You'll see that I had to get Nigel here to bust the door in."

A distant bell alerted them to the arrival of the lift at the floor. The doors opened and a pair of paramedics exited the lift for the corridor with their gurney. They both smiled and nodded their recognition of Reymond, and one grunted the room number.

"You guys took your time," said Reymond.

"You done?" the paramedic dragging the gurney asked.

"Not yet. I haven't even been in to see the scene."

"Then what does it matter that we took our time," the paramedic replied smugly. "Based on the call, I didn't figure he was going to need immediate care, so we allowed ourselves to be distracted by more pressing, and living, patients."

"Touché!" Reymond smiled. "You guys go and have a smoke, and I'll send for you in a bit. On that point, Morris, your offsider can go too, but I'd like for you to wait a while. Just give me a moment on my own."

Reymond watched the others leave via the lift as he started to fit gloves from his pocket. He pushed the ajar door open wide enough for him to enter, and started to take stock of the room.

Had his eyes been closed on entering the room, Reymond would have felt his senses heighten in sensitivity based solely on the pervasive smell of blood. Nothing smells like it, not even other bodily fluids, and in this room, there was a smell, not just a scent, that indicated a sizeable volume of it. *Angie had that right.* Eyes open, the room amounted to a frightening sight, reminiscent of a farcical b-grade horror flick. Blood covered what looked to be the whole room, almost floor to ceiling. There was a single body, a man, lying impossibly comfortably on the blood sodden sofa.

Detective Reymond checked the door and its damaged frame, confirming what he'd been told about it having been forced open. He stepped forward carefully towards the body. There was no way to avoid interfering with the crime scene, but he did need to minimise contaminating the site if at all possible. He felt the squelch under his shoe, and then the residual stickiness of the congealing blood with each step. Up close to the body, it was even more obvious that the man was dead. A film of dried blood over much of the glass window wall tended to give everything a magenta hue, but even so, the man had a distinctly lifeless colour about him. Reymond checked for a pulse as a matter of routine, but he was realistic about his expectations, particularly when at first touch it was obvious that the body was at room temperature.

Primary formalities over, Reymond set about his immediate secondary purpose, confirming the cause of death. More importantly, he needed to confirm that it was indeed suicide. He inspected the wounds, which all appeared to be self-inflicted by a right handed individual, but the wounds would have been far from painless, particularly as they were being inflicted. The incisions had been made by a sharp, but far from surgical blade and it was apparent that it had taken quite a lot of effort, in much the same way as a standard cutlery knife would struggle with a gristled piece of meat. If the man did die at his own hand, it proved only that he was committed. He'd need some kind of pain relief too, but judging by the plentiful array of empty bottles of wine and spirits spread on the adjacent coffee table, Reymond figured that alcohol had sufficed.

Morris said he'd cut the man down from the fan, but Reymond was interested in what this meant in terms of the chronology of the man's death. He scanned the room after looking at what remained of the haphazard noose around the man's neck; fashioned simply as a long loop out of a bed-sheet. Judging by the smear of blood on the fan switch on the wall, Reymond theorised that the last few steps that the deceased had taken were to turn on the fan after cutting himself. He'd then slung the sheet over the fan and waited for the slack to be reeled in, lifting him from the ground and spinning him around until being discovered. There was no significant damage to the man's throat or neck and it appeared to him that the noose had little to do with the man's death, other than to expedite the bleeding.

Reymond was satisfied in as much that it was in fact suicide. He removed a camera from his pocket and started taking photographs of everything. He called the paramedics, inviting them to do their job and left the room.

Chapter - 35.

Devlin was keen to provide some support for Lori, though he knew the feeling was mutual. He was getting the support that he himself needed by just being among friends. Ikel had joined them in the bar which seemed the only appropriate place to be. They sat, quiet on the main, but periodically breaking into casual, reminiscent banter about David. "Remember when …." With each outbreak of talking, the mood would lighten temporarily and smiles would appear from nowhere, only to retreat with the greyness of silence.

Not surprisingly, the collective recollection, spoken at least, was overwhelmingly positive about David. Just as eulogies tend to focus on the good in someone, there was no talk about what everyone knew. Devlin was tempted to ground the conversation and add a little sobering honesty about what he thought about David. He could have said that David was difficult to get on with, bordering on obnoxious, self-righteous in the extreme, and as it turned out, was probably a closet sex addict. Devlin decided that now was not the time or the place and it would serve no purpose other than to distance himself from the others. He opted to keep his malevolent thoughts to himself.

It was early evening when they were joined in their corner in the bar adjacent to the restaurant. They had the perfect vantage point to see each and every person entering the area, and it was obvious that the newcomer was making a direct route to join them. An old guy in a cheap suit, coming towards them with a purpose could only have been Police.

"My name is Detective Alan Reymond, and I'd like to talk about David Yeardley," the newcomer announced. "I'm assuming that at least two of you are Ms Hinkley and Mr Bennett."

Ikel rounded out the Detective's information. "I'm Michael Donovan. I work, or *worked*, with David. But I was in my room when he was found."

"That's fine. I'd just like to talk to you all for a while." Reymond made himself comfortable, sitting in one of the deep armchairs around a central drinks table. He ordered a soft drink from the waitress and casually looked over the others as he waited for the drink to arrive. "Can each of you please start with your name, and then tell me anything that you think that I need to know."

Lori was the least composed of the three, so she paused expecting either Ikel or Devlin to start briefing the Detective.

"I'm Devlin Bennett. I live just down the corridor from David, and I worked with him, until today." He thought about continuing, but once more he resisted any inclination to oversupply information. He allowed himself a moment to have a drink and wait for the Detective to steer the passage of disclosure.

"Where do you work?"

"We're all employees of Independent Media Analysis," Lori answered on behalf of Devlin, finding her voice. "We're media analysts. We live down the corridor too." She pointed her finger erratically, alternating between Ikel, Devlin and herself.

"You worked with David until today. What happened?" Reymond continued questioning Devlin directly after an acknowledging nod to Lori.

"He left," Devlin answered succinctly, glancing briefly at Lori for her concurrence. "An internal matter, or perhaps a personal matter. It doesn't matter which."

"It might," Reymond encouraged subtly.

"He broke a well understood, internal company directive. As much as any of us know, either he was asked to leave or left of his own choosing when confronted on the matter. In any case, he left."

"When was this?"

"Earlier this afternoon. I left work a while after. We work in a small office, and having someone leave left a bit of a cloud in the air. I figured that I'd go and clear my head. I came back here and then I went to speak to David."

"Why?"

"Why not? He was a workmate who just upped and decided to leave. I've only just joined the company and so I was interested. He didn't say much, and he was hitting the wine way too hard, and early, for me. He gave me a note to give to Lori here, and then I left."

"What time was this?"

"Mid-afternoon I guess. I didn't look at my watch. I just made a bee-line for the office. Our boss filled us in, of sorts, as to why David left and then he sent us all home for the day."

"So when did you make the discovery?"

"When we all got back here, I remembered the note that I was supposed to give Lori and I gave it to her. It spooked her, we rushed to his room and the rest you know."

Reymond's attention turned to Lori. "What did the note say?"

"It was nothing really. You're welcome to it." She offered the note to the Detective, passing it across the table.

"So who's this Derrell?"

"Derrell Kendrick. David knew him. I knew of him. I know he committed suicide and that he was a past employee of our company. Other than that, I know virtually nothing about the guy."

"So when did you last see him? David, that is. Alive," Reymond broke eye contact with Lori only long enough to check the notes he'd been taking were legible.

"Today at work. We work pretty closely together."

"So was he there at work all day?"

"Yes, or at least he was there when I got there. I tend to get in later than the others generally, and David is, or was, routinely on the night shift." Ikel smirked at mention of the night shift and Lori sighed in response at his immaturity. She offered an explanation for the benefit of the Detective. "We found out today that David was, well, using his time on the night shift on ..."

"Personal development," Ikel said, trying to help.

"I was going to say *inappropriate activity at odds with our company ideals*," she scowled at Ikel. "That's why he left, or was sacked."

Ikel took his cue from Reymond for his account. "I last saw him this afternoon. He and Glen had words and then he left, and I haven't seen him since, other than the video. Dev' rang me after they found him and I met them here."

"Glen who?"

"Glen Scott. He's our boss."

Reymond continued taking his notes, as if he knew the name but just needed to write it down. "What's this video?"

"Company internal security footage," Lori answered quickly, as if considering herself the best to explain this appropriately, for all concerned. "We were shown it today by our boss. David breached our security rules. That's all, but it's a big deal in our work."

"Anyone got anything else to add?"

There was silence at the table. Devlin watched as Reymond looked at everyone in turn and collectively, gauging what intangibles he could. He theorised as to what the Detective might be thinking, but he figured that they all looked just like people who'd just learned that a colleague had died, committed suicide. There was an obvious sadness among everyone and they all just sat silently, not really waiting for the Detective to go, not really waiting for anything.

"I'll be in touch if I need anything, and likewise, let me know if you think of anything else." The Detective stood and exchanged business cards with the others, as a matter of routine. "I'm sorry for your loss," he offered.

Chapter - 36.

Dinner that evening for the remaining trio from LastGasp' was a quiet affair. The reminiscing about David had stopped and nothing filled the communication void except the silence. In many ways, Devlin reasoned, it was probably just like the drive home from a wake. The topic of conversation that did rise above the distant din of the kitchen was talk of the funeral and who, if anyone would need to contact David's family. This in turn gave rise to speculation about what family David had, the answer to which no-one it seemed really knew. This sad fact further deflated the dinner mood as it reinforced the fact that ultimately no-one knew a great deal about David Yeardley.

Devlin returned to his room substantially earlier than the previous evening. An early dinner following their meeting with the Police, and without the frivolity of pre-dinner drinks and lively mealtime conversation, he was in his room by 8pm, bored as hell by 8:10, and in bed but clearly unable to sleep by 8:30. He'd neglected to turn off his phone for the evening as suggested by Ikel.

A steady stream of messages began to arrive, each marked by the familiar sounds, and punctuated by relative silence. With the receipt of the second, Devlin was summonsing the motivation to find his phone, but eleven messages had been received by the time he'd actually found it. He considered deleting them, as Lori and Ikel had suggested would become standard practice, but instead he opted to browse them. Curiosity was getting the better of him.

The first few messages were familiar. He'd read the messages about Leon, Casey and Carson before and his thumbs instinctively pressed the key sequence on his phone keypad to delete each without any further consideration. The next two were similar, but new.

```
Derrell Kendrick is
dead.
```

```
David Yeardley is now
dead.
```

This was hardly news, but it was disturbing nonetheless and Devlin pondered it for a moment before continuing with the rest of the messages. He knew that suicides invariably only ever made the media if it involved some celebrity or innocent bystanders. This begged the question of how the sender of the message could have learned of David's death so quickly. It was reasonable that the cause of Derrell's death would eventually make it to the public domain, but David's death would not have even made it into a register in the morgue yet. Furthermore, Derrell had died some time ago, but until that afternoon he'd never received any message relating to him, and for that matter he was unaware that he'd actually died at all, let alone even existed, until Lori explained en-route to David's room. He was perplexed as to why Conrad would wait until now to send a message relating to a long dead person. He continued reading.

```
All readers.
```

```
All dead.
```

```
All suicides.
```

```
All guilty.
```

```
Too late for Ikel.
```

<pre>
Too late for you?

Be sure you
understand the
greater good.
</pre>

Devlin considered phoning Ikel, but given that it was still only early evening he decided to visit him instead. He knew that personal contact was perhaps the only thing that would prevent a panic setting in completely. He burst through his door and bounded down the corridor to Ikel's room.

Ikel was dozing fully clothed on his bed when he was aroused by manic banging on his door. He opened the door and stood back as Devlin rushed in and frantically started looking for his phone. "What's the problem?"

"Where's your phone?" Devlin asked desperately.

"Beside the TV," Ikel replied calmly, repeating his question, "What's the go?"

"I got more messages. Did you get them too?" He retrieved the phone and straight away looked to access his received messages.

"I didn't get any," said Ikel, understanding Devlin's frenzy. "If you're still spooked by messages, why don't you turn your 'ken phone off?"

"Has your phone been on the whole time?"

"Yep. I ignored the messages you're so spooked about for a while, and now I generally don't get any that aren't actually for me. Well, not very often anyway." Ikel said, heading for his bar-fridge. "Can I get you something?"

"And you haven't deleted any?"

"No. Not tonight anyway," Ikel removed the cap from a bottle of beer and drank a long mouthful.

"Why don't you get those messages about Casey and co?"

"Remember when you were little and scared of the bogey-man and your Dad would tell you to ignore him and he'd go away?" Ikel offered.

Devlin could see where this was going. "I haven't even had a chance to ignore them yet. Tonight I got twice as many as last night. You were mentioned in one of them and ..."

"Let me finish. I tried ignoring them, but they kept coming. Like you, I didn't know who was sending them until Conrad said something. I had a bit of a chat to him about it, and amazingly the volume of messages I received dropped off. Admittedly, not straight away, but I guess he figured he was wasting his time. I would have preferred for them to stop completely, but that's OK."

"What did you say to him?"

"Not much. But he got the picture just the same. He denied sending them of course. After last night, I figured he was just giving you a quick burst and if they continued I'd just have another chat with him."

Devlin thought more about the message content. The fact that Ikel wasn't interested in them had done wonders to reduce his concern, but not entirely.

"What exactly did the message say?" Ikel asked, displaying only a modicum of interest.

"That it was too late for you, and some crap about a *greater good*." He offered his phone in case he wanted to see for himself, but Ikel shook his head, shunning the offer. "So what's *that* all about?"

Ikel sighed and stood up. "I might go and have another *chat* with Conrad."

"Thanks. But perhaps it's my turn to speak with him."

Chapter - 37.

Conrad Tran was alone in his home office when his phone rang. Devlin had been a little abrupt, but he was insistent on a meeting, and that suited Conrad perfectly. He was desperate to speak with Devlin, and now was as good as any other time. He knew he was onto something, and without a personal life, it didn't really matter what time of the day they met. He tended to work a cyclic twenty hour day for weeks on end. This meant that periodically he slept the remaining four hours during daylight, or during the night, or whenever he tired to the point of exhaustion, without any regard for the normal hours kept by most of the population.

Conrad rehearsed his big sell in anticipation of one more chance to impress Devlin. He knew the best time to approach Glen's people was just after they'd joined. He knew that there had to be a purpose to Glen's recruitment strategy, but he was still to work it out. There was no chance to intercept his potential recruits before they'd joined. However, just after they joined, they were still sceptical enough to challenge what they thought about anything, particularly what they thought about LastGasp' and Glen. But, he'd blown it with Devlin. His one good opportunity was looking promising until Devlin got suspicious, upped and left. Ikel Donovan had been more physical in avoiding a meeting, but he'd hurt Conrad's pride more than inflicting any lasting physical injury. Devlin, on the other hand, had just avoided him. There was hope with this one.

I can't blow this, Conrad thought as he tried his best to form his thoughts into something logical. He knew he was thinking erratically, invariably on par with his racing heart, the result of fatigue, excitement and way too much caffeine. To him, the result of his research was clear, irrefutable really, but so far he'd not managed to convince anyone to understand his theory and ultimately share his concerns. For whatever reason, they'd either been unwilling or unable to understand. It was true that it was just a theory, but with a little insider help he'd be able to convert theory to proof.

It wouldn't take Devlin long to arrive, particularly given the urgency in his tone, and until then he could do little more than tidy some of the filth that tended to accumulate in his home office. Long work days did not lend themselves to fastidious attention to housework, and had it not been for a weekly visit from his mother, he surely would have been naked for a lack of clothes and fighting off rats for sure. His mother had come from Vietnam after the war and assimilation into a new country had done nothing to dampen her cultural attachment to what was most definitely woman's work, and a mother's lot. But his mother was not due for a few days, and while he still had enough food and clothes, it was going to take a little while to make the place hospitable for guests. Worst case, Devlin would stay for a moment say his piece and leave soon after, without even coming inside. Best case, he'd listen and want to come inside to hear more. Conrad reasoned that there was no avoiding the need to tidy at least some of his home; the lounge for starters, on his own, for the first time in several years.

*   *   *

It would have been faster to catch a taxi, but Devlin figured that a walk would do him good. The streets weren't the best, but they were lit adequately and nowhere near as bad as those behind LastGasp'. In any case, he was feeling brave and hyped from Ikel's pep-talk primer before he left. If the truth be known, he needed the time to prepare what he needed to say and clarify what he needed to know. It didn't take him long to travel the ten or so blocks to Conrad's office as described on his business card. By the time he arrived, he knew what he needed to say.

"I was hoping you'd call," Conrad began as soon as he opened his door. "I've needed to speak to you."

"Me likewise. But first I want to talk about the messages," Devlin prepared himself for a confrontation.

Conrad smiled. "You know, Ikel accused me of sending the messages too. The guy even punched me when I told him I didn't send them. But it wasn't me."

"But you know about them?"

"You work there, you get the messages. Others have told me about them."

"And they're not from you?"

"Nope. And to answer your next question, no, I don't know who they're from."

"You know that Ikel has received fewer messages since he *spoke* with you. With that in mind, wouldn't you assume that you'd found the message sender?"

"Maybe. But why the interest this late at night?"

Devlin considered leaving it at that. After such a cold denial, it seemed fruitless to continue on the matter. Conrad's face expressed honesty, and Devlin was certain that he was telling the truth. However, he was also mindful that Conrad had been surprisingly zealous in his efforts to make contact that day. "So what do you want to talk about?"

"David's dead," Devlin began, pausing for effect and to gauge Conrad's reaction. It was apparent that this was news to Conrad, evident in the way his shoulders sunk and his natural, perpetual smile dissipated into blankness.

"I'm sorry to hear that. I liked David. He was a nice guy." Conrad rubbed his face with his hands. "When? How?"

"Today. Lori and I found him in his room. Suicide."

Conrad focussed. "And David was mentioned a message?"

"One of them. I received eleven messages tonight, and one of them mentioned David. Many of the other messages were ones I'd received before, that Casey and others were dead, and a series of new ones telling me that all the other readers were guilty and all suicided."

A spark returned to Conrad's face, and he smiled. "Well that's not true." He leapt from his seat on an old armchair, and headed for a cluttered computer desk behind him. "Come and look at this." He took his seat at his keyboard and began to click and type frenetically as he spoke. "I've had an interest in LastGasp' for some time," he began.

"Professional or recreational interest?"

Conrad stopped typing before answering. "I know what you're asking. Technically, it's '*recreational*' in that I have no formal mandate to exploit any of my professional expertise or contacts in any related investigation. But it came up professionally enough."

"How so?"

"Well. I was doing forensic technology assessments for the police when I noticed a pattern." Conrad looked at Devlin, as if expecting to see puzzlement and his expectation was realised.

"Forensic technology assessments are like a fishing expedition on the internet for anything about someone who's died. Throw out a big net and see what gets caught. OK so far?" He looked for a nod from Devlin before continuing. "Anyway. I noticed technical interaction with LastGasp' and did a little homework."

"Given what LastGasp' does, I wouldn't have thought that would surprise anyone. It seems reasonable an organisation that sends emails after someone dies would get implicated somewhere."

Conrad sighed. "That's what the police said. That it was *'reasonable interaction'*, to use the official term. Without wanting to abuse my fishing analogy, we caught a common but inedible fish. So I moved on, but the same pattern came up, over and over.

"I'm allowed a little latitude with my investigations, primarily because there's nothing definitive in what I *should* be looking for, and so I kept at it. I sunk a lot of time into it, but then I had to move on."

"So if you came up with nothing, why are we having this conversation?"

"That's not what I said. I moved on because I was told to move on. But I didn't come up with nothing." Conrad looked for roused interest in Devlin. "Look at this and tell me what you see." He slid to his left slightly to allow Devlin a better view of the screen.

"I see a web," Devlin said, describing what he saw; a matrix of lines and coloured nodes randomly interconnected such that each node was joined to a variable number of adjacent and non-adjacent, disconnected nodes. "What am I looking at?"

"You got it in one. It's a contact matrix. The nodes represent people, and the lines represent contact between these people. It shows how potentially each of these people are known to each other, within a few degrees of separation anyway."

Devlin accepted what he was being told, but was cautious to give any indication as such, verbal or otherwise. "And?"

"OK. The red dot in the middle represents Glen." He used the mouse to point to the only node in the matrix coloured red. "The node colour represents an indication of the degrees of separation from the red node. You are one of the blue nodes, which one is not important at this point in your education." Once again Conrad looked for cues of understanding before continuing. "What does this tell you?"

"That Glen is known to me and a lot of others?"

"Well, technically the matrix represents *contact*, so it doesn't actually show that these people *know* Glen, but you're on the right track."

"OK, so it shows that Glen is *'influential'*?"

"Perfect! He's an *influential* guy."

"And? I wouldn't have thought that was too surprising given the volume of semi-solicited email LastGasp' sends."

"Actually emails don't count. In this context, the definition of contact is human to human interaction. So face to face is obviously in, as are phone calls. But emails are out, rightly or wrongly."

"But it still shows that Glen is influential. Right?"

"Yes. But look at this?" Conrad typed on his keyboard some more and clicked his mouse, and the interface changed slightly, such that a number of the coloured nodes started to flash. "Remember what I said about the blue nodes? Well I know you aren't one of the *flashing* blue ones. Wanna' know how I know?"

Devlin only shrugged, though he no longer feigned disinterest. He looked at Conrad and waited for the answer.

"Because the flashing nodes are all dead."

"Bullshit."

"What part of this do you think is bullshit? The contact, or the fact that a surprising number of them are dead?"

"Both," said Devlin, interested but not convinced. "It's not just blue nodes that are flashing. And people die every day!"

"So? That should make this information more interesting to you. For comparison, look at my matrix." Conrad typed and clicked once more. The display of the screen changed noticeably, but presented a similar matrix. There were a number of flashing nodes, but not nearly as many as there had been previously.

"See! You know dead people too, or, *sorry*, have had *contact* with dead people," Devlin commented smugly.

Conrad was visibly saddened by the comment, but he said nothing.

On seeing Conrad's reaction, Devlin was lost as to what he'd said wrong. "What? What did I say? I only pointed out that you've *contacted* people who are now dead too. So what's the big deal about Glen's matrix then?"

"The flashing dots on mine are some of the same dots on Glen's," Conrad pushed himself away from his desk. "They were all readers, like you," he said as he edged past Devlin. "I didn't convince them and so couldn't help them, but I can help you."

Devlin remained fixated on the screen for a while and reached for the mouse in an effort to use the computer. Glancing over his shoulder, he looked at Conrad for some indication of approval or concurrence, but Conrad only reached for the television remote control after briefly locking eyes. Devlin took the passing eye contact as tacit approval, and he started using the mouse. He very quickly worked out that if he moved the mouse cursor over any of the nodes, flashing or otherwise, a name, presumably that of the person that particular node represents, was displayed, along with an array of personal information. He gravitated to the first of the flashing blue nodes, and recognised the name, Casey Lawrence. He knew the names represented by the second, third and fourth flashing nodes subconsciously before he confirmed them.

"Leon, Casey, Carson, and now David," said Conrad as he turned off the television.

Devlin was lost for something to say. "Who are the others?" he asked, pointing to the flashing nodes. He could have found out with his mouse, but after the latest revelation, he felt more inclined to ask.

"Relax. The others are my uncle, and a guy I knew from the gym. And it doesn't mean that I killed them."

"Well, it doesn't mean that Glen killed them either."

"You don't think that it's a little odd that so many readers are dead?" asked Conrad emphatically. "What would convince you? Surveillance video of Glen actually killing them?"

"Perhaps." The thought dented his façade of confidence. "How did they all die?"

"Suicide. Mainly suicide anyway."

"Suicide? I thought the important definition of suicide was that the perpetrator killed himself, or herself. So how is it that Glen was, or *is*, implicated?"

"That's still open."

"Do you mean that the police investigation is still open, or you haven't managed to pin it on him?" Buoyed by Conrad's silence, Devlin continued. "I'll assume then that the Police don't think that the suicides were anything out of the ordinary." He felt his anger rising that he'd allowed himself to be taken into a fairy-tale. "What a waste of time!"

Conrad found a voice. "You don't think the suicide rate of those that work for him is even remotely interesting?"

"It's a stressful job. Glen and everyone else have been up-front with me about that from the beginning. Based on David and what you've been telling me, clearly I need to get out before I burn-out!"

"Devlin," Conrad began with a condescending tone. "Futures trader and air traffic controller. *They* are stressful jobs. You and your reader mates only read emails. You get to sit in your little bombproof box, read emails, and for this you are overpaid. That doesn't constitute anywhere near enough stress to warrant such a high suicide rate amongst employees! Dumb I can handle, and you wouldn't be the first to not believe me, but don't be so naïve!"

Devlin took a deep breath to begin his retort, but the momentary pause also gave him time to reflect and think. Conrad had a point.

"I'm deadly serious about this, particularly as I'm not absolutely sure that they were suicides. But I may never prove that much."

"David looked like a suicide to me."

"Would you know? Whatever your background, I doubt you could tell."

"Are you thinking Glen?"

Conrad smiled. "I'm happy that I've at least got you thinking. But as much as I hate the prick, sadly he can't be responsible for all of them. I know that he was out of the country for at least two reader's deaths."

"You sure?"

"Yep. I have access to virtually all Police systems, state and federal, and the systems that each interface with. He was definitely out of the country when at least a few of the bodies were discovered, and also when the coroner's report confirmed their time of death."

Devlin thought some more, his arrogant confidence now absent. "So what now?"

"I've been so fixated on making a convert out of you that I'm not entirely sure. Will you help me?"

"I can hardly say no can I?" said Devlin. "It sounds like I stand to gain more than you."

"Fine. Go now and I'll be in touch."

Chapter - 38.

Too tired to stay awake and too anxious to drift off, Devlin was in that restless no-man's land between being alert and asleep. He thought about David and his passing for a time, but the law of self-preservation inevitably made him focus on Conrad and what he'd said. The more he thought about it, the more he was convinced of only one thing; that he didn't really know anything for certain.

When there was a knock at the door, he was both thankful for the distraction and angry for the interruption. It was 5am and only after acknowledging the time did it dawn on him how little sleep he'd actually got. He cautiously opened the door to the hotel manager insistent on entering his room.

"You might want to look at this," the manager said, handing over the early morning edition of the newspaper.

Devlin was about to challenge the necessity for such a personalised delivery service, when he registered his own image on the front page. Crystal clear, the picture showed him crossing the road outside of Tania's apartment by the looks of things. Had a child's playground not been clearly visible in the background it wouldn't have warranted any photo-journalistic merit. But the swings were there, as were several children; at least *their* faces were hidden or obscured.

Deep down he knew this would come; that he'd be identified and tracked down. Moving interstate might have bought him time, but it wouldn't buy him absolution. His acquittal was old news, but his label would persist and apparently follow him for some time to come. Political and geographic boundaries would not stop the transmission of information.

"The media are waiting in the lobby, so you might want to steer clear," offered the manager.

"Does this mean you want me gone?" Devlin asked, expectant of the answer.

"Not at all. Glen pays me well to look after such matters, and in the meantime, the hotel will make a fortune selling coffee to them."

"Thanks."

"Reporters, paedophiles. You know they're not that dissimilar."

Devlin ignored the comment. He was too tired to bite.

"You know, you're not the first," the manager said, no doubt seeing the disappointment in Devlin. "Glen attracts them, like puppies."

"What? Reporters or paedophiles?"

"Neither. Most of his people have a history that tends to attract media attention, given half the opportunity. Perhaps time with Glen gives them the chance to lie low so they can get on when the heat dies off."

"Maybe, but in the meantime I'm trapped here."

"Don't worry about that. We've got more than one service entrance for just such a … service."

Chapter - 39.

Albert woke, as ever, to his watch alarm. His watch was his last possession, and not while there was breath in his body would he part with it, even if those breaths were laboured and his body effectively pickled. Waking each night to the alarm was his small ritual of remembrance. It made him remember his friend.

With each bloodied lung oyster that Albert coughed up and either spat out or swallowed, he thought of his friend. Robert. Rob. They were more than friends, but Rob had a family before they realised it. Closeted for as long as they were, it was never going to happen. Their friendship, he never once called it love, was restricted to stealthy meetings and a casual knowing between them. Moonlighting together gave them extra time, but not really any additional opportunities.

The night of the fire was cold. They'd taken it in turns to wander the facility then warm themselves in the office, sharing only five minutes or so together watching TV before swapping roles. That was the way it was. This division of time gave them each a balance of companionship and time to think. Rob would get time to think of his family and manage his guilt, while Albert would consider how his life would be shattered if their secret ever surfaced.

Ten minutes earlier, Albert himself could have been the one killed. Oxidising substances and limited ventilation; the post incident report said it was inevitable, sooner or later. He couldn't blame foul play or terrorists, it was just fate that took away his friend. Fate is cruel too. It took away his friend and denied a family a father and husband.

When Albert received a LastGasp' message from his friend Rob, he was very appreciative. Glen hand delivered it, and when he later read it in private he was even more thankful. That Rob wanted to share what Albert meant to him was special, but he feared for how the message would be received if read by anyone in the force. One of the last bastions of homophobia, the Police force would not take too kindly to him if he was covertly outed. As it was, he'd been completely isolated after the incident. Perhaps they'd worked it out. Perhaps his secret was still a secret.

The message that Albert received was different to the one that Rob's wife received. Albert tried to keep in touch with Rob's family, his wife in particular, but she wasn't interested. Whether she resented that she was now without a partner while Albert was still alive or some other reason was irrelevant. She did, however, share the message that *her* Robert sent. Content aside, the tone in her message was different. He expected differences obviously, but when he read them both, it was clear that he could not account for the differences with any simple psychological struggle. He knew in an instant that the two messages had been drafted by two people. He felt confident at least in the authenticity of his message; it was too human, too Rob.

He raised the matter with Glen immediately. The realist in him understood that Glen would have read his message when he delivered it, and the odds were that he'd have read the other one too. Glen was sombre, and that little bastard Sam, before he changed his name, had that smug look about him. Glen disregarded his concerns, despite Albert's insistence. As he recalled it, Sam revelled in Albert's efforts to explain how he knew something wasn't right. It was hard for him to make a point without drawing attention to his own message for comparison.

A casual comment from Sam changed everything. "Of course it makes you think which of Rob's messages are actually from him, doesn't it?" Albert remembered the knowing way that Sam raised his eyebrows and stared at him, watching for his reaction. Albert understood immediately that Sam knew about Rob's message. He tried to consider that maybe, just maybe, Sam had simply only read Rob's messages. He tried to take comfort in what he knew of LastGasp' security.

Glen made to silence Sam like a child, but the comment had been made. The damage was done. He asked Sam to repeat what he'd said, as if he hadn't heard correctly.

"Don't you wonder what could be said in your message?" Sam asked.

It changed everything.

Chapter - 40.

Despite being awake the entire night thinking about matters as he understood them, Devlin decided that he needed to be upfront with Glen. Beyond this, he wasn't entirely clear on what he wanted to know.

Glen opened the door at LastGasp' with a friendly smile and "What did Conrad tell you?"

"I'd like to talk to you about that too," Devlin replied.

Glen blanked the bank of televisions in the lounge room and began his own line of questioning, not waiting until Devlin was actually seated. "What did he say?"

"Aside from the fact that I'm more than a little surprised that you even knew that we'd met, he just wanted to warn me, I guess. And for the record, '*Yes*' I was going to tell you and talk to you about it. That's why I'm here so early."

"You're here early because you couldn't sleep. I can see the fatigue in your eyes." Glen drank of his coffee, not seeking any confirmatory response. "But I'm not your keeper, and you're free to meet with him obviously. I'm just interested in what he told you, and more importantly how you responded based on what I told you yesterday."

"I met with him because I assumed he was sending me these messages. Ikel said after he approached Conrad the messages magically stopped. So I went to meet him, and he bombarded me with his concern that I was at risk."

"So what did he say?"

"He said life expectancy among readers was a little, *limited.*"

"And you believe him?"

"I don't know what I believe! He might just be one of a sinister horde wanting '*in*' to LastGasp', but I don't see it. He, on the other hand *shows* me that most readers are dead. I don't recall you telling me this."

"Conrad would never have said most reader's life expectancy was limited. Tell me what he said and showed you." He raised his remote control to turn off all of the televisions.

Devlin paused for moment. He was aware that he was being directly asked to disclose all, and Conrad's warning sprung to the forefront of his mind. He was implicitly being asked to choose a side. To be anything less than up-front with *all* of the details with Glen would be paramount to siding with Conrad. It was reasonable thereafter that Conrad's warning might truly be warranted. Alternatively, why wouldn't he side with Glen and disclose all about his brief meeting with Conrad? If nothing else, Devlin figured he owed Glen the truth. The man had given him a chance and a job when he had nothing else, and at that moment his gratitude outweighed any concerns for himself that he felt.

"Can I start with the fact that I went there under the premise that he was sending me the messages. It turned out that he wasn't," Devlin started. "I plan to try to trace the messages from the phone company today." He felt immediately that he'd proven his allegiance.

"He showed you the matrix? The dots on the screen?"

"You know about it?"

"I know a lot. What else?"

"He thinks you're involved, or at least to blame, for all the reader's deaths, *apparently*."

"Do you remember how many flashing dots there were?"

"I didn't think to count. Why? Are they dead or what?"

"Just ask what you want to ask me, Devlin!"

"Alright. Am I at risk?"

"I appreciate the candour in your question." He drank slowly from his coffee, drawing out his reply. "No, you're not at risk." He turned on the bank of televisions once more, teasing Devlin with the distraction.

"So Conrad is a liar? What about the fact that all of the other readers are dead?"

"Sadly, some have died. Thus the flashing dots on the screen that you would have seen."

"I saw a lot of dots!"

"Sadly, a small percentage of my high staff turnover over many years."

"Conrad said they all killed themselves!"

"That's not what he said. Conrad is misguided, but he's not a liar. I'd suggest he said *many*, not all, have in fact committed suicide, because it's true."

"Why did they kill themselves?"

"Stress is sure to be at least a part of it. But it's just as likely that LastGasp' was not the source of all their stress."

"That's a joke! Boredom is more likely!" Devlin laughed.

"I'm glad you're laughing about it. I'll keep tabs on your stress levels, just the same. In the meantime, I'll see what I can do to make it interesting."

"So what are the rest of the readers doing now? The ones that aren't dead."

Glen presented his total attention to Devlin, albeit without eye contact. "How about if you go and learn about the other readers yourself. I'll even give you a list of names. You'll learn something from all of them. I'm sure that Ikel wouldn't mind if you borrowed his car. Thereafter, you can make up your own mind."

*   *   *

Glen seconded Ikel's car with a spare set of keys and sent Devlin off with a manila folder filled with a list of people, their contact details and home addresses. He purchased a latté to go, retrieved the car from Albert's guard and drove off without any clear plan or having even examined the list. As soon as he was stopped at a traffic light, he returned his focus to the obvious need to formulate a plan, if only to define a route to at least some of the past readers on Glen's list.

Just as he was about to close his eyes and randomly point to one of the listed names, he was alerted to the arrival of a message on his phone from Glen.

TRY WHITELY MASON.

Devlin scanned the list looking for Whitely and on finding it confirmed that his address was on his shortlist of those immediately visitable. He considered whether to take up Glen's recommendation, cynically weighing up what Glen stood to gain by such a suggestion. It may well have been that Glen knew the most likely person to provide him with the information that he desperately sought. Alternatively, Devlin theorised that Whitely could well be the person that Glen knew would reinforce his own agenda and bias, thereby largely defeating the purpose of having Devlin speak with him. He decided that for whatever Glen's intent, Whitely was as good a name as any to begin with.

Chapter - 41.

On arrival at what Glen had listed as Whitely's house, Devlin made a reasonable assessment that the guy had let himself go. An alternative explanation was that Whitely was out of place in his current locale. In a leafy street in a moderately affluent suburb, Devlin marvelled at how obvious it was that Whitely did not belong. He was clearly not big into home maintenance or gardening. It also appeared that he wasn't interested in collecting the mail, putting his rubbish out for collection, or doing anything about the layers of graffiti that covered the front of his house and surrounding picket fence which was partially burnt in several places. Devlin resisted the urge to read the graffiti under the pretence that it might prejudice his meeting. He parked his car outside a neighbour's house and walked back to Whitely's door, noting the movement of curtains in surrounding houses. It occurred to him that if he was being watched so closely, then why hadn't such community policing better protected Whitely's home too.

The closer Devlin got to Whitely's front porch, the more he noticed. Dead vermin were scattered around the brickwork of the house and in the garden, all attracting their share of insects, flies in particular. Occasional movement in the overgrown undergrowth suggested that there were perhaps more vermin living in the environs. Only the heavy moisture laden morning air prevented the associated smell. Devlin made a mental note that it would be in his best interests to keep his time with Whitely to a minimum, if only to avoid the smell that would hit as soon as the sun fell on the rotting carcasses. All of the front windows had been broken to at least some degree. While some had subsequently been haphazardly covered in wooden boards or tin sheets, others were just left with projectile sized holes and long cracks indicating the fragility of the remaining panes. As much as Devlin didn't want to succumb to prejudice, he couldn't help but figure that Whitely was not very popular.

The front door was wide open, but on closer inspection Devlin discovered that there was, in fact, no door. The door frame remained intact and undamaged, as if the door had been intentionally removed. There was no door-bell, knocker or chime, and after a moment's hesitation, Devlin called out as non-committally as possible. "Is anyone there?" There was no reply, but on hearing the sounds of a television, he called out again, this time a little louder and a little more confidently, "Whitely?"

"Come in then, or fuck off!" came an obtuse reply. There was no face visible to accompany the voice.

"Glen Scott sent me. I'm coming in."

"Thank fuck for that," came the reply from inside. "Come and put me out of my misery."

Devlin started to walk down the hall, heading in the direction of Whitely's voice. The hall was unlit, and the further he ventured away from the reach of the morning sunshine, the darker it got. He stepped cautiously, expectant of some obstacles on the floor. He felt several things underfoot and immediately he hoped that there were less vermin inside the house than out, but his hopes were not high. "Is there a light?"

"Third door on the right," Whitely called out. "And there's no light."

Resigning himself to the fact that help, by way of illumination or guidance, was not forthcoming, Devlin continued to feel his way along the corridor carefully. He was now less concerned about what he might damage with each step, and more about how he might be injured by something unseen. Gradually, as his eyes adapted to the available light, he got braver and started making faster, but still undeniably slow progress.

The third door on the right was the only room lit with the morning's natural light. Devlin had passed two other rooms, each with their doors removed and their windows shrouded with blackout curtaining. Try as he might, he couldn't make out the contents of either of these rooms, but on reaching Whitely's doorway, he felt comfortable that he hadn't missed much. The room was strewn with rubbish and decay, ankle deep generally, but in places Devlin saw that the waste would extend above his knee. Scattered amongst the refuse were piles of books and newspapers.

Whitely sat in a high-backed, filthy looking, upholstered armchair that was positioned in the corner of the room such that he could see the window, the door and an old television all at once. He was unshaven, dishevelled and looked as if he hadn't slept in some time, despite being barefoot and wearing a dressing gown of some description over what may, or may not have been pyjamas. He gave Devlin a cursory glance, and then returned his attention to the television, changing the channel using a remote more out of habit than any real need. "Get this the fuck over with, and fuck off!" he muttered.

"My name is Devlin Bennett. I'm a reader," Devlin started an explanation without physically entering the room. "Can we talk?" He wasn't expecting to be turned down, but he felt the need to ask just the same. He edged his way inside the room looking for any indication of hospitality, or even civility. Once inside, he finally got a chance to look at Whitely properly. He was drawn to look at the man's face, but immediately felt bad for doing so.

Devlin figured that Whitely was about his age, but his face bore old scars and recent wounds suggesting injuries spanning a protracted period. Whitely returned Devlin's stare, as if to guilt him into averting his eyes and it took Devlin some time to realise what he was doing. "What happened to your face?"

"None of your mother fucking business."

"But who would do that to you?" He couldn't stop looking and he reasoned that the more questions he asked, the more he could justify continuing his stare.

"What's to say I didn't do it to myself?"

Devlin decided to return to his original line of questioning. "Can we talk?"

"Then will you fuck off and leave me alone?"

"I thought you'd appreciate the company?" Devlin assumed tacit approval and started scanning the room for a place to sit. There was no obvious seat and Devlin looked to Whitely for a cue.

"Company is over-rated." He pointed to the corner adjacent to the door.

Looking a little harder, Devlin noticed an old dining chair hidden under a mass of newspapers and clothing. He pushed everything off the chair, figuring that Whitely wouldn't mind a little extra strewn over the floor, and lifted it so he could sit with the chair reversed.

"What do you want?"

"I came for a chat. That's all."

"Why?"

"I just want to know about LastGasp', and some other readers."

"Why?" Whitely finally offered some promise as he turned off the television.

"Where to begin. I've only just joined, as a reader, and I guess I'm a little paranoid. I started getting phone messages. Meanwhile, Conrad ..." He stopped talking as soon as he saw the hint of recognition in Whitely. "This sound familiar?"

Whitely smiled and nodded. "You got the messages and Conrad planted the seed of doubt in you. Right?"

"I'm just a little spooked. That's all."

"Rightly. So why are you here?" he asked. "And I'm not being philosophical." He locked eyes on Devlin.

"I just thought you might help explain my concerns, and whether they're justified, if only a little." Devlin looked for any sign of relaxation in Whitely's gaze before continuing. "I needed a job and Glen's helped me out with what looks like a great job. But it's a shit job if I'm not going to survive it. I guess I'm looking for something, or someone, to tell me to cut my losses and run, or that I've nothing to fear."

Whitely looked Devlin over again. "I can't tell you have nothing to fear. Only you can do that. But I can help you out a little, I guess. Do you trust Glen?"

Devlin appreciated that Whitely was starting with a simple mind game. However he answered, he knew he ran the risk of biasing anything that Whitely might say, or alienating Whitely altogether. Knowing that any delay in an answer might betray him just as much, he decided to answer with honesty. "I do trust him.

He's been good to me, and I've no case to not believe anything he says."

"Good answer," Whitely smiled. "He's a good man, and as I'm guessing he's told you, he'll always tell you the truth." He drank from a can of Coke that appeared among the refuse on a small coffee table. "I'll do you a deal. I'll answer your questions just as Glen would, and as with Glen, the trick is to ask the right questions."

"Fair enough." Devlin arranged his questions into a logical sequence, starting with the most pressing first, in case he got cut short. "I got a message that said it was too late for me."

"Is there a question for me then?"

"Am I in danger?"

"Everyone's in danger. Crossing the road can be dangerous."

Devlin sighed. "OK then. Am I in danger from my work at LastGasp'?"

"No," Whitely answered with barely any interest.

"Are the others dead as a result of LastGasp'?"

"Yes," Whitely was playful. "And no."

"Are you going to explain?"

"You've got to ask the right questions. If it teaches you anything, LastGasp' needs to teach you that."

"Why did David die?"

"I'm assuming we're talking about David Yeardley." Whitely was visibly saddened. "He wouldn't be the first. And chances are he won't be the last. Next question."

"So was it actually suicide?"

"With the caveat that I haven't seen the Police report, it probably was. If you're implying that he might not have died at his own hand, I'd suggest you're barking up the wrong tree."

"So why would he do it?"

"Do what? Specifics please, or I can't help."

"Why would he kill himself?"

Whitely sighed, "Don't underestimate the power of guilt as a motivator."

"What was he guilty of?"

"I don't know. Who says the guilt is his."

"So what killed the other LastGasp' employees?"

"Who said they were killed? A lot of us, most of us, are still alive and kicking."

Devlin sighed while his stress heightened again after a temporary reprieve. "How many of them are dead then?"

"That's hardly relevant."

"Why not?" Devlin challenged.

"It's not relevant because you don't give a fuck. Why would you care how many died?"

"My next question was going to be ..."

"Your next question should be dependent on your evolving understanding. That said, I sincerely doubt you could have a relevant question prepared." Whitely was strangely incensed. "If I said 10, that means nothing just as if I'd said 100. Neither would contribute to your understanding. If LastGasp' employed one thousand people, over a period of time some will die of natural causes, in car accidents, whatever. So what does a simple count of the number that have died tell you?"

"Not a lot."

"And don't bother wasting my time asking *how* they died. That's not relevant either. I won't pander to any morbid fascination that anyone might have. I'll help you out though, because I'm that kind of guy."

"Thank-you." Devlin waited for Whitely to say something pertinent that wouldn't make him feel like a ten year old in trouble.

"Don't thank me until I actually do something for you."

"Why did you leave?" As soon as he'd asked it, Devlin knew that the question had found its mark. He watched as Whitely, previously arrogantly comfortable in his chair began to squirm.

"I had a life changing experience. The details of which are either personal or a matter of public record. After that, I didn't feel like working, or being with people either for that matter. I bought this house, cash of course, thanks to the money Glen gave me, and that's it. And clearly I'm still alive."

"How long have you known Glen for?"

"Does *that* matter?"

"Just curious is all."

"I've been waiting for years to be put out of my misery." Whitely's tone was angry. "Good enough answer for you?"

Devlin looked around the room once more, as much a distraction from Whitely's intermittent looks, as he marvelled how anyone would live amid such filth. While he hated himself for thinking it, he figured that much of the damage outside the house could reasonably have been a series of hints from neighbours interested in their own property values. Perhaps Whitely was the quintessential neighbour from hell.

There were no clues in the room as to why Whitely would live as he did, or to explain his facial wounds. It was not a human way to live. He recalled seeing commercials and documentaries about unfortunates from the third world living in rubbish dumps, but to the best of his memory those people would still have a 'home' than was devoid of waste, as much as possible. Whitely on the other hand seemed willing to live surrounded by rubbish of all descriptions. His injuries obviously contributed to the waste. There were bloodied tissues around the room, but they were certainly more prevalent within what amounted to tissue throwing range from Whitely's armchair. On some the blood was still an off red colour, on others the colour had dried to a dark magenta, on still others they were near black, but on all there was no mistaking the source. The volume on each was another matter entirely, easier to quantify, but more difficult to qualify. Devlin figured that the tissues had been used for more than a shaving cut, but less than a gunshot wound. He appreciated that there was a large grey area in between, and this made him look for fitting wounds all the more. Judging by the sheer volume of frozen meal containers scattered everywhere, rodent bites, or possibly dysentery, would be understandable. Once again Devlin had a closer look at the wounds on Whitely's face.

Devlin tried to think of more polite questions than the most obvious ones, but the longer he tried, the more reasonable they seemed. He convinced himself that asking anything would be acceptable, particularly as his visit was sanctioned by Glen. The worst that could happen would be that Whitely would put him in his place. He could at least try to ask the impolite questions politely.

"Whitely, why do you live like this?"

The question didn't appear to fluster Whitely. "Now *that* is none of your business."

"Well, I tend to think that it is," Devlin got brave. "I'm looking at you and wondering if I'm looking at myself in the future if, or when, I leave LastGasp'. You live in shit and someone, or a lot of people, hate you. So what's your story?"

"My story is exactly that. *My* Story. None of your business. Suffice to say that my story was decided long before I left LastGasp'"

"But …"

"How about you shut-up for a bit and let me tell you some things," Whitely interrupted. "I can't and won't speak for the others, but Glen didn't make me who, or what I am. Neither did LastGasp'. That much I did myself." His tone softened, as if there was a certain catharsis in talking. "I understand your concern, but I can't say you have nothing to fear. The worst thing is that the things that I can tell you will only heighten your anxiety.

"Perhaps it would help if you knew that I don't think you'll end up like me. I have my regrets, but regret doesn't change what's happened. I live like I do because I don't care." Whitely looked weary. "It's a funny thing. Do you think that suicide is brave?"

"I hadn't thought about it."

"Sure you have. But anyway. Whether out of bravery or cowardice, I couldn't do anything about it myself. So I'm still here. I spend each day waiting, but nothing ever happens."

"That doesn't explain your face."

"It's the face I was born with. But sadly I still have to look at myself in the mirror. A lesser person might not look in the mirror, but that didn't seem right. I guess it's part of my absolution. My way, I get a reminder every time I see my reflection. It doesn't help the time pass any faster, but it helps me focus as the hours and days roll on."

Devlin thought about what he'd just heard. If he understood correctly, Whitely's injuries were self-inflicted. He couldn't think of an appropriate comment on the matter.

Whitely revealed a contented grin, but as the grin broadened further, several ill-healed wounds on his forehead ruptured, releasing a trickle of fresh blood. He relaxed his face to a more comfortable vacant expression and reached for another handful of tissues. "So what are you going to do now?" he asked, partially muffled through some tissues.

"I guess I'll have a chat to someone else on Glen's list."

"They won't tell you any more, or less, than me. Unless you find Malcolm Venn."

"Why?"

Devlin scanned Glen's list for the name. He was on his third pass before Whitely commented. "He won't be on your list because Glen doesn't know where he is. Glen wouldn't want him found either."

"So how do I find him?"

"I would have thought a more logical question would be '*who is he?*'"

"OK. So *who* is he then?"

"If you can find him, and that's a reasonably big '*if*', he might make a lot of things clearer. I might add that you won't be the first to look for him, and you won't be the only one."

"So what's so special about Malcolm?"

"How can I put this simply?" Whitely feigned a pensive expression, immediately regretting doing so and grabbing another handful of tissues. "Ok, how's this. You're a *reader*, and you *read*. You only read. Malcolm is a lot less passive." Whitely smiled, quietly satisfied he'd made his point as clearly as he was going to make it. "On your way out, can I ask *you* a few questions." Whitely made it clear that their meeting was effectively over.

"But …"

"First question," Whitely began, interrupting. "Where does Glen live?"

Devlin accepted that the question was a little odd, but he gave Whitely some latitude. "I'm pretty sure he lives on the top floor of LastGasp', or at least a room there somewhere. I don't rightly know really. From all accounts he doesn't sleep much anyway."

"Next question. Where and when did you meet him?"

Again, Devlin marvelled at why Whitely considered these mundane questions to be necessary. "I met him on a train, a few days ago. We started talking, he gave me his card, and later that day I called him and he offered me a job."

"Interesting," Whitely replied succinctly, disinterested. He took up his remote control but stopped short of using it. "One more thing, Devlin. Only knowledge comes with death's release. Don't confuse knowledge with truth. Remember that."

Devlin couldn't help raising an eyebrow at the obscurity of the comment.

"Goodbye, Devlin." Whitely turned on the television and started cycling through the channels. As a final parting gesture, he farted.

Devlin took the hint. He navigated his way through the dark corridor and into the bright sunshine.

Only after his first breaths of fresh air did he realise just how bad Whitely's home, his living room in particular, actually smelled. On entry, his many breaths walking slowly along the hallway had gradually introduced him to the pungency, but with his faster exit, the freshness of the dew heavy air was all the more noticeable. He scratched his hair sub-consciously just thinking about the way Whitely lived.

Chapter - 42.

At the first traffic light, Devlin checked the glove-compartment and console for some air freshener. He still had a bad taste in his mouth from Whitely's house and while he knew that it would pass, he wasn't prepared to wait. The odour in Ikel's car was nowhere near as over-powering as he remembered, in comparison at least, but surely Ikel would have something. He found some car deodorant and sprayed it liberally on both the car interior and himself.

He reached for Glen's list looking for the next ex-employee to visit. Whitely's words about the limited value of visiting the others were loud in his mind, and he lost interest in any other impromptu visits. He pondered the rest of what Whitely had said, and in particular, he thought about his last questions. Even in hindsight, the questions were pointless. Whitely clearly had a long history with Glen, and as he rarely, if ever, ventured out of the house, then surely he was beyond the need for the mundane banter that Devlin's answers clearly constituted. Unless, he thought, Whitely was genuinely interested in what he'd said, despite his apparent disinterest. He thought over his replies again, obsessing that it was he who'd missed the point. The traffic light changed and in an instant Devlin had an epiphany. Whitely had asked the questions not for himself, but instead to subtly make a point. *If Glen lived and worked at LastGasp', then why would he be on a morning suburban peak hour train?* Devlin suddenly doubted that their meeting was purely one of chance.

Five minutes passed, then ten and Devlin was no closer to being able to understand either *what* was happening or *why* it was happening. Most importantly, he couldn't understand where he himself fitted into the situation. He tried to consider himself as just a casual passer-by, and one who could easily move on and forget about it all. Whether he was willing to turn his back on the money, legal money, on offer from Glen was another matter entirely. Whether he fully understood why or not, deep down he knew that he was involved in some way. More importantly, the messages that he'd been sent, conceivably from his stolen phone, and the information from Conrad told him enough to know that he couldn't walk away.

Devlin started to fidget, anxious for his own well-being. He considered his options, superficially at first, and then with increasing granularity, weighing up the potential upside and downsides of each. Leaving LastGasp', possibly without a word to anyone, was a very reasonable option. If he was truly *that* fearful, then it was possibly the only option. However, the fact that he had nothing *definitive* to actually be fearful of made him look further into other courses of action. His concerns were logical, but only circumstantially. The messages themselves meant nothing, but suggested a great deal. The death of David and possibly others did not constitute a legitimate threat to himself, particularly when he was still to confirm anything that Conrad had said. For all he knew, he could well have been played by Conrad, and Whitely, and even Glen for that matter. Being honest with himself, he knew that he was prepared to discount this avenue because of his reluctance to leave LastGasp', but he was content just to have identified it as an option.

He felt the minutes drag on as he deliberated his choices.

Chapter - 43.

Devlin described his actions as 'selectively indecisive'. He couldn't decide what to do, so he undermined his own thought process, added a new option and ran with it. He opted to ignore his current concerns, do nothing and return to work. He took a roundabout route, concentrating on the banal banter of some talkback radio station, ever hopeful that he'd think of a solution as soon as he relaxed. No such solution occurred to him; he was unable to truly relax.

Pulling into the laneway behind LastGasp', Devlin saw Lori talking with Albert outside the car-park. They stopped talking when seen, and just stood awaiting Ikel's car to pull in. Lori showed no surprise that Ikel was not the driver, so Devlin accepted that they'd been talking for some time and Albert had told her of his dawn expedition. Devlin parked and quickly got out of the car-park, holding his breath from the moment he turned off the ignition until he joined the others away from the smell.

"Find out what you needed?" Lori asked.

"Not really. I just wanted to meet some other readers."

"Why the fuck would you want to do that?" asked Albert abruptly.

"What 'Bert here means is, why?" Lori softened the same question.

"I'm still getting the messages, and I'm still more than a little stressed over it. I asked Glen about past readers and he suggested that I go and meet a few."

"Who'd you see?" Albert asked, interested.

"I had the whole list and I had to start somewhere, and Glen suggested to start with Whitely. I can't remember his surname."

"Mason. Whitely Mason," Lori grimaced subtly at Albert. "I didn't think he was still alive."

"He is. Of sorts." Devlin considered how the definition of 'alive' could be equally both applicable and inapplicable, but he didn't digress. "Anyway. I met him hoping that my concerns would be put to rest, but I left there wondering if I'd be in Whitely's shoes down the track some time. And as a parting gesture, he sent me off with a little riddle that made me wonder if me joining LastGasp' wasn't entirely the result of a chance encounter with Glen on a train."

Devlin felt relief. Nothing had changed, but he felt different. He waited for wise words to flow in reply, but none came. Devlin appreciated that there was truth, but certainly not the whole truth, in his concerns. "Who's Malcolm Venn?"

Lori didn't avoid the question. "This isn't the thing that we should discuss here." She looked to Albert for his concurrence.

"Does this mean you want to discuss it with Glen too?"

"Unlikely," grunted Albert.

"I'd prefer not, and I don't want to talk about it with Albert. He understands."

"I'll be here later if I can help," Albert commented with resignation. He returned to his seat in the car-park, leaving Lori and Devlin to walk off, but not in the direction of LastGasp'.

Devlin allowed himself to be casually led by Lori out of the laneway and onto the main strip, past cafés with mid-morning hyperactivity, and evening venues cleaning up from the night before. Eventually, Lori checked over her shoulder and stepped into a nondescript coffee shop long overdue for renewal or refurbishment. She chose a table partially hidden from the street and ordered two lattés without even confirming Devlin's preference. He took his seat.

"I've never met Malcolm. But I've heard about him too," Lori launched into what she had to say. "For the record, I'd like to meet him, along with everyone else who'd like to meet him."

"Is that it? We came here for you to just say you've heard of him? So who is he then?"

Lori shrugged. "Malcolm is everyone, and no-one. Of course Malcolm isn't his real name. That would be too easy."

"So what's the big deal about him then?"

The coffees she ordered arrived, and for a while Lori seized the opportunity to avoid the question. Eventually, she started to speak, though not to answer directly. "I've been with LastGasp' a lot longer than you. I've not done anything wrong."

"I wasn't accusing you."

"The name 'Malcolm Venn' came up in conversation with Albert a few weeks ago. It was just a passing comment. 'Bert knows what goes on at LastGasp', and we were just talking about being able to identify people. I told him sometimes people mention names, and there's a protocol for any mention of names." The noise of a siren from the street interrupted them, and they both drank more of their coffees until the wail died down. "He asked if the name 'Malcolm Venn' ever came up. And it hadn't."

"Hadn't or hasn't?"

"Hadn't."

Chapter - 44.

Suicides are not like lightning, Detective Reymond theorised as he crossed the parquet flooring of the hotel he'd left a little over twelve hours previously. Everyone knew the cliché that lightning never strikes twice in the same location, and generally speaking his experience had proven this to be true. However, his experience with lightning was decidedly limited, whereas suicides were a different matter. Not only was it conceivable, and probable, that multiple suicides could occur at the same place, but his experience in this subject was considerable.

The suggestion by the manager the previous day that there had been another suicide there at the hotel had kept Reymond awake at night, and first thing in the morning he'd done some background checks. There had been a number of incidents at the hotel, not an unreasonably high number for a hotel, or enough to make him immediately reconsider his assessment of suicide, but enough to force his due diligence to investigate further. The more he looked, the more he recognised anomalies that, in all reality, should have been identified earlier. If this hotel had always been part of his patch, he would have picked up on the peculiarities immediately, but incessant jurisdictional changes meant that technically the hotel had slipped in and out of his *patch*.

It was an easy thing to miss, Reymond sub-consciously defended his predecessor, but it didn't work. Multiple suicides, same location, and same floor that the hotel manager had described as being for longer term residents. Questions needed to be asked then, and still need to be asked. He had to start somewhere and he decided to start with the hotel manager he'd met the day before.

*   *   *

The hotel manager was helpful. He made available everything that was at his disposal, including the security footage, and also that which was not legally his to share, including guest registers.

Reymond noted the guests whose billing was met by David Yeardley's employer. With each name, the hotel manager shared whatever he could remember of them in an effort to help. While they all stayed on the same floor without security video, access to their floor was still subject to surveillance. Reymond scanned the footage of the previous day, slowing the fast playback to see individual faces before returning to the animation of real time being played extra fast. With each face, the hotel manager would share a commentary. He saw Ikel and Devlin's near dawn departure and also Lori returning to the hotel lobby at a more reasonable time. He watched David return, just as the others had described, followed not long after by Devlin. When Reymond saw Malcolm Venn on the screen, he paused the playback.

The hotel manager continued his commentary unabated. "Sam Burbino. He was a guest here some time ago, but he periodically visits."

"Are you sure?"

"Sure that he visits? Yes, he's a regular. I've known him to have a coffee with many of the guests."

"But you're sure of his name? When I met him recently he called himself 'Malcolm Venn'."

"Never heard of him by that name, but it's definitely him."

"Dammit," Reymond mumbled as he scribbled in his notebook.

Chapter - 45.

Nebojsa Kendic was in the clear. He knew from the moment he woke that *lay time* was over, and he responded with his usual fervour. Yesterday, he'd been on his best behaviour when lay time began, but as the hours passed, his confidence had evolved into arrogance, and by the end of the day he'd drawn the attention of sycophants and superiors alike, all wanting to share in his presence. By early evening he knew that Angie was going to keep her mouth shut. She wasn't a good girl, but she'd proven herself to be a smart one.

Sleeping alone was a fact of life for Nebojsa, though this suited him just fine. He got all the sex he wanted, and having space between the sheets for him to sleep was hardly a difficult price to pay. But lay time was always a difficult time, not because he'd miss the solace of companionship during a time of stress, but rather he was denied his usual outlet. What made the end of lay-time particularly bad was that he'd be so aroused by his own confidence that sleeping was impossible. Even during yesterday's lay time he'd shunned advances by several female colleagues purely because this was a rule, a line that should never be crossed. He didn't shit where he worked. Despite the offers, he resigned himself to the necessity to take several whores for the evening. This he'd done, and sent them on their way before ordering a pizza. He was in bed by midnight, alone once more, and appreciative that the prostitutes had served their purpose and earned their pay. He'd lain awake marvelling at how common *women-for-hire* could reasonably be expected to keep their mouths shut. If only all of his acquaintances could be this trustworthy.

However, this lay-time was different. He sensed it from the moment that he learnt that Angie had been admitted to hospital. Others in her situation had allowed themselves to die, but not Angie; she wasn't going to give him the satisfaction. It was a testament to her really. He decided to send her some flowers.

Chapter - 46.

Devlin was now more confused as to his next course of action. Lori had apparently passed on everything she knew about Malcolm, but this amounted to little more than the fact that the LastGasp' Research Interface hadn't helped. She either didn't know or didn't share who he was. All she said was that there appeared to be an ever increasing list of people interested in finding him, regardless of whether they confessed their reasons. Devlin was too distracted to press her to explain how she came to know of the others apparently looking for this Malcolm guy.

"So if you know nothing about him, this Malcolm, why didn't you say so in front of Albert?"

"Albert is another matter," Lori began. "I asked Glen about Malcolm, largely as a favour to Albert."

"And?"

"And nothing. He just kept watching TV like he does."

"So?"

"But then he gave me a newspaper article." Lori fumbled in her handbag and produced a newspaper clipping.

Under the pretence that newspaper headlines get smaller and less impressive the further from the front page, Devlin gathered that this was not a particularly important headline. *Moonlighting Policeman Likely to Recover'*.

Lori added a commentary as Devlin read. "It's about Albert. He's a Policeman, or at least he was. He was working after hours as a security guard babysitting a chemicals storage facility when there was a fire, some explosion. He came out of it relatively lightly. Some scarring, moderate respiratory damage and a totally destroyed sense of smell, thanks to Chlorine gas exposure at the scene of the incident. He's still better off than another guy who didn't survive the blast."

"That explains a lot," Devlin mumbled as he read. Actually it explained very little, except to justify his periodic coughing fits and answer the question why Albert would tolerate the smell of the car-park.

"That article was dated a few years ago."

"So Albert left the Police force, lost his way and became a derelict pseudo-security guard for LastGasp'. I'd hate to think that he'd let himself go so quickly if it was any more recent."

"Quite," Lori ignored the quip. "Glen refused to talk about the article. All he said was that '*I'd work it out*.'"

"That sounds like Glen."

"Well yes, it's very much his style. He likes for people to discover things for themselves, but you're missing the point. I traced the details of the accident, if that's what it was, through the details in the paper. I found the incident site, and other miscellaneous details. That much was easy."

"And?"

"And nothing. The story disappeared from print very quickly, hidden with interest rate concerns and the rising cost of oil. The Police lost interest remarkably quickly and needless to say that no-one saw justice over it."

"So what does this mean?"

"I don't know." Lori sighed. "What I do know though is that the guy did actually die. I met his widow and children and I recognised genuine loss in each of their eyes."

"Sad of course, but I don't see how this affects me, Albert, Glen, or LastGasp' for that matter."

"I don't understand it either," Lori conceded.

Chapter - 47.

Devlin returned to LastGasp' with Lori. For a new employee determined to prove his worth, he felt more than a little guilty about the fact it was now after lunch and he hadn't done any real work. He felt obliged to head straight to the bunker, saying only passing greetings to Glen in the sitting room engrossed in the bank of televisions, ambivalent but not oblivious, as they joined Ikel in the bunker.

"You looked after my car, right?" Ikel asked, barely drawing his eyes from his screen.

"Yes, and thank-you. It wasn't my idea, Glen just threw me a set of your keys. And…"

"It's not a biggie. I trust you." Ikel interrupted, saving Devlin from continuing.

The atmosphere in the bunker was laboured, as if everyone was determined to continue as normal despite David's death. Despite their best intentions, no-one was convinced.

Devlin focussed on his reading and within the first few messages, he settled into his rhythm of the day before. He read a message, considered the content and whether a protocol was necessary or appropriate, and then moved onto the next. By the time he'd started the next message he'd largely forgotten the last. He knew it was only early days, but there would be little chance of his stress levels reaching any tangible level if he could continue in this manner. He started keeping statistics in his head. *Five messages without flagging any. Six messages without flagging anything, four male, two female.*

Seven messages, four male, three female, three happy, four sad, none identifiable. Eventually, he realised that the statistics were becoming more of a distraction than their worth and he decided to just keep a running count that he read.

After twenty messages Devlin remembered the tedium of yesterday. His abstraction from the message content was still present, but his clarity to separate each was starting to wane. *Was this one being written by a man or a woman? Married or single? A charmed life or a regrettable one?.*

Devlin's seventy first message for the day began like the rest. Whoever had written it was obviously finding it difficult to find a context or perspective to writing what was surely a mix of private letter, eulogy and epitaph. It was written awkwardly, but gradually she, Devlin assumed it was a woman, found her rhythm and he prepared to glimpse at what she found important enough to share in a final message. She teetered between the first and third person perspectives and in so doing she shared her name, Angela Clarke, more commonly known as Angie, and implicitly thereby earned her message his first protocol for the day, and first definitive sender identification. This particular message was suddenly more interesting than the others.

As he started to read and actually concentrate on the message, it seemed to Devlin as that Angie had written her message mindful of her mortality. She knew that she would die sooner or later, but when or how was far from clear. As certain as she was that she would die, she seemed less certain who the recipient of her message would be. There was no familiar hint of who she expected or wanted to read her message after her passing. Devlin read the message aloud in his mind, trying to capture Angie's tone. He couldn't help but try to picture her too. She didn't sound old, nor young and gradually he pictured a nice looking, but not gorgeous, nubile but not emaciated woman about his age, a non-committal brunette with long hair and grey-green eyes. He also saw a short skirt, revealing blouse, sweet smile and more than a little confidence born of happiness.

Angie shared memories of a reasonably happy but as yet incomplete life featuring family and friends such that she was never on her own, more 'ups' than 'downs', and money enough to pay the bills without the downside of wealth. While she wasn't on her deathbed, Devlin pictured her, when that day came, with a contented smile on her face. Devlin shared the smile, content that he'd been allowed to share the joy.

The tone in Angie's message turned sour very quickly. No sooner had he started to smile inwardly that Devlin was shaken with Angie's revelations. There was suddenly a sadness in her message exacerbated by her contrasting memories, and an anger about her inability to do anything about it. He kept reading, fixated, as Angie divulged details of her life clearly not shared with anyone else. She told of her landlord, a man named Nebojsa, though he answered to many names, but whom the title bastard would be an understatement. She described pain and bruising and isolation, and frustration at the inability of the Police to help. Reading between the lines, Devlin could however detect more than a little pride from her that she had stuck it out for as long as she had, but also sensed that her resilience was on the wane.

Now when Devlin pictured Angie, he focussed less on the look of her face and more on her demeanour. She still looked the same, but now her confidence was gone and the previously imagined sexual fire in her eyes was definitely absent. She no longer wore short skirts, opting instead for something capable of hiding lingering bruising.

Devlin was beyond hoping for a happy ending as he neared the end of the message, though he did hope for something to indicate that Angie had not all but given up. Instead, Angie shared that she hoped that 'Malcolm' would help, ending her message abruptly and simply with her name and phone number.

The mention of 'Malcolm' caught Devlin's attention briefly. Had he been identified with his surname then that would have been too much of a co-incidence to be reasonable and Devlin knew it. He wrote off the name as being not worthy of further consideration, particularly the odds of this 'Malcolm' being the same guy that Whitely had spoken of.

Oblivious to a discussion between Lori and Ikel, Devlin sat back in his chair to ponder all that he'd read. He assigned all of the protocols that he considered appropriate, but fell short of adding a suicide protocol. As bad as Angie's story was, he still felt that enough fire remained to sustain her, though for how long was anyone's guess. He noted that this message had previously been edited and was actually Angie's fourth iteration. Clearly Angie thought enough of her future to warrant investing in something other than a free LastGasp' account.

The fact that Angie's message was signed off with a phone number, her phone number presumably, perplexed him. If the message was purely intended to be seen only after her death, then surely the addition of the phone number was pointless. He waited for a lull in the discussion between Ikel and Lori before asking, "Guys, what do I make of a message signed off with a phone number?"

"Ghost," Ikel answered succinctly.

"It's probably a ghost." Lori added. "You ring a number known only via a LastGasp' message and *voila*, LastGasp' and its associated privacy concerns are exposed. What was the rest of the message text?"

"Some abused woman." Devlin fell short of disclosing that he felt for the woman, opting instead to keep his summary objective. "I've already flagged a few protocols."

"Do you want us to look over it?" Ikel offered.

"Don't worry. I just haven't seen one like this before, but undoubtedly you would have."

"Add the ghost protocol, and move on," Lori demonstrated the abstraction that was unexpectedly absent in Devlin. "We've got a lot to clear today."

Devlin did as instructed, but only after making a mental note of Angie's number. He needed some fresh air.

Chapter - 48.

As soon as Devlin was out of the bunker, he began to key Angie's number into his phone and deliberated actually making the call. The wheels in his mind were spinning, searching for something that could or should be done now that he had shared Angie's life. He didn't want to be the one to bring down LastGasp' for want of proving a message or learning more. It occurred to him too that he might be too late, and that Angie might have met her end at the hands of the bastard she'd described. That thought clicked his mind into overdrive. What if he made the call and it wasn't too late? Then what would he do?

Devlin had only just entered the fresh air outside LastGasp' when his phone rang. He couldn't get Angie's message out of his head and he reached for the phone out of conditioning rather than deliberate action. He answered it, suspicious as ever, but was comforted in as much as the calling number was not familiar. Still distracted, he passively listened to a woman's voice and even though she'd stated her name, Tania Wilson, it still took some time for him to put the name and voice to a face. She spoke, he listened, still miles away. She wanted to meet to talk, now. He agreed, if only to allow him to return to his headspace. It was only after he'd ended the call that he fully realised who she was and what he'd actually agreed to.

Ikel offered to drive Devlin back to Tania's house, but as the offer was accompanied by wisecracks, Devlin declined. Instead, he asked to borrow Ikel's car, primarily under the pretence of needing some 'alone time' after what was, without question, the most stressful message he'd read. His claim had merit and he'd been thrown the car keys without any further questioning.

*   *   *

Devlin had no recollection of anything from their brief talk on the phone, but he'd naïvely expected Tania to be in a mood comparable to how she was after their meeting the previous day. Instead, he could tell from the moment that she answered her door that she was anything but appreciative or happy. She invited him in and essentially instructed him to take a seat on her couch, but at least she offered coffee which he accepted out of habit. The burst of caffeine did wonders to focus him.

"The message I got yesterday from you was lovely," Tania began. "But today's one just makes me think that I'm either being stalked, or perhaps you at LastGasp' think that I'm ripe to receive spam from you every day. I just thought I'd stop it before it began." She eased off her tone to add, "I figured that if you were nice enough to hand deliver your message yesterday, then I should at least cite my case to you in person."

"I'm sorry Tania, but I don't know anything about your latest message." Devlin quickly understood that someone else known to Tania had died. "Would you mind if I read it?"

Tania handed over a message printed on recycled paper and Devlin accepted that the email issues that had warranted his hand delivery yesterday had been resolved. The message had all the makings of a near anonymous apology similar to many that he'd read in the bunker and he scanned the text accordingly without really concentrating on any of its content. Then it dawned on him that he should be reading this particular message like a concerned friend and not like a LastGasp' reader. He started to read from the beginning once more.

On his second read, Devlin failed to understand Tania's concern. If she'd accepted yesterday's message without question, then why would today's message be such a leap of faith? And then it struck him that yesterday's message was technically from her belated brother, whereas this one was apologising for her brother's death. There was nothing explicitly confessional in its nature, but there was little doubt that the sender of this particular message felt guilt for the death of one Tim Wilson, brother of Tania. The message ended with a name, David, and his phone number.

"Do you know who this *David* is?" Devlin asked.

"No, but I thought you might."

"Why?"

"No reason, other than the fact that it's on your letterhead."

Devlin nodded. "That's not how it works," he started to explain. "LastGasp' is effectively just a delivery service. Messages get sent after someone dies, on their behalf."

"So this isn't a prank?" Tania asked earnestly.

"I can't vouch for the sender or their intent. If it's a prank, then it certainly isn't sanctioned by LastGasp'. There's not a lot more I can say."

It took some time for Tania to digest this new information. "So who sent it?"

"I've got no idea of who sent this or any other message." Speaking to an outsider, Devlin finally understood the purpose of message anonymity. "Have you rung the number for this *David?*"

"Yes, but there was no answer. I'd just like to speak to him, whoever he is."

Devlin considered correcting Tania in that this David, if he ever existed, was now dead if his message had been sent, but he decided against it. "Would you be offended if *I* tried his number?" he said, reaching for his phone in his jacket pocket. Acknowledging a nod of approval, he dialled the number. His phone immediately associated the number with a stored name. *Yeardley, David.* Shaken, he maintained a façade of waiting for the call to be answered, as if he wanted to prove for himself what Tania had reported, but he knew there would be no answer. He returned the phone to his pocket as Tania shrugged approvingly that she'd been proven right.

Devlin was lost for what to do with this new information. "I don't know what to say. LastGasp' really is just the messenger." Tania said nothing, so he continued. "I can't think why someone, this David, would send a message like this."

"So is there *any* way that I can track down David?"

"How would that help?" Devlin replied defiantly but politely. "Sorry, I understand *why* you'd want to track him down, but perhaps I hadn't made something clear. LastGasp' messages are only, can only, be sent posthumously. Whoever wrote the message, in this case this *David*, is dead."

Devlin fidgeted, re-reading the printed message in his hands. "How exactly did your brother die? I mean there's nothing actually in this message."

"Someone, a no-one, killed him. Beat him to death one night." Tania wiped away an imagined tear before they appeared for real. "The guy heard voices singling out my brother, apparently. Why, I'll never know."

"And the Police got him?" Devlin couldn't help a doubtful tone.

"Yes. The Police quite literally followed a trail of bloodied shoe prints once they found my brother's body, courtesy of him having kicked the shit out of Tim. You know his skull was crushed?" Tania sighed. "They found him, sitting kerbside, crying … and scraping pieces of brain from the welts in his boots. Apparently he was very remorseful."

"When was this?"

"Doesn't matter now anyway. He's dead now, the guy who did it. He got *his* on remand. Eddy Stantoch. Rest in peace, but with stab holes you bastard!" She drifted off and into her mug of coffee.

"Who got him, this Eddy?"

"No idea and not that it matters either. It won't give me back my brother." Tania relaxed herself into her couch.

Devlin was silent for a moment in recognition of Tania's grief. "I don't know what to say, other than to say that I'm sorry for your loss. Perhaps this David guy got you, or Tim, confused with someone else."

"Perhaps," Tania replied solemnly.

Devlin felt that he had reclaimed some level ground in his meeting with Tania. He saw that she was no longer braced for an argument and he figured that he should move on. "Do you mind if I take this?" he asked, holding up the printed message from David.

"Fine," Tania replied. "I guess if I need another copy I can always print it off." She nodded a vague indication to her computer on her study desk. The Police didn't really sound interested either, but someone is coming to have a look anyway." Tania thought for a moment. "Can you believe that they couldn't, or wouldn't, give me an email address to forward the email on to! So I have to wait until he comes to pick it up." She tuned out once more and drank some of her coffee.

"I guess they know who you are and want to show a personal face to the Police force, for what it's worth. Can I add that I see a lot of messages at LastGasp', and before I joined I never realised the subtleties that are hard to explain in words. More than likely they'll just want to ask you more about your brother and David, and any possible relationship there could be between them that you know of."

"You're right. I'd understand why they wouldn't be interested. They have their man and they certainly don't need any more evidence to deal with him."

Devlin and Tania both appreciated that their meeting had met its natural conclusion. He stood to say his goodbyes when there was a knock at the door. "That'll be the Police now," Tania said, making her way casually to the door and greeting the new arrival.

"Hi Tania. Is this the kind of personal service you expect from the Police?" Detective Alan Reymond entered with a smile and the ubiquitous small-talk necessary to lighten the mood with the arrival of anyone from his profession. Devlin figured that it would have been one of his standard lines, but it obviously served its' purpose well.

Devlin listened to Tania and the Detective's discussion and managed to piece together the extent of their recent history. They clearly had history, but most recently the Detective had not seen Tania since that initial flurry of Police presence after the death of her brother. He'd been the one to first pass on the news of her brother, and thereafter he had kept in contact with updates on the subsequent investigation, most notably the arrest of Eddy Stantoch and his redundant confession. He apparently also had the dubious honour of advising Tania when justice for Eddy, of sorts, preceded any trial. With Eddy's demise however, the investigation was abruptly concluded and Detective Reymond's obligations to maintain contact with Tania also disappeared.

Reymond then progressed into more human banter, commenting on how he knew how difficult a time Tania had been through. He saw that she looked thinner, but her eyes no longer looked red and puffy from endless tears. He shared some analogy likening her grief to a tunnel and surely she was on her way out of the tunnel. Only then did he scan the room to notice that Tania had company.

Devlin raised his hand in greeting, but said nothing. He'd said his goodbye and the arrival of anyone did nothing to make him want to stay. That the new arrival was the Police just made him feel uncomfortable. "I'll be off then Tania." He moved for the door, naïvely hopeful that Reymond would stop him. When Tania smiled and waved, his confidence grew.

"Actually, I was heading to speak to you again next," said the Detective. "Perhaps if you stick around, we could talk a little more over a coffee. There's a little café over the road. I'm sure that this won't take too long with Tania, so I'll meet you there shortly."

Chapter - 49.

Devlin reluctantly headed to the little café. Wiser after yesterday's coffee, this time he bypassed anything prepared by people who clearly had no idea what they were doing. He bought a can of Coke and sat at the same table in the garden courtyard and prepared for what would hopefully not be too long a wait.

He found the wait for Detective Reymond difficult. The minutes dragged on long after he finished his drink and now the wait was painfully slow. He fidgeted a while before he looked for something else to help pass the time, grabbing a newspaper and puzzle book from the adjacent table. He turned his attention to the newspaper, ignoring the cover story. He was well past the news pages and into the lifestyle section before it occurred to Devlin that he was reading the paper differently. Whereas previously he focussed on the news-worthy content, now he found himself obsessed with the people behind the stories. Today, just like every other day, he knew that LastGasp' messages would be sent and he wondered what their content would reveal and lead to. His final thought, just as Detective Reymond arrived, was almost surprise that he didn't recognise any people from their stories, or associate them with any LastGasp' messages.

"We need to talk Devlin," Reymond began as he sat at the table. He ordered a coffee by gesture to the waitress, and Devlin made no motion to warn him against doing so. "I was more than a little surprised to see you there today."

"It was a purely professional visit I can assure you," Devlin commented defensively. "What's the problem?"

"No real problem I guess, except that I've been police since before you were born. Look at it my way. Yesterday I meet with you following the death of one of your work colleagues. Today, I bump into you on the other side of town at the home of a woman who has recently lost her brother. It doesn't take that to bring out the suspicion in me, to say nothing of your exposure in the newspaper. So let's start with how well you know Tania?"

"I don't!" Devlin exclaimed. "We met yesterday. I delivered a message from LastGasp' to her, we talked for a little about her brother and that was it."

"What reason did you have in delivering a message to her."

"I'm just a messenger. I made a delivery that couldn't be emailed, that's all."

Any innocence in Devlin's explanation was lost on Reymond. "In my line of work typically the title *'messenger'* routinely equates to *'courier'*, drugs courier more specifically. Care to elaborate?"

"I'll assume you don't know how LastGasp' works. We deliver messages drafted by members to be sent after they die. Ordinarily these messages are simply emailed, but on occasion they need to be hand delivered. That's how I met her yesterday when I delivered a message from her brother."

"What did it say?" Reymond asked sceptically.

"It's a private message. If you want, or need to know more then you're going to have to ask Tania." Devlin was curt. He knew that there were probably no legal grounds to prevent such disclosure, but he decided to err on the side of caution.

"And today? Tania tells me that you forwarded something of a hoax."

"If it was a hoax, then it was not of my doing, or anyone else from LastGasp'."

"She tells me that you have a copy of the message."

"Yes. And I'm not going to show you for the same reason as with her brother's message. It's private."

"And apparently a hoax, purposely and deliberately delivered to a bereaved woman who has invited Police involvement."

"But it's private."

"Private possibly, but private for Tania, not you. I could just as easily get another printout from her."

"True," said Devlin, confident he'd created a stalemate.

"Thanks Malcolm," Reymond mumbled.

"Did you say 'Malcolm'?"

"It's nothing. For a moment you reminded me of someone I met recently. He too was annoyingly in tune with legal matters where it suited his purpose," Detective Reymond revealed a childishly smug smile.

"Malcolm *Venn?*" Devlin's interest was now well aroused.

"He's a friend of yours?"

"No, but I'd like to meet him."

"Well let's just complete our little chat, co-operate a little, and then perhaps we might be able to arrange a meeting." The Detective folded open his notebook and clicked his pen in anticipation.

"What would you like to know?"

"Can we start with what you know about him?"

"Until this morning I'd never heard of the guy, but..." Devlin was reluctant to say too much too soon.

"And now?"

"And now ... I have no idea."

"What's the problem?"

"Are we talking or are you interviewing?" Devlin asked suspiciously.

"Does that matter? I was planning to talk to you about David Yeardley and your employer later today, but I was more than a little surprised to bump into you at Tania's home."

"*That*, I have explained."

"Yes, you have explained it, but not the fact that when you dialled the number for the 'David' on Tania's email, the number was replaced with a name. Tania noticed it, but not the name. She also mentioned you didn't say anything about it, as if you didn't want her to know. I'm guessing that if I was to check the number you dialled on your phone it would tell me that you dialled David Yeardley. Tell me if I'm wrong somewhere?"

Devlin didn't waste his time challenging the Detective. "So does this mean that this is turning into an interview?"

"Your call. At this point I'd say that I know as much as you, but not the same things. So perhaps we could help each other. What can you tell me?"

"You first," Devlin replied coyly.

"This isn't poker. I'm a patient man, but one who's more than capable of turning this formal if necessary or if you'd prefer."

"Alright then, let's keep it to a chat." Devlin took a deep breath. "Until this morning I had never heard of Malcolm Venn. I met a guy called Whitely Mason, who's an ex-LastGasp' employee that Glen, my boss, suggested I meet. Whitely ultimately suggested that if I want to understand anything I need to find 'Malcolm Venn'"

"What's to understand?"

"I guess I'm having difficulty coming to terms with my new role. I trust you know who I am and my recent past. I've got no friends, no family and no future, and then from out of the blue I land a well-paying job that a semi-literate monkey could do. My boss may, or may not, be a little odd and I'd be lying if I understand what seems to be happening around me. One colleague topped himself yesterday, and apparently there have been others, though the one past employee I've met, this Whitely, was coy with the details. I don't rightly know whether I should be concerned, or happy and just keep my mouth shut."

"And?"

"David wasn't the first LastGasp' employee to die."

"People die everyday."

"From their job?"

"*From* their job or *on* the job? It's one thing to blame an employer for a suicide, but it might be a stretch to imply criminality."

"What if I said that I'm being warned not to follow suit?"

"Warned by who, whom?"

"God knows. I've been getting phone text messages from someone about it."

"I could look into it if you like? If you're genuinely concerned. It is what Police do, you know."

"I doubt that would help. I had my phone nicked a few days ago, and the messages are being sent from that number. It was only a cheap pre-paid thing anyway."

"I'll see what I can do," commented Reymond.

Devlin shrugged, wholly expecting that any such investigation would amount to nothing. "*Quid pro quo*, Detective. What *would* help is telling me about Malcolm."

"I'll tell you what I know," Reymond began, "and then if you're interested I'll tell you what I think."

"Both would be good."

"I met Malcolm a few days ago in a psych ward. He'd been in there for a few days. It wouldn't have rated a mention, and certainly wouldn't have attracted any enforced stay, particularly with hospital beds at a premium as they are, except for the fact that he was covered in blood on admission."

"Whose?"

"No idea, on the main it wasn't his, but your thoughts were shared by many, including me. It deserved a little investigation, at least until a body or two surfaced."

"He killed two people?"

"Not that I know of, but it's hard to say. There was a mixture of blood samples on him. The source was a separate matter, or story, entirely. Nothing conclusive enough to confirm his involvement in any of the several bodies that appeared around the time of his admission. They at least have been accounted for."

"So what did you find?"

"I didn't have grounds to hold or arrest him, but I was obligated to prove his identity to at least gauge who he is. That's when I met Angie."

"Angie?" Devlin questioned out of surprise. "Angie who?"

"The deal was that I'd tell you about Malcolm, not Angie." He waited for some acceptance before continuing. "Anyway. I found Angie. She'd been assaulted, and over a long period by someone. Of course I wanted to finger Malcolm for it, but the timelines didn't match. Thereafter he was released under the pretence that I could find him if I needed to, but he's since disappeared."

Devlin recalled Angie's message. She had disclosed the names of her attacker and Malcolm was not among them. It dawned on him that it was possible, if not likely, that the Angie from the message and Malcolm's friend Angie were invariably not the same person. "I don't think that I'm thinking of the same Malcolm, or Angie for that matter."

"Why do you say that?"

"The Angie I know named her attacker, and it isn't Malcolm. *My* Angie even described her 'Malcolm' as some kind of friend."

"A pity, I'm sure." Reymond sighed. "I was obviously hoping you'd be able to assist me to at least some degree. I get few enough tangible rewards in my job to be able to turn my back on the prospect of being able to put the finger on any man so capable of beating a woman. I figured that Malcolm was implicated in at least some way, irrespective of whether he had a half plausible alibi or excuse on this particular occasion."

Devlin felt a weight lift from his shoulders. "So. Is there anything else that we need to talk about?" He was tempted to stand, but instead opted to wait for an answer.

"You know. It's a funny thing." Reymond ignored Devlin's obvious attempt to cut short their meeting. "I'm no fan of all of this technology. I'm 'old school', you see. Not a dinosaur, mind you, but I've just been a little slow to embrace computers in everything we have to do. The purists argue that all this technology makes it harder for the guilty to hide, but I've seen bad guys protected by a computer hard disk 'crash' just the same." Reymond zealously emphasised his use of modern terminology with gestured 'dittos' in the air. "They're right, of course. I'm not denying that. But, Malcolm's situation surprised me is all."

"How so?"

"You know. Everyone has a history. When I first started in my game it would take a lot of time and effort to learn of anyone's past. It took contacts and time, and generally speaking you could find out what you needed to know. It wouldn't be everything, sure, but it would be enough. You could prove a man has a history of violence, or trouble with substance, or perhaps that he's indebted to the wrong people. Now of course you can find out substantially more, almost instantly. And that's not just the police either. A simple Internet search by anyone could find out just as much. Sometimes I wonder if the Police capabilities would be better if they actually just did a *Google* search!

"But not Malcolm Venn. The guy's got no identification, nothing now or ever. Not known to police, here or overseas. No medical records, driver's license, no passport. Not in any high school yearbooks or rolls. Nothing."

"Did you think that perhaps Malcolm wasn't his real name?" Devlin commented mockingly.

"I'm old, but not senile and certainly not stupid. It wasn't hard to justify getting the fingerprints off a man admitted covered in blood. The DNA test took a little more time for the approval, but not even that bore fruit. Incidentally, I've since learned that he's known by at least one other name.

"Sure, I found other people named the same, but not my guy. Many years ago it was substantially easier to live under the radar, but now it's almost unheard-of. It's your turn to talk, Devlin."

Devlin attempted another sip from his long empty can. "I don't know who Malcolm is, but I'd like to meet with him just the same. When I told Lori, you remember Lori, that Whitely mentioned Malcolm she said me that others were looking for him too."

"In spite of how committed I am to my job, I have no interest in playing nursemaid to you as you struggle with life's mysteries. I am however willing to help you where it helps me."

"How so?"

"Help me to help Angie."

"I said I don't think it's the same 'Angie'. All I have is her number, and the rest is just what I've read."

"So what did you read?"

Devlin felt the challenge of flaunting privacy. "I just read a message that she, the Angie I'm thinking of, left with LastGasp'. The details were private, but I felt for her."

"Felt for her enough to be a bystander, or to actually do something to help?" The Detective paused to allow Devlin to think. "Would it help if you could put a name to a face?"

"Probably not."

"What about if you knew *your* Angie and *my* Angie were one and the same? You mentioned you had Angie's number. If you tell me her number, *your* Angie's number, then I'll tell you if your number matches my contact details."

"You're assuming that I trust you to tell me the truth. There's nothing in that to prove to me you've even got a number."

"Well I'm not going to tell you my Angie's number. I'm not a dating service. How's this then. An eight digit number, here's the last five digits."

Devlin couldn't hide his acceptance that he'd found his Angie. "What now?"

*   *   *

Devlin tried to relax in Detective Reymond's car, but he was un-nerved. He'd reasoned initially that his decision to make a few visits with the Detective was 'against his better judgement', but in reality he could just as easily have argued staunchly in favour of joining Reymond. It implicitly meant that he needed to weigh up what he could gain from meeting with Angie, and possibly Malcolm, relative to what Glen and the others might make of it. It was a moot point now. He'd left Ikel's car parked near the café and set off with the Detective.

On the road, Devlin amused himself with the thought that at least he was in the front seat of the Police car and not in the back seat. He remembered his first ride in the rear seat of an un-marked

Police vehicle as if it were yesterday. In particular he remembered the vandal proofing on the rear of the front seats, the smell of sweat and fear that permeated the vinyl seating, and the non-functional inner door handle. It occurred to him that his recollection was restricted to the view from the rear as would be seen subdued and head down, as he was. This time however, he was in the front seat, but he instinctively grasped the door handle to prove to himself that it would work.

"Where are we going?" Devlin asked.

"I just want you to meet Angie. After that… we'll see."

"I'm not committing to anything remember. The only reason I'm here is to meet Malcolm, or at least get on his trail." He was more interested in setting a realistic expectation of his involvement, no matter how limited, than rescinding his offer.

"Meet her and then we'll see."

Chapter - 50.

Angie was singularly unimpressed to receive her flowers. More correctly, her initial delight at the delivery was replaced with a confused mix of anger and disillusionment as soon as she read the card to establish who had actually sent them. Nebojsa. She imagined just how the man would find it amusing, and the thought of it all made her feel sick.

The hospital resident barely looked old enough to be out of high school, but he'd made it abundantly clear that her bed was ripe for vacation. She tried to argue the point, but she was the patient, and as such, what would *she* know. Without medical grounds to stay and her reluctance to disclose any other reason why she shouldn't leave, the hospital was sure to get their way. Under those terms it was difficult to blame the medical fraternity entirely.

As selfish as it was, Angie felt the desperation of her predicament such that when she saw Detective Reymond enter her room, she saw potential to use him to prolong her hospital stay. The Detective raised his hand in greeting, but first went to speak to one of the staff. His young offsider, she presumed it was another cop, stood staring at her from the doorway. She smiled and returned his gaze, but he seemed oblivious to what she was doing, as if he was trying to place her face somewhere in their common history.

"They tell me you're well enough to be discharged," Reymond announced as he made his way to Angie's bedside. "I tend to disagree, but alas I'm not a doctor, and the party line with the public hospital system is that beds are at a premium but home visits are easier, that is, *cheaper.*"

"You don't sound convinced."

"Well I'm not, Angie. I think it's criminal that anyone would consider sending you home after what has happened, and even more so when doing so is putting you potentially back into harm's way." Reymond looked her over, "you know with just your forearms and face exposed above the bed-linen you really do look fit and healthy. And your fairy-tale explanation for your injuries hasn't convinced anyone, nursing staff included." He glanced to a wandering nurse to suggest that they would happily provide confirmation if necessary.

"Your pride or fear is going to see you discharged whether you want or not." The Detective softened his tone. "Of course, legally you can't be discharged to home care if this would be putting you at risk." That was as subtle as Reymond could be.

"Who's your offsider?" Angie ignored the hint.

"My name is Devlin," he said, stepping forward to introduce himself. "The Detective here wanted me to meet you. It may be that you know someone that I'd like to meet."

"I know who you are," Angie said as soon as she registered the name. She looked to Reymond, "You're wrong about Malcolm, Detective."

"I'm just trying to help. Malcolm and his friend, or friends, won't stop. I would have thought you'd understand now how close you came."

"Malcolm's more likely to help me than you are, but thanks for introducing me to Devlin here. Malcolm's already told me about him."

Devlin stepped forward and spoke up. "Angie, I'm only here at the request of the Detective here. But if the opportunity came up, then I'd be keen to meet with Malcolm."

"Quite," said Angie. "I'd like to talk to you too, but only after Detective Ghoul here leaves."

The Detective raised his hand in acceptance that he was being sidelined. "My offer stands, Angie. And just because you can't see it or won't see it, won't stop it from happening. I'm going to get him with or without you because if it's not you, it will be someone else." He left the room, summoning a nurse to follow him.

"Why didn't you tell the Detective about Nebojsa?" Devlin started as soon as the Detective was out of sight. "I'm assuming you're the same Angie who described Nebojsa in a LastGasp' message."

Angie nodded while touching the most painful of her bruises under the covers. She held back a wince, but used the pain to focus her thoughts. "Malcolm said you were different."

"I have no idea why he'd say that about me."

"He said you'd be oblivious too."

"Why would he say that about someone he didn't know?" Devlin asked, frustrated but composed.

"I don't know. Perhaps if I knew then I could make him stay."

"The Detective seems keen to help … If you'd let him."

"Detective Reymond is well meaning, but he's chasing the wrong person. He was nice enough to save me the other day, but he needn't have bothered."

"Was Malcolm going to come to your rescue?"

"Malcolm has it in hand," Angie said solemnly.

"I would have thought that any man worth their salt would have wanted to be there for you. I tend to agree with the Detective and his low expectations of the guy."

"You know nothing about Malcolm, so who are you to say?" Angie closed her eyes and sighed. "I'm sorry. That came out all wrong." She took a deep breath and composed herself and relented a regret filled look to her visitor. "I know you're only here to meet Malcolm."

"That's not entirely true. I read your message, and when that cop mentioned your name, I guess I wondered how I might help."

The comment hit a raw nerve and try as she might, she could not contain her emotions. "Were you prepared to extend your wonder into action, or just sit idly by thinking about it?" she said angrily

"I wanted to help, but …"

"I'll bet you think you're so fucking good, just because you at least *wanted* to help!"

"I don't need to take this from you, Angie."

As he stood to leave, Angie felt her rage bubble over and be further inflamed with every step that he took from her bedside. She unleashed the vitriol that welled up from inside her. "I hope he finds you!"

Devlin paused for a time with his back to Angie as if considering asking for some clarification. That he didn't say anything and eventually continued on his way was typical.

* * *

Malcolm waited until he saw Reymond and the new guy leave before he made his way from the ward waiting room. It was just as well that they didn't stay longer really as he had too much to do to sit idle and he'd completed every puzzle in each of the available magazines on offer. It was true that he could have just left, but he needed to say his goodbyes to Angie; she deserved that much. He could have joined her while they were at her bedside, but he didn't want to see the Detective or Devlin really.

One thing that was good about hospital waiting rooms was the volume and assortment of newspapers. Malcolm had managed to piece together the complete chronology of everything that he'd missed during his *sabbatical* and also checked the progress on his other projects. Others might not have been able to see through the gloom and doom of the news, but Malcolm found the read very positive. What was more, he had managed to do this without any digital signature. There was a lot to be said for such traditional media.

There was no time to procrastinate. Angie would not be happy at what he had to say, but there was no avoiding the fact that it needed to be said. It was just unfortunate that he needed to say it now when, judging by her tirade, she was a little emotional. Malcolm just hoped that she would be able to stay objective and understand the bigger picture; the greater good.

Chapter - 51.

Devlin refused to be engaged by Detective Reymond in the car on anything beyond banal comment on the weather and traffic conditions. He wasn't being rude, and it wasn't on account of his usual innate apprehension with regard to authority. This time, Devlin was busy thinking, but he was finding it difficult to focus. His thought processes were a scattered array of confusion; debating his stay or run options, replaying Angie's words and perspective, Lori's revelations about Albert, and the disparity in driving style between Ikel and the Detective. Devlin also thought of Glen and Whitely, picturing them each with a knowing grin.

A phone rang and Reymond answered it using some wireless, cordless, hands-free thing that Devlin never understood. The use of such technology enabled him to share in the conversation initially, though as soon as Reymond realised it was Angie on the line, clearly in more of a state than when they'd left the hospital, he reverted to the use of the handset. Devlin tried to make what he could of their exchange, but the surrounding hum of traffic made that next to impossible, particularly as Angie was doing all of the talking. He resigned himself to the necessity to wait.

The smug look on the Detective's face as soon as the call was completed was enough for Devlin to be concerned. When he pulled over to side of the road and switched off the engine, Devlin just braced himself for what could only be bad news.

"That was Angie, obviously," Reymond began. "And she's more than a little upset." Devlin said nothing, waiting for the kicker.

"She's finally decided to tell me who her attacker is. I have to say that this is good news and it makes me happy. Today might just have an upside after all!"

"Why do I sense there's a '*but*' coming?" Devlin tried a smile, as much to relax his mood as that of the Detective, but one never eventuated.

"Can you please account for your whereabouts the day before yesterday once more for me?"

Devlin felt for the door handle, but he stopped short of actually exercising it, and oddly enough there was little comfort to be had in stroking the handle. Angie had set him up, and a cursory recollection suggested that proving things might be difficult. Amongst the small talk that the Detective had tried to encourage further discussion had been to share how he had come to meet Malcolm and then Angie. He described Angie's house and locale, and Devlin reasoned that it may well have been within a few blocks of the LastGasp' office. It would be just his luck that he walked right past it as he made his way to meet Glen at LastGasp' the first time. In fact, he may well have walked past just as she was being assaulted. It wouldn't take too much digging to come up with witnesses to place him in the vicinity, and that would be enough if Angie cared to finger him. He knew enough of the procedure to be worried.

"Convince me now and you just might save yourself having to do this at the station."

"What exactly has she said?"

"Here or at the station, Devlin?"

"There's nothing to tell. I read her message, I bumped into you on an unrelated matter and the rest you know, including the part where the only way that I managed to meet her at all was via you."

Devlin couldn't help his exacerbation. "I only met her in the hospital, so please don't tell me she's saying that I'm responsible in some way for her injury. I don't know what else I can tell you, but more than ever I'd like to speak to Malcolm." He wound down the window as a safe alternative to opening the door.

Detective Reymond watched Devlin with the maturity of an old dog on a porch. "Angie's injuries could well have been the result of a drug deal gone wrong. But they weren't. You could well have been involved in her latest injuries, but not the rest of them." The Detective held up his hand to quash any potential interruptions. "It's interesting that when you were… elsewhere, Malcolm was potentially in the frame." He produced a single sheet of paper from the inside pocket of his jacket. "What can you tell me about this list?"

Devlin took the sheet after the Detective baulked briefly at his attempt and then relented. Within the first few lines he recognised Glen's list of past LastGasp' employees. This was a photocopy, hand annotated with some indecipherable scrawl and copied, but it was definitely the same list. He resisted the urge to compare it line for line with his copy, still folded in his jeans pocket. "Where did you get this?"

"My sources are my business. What do you know about it?"

"Not a lot. I said before that Glen gave me a list of past employees to visit. Well, this is the list. Why would you have it?"

"Angie had it on her person when I found her." The Detective thought for a moment then added, "You know I can help."

"Frankly Detective, I'm not entirely sure I need help. "

"How many names on this list have you visited?"

"One. Only Whitely. I saw him this morning. Are you suggesting that I should visit a few more?"

"Perhaps, but you might like to choose carefully. A number of the names on the list were familiar, which invariably means that I've come across them in my work."

Chapter - 52.

Devlin thought he would feel relief when the Detective returned him to Ikel's car, but instead, he felt more than a little abandoned. Reymond hadn't said another word after suggesting that he needed to meet with others from Glen's list, and so the entire trip dragged on and seemed to take substantially longer than the ten or so minutes that it actually took. Devlin had spent every one of those long minutes trying to come up with a plan while half expecting to be taken directly to the Police station. It wasn't until the Detective pulled up gently behind Ikel's car that he realised at least that particular element of his stress was in vain.

Now alone with his thoughts seated in Ikel's car with the engine running, Devlin had no idea what to do. He saw the playground that provided the backdrop for his picture in the newspaper and theorised as to where the photograph was taken from. From where he was parked he could also see many windows in the adjacent apartment complex, one of which was possibly Tania's. He considered visiting her for more information, but that seemed both pointless and inappropriate.

A knuckled knock on the passenger side window abruptly ended Devlin's daydreaming. By the time he made a motion to see who was attracting his attention it was apparent that, whoever it was, a man, was opening the door. By the time Devlin thought to wonder what was happening, the guy was seated, eyes forward, looking at the street ahead, and reaching for his seatbelt. Devlin struggled for the most appropriate words to express all that seemed necessary. "What the fuck are you doing?"

"My name is Malcolm Venn." He spoke clearly and succinctly, but kept his eyes forward, looking through the windscreen. "I want you to drive away from here."

"Where to?"

"It doesn't matter. Just drive."

Devlin slipped the car into gear and did as instructed.

Chapter - 53.

Angie was true to form, thought Nebojsa as soon as he learnt that she had checked herself out of the ward. The nurse then proceeded to describe how she'd grown angry with a few visitors, but then went completely irrational and left, but he wasn't really listening to anything that she said. Instead, he was focussed on another nurse in an adjacent office with the door ajar briefing an older gent. The usual lack of respect for patient confidentiality was very beneficial. It was obvious that the older guy was Police, of some description, judging by the fact that the staff were comfortable disclosing all to him; in so doing they shared everything with Nebojsa himself too.

It was refreshing to hear the old guy's frustration. He was annoyed that Angie was gone, and Nebojsa shared that sentiment, of sorts. That Malcolm was of interest to the Detective too was obvious. Nebojsa wondered if the Police found Malcolm to be as good a source of knowledge as he did. If Malcolm wasn't such a veritable source of *seeds* he wondered if he wouldn't have wanted to coax all the knowledge that he could from the guy.

So engrossed in listening to what the old guy was being told, Nebojsa didn't notice when the nurse addressing him actually stopped talking. The nurse quickly understood that her banter was little more than background noise to what he was really listening to. She closed the door, and only after she had done so did he realise that his veneer of cover had been blown. He shrugged off her evil stares, but noted her name just the same, in case a later visit was to be considered. He pushed the basket of fruit and 'Get Well Soon' balloons across the counter and calmly left the ward.

Chapter - 54.

The knock at the door broke Conrad's concentration completely. Used to working on his own, he often surprised himself at how familiar sounds would not distract him from his train of thought. He worked best iPod in ears, some pirated DVD playing in the background and the periodic whir and bubble of his coffee machine or a beeping reminder that some reheated food remained in the microwave awaiting retrieval. However, he didn't get many visitors and the rap at the door took him completely off guard. He responded poorly, spilling his coffee over his lap, and had it not been for his much soiled dressing gown, he would certainly have burned his nether region. Instead, it might just have provided the necessary impetus for his dressing gown to be washed.

Malcolm's visits were always unexpected and this time was no exception. He pushed his way inside much like he usually did, this time all but dragging Devlin with him. He coaxed Devlin to the couch and then made himself at home at the desk. Quicker than Conrad could object, he rebooted the computer after first inserting a memory stick into the machine.

"What are you doing, Malcolm?" Conrad asked desperately. "Do you have any idea how close I was?"

"Yes," Malcolm replied with disinterest. He typed as the machine started, oblivious to Conrad's confused mix of professional contentment that he'd made independent progress and resentment that he may well have lost much of it with a reckless reboot without first saving. "Would it help if I said you weren't close?"

"How would you know? And why's Devlin here?"

"God knows! Malcolm let himself into my car and told me to drive. He hasn't said anything since, other than to direct me here." Devlin accepted that Malcolm was too engrossed at the keyboard to contribute to any discussion, so he continued. "Of course, I was more than a little surprised when we came to visit you, but I guess that I shouldn't be surprised at anything really."

Conrad's attention was divided between more than cursory interest in what Malcolm was doing, unrestrained on his computer, and feeling obligated to explain things to Devlin. He knew much of what Devlin would have to be feeling.

Devlin wriggled uncomfortably in his seat. "Can one of you please tell me what's going on?"

Conrad looked to Malcolm, still madly typing away with the screen angled so as to obscure the display to all but himself. Malcolm held up his hand to acknowledge the prompt, but continued to type one handed before removing his memory stick from the slot and rebooting Conrad's system. "Done," he mumbled.

"So what's going on?" Devlin reiterated.

Malcolm stood, rolled his shoulders and stretched his fingers. "Glen's not a bad person. You can make your own mind up about him, of course, but his intentions are good. Whether you can see it or not, he's trying to help you."

Devlin looked to Conrad, expecting to see a reaction to the comment, but Conrad said nothing.

"I was a reader, like you, and I used to marvel at the messages that I would read. At first, I naïvely read, believed and applied Glen's protocols. I expected things to happen, and I slept soundly at night, happy in the knowledge that I had done my part. I'm assuming that this is all familiar.

"It exposes a different side of people, and I'm not just talking about what you might glean from people through reading their messages. You'll read the confessions and the secrets and the thoughts, and it changes the readers themselves."

"Glen suggested that stress was going to be a big deal."

"At first, possibly. There's a certain helplessness that comes from reading messages, particularly when there's nothing you can do about them."

"Does anyone try?"

"Do you like your job?" Malcolm asked, changing the subject.

Devlin shelved his immediate disappointment at the question. "I expected a little more than career guidance from you."

"Do you like your job, Devlin?" Malcolm repeated calmly.

"I'm only new in the role," Devlin attempted to buy himself some time to assess the bias in the question. "It seems OK, but there's no shortage of people trying to convince me otherwise."

"I'll take that as a 'yes'. Tell me what you like about it?"

"I like the money. Not wanting to appear fickle, but …"

"Let me guess," Malcolm interrupted. "Glen's said 'there's more to life than money'. He's right of course."

Malcolm said nothing more, leaving Devlin with a confused look on his face as if expecting some continuation. He watched with disbelief as Malcolm returned to the computer and continued reading the on-line versions of several newspapers.

Conrad felt the stress rise in Devlin until he could actually see the thumping of his elevated blood pressure in his temples, and his neck cramping at the weight of his head. He saw that Devlin had edged forward on the couch in nervous anticipation, expectant of wisdom of some description, but now he slunk back into the couch, and rested his head on the cheap fabric of the back. After a few calming breaths, he spoke, eyes closed, as if absolutely focussed on saying something rational. "Can someone please tell me what's going on?"

Malcolm was unperturbed at the question leaving Conrad to comment, "Don't ask me!"

"This is so stupid!" said Devlin, finally having had enough. He stood and marched the few steps to the door, muttering as he went, obviously hoping that someone would call his ruse and stop him before he reached the door.

Conrad took his cue from Malcolm and allowed Devlin to leave.

*   *   *

Malcolm felt no obligation to stop Devlin. He didn't really care that Devlin didn't understand, nor did he care. He remembered that Glen too was so focussed on what was in LastGasp' that he was unable to see where the real power of his creation lay. It wasn't the blissful ignorance of the greater population. Instead it was like a naive expectation that things would work themselves out. Describing it as 'naive' had upset Glen at the time. They'd debated the point for a long time, primarily because he himself had suggested that Glen's mentality was little better than childish. They'd settled on the word 'misguided'. He accused Glen of being *misguided* in his expectations, and in return Glen suggested that it was he who was misguided.

A little older but a lot wiser now, he understood that in so doing Glen was making another ever so subtle point. That it had taken him time to come to this realisation was testament to how little

249

he understood at the time. Glen understood more than he'd given him credit for.

He'd met Glen at a community support group. Attending wasn't his idea and he didn't really want to stay, but his television had finally died and the venue offered shelter from the cold and human warmth when he lacked these things in his own hovel. He'd bypassed the cheap coffee in favour of a comfortable looking lounge and in so doing had unwittingly joined the group. It was counselling with a friendly, albeit amateur face. Sixteen people assembled in an open circle, the lounge completing the ring. By sitting on that particular chair he as much as indicated that he had something to share.

He pretended to be shy, but that day was a good one and he was not at all intimidated by the prospect of having to talk in front of an audience, but he did need to know *what* to share. He could have said anything. All of them had issues, especially the most vocal of them, apparently the group leader. It wasn't Glen, though Glen was without question the most rational of them. He didn't burst into tears at the slightest provocation or escalated tone, and he didn't nod or make noises of approval or acknowledgement when the speaker paused momentarily for reflection. Though Glen was the most cryptic. A lifetime of listening to people to gauge what they wanted to hear made Malcolm very good at understanding their intent. But Glen was different. He wasn't guarded, which Malcolm would have spotted within the first sound-bite. Malcolm also sensed that Glen wasn't fishing for medication or carefully composing feigned thoughts to avoid medication or battling the suppressive effects of medication, all of which Malcolm himself had variously done, tried or experienced.

Malcolm felt guilty for the way that he'd taken a liking to Glen and ignored the others. It wasn't him really. It was the day, or the meds or the lack thereof. On another day, the day before or the day after perhaps he might have focussed on someone else. Who knows where he'd be now if that had happened. He tried not to dwell on it though, just as he didn't stress that had he paid the gas bill he possibly wouldn't have been wandering the streets for company. The upside, the greater good in its most basic incarnation, was that he'd met Glen. This was the first thing that Glen had ever taught him.

The next thing that Glen suggested was that he should look forward, not back. Malcolm warmed to his eternal optimism. On that particular day, Malcolm saw his positivity being appreciated rather than psychoanalysed, and he felt sure that his down days would be accepted equally. Indeed they were. Within a week he'd lost his job, as menial and below him as it was, but to be employed he needed to leave the house and he just wasn't capable of facing the world. He just sat alone in bed crying at the prospect of needing to close the curtain a little more.

However, Glen came and stayed. He brought a thermos of coffee and a pillow and talked through the door for hours. Others, not many, but a few people had reasonably assumed that Malcolm was holed up in his room and made a token effort to coax him out, but when he kept quiet, they left. Perhaps they reasoned that he'd been successful, this time, in leaving. But Glen wasn't perturbed at the wait. He talked knowing that Malcolm would be listening despite an absence of any signs of life from behind the door.

There was nothing in particular that Glen said that made Malcolm open the door. It could have been just reward for his persistence, but it was more than likely what he'd said about his mother.   His mother wasn't directly mentioned, but Malcolm understood the veiled references. Glen spoke of family exposing the darker side of people. He later learnt that Glen was possibly talking about himself, but that sentiment was also true when he thought about his own family.

Malcolm had never known his father. The guy had died before Malcolm was born, apparently. He'd doubted his mother's story but not enough to seek the truth for himself. It wasn't a significant problem as a child, primarily because in his 'passing' he'd provided for his family, even if he hadn't shared his surname. Of course as a child he didn't understand the concept of wealth, but there was love in his mother's heart and food on the table.

He was a teenager before his health became an issue. It wasn't a problem in his education as his mind was largely idling at school but he was still doing better than just keeping up. His social development, however, was different. He always tended to think a little differently to his peers, which was fine, but not if he lacked the confidence to carry himself. His good days weren't a problem; he had friends. Irregularly but often though, he had his down days when he was not capable of leaving his room, much less the house.

Even worse would be when his mood was on the turn, when he was liable to be erratic and impulsive. Like falling barometric pressure, the swing would give warning but there was nothing that could be done short of battening down the hatches. That his mother didn't need to work was a blessing. She would allow him his bad days, riding them out, until the sun came out. Like any concerned parent, she sought professional help but that invariably resulted in medication, no matter how many second opinions she got. Fear of air travel was the only thing that prevented her trying foreign specialists. Eventually she reluctantly conceded that her only son would require medication.

His troubles made it difficult for others to understand him. Was he the average of his vivacious, exuberant highs and his desolate, hide from the world lows, or was he something else entirely without the tidality? His mother didn't really know either, but she knew that he was not the docile, zombified adolescent that looked back at her while on medication. Wealthy as she was, the price of the near perpetual sedation was too high. She removed her son from the doctor's care, purchased a little cottage in a remote seaside village and lived away from the less than supportive talk or thoughts of others. On their own it didn't matter if he was up or down.

Home schooling sounds so alternative, but Malcolm got a better education away from the greater teenage population. Every few weeks his mother would make the short trip to the city to see friends, meet with her financial advisor and enjoy the different pace of life. Malcolm would come along on each visit. If he was not well enough to travel, his mother would delay the trip.

One of his father's investments, some mining company, hit pay-dirt one day and overnight their comfortable existence was changed forever. Suddenly they were *decidedly* wealthy and his mother felt obligated to do more than hide away. She looked for ways to share their good fortune. Malcolm could not fault her approach, even now. She didn't want attention; that was not why she was doing it. She just wanted to do the right thing. Had they ever met, Malcolm was sure that his mother would have gotten on well with Glen on that point alone.

Despite her best efforts for anonymity, soon she was being courted by all manner of foundations desperate to impress of the worthiness of their cause. She was not prepared to compromise her lifestyle, or her dedication to her son, and soon it became common for visitors to appear at their home. They would stay for a time, typically after lunch, which gave them time to drive from the city in the morning, push their case and then drive back to the city in the afternoon. Some would make the drive home considering the trip worthwhile, but most would call it a pleasant drive but a wasted day.

One day, Malcolm's mother hosted an effort by a refugee advocacy organisation apparently in search of a patron but they'd settle for a sponsor. Two men arrived to lobby their case, one was a nervous looking individual who just sat quietly allowing the other to talk. Malcolm didn't feel up to meeting anyone, so he just listened to their discussion from his room. The case for their organisation was that without support, refugees and asylum seekers would be marginalised in this foreign land and their charitable organisation was the best to provide this support. About the only thing constructive that the quiet one offered was to present his colleague who then took centre stage, describing himself as proof positive of successful assimilation of a refugee. The organisation was legitimate, as were the credentials of the quiet one, but the other guy was a charlatan at best. Not that a lack of confidence is the hallmark of a refugee, but he didn't seem to fit his story. His mother too saw a dubious story, as if his press release didn't match reality. They left empty handed.

The next day Malcolm felt much better and opted to clear the grey away completely with a long walk on the beach. He made a day of it and didn't return until it was almost dark. He turned down his street just in time to see a car, the same car from the previous day, pull out of their driveway. His mother was tearful as soon as he entered the house but put on a brave face that didn't convince or help either of them. She spent much of the night on the phone with the door closed. She was not ordinarily secretive and Malcolm was un-nerved more for her sudden demand for privacy than the sobbing that couldn't be contained behind closed doors.

In the morning, his mother was distracted, edgy, irrational and she resented Malcolm's presence. From the moment he surfaced he sensed the difference, and try as he might, he couldn't account for it with something as simple as hormones. When she rushed to the toilet to throw up after staring at him for a time, he decided it was time to confront her. He wasn't a child, and that she would shun him suddenly was disconcerting.

She didn't say much, only that she hoped that he would understand. Their solitude was broken by the arrival of her lawyer. Malcolm was sent on an un-necessary errand to allow them some privacy which he accepted but resented.

Malcolm was orphaned at the age of eighteen. Legally he was responsible for his actions, emotionally he was more than adequately developed, but was ill-prepared nonetheless. That she killed herself was a low blow. That she left him with nothing was even lower. Before her body was cold, his mother's lawyer executed her will and intent. He was, quite literally left on a street corner with a wallet half full of cash and a puzzle book. In the space of a few days, her assets that had attracted no end of interest as a source of philanthropy was gone. The stocks and shares sold, the real estate sold, and the proceeds of the sales and outstanding cash assets gone.

Malcolm learnt that he had amazingly few grounds to trace the proceeds. No crime had been committed, beyond the arguable crime against God's will in her suicide, and everything else had been entirely in accordance with his mother's wishes. This didn't help him, and it was through this that Malcolm learnt first hand that the world didn't care. Had he gained anything in her death, the finger of suspicion would have been squarely pointed at him, but without gain he was apparently above such suspicion.

The stress of such an upheaval inevitably dragged Malcolm down. That in itself had an upside in that it prevented him from frittering away his money, his limited inheritance. He found a cheap boarding house at the first onset of a sliding mood and prepared for a long time of isolation. Sometimes he'd manage a month or more of wellness and he'd try for some work. Nothing too taxing, physically or mentally; it wasn't worth the effort. He knew it wouldn't last and that he was unexpectedly poor had also made him cynical for the pursuit of wealth.

It was on one of these 'up times' that Malcolm met Glen. Perhaps their meeting was a chance encounter. Glen had cause to share what he did in the group session, but Malcolm didn't. D.A.G.S. Domestic Abuse Group for Survivors. Malcolm didn't have any grounds to be there. As much as he derided the others for their recollections, it did introduce him to something that his isolation had denied him. It could be worse.

When Glen said that he'd been searching for him, Malcolm, initially at least understood the comment to be subjective. He later learnt that there was more truth than rhetoric in the comment. His protracted ill-health had made him impossible to trace, but Glen couldn't believe his luck when Malcolm sauntered into the DAGS session.

Malcolm joined LastGasp' without any hesitation, lured by the prospect of learning about his mother, if not to trace the money that was rightly his. Glen promised nothing tangible other than to suggest that Malcolm would be best positioned to learn all with him.

Money became less important with every day at LastGasp', not only for the money that he was being given. Immersed in other peoples' lives, thoughts and secrets, Malcolm came to understand for himself that money wouldn't change his past and while it would surely change his future, money would not buy peace of mind.

Malcolm wondered what it would take for Devlin to find this same peace of mind.

Chapter - 55.

Detective Reymond was back in his office. Without a partner, there was nothing obligating him to routinely visit his desk at the station; there wasn't even a picture of family or friends on his desk that might make any time there more comfortable or homely. However, his desk did offer a computer terminal, and he knew that he'd need to validate the list that he'd obtained from Angie's personal effects on admission to the hospital. Too many of the names on the list were familiar to ignore, and while legally he had no grounds to actually confiscate the list, technically, photocopying it wasn't actually taking it.

On top of the indecipherable handwritten notes on the list, Reymond had added his own simple annotation following a quick investigation using the Police search tools. It didn't take long, and not just because of the technology. The first name, the name at the top of the list, meant nothing to him personally, but it came up trumps with the *system*. Kendrick, Derrell. The guy was deceased, and the listed address matched his last known address, which was also where his body was found. Non-suspicious death, suicide. Cut and dried. Reymond scanned the rest of the details, not really looking for anything in particular, but looking to assimilate all of the information *en-masse*. The guy died alone with a sizeable fortune in the bank, and quite an amount of cash on his person, and without any family or a will, the state had all but commandeered his assets.

Reymond moved onto the next name on the list. Then the next. Virtually all were dead, each having met their end in different ways, and often, but not always, at their own hand. This explained why so many of the names were familiar. He decided immediately that each of the survivors on the list, including Whitely, were worth a visit, perhaps after first visiting Angie. It was nearing peak-hour and the drive across town was sure to be slow, so he printed off a mass of reports and background on each of the listed individuals to while away the minutes bumper to bumper in traffic.

He tried to mentally order what he'd read, looking for similarities and peculiarities. As well practiced as he might be, this particular scenario was not familiar. The people involved did not represent any logical single demographic. Men and women, old and young, rich and poor, immigrants and others. About the only thing that they had in common was that they were no longer among us, but even that didn't help. A few suicides, a few road traffic accidents, a few victims of domestic violence, and a spattering of other unfortunate, but undeniably random acts, including a drive-by shooting, and a good-old fashioned shanking while on remand. *Unfortunate*, Reymond thought, *but nothing conclusive.* A statistician might raise an eyebrow that the rates of the various causes of death were high, but then the sample size was sure to be too small to be conclusive for them.

This was just a list of people, and the fact that they were past LastGasp' employees could easily have gone under the radar, or perhaps remained under the radar. Legally they possibly weren't even employees, but the hotel manager had confirmed as much and the money trail for the assets of each individual stopped at the bank branch less than a block from LastGasp'. Reymond marvelled again that these things had gone un-noticed by his predecessor, and wondered if he would have made the same mistakes if he was still driven enough to resent shit assignments in favour of more meaningful work. Would he have bothered to do his homework when each of these cases were so straight forward, and when something better for his career was calling?

He was comforted that any result would surely consolidate the important role that he could still play, thereby further prolonging his stay of execution, of mandatory retirement. Each day he would feel the pressure on him to retire, from his colleagues and superiors alike, and each day he'd avoid the issue. His few friends didn't understand his obsession, his commitment to justice, particularly after what happened to his daughter. Neither did those in the Force for that matter. How could he retire *until* he saw justice.

* * *

Next of kin notifications were never a high point in Police circles, and as ever, they fell among the tasks that Detective Reymond would just assume responsibility for in anticipation of formal tasking. With such a volume under his belt, he had over the course of many years become very good at breaking the news, but even more so since age had softened his appearance. He no longer looked like a junior police officer, or a grizzled old detective. Now he looked more like an old 'friend of the family', which married well with his seasoned but empathic manner of dealing with what was always an uncomfortable situation.

The latest notification was nothing particularly special in an official capacity. The untimely but natural death of a family man was sad of course, but it wasn't front-page news, and just as it wouldn't attract media attention, it wouldn't warrant priority of effort, particularly when the whereabouts of the next of kin was not necessarily known.

Ordinarily Reymond would not have dropped everything to break the news on the death of family, anyone's family, particularly with matters such as Angie and her accusations pending, and especially when finding the family was going to require some degree of effort. On this occasion, the last surviving relative was known, but technically listed as un-located, thus requiring the enlistment of at least some resources to track them down. However, never one for co-incidences, when Reymond saw the name, 'Michael Donovan' as the target next-of-kin, he immediately assumed that this would be the same Michael Donovan he'd interviewed the previous day following the death of David Yeardley. While he had spent his career fighting the temptation to become un-reasonably suspicious, he was still a realist. Angie would have to wait.

Chapter - 56.

Devlin found himself alone in the bunker, and as obligated as he was to do some work, his rudimentary understanding of the LastGasp' system indicated that there was nothing to do. Ikel had said as much, that work would be based on changes by LastGasp' system users, and so if no-one was changing the system then there wouldn't be any changes to read. He explored all aspects of the user interface, and ultimately he ended up at the Research Interface, and he decided to try it once more. It didn't seem to make any sense to retry a search for himself as he'd done before, and so he thought about what else, or *who* else, he could search for.

Movement on one of the security monitors alerted Devlin to Glen's return. He watched as Glen disappeared from one screen and re-appeared on another, clearly en-route to the bunker. Eventually the door opened.

"There's nothing to do," Devlin felt obliged to announce, not wanting to appear idle in front of the Research Interface.

Glen ignored the comment, and Devlin for that matter, sliding into a chair at one of the computers. After a few moments of typing, Glen broke his silence, but not the rate of his keyboard activity. "Ikel's left, and Lori's heart isn't in this."

The stress in Glen's tone was not lost on Devlin and he sat patiently waiting for Glen to continue. "Anything I can help with?" he offered, but the offer was ignored and he returned to his wait, hopeful that Glen would eventually provide some clarity. The wait dragged on for a few minutes before Glen pushed off from the keyboard with a pensive look on his face.

"You'd think that it would be simple to find employees, but it is more difficult than you'd imagine. The *right* people, at least, are surprisingly difficult to find. People like you are few and far between and it takes work to find them. I'm down to one reader, you, and I know that you're considering jumping ship too."

Devlin didn't bother denying the comment. "Why did they go? Why *do* they go?"

"To answer that wouldn't help my predicament now, would it?"

"Not that I'm thinking of leaving," Devlin began. He knew that he wouldn't have convinced anyone, but Glen smiled subtly for the attempt. "But why the big deal for readers if everything essentially looks after itself? Why the urgency? Why not just sit back and take your time to find the right people?"

Glen was quiet for a moment, thinking. Eventually, he settled back into his chair and relaxed his shoulders. "What have you seen and learnt these last few days?"

"I'm assuming you mean work related?"

"Just answer the question," Glen made it clear that he would not be tolerant of any of Devlin's delaying tactics. "And please don't dwell on the unfortunate passing of David."

"Alright. I've read masses of messages, seen bleeding hearts and guilty memories, and frankly nothing that's changed my life." Devlin deliberately fired Glen's own words back at him.

"I think you've learned more than that."

Devlin started to recap on his recent history, looking to find whatever it was that Glen wanted to broach. "Whitely said …"

"I don't care about Whitely!" Glen interrupted.

"Conrad thinks ..."

"I don't care about Conrad!" Glen interrupted once more.

"I don't care about you, Glen! What do you want me to say or do?" Devlin wasn't angered so much as frustrated at the interruption and the fact that he was clearly missing something important or obvious to Glen.

"I'm tempted to go, not because I really want to, but because I don't want to end up like Whitely or David or any of the other readers who seem to have met with an early demise. I appreciate that their deaths are, more than likely, not directly caused by you, but when you look at it from my side, LastGasp' doesn't look like a good option.

"Whitely told me to find Malcolm, and essentially that our meeting wasn't purely by co-incidence."

At this, Glen stopped typing. "I needed you Devlin. I still need you and it would be a concern for you to go. I also don't want you to go." He pushed off from his keyboard and edged his chair closer to Devlin. "I know you've been honest with me and you haven't told me anything that I didn't already know. But I appreciate your effort to convince me."

"You haven't convinced me as to whether my concern is founded."

Glen thought for a moment before scanning the nest of security monitors. He closed his eyes and breathed a few slow calming breaths. "Devlin. You and I are not dissimilar. You have trust issues, well founded trust issues I might add, but that's largely irrelevant. And you've got a good heart. And it's your good heart that has betrayed your cynicism. I know about your interest in Angie. And before you go getting all defensive, this is a good thing. This is what I knew would happen. This is what I wanted."

"So me taking an interest in Angie is good," Devlin thought for a moment. "And how's this different from David's interest in Tania's brother?"

There was no surprise on Glen's face as he spoke. "I can't tell you definitively what was going on in David's mind, but I can guess. I'd prefer it if we left it at that. Would it help if I said I expect you to do what's right? That's why I employed you, and that's why I need you to stay."

"So who's Malcolm then?"

Glen thought for a moment, as if considering whether disclosure was warranted. "He was a Reader."

"So why all the mystery about him?"

"We had a difference of opinion."

"What's that supposed to mean?"

"It's not supposed to 'mean' anything. It's just a statement of fact and I'm sure that you'll work it out eventually. Do what you need to do. There's nothing here that won't keep until you get back."

Chapter - 57.

Devlin left the bunker and headed for the street. His plan was to get a decent coffee, but thereafter his plan was decidedly limited. As he crossed the street, he was oblivious to the opening and closing of a car door to his rear. Only after he'd ordered his latté, to go, did Detective Reymond make his presence known, ordering his own coffee. Devlin acknowledged the Detective but said nothing.

"I'm actually not here to see you," said the Detective. "I'm looking for Michael Donovan. I know you're driving his car, so it's reasonable to expect you to have an inkling you might know where he is."

"Sorry. I can't help. I don't know where he is."

"So where are you going?" Reymond enquired.

"I don't rightly know. I'll let you know if I see him."

"That's interesting, Devlin." Reymond scratched his lip as he thought. "You work with him, you drive his car, and Morris at the hotel described you as Michael's, *Ikel's*, close friend. So why would it be that you'd use the term '*if*', not '*when*', to describe when you expect to see him next."

"Would you believe that I really don't know where he is?"

"Possibly. I'm just a little concerned, particularly given that you work for an organisation where employees die at a rate far above the norm." Reymond took as large a gulp of his coffee as its temperature would allow.

"I honestly don't know where he is."

"So do you know what's going on with you and LastGasp'?"

"I have no idea," Devlin replied earnestly.

"I believe you. What's happening here precedes your arrival on the scene. You're just the latest."

Reymond slipped into a more comfortable but formal mode. "What I do know is that Donovan's uncle died today. Nothing suspicious, just a heart attack apparently, but now I know that virtually all of the names on your list are now dead. Call it a duty of care or what you like, but I'm obligated to take an interest."

"So how many of them are dead?" Devlin enquired with genuine interest.

"All but three, including Whitely."

Devlin reached for the list from his back pocket and scanned the contents. He looked top to bottom over the names, and then bottom to top. "Malcolm isn't on the list!" Devlin couldn't hide his puzzlement.

"I've shelved my interest in Malcolm for now. I'm actually looking into the whereabouts of your friend Ikel. This might affect you too."

"You don't understand. Malcolm isn't on the list!" Devlin put his lidded take-away cup onto an adjacent table and laid out his list on the table for Reymond to see. "Whitely said Malcolm was a reader, but he's not on this list."

Reymond verified the point, checking his own copy. "So what does that mean?"

"I have no idea!" Devlin grabbed his coffee and drank until he was doing little more than sucking the residual froth through the lid. "But I figure Whitely will know. You might like to come with me."

Chapter - 58.

Tania Wilson received the days post with a little apprehension. Not long before Tim died she received word that her landlord was selling her apartment and today was the day for the completion of the sale. As such she expected to receive a hand delivered note of some description from the new owner, realistically or not. It technically didn't really affect her as the new owner was apparently keen to see her continue as a tenant. Though while it was nothing she could control, there was something stressful about it all. She resented that this was just an unwelcome reminder that she was just the tenant, and given the perpetual struggle to pay the rent, it was unlikely that her circumstances would improve either. This in turn reminded her that despite her brother's passing, she received nothing from his estate and thus being a tenant was sure to be something that she would have to get used to.

Nothing arrived by post, but sure enough the rental agency emailed her to *advise* that the new owner, cum landlord, would visit in the afternoon, provided that she was not otherwise occupied. She understood that the request was little more than a nicety, and that she was expected to meet the guy this afternoon. Of course, to formally set a time for this meeting was apparently too much to ask, and had she not been frantically preparing for the implicit landlord inspection, she would have been angry for the inconvenience of the wait.

Cleaning her flat however, was not the real source of her stress. That her sponsor cum friend, Cat, was not even answering her calls was the final demoralising blow. Her ally, someone who understood her completely, right down to similar mistakes, regrets and circumstances, was abandoning her too. For the first time, she felt that she was entirely on her own. She didn't have the support of any family, let alone friends, even from afar. It was an emptying thought.

Chapter - 59.

Devlin sat uncomfortably in the passenger's seat of the Detective's car as before. He'd left Ikel's car in the car-park, hopeful that Ikel would return to claim it, but the more he thought, the more concerned he became. "Why are you looking for Ikel?"

"Like I said, initially, I just needed to pass on some bad news to the listed *next of kin* of his uncle. Had it not been for our meeting the other day, I would have needed to search for your friend, given that he'd all but disappeared as far as his uncle apparently knew.

"Anyway, I still needed to do some checking. The fact that he wasn't technically earning an income, as far as his money trail was concerned, interested me. He described himself, as did you, as essentially an employee of LastGasp', and that made me wonder where his money was coming from. I'm not necessarily distrustful, but I thought his past might not be entirely behind him, in which case perhaps all of the LastGasp' employees are implicated in the same way. When I checked all of the names on the list we discussed earlier, it was clear that something wasn't right."

"How so?"

"I know you have concerns, whether or not you're prepared to share these concerns with me is another matter, apparently, but don't play me as stupid or yourself as naïve. I've been in this game for too long to be played by amateurs."

Chastised, Devlin kept quiet. "I'm interested why so many former employees are …"

"They're not all dead!" Devlin interrupted.

"Actually, I was going to say that it was odd that so many of them are so unfortunate. But your version is perhaps more appropriate. It also explains your edginess."

"I don't think Whitely is big into visitors," said Devlin, changing the subject. The fact that Reymond didn't question the comment was puzzling. "You know him?"

"It was a long time ago, but I couldn't forget Whitely."

Chapter - 60.

The massed blooms of Whitely's neighbours gardens offered promise as Reymond and Devlin walked past, but the reality was that his house smelled significantly worse in the early evening. He braced himself and tried to exert whatever control he had over his senses, but he feared it wouldn't help. He considered briefing Reymond about what to expect, until he saw the Detective up-end an entire container of breath mints from his pocket into his mouth as he walked through the garden. He fell in behind Reymond, allowing the Detective to take the lead.

"Hi Whitely, it's Alan, Alan Reymond." He announced his arrival and marched down the hall, pausing only for his eyes to adjust to the changing light rather than waiting for an invitation. Devlin gingerly followed, buoyed only after hearing Whitely's reply, even though the reply wasn't friendly.

Whitely was exactly where he'd been when Devlin saw him last. "I'm interested you're here only because you're here with the Detective," Whitely took his aim at Devlin, ignoring Reymond.

"I got your message about Glen," Devlin answered. "But that's not why we're here."

"You know a lesser man might have worked out what I was saying before he left."

"OK," Devlin accepted. "So why didn't you say that Malcolm started LastGasp' with Glen?"

"It wasn't relevant."

"Whitely," Reymond tried to deflect the sniped responses. "What can you tell me about Michael Donovan, otherwise known as 'Ikel'."

"Not a lot," Whitely replied, his focus still fixed on Devlin. "But can I prevent a mass of bullshit questions and pointless provocation by saying up-front that I won't help you interfere with anything that doesn't need to be interfered with."

"You'd appreciate that comments like that make me think that I *need* to ask. I can fix whatever it is that …"

"If it's not broken, it doesn't need to be fixed."

"David Yeardley's death seems to be only the latest in a long line of anomalies."

"Anomalies? What shit! You were both at the scene, and while the monkey here mightn't know better, you, Detective, do."

"The coroner's report hasn't been finalised."

"You know full well that David's death was a suicide."

"But why?" Devlin asked, finally finding a voice.

"We've had this discussion before Devlin, but we'll entertain the Detective if you like." Whitely yawned. "I can't vouch for why David would kill himself. That much might have died with him."

"Perhaps yes. But it seems that he prepared a message to be sent after he died," said Devlin.

"Who did the message go to?"

"I would have thought you'd be interested in how we know this, or perhaps what secrets were revealed?" Reymond probed.

"You'd be wrong. Who did the message go to?"

"The message went to Tania Wilson," said Devlin. When Whitely darted a look to the Detective, Devlin interpreted the silence as a cue to continue. "She's the sister of a guy, Tim, who was killed."

"How unfortunate," Whitely smirked. "What did the message say?"

"Not a lot. David clearly felt some sadness over the brother's death. Others might have described it as guilt, but I wouldn't know."

"Give yourself some credit, Devlin." Whitely closed his eyes and stretched his arms towards the ceiling. He looked at his watch and then paused to think for a moment. "How about I ask you a few questions? And sorry Detective, the offer doesn't extend to you, but I'll let you sit in." He didn't wait for a reply. "First question. Why are each of Glen's employees different?"

"Shouldn't I be interested in how they are alike?" asked Devlin.

"I'm not offering a discussion on the subject and frankly I don't even care if you answer or not. But I'll give you this for free. Glen's not the bad guy, he's just the most obvious common link between you all."

Whitely appeared to think things through a little. "Actually, fuck this. Fuck the questions. Glen needs you for his own conscience, just like he's needed the others. Whether you turn out to be part of the problem or part of his absolution is entirely up to you. The messages I sent you were not intended to scare you, but were just a warning. If nothing else I wanted to make sure that you were aware of what you were getting yourself into."

The realisation came as a shock to Devlin. "Does this mean that you took my phone too?"

"Well not me personally. I slipped some kid a little cash and told him he could keep the phone, provided he gave me the SIM card inside. If it's any consolation, your phone was such a piece of shit I actually had to give him extra to keep it."

"But why take my phone?"

The question silenced Whitely for a moment. "Did you believe the messages more because you understood their source?"

"Perhaps. You know Ikel beat up Conrad because of the messages?"

"Ikel," Whitely sighed. "Glen will be disappointed. It won't really matter now. It never does."

"What do you mean it never matters?" asked Devlin.

Whitely looked clearly un-impressed at the question. "Glen gives you more credit than I think you're worth."

"So you won't help?"

"There's nothing to help. Ikel has his path, as do you, as had all of the others. Myself included."

"You're not filling me with confidence!"

"Frankly Devlin, I couldn't give a shit about anything, your confidence or lack thereof included." Whitely cast a disapproving eye over Reymond as he fossicked through the refuse in the room.

"So what happens now?" Devlin asked.

"Ask 'em if you've got 'em," Whitely said with disinterest. "Try your luck."

Devlin fidgeted as he thought what he should ask. He thought about how odd it was that he'd had the entire drive to consider, and rehearse, such questions, but now he didn't know where to start. He looked to Reymond, as if to indicate that he should take up the opportunity.

"Tell me Whitely," Reymond said as he settled himself into a chair. "Why would you say that Ikel is not dead? The indications that I have would suggest otherwise."

Whitely mocked. "If there was any genuine concern on your part, to say nothing of actual evidence, your visit would not be as a passenger to this idiot."

"Ikel's missing and others…"

"Who, pray tell, has formally listed him as missing?" Whitely interrupted as he juggled the remote control. "The guy's got no family, I know this because that's how it typically is with Glen and his monkeys."

"Alright. I'll try that again," Detective Reymond thought about re-posing. "In the immediate term I want to find him as the next of kin of his uncle, but Ikel's absence comes hot after the death of another employee. Instinct tells me that I should be asking questions."

"So ask them!"

"How's this. David left a note for Ms Hinkley indicating that 'Derrell was right'," Reymond said, half reading from his notes. "I know the 'Derrell' in question also took his own life, but I'm not clear as to why."

Whitely thought for a while. "Detective, it's not my place to say anything more." He pointed to the door and turned to face the television. "Fuck off and leave me alone."

Chapter - 61.

Angie all but dragged herself into her home after being dropped off outside. It was only 30 paces from the curb to her door, but she felt each step across her entire body. Once inside, too pained to be concerned as to the possibility of her not being alone, she slumped into her bed, after a momentary consideration of whether the couch was closer.

Alone with her thoughts on her bed in the dark, she felt torn between wanting to turn on a light and continuing the peace of the darkness in the vain hope that she might sleep. The reality of it was that she knew she would never be able to sleep, she was too bruised, both physically and emotionally. If anyone was to ask her what hurt more, there would be no question that it would be the betrayal that now had her mind in an exhausted but perpetual spin.

Nebojsa, she could handle. She'd put up with him for some time now, and while it wasn't getting better, it wasn't getting worse. She could see the light at the end of that tunnel; that he would lose interest when he became aware that she had nothing else to give. She hoped that he would come to this realisation sooner rather than later. But Devlin and Malcolm were a different matter. Devlin couldn't hide behind ignorance or anonymity, he just didn't want to help. And Malcolm. She expected more from Malcolm, more from her saviour. Why did Malcolm tell her that Devlin was one of the good guys, when he clearly had no desire to be anything other than an on-looker. As if she didn't have enough of them already, and the mere thought of them caused her lip to sneer. The 'friends' who managed to keep their distance rather than get involved and then gradually disappeared from her life. The Police who took one look at her history and subsequently did their level best to bury her in a mass of bureaucracy. And then her family who had demonstrated a sordid mix of ambivalence and reluctance.

It was odd that just thinking about her family made her think of the words of her father, *'what goes around, comes around'*. Her father had meant that good things come to those who are patient enough to wait, and as a child, rightly or wrongly, she'd found those words comforting. Malcolm too described those words as timeless.

Chapter - 62.

On return to the car, Reymond and Devlin were quiet. They both sucked in fresh air and contemplated what Whitely had said, but they felt no need to share any of their thoughts with each other. Reymond started the car and began to drive, and his offer of breath mints eased the air between them enough for them to communicate. "Based on what Whitely said, it might well be premature for me to have a professional interest in Ikel at this point."

"I wouldn't have thought he'd be the best witness for you to make that call. Did he fill you with the same confidence when last you met him? And incidentally, which of the others on the list attracted you to him?"

"None of them." Reymond's face softened, but he kept his eyes on the road ahead. "He was almost my son in law, but that seems like a lifetime ago."

"He doesn't seem like the perfect son-in-law type."

"Aside from the fact that you don't get to choose your son-in-law, he wasn't always as he is now. My daughter loved him, and I was quite partial to him. He was a good partner and good father to my grandchild."

"Was he working for LastGasp' then?"

"No. That came after."

"After what?"

"After my grand-daughter died. Cot-death. It was just something that happened. A healthy little girl, loved by all, but one morning she just didn't wake up." Reymond proved his reluctance to shed a tear as he retold an often repeated memory. "My daughter didn't cope, and he struggled to keep it together himself."

"So Whitely and your daughter drifted apart?"

"Officially, my daughter died of an overdose. Whitely and I were effectively taking it on shifts to console and support her. We didn't realise she was suicidal and we kept tabs on her meds, but in the end we couldn't stop a grown woman doing what she wanted to do."

"I'm sorry."

"There's nothing for you to be sorry about. Whitely blamed himself and I blamed myself. We had nothing in common except blame, anger, and sadness, but it wasn't enough to warrant feigning a friendship that wouldn't sustain itself. After that, Whitely and I drifted apart. The depressants he was on lost him the spark that made him good at his job and eventually he lost his job too. I kept my job only because by this stage I'd long since been passed over for promotion, but was in the unenviable position of having experience that was in demand."

"And then he joined LastGasp'?"

"At the time I thought he was lucky just to secure employment, but it turned out to be pretty lucrative, even though he wasn't there long. He owns that house, out-right, and it wasn't always a shit-hole like it is now. A nice place, good street, good suburb. I periodically get involved officially. Pissed off neighbours wanting something done about him, but there's amazingly little that can be done. The only reason that he hasn't appeared on some tabloid current affairs show on TV is that would invariably drag down real estate prices, particularly when Whitely won't be swayed.

The real criminals are the ones who are systematically looking to force him out."

"But why is he … does he?"

"Guilt. He feels responsible, and guilt drives people in different ways. But enough about Whitely."

Devlin took the hint that it was time to change the subject and his thoughts strayed to Whitely once more. "I'm just thinking it's interesting that he's the one who's been sending me the messages."

"There's an excellent talking point. What were these messages? I didn't realise that your friend Ikel had a violent side."

"I don't think it's fair to describe him as violent. I'd say the messages amounted to provocation."

"So what are they?"

"As soon as I joined LastGasp', I started getting these text messages on my phone. Like Whitely said, they were intended as warnings, but they were un-nerving particularly when I didn't know the sender. You're welcome to read any that I've still got."

"I thought you'd be able to identify the message sender."

"So did I, but apparently not." Devlin began to think more about what Whitely had said, looking for the pearl among the banter. This time he couldn't identify any subtle message. "Detective. What was the most interesting thing that Whitely said?"

"I thought it was interesting that he was so convinced that David would have died by suicide even when he wasn't even there. Then I was surprised that he'd be interested not in David's LastGasp' message content, but in its recipient." The Detective sighed. "Tania."

"You're right. That got me too." Devlin noted the mournful look on the Detective's face, but was all the more intrigued in what Whitely had found so interesting. He thought of the last time that they'd met and his suggestion to find Malcolm. It was suddenly very interesting that Malcolm had appeared after visiting Tania. Far from being a 'pearl of wisdom', Devlin was confident that he'd at least found the oyster.

"You know it was Whitely who suggested that I find Malcolm. *Find Malcolm and he'll reveal all,*" Devlin waved his arms mockingly. "When I did meet him though, he told me nothing. And I only found out later that he started LastGasp'." Devlin drifted off trying to recall every detail of his meeting with Malcolm. He decided he had nothing to lose in enlisting a little help. "What's going on?"

The Detective reached under Devlin's seat and produced his stack of printed reports. He handed them to Devlin without saying a word.

Skim reading, Devlin quickly worked out what he'd been given. They weren't in order, but recognising several of the names on the reports he gathered that they were all invariably from Glen's list. The structure of the Police reports made them easy to read.

The stack depleted, Devlin was more than a little seedy from reading amid the movement of the car, and frustrated that he was no wiser. "Does this mean that the Police cases are still open or are to be re-opened?"

"No. There's no case for them, any of them. Doing so would invariably cause more hurt for their families."

"So why did you give them to me to read?"

"Technically I didn't, and if you say I did I'll deny it. But *if* you were to read them, you wouldn't know any more than me. They didn't help me either." He reached to open the glove box, exposing another manila folder. "That might help you with background."

Devlin fingered through a series of hand written notes. "What are these?"

"I took it upon myself to do a little research *'on-line',*" Reymond emphasised his use of technology. "Impressed? Not bad for an old guy?"

As he read, Devlin mentally tried to tie together the various police reports with the respective background notes, all the while thinking of the LastGasp' Research Interface. "Can I assume that you're taking me back to the office?"

"Clearly you're not impressed at my research. That's fine. But if you read it, you'd see what I see." Devlin took the hint to read a little more closely. "I want you to look for a pattern among them. I've been doing this for a long time, but I can't see anything even similar in their backgrounds.

"To answer your question, I'm prepared to take you back to your work, perhaps to find your friend Ikel waiting, but I'm hoping that you'll lend your assistance."

"Doing what exactly?"

"Something isn't right, Devlin. You know it, and I know it. I'm not looking to rake over old coals, but I'd like to prevent anyone joining this list or becoming any other statistic. In so doing we might save someone's life, maybe even yours."

"So were they suicides or not? You make it sound like there's some doubt."

"There's more to saving a life than just keeping a heartbeat."

Devlin accepted the veiled reference to Whitely. "So what are we going to do?"

Chapter - 63.

Tania's stressed wait for the new landlord dragged on into the early evening. It wasn't that she had anything better to do, but still. There was nothing on TV and after having put so much effort into tidying her home, she was reluctant to do anything more than re-use a single coffee mug.

Inevitably, her thoughts turned to her long empty liquor cabinet. It was at times like these that traditionally she would turn to family or friends, no matter how distant or aloof they'd become, but that was no longer an option. Tim was, without question, her staunchest ally, but he couldn't help now. Nor would her friends; what friends? She also felt the shallowing emptiness of recent abandonment by '*Cat*', and the anger that accompanied it.

*   *   *

Malcolm watched Tania leave her apartment. She was muttering to herself as she always did, and he recognised the desperation in her walk as she crossed the road. The only question was whether she would head for the bar or the adjacent liquor store. The net effect would be the same of course. He closed his eyes and hoped as he watched her deliberate from outside on the footpath.

He was disappointed with her choice, but the outcome would not change, only the timing.

Chapter - 64.

Devlin looked over his list of names as the Detective stopped off somewhere for a few take-away coffees while they came up with a plan. The old guy had a self-confessed aversion to drive-throughs and so opted for some dingy little café which he knew from experience. Devlin's expectations as to the quality of the beverages was not high.

"Thoughts?" the Detective asked on his return.

"The names mean nothing to me. David was the only one I knew, but not well. Casey, Carson and Lawrence were mentioned in Whitely's messages."

"Alright. Let's start with them then," said Reymond..

Devlin separated the reports featuring names he recognised and began to read them more closely, thinking aloud as he read. "Alun and Derrell suicided, according to the reports, but Casey didn't. So what's special about him?"

The Detective scanned his own notes. "He interested me the most too, if only because he was known to have some bad ties. Habitual gambler, sooner or later he was going to end up owing the wrong people. My guess is that he couldn't pay up fast enough."

"That isn't in the report."

"The report is supposed to be objective. Associations can be hard to prove. Certainly no-one went down for his death, but maybe if they ever find the rest of him that will change."

Mention of associations prevented Devlin from asking for further, sure to be morbid, details. "Can we go for a drive? There's someone I'd like to visit."

Chapter - 65.

Conrad was not appreciative to see Devlin appear at his door with a guest. Devlin himself was expected, thanks to his call en-route, but not the company. The fact that he was clearly a Detective represented the real cause for concern. He saw the trouble flashing before his eyes, but for the moment he ignored the guest and kept focussed on what Devlin had asked. "I've got the matrix for Casey. I'll need a moment longer to compare it with all the others."

"For the moment I just want Casey compared with Carson and Leon. This is Detective Reymond, you might have crossed paths before," said Devlin as he made himself at home on the couch.

"Sadly not. My *past* involvement with the Police does not entitle me to ongoing involvement." Conrad hoped the subtle reference to 'past' would be enough to dissuade Devlin from showing his hand.

"Devlin tells me that you're something of a researcher. Researching what exactly?" asked Detective Reymond

"Nothing specific. I look for patterns in people and their relationships." Conrad kept it generic and without anything that could be played against him.

"He also tells me that you tried to warn him. So what has he got to worry about?"

Conrad left his comfort zone at the keyboard to engage the Detective as best as he could. He explained as much as he knew, but fell short of explaining his sources. It occurred to him that technically this is what he wanted, formal interest in LastGasp'.

"So you have nothing, *really*. Just a mass of conjecture," Reymond said, unconvinced. "I've seen the police reports and there's nothing there."

"You're not the first to doubt me," Conrad was unfazed. "I've had this same discussion with many of Devlin's predecessors." He felt the opportunity slipping from his fingers. "Devlin just suggested that you would be more likely to listen."

"I'm prepared to listen, but so far you've only told me what I already knew."

"Can he see the matrix?" Devlin asked Conrad from the keyboard. "That's what did it for me."

Conrad was reluctant, not that it was any more of a breach than having shown it to Devlin. In fact it was arguably less of a Police security or privacy matter showing it to a Detective. He knew that others would see a breach as a breach, regardless, though if some quantifiable good came of it, then it might provide for some justification or mitigation, if or when it became necessary. He conceded, waving his hand to coax the Detective to the computer in capitulation. He gave the same summary he'd given Devlin previously, this time mentioning departmental justification and authority. He used his fishing analogy again.

"It's pretty, but what does it actually mean?" asked Reymond as he perused the matrix on the screen while trying to associate what he'd heard Devlin ask Conrad from the car. "What did Devlin ask you to do?"

"I've been fixated on the relationship between all of the LastGasp' employees and Glen, or LastGasp'." Conrad gestured for Devlin to move from his seat so that he could continue with his task. "Devlin thinks that I must be missing something because I'm concentrating on what is so obvious. He suggested that I should look at other commonalities between them. The matrix disappeared as he started to use the computer.

"What's happened?" asked the Detective.

"I need to write a little code. It will be substantially faster and more efficient than mindlessly and manually comparing the matrices of everyone by eyeball."

"So what are you doing?" asked the Detective.

"Alright then." Conrad sized up the Detective to gauge the best way to describe what he was doing. "You're obviously pre digital age, but do you remember doing set theory in mathematics at school?" As the Detective nodded vaguely, Conrad figured that his description would be understandable to him. "Well, until now my program has focussed on presenting a *union* of known interactions. It's interesting to see who people know within a few degrees of separation. Devlin wants to look at *intersections*."

The Detective thought this through for a moment. "In my day we called them '*Venn*' diagrams."

"As in Malcolm *Venn*?" Devlin said, a spark in his eyes.

Conrad ushered the others to the kitchen. "I can't work with someone looking over my shoulder. Help yourself to coffee. I'll need about ten minutes." Left on his own, he started to type feverishly.

"Did you work out what Malcolm was doing on your machine?" Devlin asked while he sniffed the percolated coffee on offer. Conrad either ignored the question or was otherwise oblivious.

The Detective's interest was piqued, "Why was Malcolm here?"

"I don't know," said Conrad, not missing a keystroke as he spoke. "He found me initially."

"So why haven't I been made aware of this before now? Or can I assume that your interest isn't entirely official?"

"I've tried, but no-one's interested. Conflicting priorities and that shit," Conrad paused and looked to the Detective. "What aroused your interest?"

"Actually, I bumped into Devlin here a little more than is likely. First at the hotel after David's passing, and then across town. He offered to help me because we're both interested in Malcolm."

"Suffice to say that's not his real name," Devlin felt the need to contribute. "But no-one's told me if he's actually done anything wrong?"

"Legally not. Not this time, not ever. He's a no-one," said Reymond. "He couldn't have done Angie over, the latest time at least, and certainly she won't have anything against him."

"I've told you that," said Devlin. "It wasn't Malcolm."

"How can you be that certain?"

"I told you. I saw a message from Angie, and she named the guy and it wasn't Malcolm."

"It might help if I had a copy of that message. Then at least I could do some checking."

"It's not like that. This was a private message that Angie has written to be sent after she dies."

"Who to?"

"I don't know, just as I have no way of printing it off if I was in any way obliged to do so. It's only accessible from the LastGasp' office."

"I could get a warrant."

"You could try. I've been told that others have tried but still no-one's gotten in unless they're an employee." Devlin looked to Conrad, still typing away. "Some geek researcher could potentially get in, but me thinks that none of us would be here if that was the case and they'd actually been successful."

Conrad made a spectacle of waving his arms to ensure that he had his visitor's attention. He then made a point of pressing a key with a single finger after his arm had traversed a full arc through the air down to the keyboard. "I'm done."

Devlin and Reymond joined Conrad looking at the screen. "What am I looking at?" asked Reymond.

"It's exactly what Devlin wanted. The aesthetics will come later, if I'm so inclined, but right now it's just what he wanted. It's a list of common interactions, people, between the list of LastGasp' employees." The list was empty.

"Alright, so that doesn't help a great deal." Conrad thought for a moment. "But if I relax ..." He tapered off into lazy mumbling.

Reymond and Devlin kept looking on, hopeful that a result would materialise quickly. After a minute or so, they both returned to the couch.

"How's this?" This time there was a list of names. Conrad made a point of periodically pressing a button and the list would change to reveal more or fewer names.

"Why's it changing?" asked Reymond.

"I figure that it was possibly unreasonable for anyone to be known directly by all of those in your list. Rightly or not, I relaxed my algorithm to try people known by more than one of them on the list. It might not be exactly what you asked for, but it's certainly better than nothing."

"Can you make them flash?" asked Devlin.

Chapter - 66.

Nebojsa would never have likened himself to a shepherd ordinarily, but the fact is that he did tend his flock, of sorts. Those dumb individuals, those seeds, needed to be protected from themselves. He was exhausted by the time he returned to his home, but it could have been worse. He'd spent the best part of the late afternoon and early evening doing the rounds, but one took longer than normal to understand what he expected. The result was that there were many people that he simply didn't have time to visit. He knew they wouldn't go anywhere, but it was inconvenient none-the-less.

Tonight, he felt an odd mix of emotions; primarily fatigue and disappointment. He slumped on the end of his bed, kicked off his shoes and then lay back on to the bed to recap on all that he'd *learnt* today. *Stupid bitch*, he thought.

His visit started much like the last time, but then she got smart. He recognised her self-confidence immediately and it made him smile just to think about it. He knew in an instant that what was supposed to be a simple exchange, property for knowledge, was not going to be that simple, but he asked just the same. He asked once.

It was then that Nebojsa learnt that leverage can be tricky with someone with no-one. In retrospect, it was odd that it hadn't come up before. All his life, with everyone he'd learnt from, there was always something that people would value, something to trade, but this one was different. She was single, widowed, but not by him, and had no family. She had assets and up until this afternoon she had been willing to part with them without much coercion; he only had to ask. But then she changed her mind. Just like that, she said she wasn't willing to complete the deal. That much was fine, and it wasn't the first time he'd heard that kind of response from her, and others. She was so confident about it too, even bordering on arrogant. Luckily she didn't threaten him or mention any outside help. She obviously understood the implications of involving others, but it left her wide open to being convinced, to be made to understand.

She submitted immediately to a humble request for oral gratification, but this didn't bring him closer to what he really wanted. An ageing woman, dentures out just in case, salivating over his cock made for some light entertainment, but it really only exposed just how much the years had *not* wisened her. Climax over, time had passed, the deal was still to be made, and he made it clear he wasn't going anywhere. Her tears changed nothing, but it did remind him that on each of his past visits, damaging her in some fashion, regardless of the volume of blood that was spilt, while entertaining, was not going to change her mind or weaken her resolve.

The arrival of a ginger cat at the door startled Nebojsa at first. One second there was sunlight on the glassed French doors opening onto her courtyard, the next, the cat was pawing its 'let me in' routine. When the woman shook her head, as if to tell the cat to go back to chasing mice or something, he saw a new flow of tears and knew he'd found his means. He invited the cat inside, picked it up and nursed it in front of the woman for a time. It was overweight and apparently not that choosy as to its human company, judging by the fact that while it didn't purr, it didn't moan either, not initially. It did moan later though, and it moaned a lot. He didn't leave empty handed.

Nebojsa was extra attentive to his personal hygiene as he showered. It had been a long and messy day, and he had two species of pussy juice to remove. He laughed that his new home and its' language had provided such a humorous play on words.

Chapter - 67.

Conrad periodically looked at Devlin and Detective Reymond seated on his couch, looking uncomfortable. The seat itself was comfortable enough, but it was a two seater and invariably better suited to a couple than two heterosexual men thinking about a problem. Periodically, each would sit forward in an effort to increase their inter-personal space, but that didn't really allow them to speak face to face. Eventually, Devlin dealt with the matter by standing. The greater problem of the lists and updated matrices represented remained.

The lists spoke for themselves, but didn't actually say much. The addition of the flashing, as Devlin suggested, added clarity, but it didn't help. The larger the list of names, the greater the volume of flashing names.

Conrad printed off multiple copies of each list and handed them out so as to enable the others to make whatever sense was possible for themselves. Forever the technocrat, Conrad himself tried to code an algorithm which he was sure would be both simpler and more conclusive than what would be possible with three sets of eyes.

"I'm tempted to leave with what I've got," said Detective Reymond. It was late and his tone was deflated. "I'm impressed of course, but maybe I'm better off returning to the station and doing my research in a familiar environment."

"There's nothing at the station that I can't access here," Conrad said as he typed. It was true, but he was wary about drawing too much attention to the point. He hoped that the Detective might accept it, which might give him a little more time to subtly ask him to overlook the thirty five system access violations that he'd witnessed in the name of an un-authorised 'fishing trip'. If the Detective walked out the door now, he felt that his future would walk with him.

"I've got a better idea," Devlin said, much to Conrad's relief, hopeful. "I can do better research than you can at LastGasp'."

"I disagree," said Conrad, a little offended.

"This isn't a pissing contest," Devlin announced. "The messages are only part of LastGasp'. There's a whole Research Interface specifically designed to identify people." Devlin terminated any ensuing discussion by standing and heading for the door. He paused with his back to the others, "I need a lift, Detective."

Chapter - 68.

Devlin left the Detective at the LastGasp' door and went inside. He half expected him to follow or try the 'foot in the door' thing, but the Detective seemed to take it in his stride, advertising the fact that he'd be waiting. He assumed that the Detective meant it to convince of his commitment, but only as he walked towards the kitchen did it occur to him that it could just as easily have been meant to intimidate.

The kitchen and lounge were empty and Devlin proceeded directly to the bunker. He launched straight into the Research Interface and started working through the list of names. It wasn't late and there was no real urgency, even with the prospect of the Detective waiting outside, but still he felt pressured to complete his research quickly. He tried to keep a cursory eye on the security monitors on the wall, hopeful that he would be able to avoid the appearance of secrecy if Glen or anyone else returned, but doing so only further exacerbated his stress.

Page after page of personal information flashed past as he read as quickly as possible. The first ten minutes made for interesting reading, much like the first few minutes of reading messages, but the rest was substantially less so. Devlin exhausted his list of names and associated perusal of their information without finding what he was looking for. *'It's hopeless'*, he thought as he rested his head on his forearms on the desk. He wondered if Conrad would have any more luck, or if Malcolm would be back to taunt him. The thought made him think of the task he'd set Conrad, sure as he was that commonality between the names would reveal all.

It occurred to him that LastGasp' was sure to have access to the same data that Conrad was accessing, which meant that for all of Conrad's suspicion, he was just as capable as Glen. Using the Research Interface for the same task was worth a try. He tried a selection of the most recent names on the list and there was a delay in a response from the Research Interface, but eventually it returned a single name. Tania Wilson.

It took a moment for Devlin to register the name, and still longer for him to contemplate what it meant. He'd expected the name of a reader, or Glen, and he felt some disappointment accordingly. He tried to ring Conrad to share his findings, but the phone reception in the bunker hadn't changed in his absence. He decided to head for the kitchen, possibly just as a temporary staging area for his departure. He marched along the corridor, checking his phone for some visual indication that he would be able to call. He knew he could just as easily head outside where the Detective would be waiting, but for the time being he was comfortable with maintaining the distance that a phone call would provide.

"I ask only one thing, Devlin," Glen revealed his presence in one of the armchairs, aware that he was yet to be noticed. As ever, he didn't look directly at Devlin as he spoke.

Devlin couldn't help but be a little surprised, and he knew that it showed. In his fixation in the bunker he had forgotten to watch the monitors, and while Glen didn't look like he'd employed any stealth to enter the building, Devlin felt for how his surprise would be perceived. "I didn't see you come in."

"I ask only one thing," Glen repeated himself. "I ask only that you don't interfere with what you don't understand."

"What's that supposed to mean?"

"It means only that," Glen replied solemnly. "I know you've met with Malcolm. Just don't interfere with what he's doing."

"Interfere with what? I'm actually interested in Tania, and why she would come up in your Research Interface."

"Just don't interfere."

That Glen didn't question who 'Tania' was spoke volumes. "So who's Tania?"

"Perhaps she's Malcolm's acquaintance."

"So what does Malcolm have to do with her?"

"Possibly nothing. I'm not his keeper?"

"Bullshit!"

"Bullshit nothing. I have no control over him and he does as he sees fit." Glen took a deep breath, as if to begin talking, but he remained silent. "Take a seat Devlin," Glen said as he patted the arm of the adjacent armchair.

Devlin sat as instructed, fidgeting with his phone and tapping his fingers on his chair arms while Glen watched a number of the assembled televisions simultaneously. Eventually, Devlin too started to watch, his eyes darting between the screens. The evening programming presented a cross section of news and current affairs, to sit-coms and game shows. Scanning the various channels wasn't relaxing, but Devlin was oddly appreciative for the distraction.

"Tell me what you see, Devlin."

"I see crap. I don't see how you can take any of this in!"

Glen largely ignored the comment. "I see potential *Malcolms* everywhere. But there's only been one. Others like him are hard to find."

"I found him without any problem at all!"

"Technically, he found you."

Glen was right. It was a point that Devlin had overlooked, and while his initial reaction was to argue the poignancy of the difference, he decided against it and kept quiet.

"Malcolm is ..." Glen paused, as if deliberating his choice of words carefully, but couldn't, didn't finish. After a few moments, he tried again. "Malcolm's a friend."

"If he's a friend, why don't you introduce us?"

"What's to introduce? You've met him. Say what's on your mind, Devlin."

"I just want to know what's going on."

"So does that mean that you're concerned for yourself or others?"

"Does *that* matter?" Devlin enquired.

"It means a great deal."

"A bit of both probably. I'm concerned for Ikel, but I'd be lying if I said I wasn't concerned for myself too."

"Have you done anything wrong?"

"No." Devlin was proud that he'd replied quickly, knowing that it would surely represent honesty, or perhaps denial, but in either case it would represent conviction.

Glen shrugged off the reply and kept watching the televisions. Devlin watched a full commercial break on two different channels before he felt that Glen was going to say anything. "I don't know where Ikel is, so I can't help you on that front. Perhaps your Detective friend might be a better help."

"And Malcolm?"

"And what?"

Devlin felt his frustration rise as he tried to determine whether Glen was being deliberately annoying, or just playful. The net effect was the same.

"I'm not going to tell you anything about Malcolm or Tania."

"I just don't want to be like the rest of your readers, Glen."

"You're not like them Devlin, that's why you're here," Glen offered some consolation. "Give me a name, and I'll tell you why you aren't like them."

Seizing the opportunity, Devlin fumbled for his list of readers, but began with the first name from the top of his head rather than the listed sequence. "OK, Casey. I can't remember his surname."

"Lawrence. Casey Lawrence. But I've got a better idea. How about you start with Keegan Kirkby."

"Why him?" Devlin scanned the list, but the name wasn't even listed. "Actually, who's he? *Was* he?"

"He *was* my first real employee after Malcolm, and he *is* alive. Still."

"So where is he, and why isn't he listed?"

"The point is that it's not a complete list of employees, intentionally, and just because a few are not available for your interrogation doesn't mean they are all dead."

"So what's so special about him?"

"Nothing. He was a decidedly un-remarkable man. God knows where he is now, or what he's doing. He made sense of his life and continued on his own path. You could end up like him."

"So why did he leave? Money?"

"There are limits to wealth."

Devlin felt no obligation to argue, opting to move on. "Alright, who's next?"

Glen turned off one of the televisions. Casey Lawrence. He's on your list."

"What's his story?"

"He had to go. You wanted to know why I did my homework on you before I offered you a job? Blame Casey."

"So what did you do to him?"

"Spare me your accusations. He made some bad choices. Check with your Detective, again, as I know you must have already. Next I'll tell you about Alun Boyle and Leon Newman," Glen turned off another two of the televisions. "I had high hopes for both of them. I figured them for their commitment to the law and doing the right thing, and they didn't disappoint."

"So where are they now?" Devlin asked as he scanned the list.

"They found the waiting difficult."

"Waiting for what?"

"They thought more would happen, and when it didn't … they reacted."

"What happened?"

"Alun was clearly disappointed with my protocols and thought he could do better."

"And got LastGasp' un-necessary attention. Right?"

"He wasn't that blatant. He just figured that he'd pass on information, sit back and be the better for his role in making things happen."

"Sounds fair."

"You know I understand people better than most, and certainly better than Alun. He *thought* that if people knew, then things would change. The reality was that it didn't. It saddened him, and he left."

"So if they're similar, why isn't Leon dead too?"

"He and Alun, were similar, but in the end they were also very different. Where Alun was committed to the law, Leon was more interested in justice."

"So where's he?"

"Jail."

Devlin gwarfed. "How does that work?"

"Leon described it as *activism*. Purists would have called it *vigilantism*. You'd have to understand by now how it was, how it is. You read messages, guilt in varying degrees and various strains and sooner or later, in spite of the lack of identifying information, you'll be able to work out who the bastards are. Looking back, it was just a matter of time before someone would want to do something about it themselves."

"And he got caught," Devlin pre-empted the story. "So how did you and LastGasp' not get implicated?"

"I'd like to say that good management kept LastGaspStore clear, but it was largely luck. There was a like-minded Detective in the mix in charge of the investigation. One who understood."

"Albert?"

Glen nodded. "A good guess. He kept LastGaspStore free of implications, but he couldn't prevent Leon from going to jail. It cost Albert all the favours he could call in, and forced him into professional purgatory.

"Alun would have got himself into trouble in much the same way eventually, but his exuberance was tempered somewhat when Leon got into trouble. A different guilt is what killed him, but not before talking to Conrad. Then I should tell you about Derrell."

"Ikel told me that you actually shed a tear for Derrell."

Glen turned off the entire bank of televisions. "You know I've learnt a lot from the various readers that I've employed over the years. Most importantly, I've learnt never to be surprised by people."

"So what was so special about Derrell?"

"You understand that I'm telling you this happy in the knowledge that you'll surely pass all of this onto Conrad and the Detective. But I have nothing to hide." The leather on Glen's armchair creaked as he wriggled in an effort to get comfortable. "The fact is that Derrell represented the changing of the guard. The readers before him were different to those who followed."

"Does that include me?" Devlin asked.

"I hope so. But anyway. Derrell." Glen took a mouthful from a bottle of beer that he'd held inconspicuously on his lap. "Derrell believed in the law. Father was a cop, grandfather was a cop. I thought he'd be perfect."

"So what happened?"

"He started passing information to his family, which essentially, indirectly, meant the police. That in itself didn't concern me, but it had all the makings of others, like Casey and Alun. I didn't want that to happen again."

Devlin kept watching Glen. He'd grown accustomed to a lack of eye contact, or at least a lack of reciprocated eye contact, but still he tried. If nothing else, it made him *feel* that Glen was being honest. He also sensed sadness in his tone, like he was peeling the scab from a wound that just wouldn't heal. "So what did you do?"

"Nothing," Glen replied indignantly. "I spoke to him. It wasn't like I read him the riot act or anything. I just tried to explain his role in the greater scheme of things. You'd understand, of course. And I actually thought I'd hit a chord. He stopped. Just like that, he stopped. He broke contact with his family, his life, everything.

"'*Kindred spirit*' sounds so, so … inappropriate. But at the time I was sure I'd found someone who was more than just an employee.

"For a time it was just him and I. He was younger than me, and I saw him as being someone who'd continue when I moved on. So I broke my own rule and explained a little of my technology. I knew my system was secure, and telling him was as much a measure of my trust in him as my trust in my system. And it was good for me. *He* was good for me. A friend who I trusted.

"Gradually, he became more and more fixated on watching TV, or the bank of TVs as I am now. At the time I remember feeling a little put out that his watching TV was interfering with our friendship."

"Was he an employee when he died?"

"He became very moody. Highs and lows so bad that I suggested medication, which he fought I might add. Then he grew more distant, more aloof. He started spending more and more time out of the office, and we drifted apart. I resented the fact that he knew so much about LastGasp', and for a time I wondered if he was going out on his own, potentially as a competitor. Eventually I confronted him on the matter."

"Was he going it alone?"

"Can I say that until Derrell came along, I believed that my system was perfect. I'd seen competitors come and go, and fail, all because LastGaspStore was perfect, for what it was intended. I'd weathered god knows how many attempted infiltrations, legal furore, bad media. But Derrell found a way to exploit it."

"How?" Devlin asked, but Glen said nothing in reply, as if he was thinking either what to say or how to say it. "How'd he get in?" Devlin asked again.

"He didn't. But he discovered that LastGasp' was geared for the truth, and I wasn't prepared for misinformation. Ikel and the others would have explained ghosts, for which I have a protocol. But when is a ghost not a ghost?"

Devlin was beyond riddles. "Can't you just tell me?"

"What happens when you have real people, but fake messages?"

"That would have to depend on the message."

"So what happens if you received a message from a relative, a friend, who described their involvement in some crime? Would you believe it?"

Devlin considered the question. "Yes." Though it made him think, and he was still thinking when Glen continued.

"The trouble was that the messages didn't change anything, and in themselves they didn't make things happen. It was some time later that he killed himself."

"Lori told me how sad you were to hear about ... *that.*"

"It was before Lori's time. I might add that Carson was worse. And if ever there was a period when I was legitimately concerned, it was then."

"What did Carson do?"

"Other than demonstrate a failing in my judgement? Where Derrell was disappointed with waiting for the messages, Carson couldn't wait."

"What is that supposed to mean?"

Glen glanced Devlin's way, and then turned on the bank of televisions, each a different channel. He said nothing.

Infuriated, Devlin considered stepping outside for some fresh air, where he was sure that the Detective would be waiting when his phone rang. He fumbled for it as he stood and left the lounge. The displayed number wasn't known or familiar, but he was beyond caring and answered it anyway.

All the Detective needed to say was that he'd found Ikel. Devlin left Glen without another word.

Chapter - 69.

Malcolm was nestled into the corner of a well-lit booth in the bar with a novel in his hand. There were others with books, a few business-men, presumably travelling away from home and weary of the surroundings of their respective hotel rooms and associated sterile confines. They sat lonely, one person per table, reading fat paperbacks. Malcolm's book was nothing special, and if the truth be known, he would have struggled to recall anything of the preceding twenty or so pages, but he wasn't there to read.

He wasn't there to drink either, though he had sampled a few designer beers interspersed with iced water and a single coffee. The coffee was decidedly average, even for a bar, and promised to leave him unable to sleep for hours, but sleep was the last thing on his mind. The evening was not supposed to be recreational. He just watched Tania, unobtrusively but not covertly.

Tania was in '*life of the party*' mode, and as such, she dominated the majority of the bar patrons. She was putting on quite a performance too. Most watched and laughed raucously, laughing at her, not with her, though it seemed that she was either incapable of, or beyond telling the difference.

The crowd around her was thinning. Gradually people were leaving, possibly because they'd had enough, or possibly because they were tiring of watching the spectacle before them. Not even increasing the frequency of flashes of her breasts stemmed their departure, and her outbursts as to their lack of staying power did nothing to endear them. It was mid-week and late at night, and soon only the sexual opportunists and very drunk remained, but she showed no sign of slowing.

Malcolm enjoyed the show. He knew it wouldn't be long now.

Chapter - 70.

Devlin recognised Ikel's car, or what was left of it, by the licence plate. He hadn't noticed it before, but it was hard to miss a plate 'IKEL' and he understood immediately that everything the Detective had said en-route was true, despite his best efforts to convince himself otherwise.

He didn't need to see the body, though Detective Reymond would have possibly allowed it. There didn't seem much point. The identity had been confirmed adequately, but not formally, by the time they'd arrived, and the ambulance and its crew was just keen to get on their way. In any case, there was too much blood on the wall for the body to be recognisable as his new friend.

Detective Reymond spoke quietly with the attending Police. He looked unfazed as he mainly listened, alternating between surveying the car wreck and looking at the uniforms as they filled him in, periodically glancing at Devlin. Eventually after what seemed an eternity, though it was only a few minutes, Detective Reymond sauntered over to Devlin, seated on the kerb with his legs stretched onto the road, away from shattered glass and debris.

"At least he died doing what he loved. He loved that car," said Devlin, nervously slipping into banality. "I'm assuming it was suicide."

"Possibly." Detective Reymond eased his older body onto the kerb beside Devlin. He made no attempt to hide the fact that he wasn't comfortable. "Traffic incidents aren't my thing. The uniforms are still checking and looking for witnesses. There's an unsubstantiated report that he might have swerved to miss a dog, so the write-up might call it accidental. Of course, we have a distinct lack of an animal, or carcass as the case may be, and there's no skid-marks to substantiate the report."

Devlin said nothing. He just sat staring into infinity.

"Penny for your thoughts," Detective Reymond asked.

"I guess I'm wondering how this fits with my understanding of what is going on at LastGasp'."

"Well." Reymond braced himself, as if about to suggest something unpalatable. "Of course you have to consider that perhaps your friend did just … *call it a day.*"

"Oh, please!" Devlin was incredulous. "Another LastGasp' employee on the list and you're telling me that …"

Reymond interrupted Devlin at the start of what was sure to be a nervous or scared rant. "I'm just saying that perhaps the suicides are real. Pure and simple. Of course, for the sake of argument, I'm not including your friend here in this list pending the formal outcome of the investigation. But maybe the problem lies in your employer's recruitment practices." Reymond took a deep breath as if in anticipation of a rebuttal.

No rebuttal came. Instead, Devlin was silent, thinking, and for a few seconds he said nothing, until, "You know Detective. I think you're right."

Chapter - 71.

Albert was so close he could taste it, but taste, like the sense of smell, was little more than a memory. He didn't really miss the sense of smell, and in his current surrounds, being able to smell anything would have been more than he could handle. To him, sloshing around amid puddles of urine was no different really than walking around after fresh rains, except that there wasn't the intangible feel of renewal and cleanliness that accompanied rain. While he didn't miss most scents and smells, he did miss the pervasive odour of cleanliness, that, and the taste of a good steak. Even just the thought of the taste of some meat made him miss his life, or what was his life. But what he could taste now was better than the best steak at the best restaurant. He could taste sweet revenge, and it was both sweet and savoury, and more than worth the wait.

It had taken forever to track Sam down, but faster than the man could be identified, he could re-invent himself, assume a new identity and disappear leaving the process of finding him back at square one. Right now he was using the name Malcolm Venn which hurt even more.

He didn't have all the time in the world for his quest either. Not only was the search wearing, but what was left of his lungs were getting worse. He was brave in the face of his own mortality, as fast as his death was approaching, but he was scared that he mightn't get to actually find Sam in time.

The most important thing in what remained of his life was that he find the guy. He needed for Sam to understand what he'd done in the last few moments of *his* life.

He didn't want to be too over-confident though. He'd been close, arguably this close before, only to have that bastard slip through his fingers and disappear. Most recently, only a few days ago, he'd tracked Sam down to where he was hiding out with some bitch, but before he could do anything about it, Sam was gone. For her part, either Sam had briefed her very well, or she genuinely didn't know anything, but she didn't concede any clues as to his whereabouts.

Albert bit his lower lip as he remembered meeting her, frustration giving way to regret as he thought of how he'd lost his temper. He tried to convince himself that it wasn't his fault, but it was no use. He could have walked away at any time, particularly when it was obvious that she wasn't going to talk. He should have walked away when she voluntarily raised her skirt, as if he would be that easily placated. And when he saw the bruises, that in particular should have appealed to what was left of him and he should have run away for fear of becoming what he loathed. And he was going to, until she suggested that he'd never find Sam. The years of anticipation, the pent up resentment at looking for him and not being able to find him, and the bottled aggression was suddenly uncapped. He couldn't even remember what he'd done to her, but it wouldn't have been pretty. Not his finest moment.

Albert wasn't even sure if she was alive, whoever she is, or was. He'd left as soon as he'd heard a car pull up outside and made his way back to his own noxious smelling cave. Perhaps the only upside was that irrespective of whether she lived or died, Sam would get the message and maybe, just maybe, it would be enough for him to make a mistake.

Chapter - 72.

Devlin was a man on a mission, or as much as was possible in the passenger seat of the Detective's car, returning to LastGasp'. The thought of Glen and his recruitment practices had left him determined to confront Glen, and to his mind, the Detective was doing little more than delaying the moment by driving at or even below the speed limit where a rush was in order.

He was fidgeting, and alternated between chewing his fingernails and looking for distractions around the interior of the car. Inevitably, he sought a distraction to the quiet of the car. The radio wasn't going to do, particularly with his thought processes higher functioning as they were. "I'm thinking," he said. "I'm thinking about what might be in Ikel's message, what he might say."

"What about it?"

"I'm wondering what he might have seen fit to share," Devlin continued. "And what might have died with him. It's just like Whitely said, that knowledge comes with death's release."

"You might never know the truth," said the Detective.

"Whitely also warned me to understand the difference between knowledge and truth. I didn't know what to make of his comment at the time, but now I'm thinking he might be worth another visit."

"I thought I was just dropping you home." The Detective wasn't very convincing as he sighed after thinking a little. "I guess he might tolerate a little more company."

Chapter - 73.

Devlin mistimed his walk from the car to Whitely's home. His plan was to hold his breath for as long as possible, but this only forced him to breathe deeply amid the detritus of the garden. He marched into the darkness of the hall corridor, lit erratically by the flickering of a television. "Whitely. It's us again." He edged towards the lounge room, ambivalent to whether the Detective followed or waited outside.

Whitely was dozing in front of the television, but he wasn't too perturbed when Devlin turned on the reading lamp that extended over his chair. Instead, he just raised his eye-brows, as much to arouse his face as acknowledge the presence of visitors. When the Detective entered the room, Whitely nodded in greeting but said nothing.

"Ikel's dead. He crashed his car tonight," Devlin announced aggressively. He planned only that much. He remained standing expectantly, as if naively sure that Whitely would break into explanation. When Whitely started cycling through the channels of his television, Devlin was less hopeful that anything would be achieved with the visit. "Ikel's dead," he repeated, more politely.

"Nothing I can do about that, but given that I could have learnt that much from the news or phone, I'm assuming you have more to say than just that." At last, he turned off the television in a deliberate final movement and returned the remote control to his chair-side table. "Ask away Devlin, 'cos I'll be fucked if I'm going to guess what you need to know."

"We're interested in why Ikel and possibly David might have died," Detective Reymond offered. "We want to understand what's going on."

"Alan, I wanted to understand what was going on years ago but I recall you told me that understanding wouldn't change things, or help," Whitely was curt. "So provided that you're not formally or professionally interested, go back to your baby-sitting and shut the fuck up."

"Don't we go back long enough for a little decorum?" the Detective asked.

"Decorum has nothing to do with this, Alan."

"I could just as easily engage my interest formally …"

"If that were a possibility you'd have done it by now, but you haven't. In any case, you and Devlin here will be clearer before too long anyway."

"There you go. As of now, that comment there, I have cause to be concerned for Devlin's wellbeing."

"Oh, fuck off Alan! How long the fuck have you known me! Do you think that I'm going to cause this guy harm." Whitely was incensed. He gestured as if to present Devlin to an audience. "Look at him. He's oblivious, sure, but he's not at risk!"

"You're not the one who I'm thinking is going to do the harm."

Whitely cooled himself down a little before continuing, his tone substantially more mellow. "He's not at risk from me or anyone that I know of. A few people's suicides doesn't mean that others are at risk, unless you're in the firing line."

"OK. So what has LastGasp' and Glen got to do with this?"

"You especially don't want to interfere, Alan. I'll not say a thing against Glen, and that's not out of fear or obligation, but out of understanding."

"Well I think ..." Reymond started.

"Alan, I don't care for what you think, but I do care for how Devlin's understanding is progressing. So how about you give it a rest and let him talk."

Devlin felt both Whitely and the Detective's stares, "Ikel was my friend."

"Move on, Devlin," said Whitely with a yawn.

"What about Tania?"

Whitely exuberantly writhed in his seat, his face beaming with a smile that would have stressed most wounds on his face. "What do you know about poor Tania?" He spoke while reaching for a few tissues.

"Only that her brother was killed."

"Tania's probably learnt that all the remorse in the world doesn't change what's happened," said Detective Reymond.

"Thanks Alan. But this isn't about you." Whitely said politely. "Go on, Devlin."

"There's not a lot more to tell, except that her name was magically singled out by the LastGasp' Research Interface when I was expecting it to reveal some pearl of wisdom about all of the past readers."

"Indeed." Whitely waved to Devlin, as if to shoo him away. "So fuck off." He turned to face the Detective. "Alan, I'd like a word in private."

Chapter - 74.

Before the interior light of the car faded, Devlin was rummaging through the case notes that the Detective had left in the back seat. Even with the privacy afforded by the absence of the Detective he couldn't make any more sense of the notes than he had previously. Despite his efforts, in reality he was doing little more than killing time until the Detective returned to the car.

Even in the dim light of the dashboard instrumentation, Devlin could tell that the Detective looked different as he drove. He looked like a man content in maintaining a secret despite the lure of disclosure.

Devlin tried to guess what Whitely could have said in private to prompt the Detectives mood. He waited for the Detective to say something unprompted, even if it was just to clarify where they were headed, but instead the Detective was unashamedly coy. Eventually, he had to ask. "So what did Whitely say to make you so …"

The Detective was in no rush to answer, and for a moment Devlin considered re-wording his question, but soon enough the Detective nodded as if to suggest that he had at least heard the question.

"It's private, and none of your concern," the Detective answered as his subtle grin gave way to a more professionally appropriate expression. "We just talked about my daughter. That's all." A reminiscent smile returned to the Detective's face.

"You just seem upbeat, that's all."

"It's just …" the Detective paused, as if struggling to come up with the right words. "I'm thinking that maybe it's time for me to retire."

"What's brought about the change of heart?"

"Who says it's a change of heart? If you hadn't noticed, I'm old enough. Perhaps it's time. Whitely just made me think, that's all."

"He didn't enlighten you further about where Tania fits into all of this, did he?"

"Yes, and no. You know it's late, Devlin, and we could almost continue this in the morning if absolutely necessary. I'm sure we'll catch up then."

"I'd really prefer to know now. I barely slept last night, and I won't be able to sleep tonight without some closure."

"Some people go for years without closure. Maybe you just need to learn some patience."

"Patience I have, but I'm not sure that I've got the time to wait for closure. Conrad suggested that others came to at least some realisation, much like I've done, just before they died." Noting that the Detective was unperturbed, Devlin pressed the issue. "Don't you have an obligation to at least sound interested? What about Malcolm?"

"I've lost interest in pursuing Malcolm."

"So what was it that Whitely told you that inspired you to forget Malcolm and finally retire?"

"My daughter." The Detective began with a sigh. "Whitely and I were devastated when she died. At the time, I was prepared to blame everyone, anyone, but all the blame in the world wouldn't bring her back. I might add that this came on the back of the death of my granddaughter, her daughter, Whitely's daughter. As fuelled as I was with anger, there was nothing I could do about it."

"You said she died of an overdose. So surely that much was out of your control."

"The overdose was part of it. The fact is that she was hit by a car as she savoured a drug induced haze before she fell unconscious. The car killed her, but as far as the coroner was concerned, it only hastened her demise. The driver was one Tania Wilson. Ably assisted by a cocky young lawyer, she even kept her drivers' license."

"I'm assuming that this is the same Tania Wilson."

The detective nodded. "They say that good things come to those who wait, and there's a small matter of karma too. But I have to say that I've been disappointed with my wait.

"Admittedly, there was more than a little irony in the passing of Tania's brother, and then that I was the one to break the news and assume the role of '*hand holder*'. But I'd moved on from my anger to such an extent that I found myself incapable of really feeling anything. I'd waited for something good, but it never came. The fact was that for the duration of my wait, I had nothing, and something happening to Tania wouldn't have helped that."

"It must have been a long, hard wait."

"Like you wouldn't know. If I was feeling more benevolent, I might also add that Tania's had more than her share of sadness too over the years. Not that I felt for *her* sadness, but I understood it."

"So what did Whitely tell you about Tania?" Devlin asked as they pulled up outside LastGasp'.

"Only that everything happens for a reason."

Chapter - 75.

Angie formulated a plan. It wasn't the kind of plan that Malcolm had talked about, but it was a plan nonetheless. Malcolm had spoken about his plans taking months to be completed, but her plan was either less grandiose or perhaps it just needed a woman's touch to shorten or fine-tune the process. Maybe it was just that he lacked the motivation, whereas Angie had enough anger inside her to fuel anything that she cared to put her mind to.

Malcolm had said precious little else about what he did. He never appeared before work or after work, or at any set time of the day. He just showed up, as if he was perpetually close by, evidenced by the fact he was around at random intervals. This hadn't been a problem as she'd enjoyed both the company and the passive protection that his presence provided.

If Malcolm had taught her anything, it was that there are those that 'do', and those that get 'done to'. More importantly, he told her that if she was being done to, then just braving up to the inevitability of it continuing was not going to improve things. That he'd said this when they'd first met at the corner pharmacy was remarkable only because he hadn't mentioned the Police or Religion. Other strangers she'd met would voice their opinion, as if they understood anything of her situation. As if they understood either the physical or emotional toll of life in her shoes. But Malcolm's advice was almost philosophically constructive, as if he really understood what she felt. She remembered feeling as if her life was on the improve after that first meeting and she felt the same surge in positivity now.

Angie was saddened when she found Malcolm's note. Except that the envelope also contained her home key, it could have been from anyone. The note did not contain an apology, but realistically she didn't expect one. Now that she'd calmed down a little and was able to be a little more rational, she accepted that he had nothing to apologise for.

On Malcolm's recommendation, Angie promised to give Devlin the benefit of the doubt. She owed him that much.

Chapter - 76.

The Detective had driven off in a hurry leaving Devlin alone with his thoughts, and a myriad of punters heading for one of the brothels on either side of LastGasp'. It was well after midnight, and for a time he considered returning to his hotel in the naïve hope that things would be clearer in the morning after a full night's sleep. Of course, that the hotel would still be blockaded to him was going to be a problem, and one that he didn't feel like embracing. The vibration of his phone in his pocket however, sent his mind racing and reminded him that sleep was unlikely. The phone call was from Glen urging him inside, and Devlin smiled at the CCTV camera above the LastGasp' door and obliged.

"It's sad about Ikel," Glen began. "But life goes on."

"You don't sound too touched," Devlin said provocatively as he grabbed a bottled beer from the kitchen. He joined Glen in the lounge but resisted Glen's suggestion to take a seat with him. "I thought you'd be more concerned, if only for the extra effort that you'll need to invest in recruitment."

"Don't be like that, Devlin. He was a nice kid, and I'll miss him, as will you. The problem is that you and I are in the minority. You're fortunate enough to be able to judge him, and remember him, with just a snapshot of his life to judge him by."

"So?"

"You seem to have become adept in the use and abuse of my Research Interface, so why not answer that question yourself?"

Chapter - 77.

Detective Reymond returned to the station. He was no stranger to being there 'after hours', but the middle of the night was always a particularly lonely time to be at his desk. To do so regularly reminded him that he had nothing or no-one to go home to, and no amount of positive thinking, religion or counselling could convince him otherwise, and God knows he'd tried. In that sense, his job was both a blessing and curse. It gave him a purpose to live, if not a reason, but it required him to avail himself whenever, and this meant the sociable daylight hours and also the lonely times when he would have almost the entire station to himself, alone with this thoughts.

Typically his thoughts were primarily of his daughter and grand-daughter, but tonight Reymond's thoughts were to recall two chapters of Whitely's words that echoed in his head. He remembered the circumstances of their parting years ago, when the wound of their common loss was still raw. Whitely had lost his child, his wife, and most recently his job, and he was living with Reymond. It was an uneasy co-habitation, but they managed only because Reymond himself found it easier to devote himself to work than offer emotional support to the man who was effectively, if not legally, his son-in-law.

That Tania was able to keep her license was the final straw for both men. Whitely swore revenge and it took all of the Detective's professional and personal experience to talk the man down into some degree of rational thought. Reymond felt the same desire for revenge of course, but at the time he knew that little would be gained in retribution. He calmed Whitely by convincing him of the inevitability that if he did do anything himself, he would be the one going to jail. At the time, Reymond added weight to his argument by suggesting that Whitely was the only family he had left. His mood softened by a mixture of acceptance and medication, Whitely calmly agreed with the line of placation.

In Reymond's memory, he sat holding Whitely for hours, though in reality it was surely nowhere near that long. He still remembered the manner with which Whitely stood, shrugging off his embrace. Raw with tears, Whitely made an announcement, calmly and rationally. "I want her dead, but the trouble with death is that it doesn't cause her enough pain. I'd very much prefer for her to die in pain, and with nothing."

With those words, Whitely packed only a few of his belongings and left. Reymond remembered those words and the way that they'd been said with perfect clarity. He'd thought about them often since then, particularly when he thought about his daughter and whenever he conjured up some pseudo official excuse to keep tabs on either Tania Wilson or Whitely himself.

In the days immediately following when those words were first said, Reymond feared that Whitely would do something he'd live to regret. However, given the conviction with which Whitely had spoken, Reymond figured that it was very possible that Whitely wouldn't live through turning his prophetic comment into reality. He reasoned that there was amazingly little he could do about it, if Whitely was to take things into his own hands. The reality was that Reymond wouldn't have really wanted to interfere.

Days turned to weeks, then months, and then years. Whitely had kept himself out of major trouble, and Reymond had assumed that he'd moved on since those words. Certainly on the infrequent occasions that he'd visited Whitely, the topic of Tania never came up, though it was obvious that Whitely's loss was just as raw as ever.

Until tonight.

Tonight, privately, Whitely shared more of himself than he had in many years. He also made no attempt to hide what he thought of Tania's brother's passing, suggesting it was not evidence of some theory of random misfortune. What he'd said required consideration, particularly when Whitely circled tomorrows date on a calendar hanging by his chair. With tears streaming from his eyes he said, "I've waited for this."

Now alone at his desk with a hot coffee in his chipped mug, Reymond was thinking about Whitely and about what he'd said then and now.

He started his usual checks on both Whitely and Tania. Admittedly, he was nowhere near as regular as he used to be, but Whitely's result was the same as it ever was. The guy rarely left his home, never had any visitors of any merit or notoriety, and short of unsubstantiated domestic disturbances where he was the victim, he was the usual clean slate. Tania's profile, however, was different.

Just like Whitely had wished, Tania was now all alone. With the unfortunate passing of her support sponsor, she too now had no-one. As ever, Reymond struggled between his professional obligation for concern and his long shelved personal indifference to her. It might be sad that Tania was now without a friend in the world, but Reymond wondered if Tania, sober or otherwise, felt anywhere near the pain that he'd felt over the years.

*   *   *

Detective Reymond felt it fitting that he would draft his resignation by hand. Short and sharp, it captured what he wanted it to say, particularly when he held grave doubts that anyone would actually read it. Handwritten as it was, or in *hardcopy* as the world would now describe it, his resignation said more than it needed to in some regards, but less than was obligatory. He didn't pander to any expectation that he reminisce over a career worth of fond memories, professional challenges, camaraderie and how the Force had evolved with a changing society. Similarly, he didn't suggest that he was indebted to those who had seen fit to allow him to stay in the force beyond what was traditional, nor did he reduce himself to using it as a soapbox.

Instead, he limited himself to a series of thankyou's, and a summary of what he believed was the most important role that he'd played in his time in the Force. He doubted whether anyone would understand, but he didn't really care.

Mr Alan Reymond left the station with his chipped mug.

Chapter - 78.

Devlin could not differentiate between surprise and relief to see Lori in the bunker. He rushed to hold her, but she was more reserved and held him at arm's length, as if wary of the gesture as some precursor to a sexual advance. "I'm just happy to see you!" he said, but Lori was unconvinced.

"You've heard about Ikel then?" Devlin asked.

"Yes, I heard. And it's sad, but right now I'm a little focussed," Lori replied as she typed and focussed on her screen.

Devlin was disappointed in her ambivalence. "You sound like Glen. I thought you would have shown more interest than that, particularly given your history."

"Frankly, my history is the last thing I want to think about at this point."

Suddenly guilty that he wasn't sharing some pending workload, Devlin logged into his machine, but noted that there were no messages awaiting review. Only then did he realise that Lori was using the Research Interface. "Who are you looking at then?"

"Save me the banter." Lori made no attempt to hide her actions, which made her appear even more brazen. "If you want to get busy, turn on the stereo."

Devlin interpreted Lori's words as a request rather than a suggestion, and he obliged accordingly. As soon as the music started, he looked to Lori for some sign of approval but she responded with a gesture indicating that he should turn up the volume. With the volume set unreasonably loud, Lori ushered Devlin closer. "I'm not being rude, but I have bigger fish to fry than just ...."

Lori stopped reactively when the stereo was suddenly silenced as Glen opened the bunker door and took a seat.

"Devlin, when I introduced Lori here, I mentioned that she was a prostitute. That she may well be still a prostitute is neither here nor there. But I could have said that she was also once a member of the Police force. And that she is still in said Police force, would that mean less or more?"

Devlin assumed that this was a matter between Glen and Lori, but he was more than happy to listen in.

"How long have you known?" Lori asked.

"I've always known. It didn't worry me then, and it doesn't worry me now." Glen edged himself closer to Lori's screen and to see what she was doing. "It's the lying that gets me though. And the turning up the volume so as to help keep your little secrets and to corrupt Devlin here is just ...wrong."

"I'm just doing my job."

"And I have no problem with you or anyone doing their job. I just don't like secrets that don't include me."

"So if you know I'm with the Police, where's the secret?"

"Lori, if you've learnt nothing in your extra-curricular time here at LastGaspStore, I would have hoped that it would be that perceptions are everything. Consider this. If I had a governing body, and I don't, but if I did, they would have seen your history and advised me that you were not the kind of employee that LastGaspStore needed. Me on the other hand looked at your history and saw proof positive of honesty. Men approach you for sex, transaction is conducted, nice and honest. You see it's all a matter of perceptions."

"I'm surprised that you didn't perceive the Police as synonymous with honesty," Lori suggested.

"Well yes, but then again I'm the suspicious one, and I'm all the more suspicious that the Police are still so determined to breach LastGaspStore for their own purposes."

"So this is not the first time?" Devlin asked. "You said *still*, as if you'd been breached before."

"Instead of asking that, why don't you ask Lori why she's here?" Glen directed his attention towards Lori and suggested that Devlin do the same. "Lori?"

"Officially, I'm here to get closer to the LastGasp' security. We couldn't breach it from outside, so we had to try from the inside."

"But why, Lori? Tell Devlin what was so wrong with my privacy, and indirectly the privacy of all of the LastGaspStore members? And if you're reluctant to disclose that, why not just tell him who you were just researching. For all you know, you might have a lot in common."

Glen stood up to leave, but on reaching the door he turned for one last salvo. "For the record, this changes nothing between us. You're more than welcome to stay Lori, if you want. Just don't interfere. It's all I ask." He left the bunker, being as careful as ever to secure the door behind himself.

Devlin looked to Lori for something, beit advice or a suggestion of some description, but once the shock of her being outed had settled, she only returned to her keyboard and continued typing. "What are you doing?" he asked, edging closer so as to look over her shoulder.

"I figure that it's only a matter of time before he locks me out."

"Is that all you're concerned about? I've spent the last few days terrified that crossing Glen or LastGasp' would be paramount to a death sentence."

"Oh God, no!" Lori exclaimed, though not pausing enough to interfere with the rate of her typing. "I'll just be replaced like the others before me. I'm not the first and I more than likely won't be the last."

"What's to work out? Why LastGasp' employees have a habit of dying?"

"People die, Devlin. My mandate is to understand how it is that Glen's managed to keep his system secure."

"So you're sure that it is secure?"

"As I said when you first joined, the fact that Glen is not awash with Law suits is proof enough for me, but professionally speaking, yes I sincerely believe this to be the case. However, I'll be the first to admit that we are talking purely theoretical here, and so my comments are technically subjective. In any case, that I'm here at all represents my highers' continued interest." Lori directed all of her attention to a single key, repeatedly tapping away, seemingly without regard to the effects. "I'm out. Glen's locked me out." There was disappointment on her face. "What were you saying?"

Devlin wanted to explain, his zeal to do so overpowering the lagging fatigue that he'd otherwise fought hard to suppress all day, but Glen re-appeared before he'd progressed much past sharing his suspicions surrounding the list of names. He was suddenly reluctant to continue.

"Don't let me stop you, Devlin, please continue." Glen edged forward as if genuinely interested and oblivious to Devlin's reticence to explain further.

"Sorry Glen, but you being here makes me feel a little seditious, particularly given that Lori here is clearly no longer welcome."

"I'd be terribly disappointed if Lori left, particularly when doing so would leave me so understaffed. Lori?"

"I just figured that given my access has been removed, then that was paramount to a warning of my sacking."

"Certainly not. I've just disabled your access to the Research Interface is all. Curiosity is one thing, but not when it's as overtly subversive as yours. Don't get me wrong Lori, I've appreciated your curiosity until now, even if it was covertly professional in its intentions, but not if you're going to interfere."

"But my access to the Research Interface is still fine," Devlin commented incredulously. He couldn't help but test his own access while listening to Glen speak. "So I'm still OK?"

"Of course. I sense you are on the cusp of learning something Devlin, and I'd very much prefer for you to make this realisation here and now."

"But …"

"The Research Interface is there to be used, Devlin," Glen hinted without subtlety, adding, "I'm not the bad guy in this."

"I just don't know how Tania fits in."

"I'm only surprised that you haven't found this out for yourself."

"I was going to…"

"And you'll do what about it?" Glen pressed.

"I don't know."

"Sure you do, and you'll do the right thing."

"But .."

"But what, Devlin? You do your homework and you make up your own mind." Glen nodded to Lori and left the room, leaving Lori initially silent and Devlin making faces to himself as if thinking.

"Who's Tania?" Lori asked, keen to coax Devlin from his distant state.

"I was going to explain Tania before Glen re-appeared."

"Who's she, and what's she to you?"

"She's no-one to *me*!" Devlin replied, sensing a hint of jealousy in Lori's tone. "To explain I have to tell you about pretty well everything that's happened to me over the last few days."

Chapter - 79.

Devlin couldn't believe how quickly Lori assimilated his protracted recap of the preceding days. He expected her eyes to glaze over as his explanation turned into a saga, but instead it seemed that she was all the more interested with every word that he said. She didn't ask a mass of questions and immediately formulated a plan. He made no secret of his appreciation either, deferring to her to take the lead and allowing her to take control of his keyboard.

The only discussion between Lori and Devlin related to the order that they undertook their research. Lori was keen to start with Malcolm, whereas Devlin was adamant that as everything and everyone pointed to Tania, then surely she should be investigated first. Only after Lori conceded that her covert investigation, until now at least, had yielded little did she agree to look first at Tania. Devlin then wanted to learn what he could of the man that Angie had described. He still felt for her, in spite of whatever she'd said about him.

"I need *everything* you know about her," asked Lori.

"I don't know a lot, really just her name. I could maybe remember her address if I tried."

"That won't be enough. If you're vague, you're punished for it. If you enter a name or a word, it tells you everything that could possibly be associated with that word from all of its sources." Lori gave a cursory look to the security camera mounted high on the wall against the ceiling. "You enter more, you narrow your search. Unlike Google, this will capture your intent."

Devlin removed the list from his pocket, anticipating Lori's interest. "Her name came up when I tried a list of recent readers names."

Lori paused a moment, her hands hovering over the keyboard. "Summarise everything you know about her."

Devlin cautiously and sparingly offered names and facts. He focussed less on the banal details of his meetings with her, and more on what he'd gleaned from what Whitely and Reymond had said. Lori executed the search as soon as she was confident that Devlin was complete.

Clearly more adept at the use of the Research Interface, Lori had managed to order the result. While Devlin noticed that the result still amounted to 38 pages worth, at least it was chronologically ordered which would make it substantially more logical than the seemingly randomised results that he'd seen in the past. Presented before him was the life, or at least part of the life, of Tania Wilson. They started to read, each silently communicating to the other when they were ready to move to the next page.

After a few pages of reading, Devlin decided that 'unfortunate' was the best word to describe Tania's life. Her employment history could have been interpreted as eclectic, as if she wanted to sample working life in as many roles as possible, but it wasn't. She'd drifted from job to job, each a little lower in profile than the last. From senior management she'd progressed to less and less responsibility, until she wasn't considered responsible enough to fetch a cup of coffee for herself. Family and friends obviously helped her get jobs but they couldn't help her keep them.

Somewhere along the way, substance abuse became obvious in her employment and life in general, though it was difficult to assess whether her decline was caused by the alcohol and other drugs, or vice versa. In any case, if her professional life was a mess, there could be no mistake that her personal life was worse. She managed to isolate herself with antisocial behaviour evident with drug induced highs, and depressive or hungover lows. One by one or in droves, friends and acquaintances gradually had enough. Tania's circle of friends, much like her circle of influence, shrank accordingly.

Devlin glossed over some of the names from Glen's list, but not all. Many recent readers knew Tania to some degree; Ikel was her dealer for a time, and David was her counsellor of some description. Perhaps the others were there too, mentioned by reference instead of name.

It could easily have been overlooked, but Devlin also noted his association to her; the guy he killed was her relative. That Tania didn't broach this point when they'd met spoke more of her isolation than any remarkable forgiveness on her part.

About the only thing that was improving in Tania's life was the volume of police interest. The more Devlin read, the more he accepted that police sources constituted at least part of the repository that the Research Interface accessed. She had a few convictions, each for relatively minor incursions against public decency, and episodes of drink-driving, public drunkenness and assault.

Devlin identified references to the accident that killed the Detective's daughter, Whitely's wife. In reading the media reports of the accident and public outcry that ensued from her acquittal, he felt renewed sadness for both the Detective and Whitely. The tabloids had obviously latched onto the story and went the extra mile to paint Tania as the one who destroyed lives, particularly the lives of Whitely and the Detective. As much as he understood the popular outrage, Devlin also empathised with Tania for how she was portrayed.

Except that the Detective's account confirmed everything that was and wasn't in the media releases, Devlin felt for how she was demonised.

She was involved in a mass of other incidents ranging from corporate fraud to theft and ultimately to narcotics, for which she'd been spared convictions, typically for a lack of evidence or dubious levels of involvement. The popular press kept her close, and it seemed like the slightest hint of Police suspicion was enough for her to return to the public eye. Devlin couldn't help but be sceptical as to whether the media was following the Police, or vice versa. There could be no denying that the media got their information from somewhere.

"So what does this tell us?" Lori asked as soon as she finished reading. She ran her fingers through her short hair, and tried in vain to draw some imaginary bulk into what would have been a ponytail had her hair been longer. "It tells me…"

Glen appeared again. "Thanks Lori, but I don't want to hear what it tells you, though I appreciate your refined instruction on the finer points of my Research Interface. It's nothing personal, I just don't want your opinion to taint the developing thoughts of Devlin here."

"So what do you want me to do?" Lori asked, clearly expecting more of a reprimand.

"Do what you like, but not here." He thrust his chin at the door. Lori stood and left the bunker, dragging her hand casually over Devlin's shoulder as she passed.

Comfortable that he was now alone with Devlin, Glen looked at the keyboard and asked., "So now what are you going to do?"

"Tim? Tania's brother?" Devlin asked tentatively, as if subtly asking for Glen's guidance or concurrence.

"Why him?"

"Because David as much as suggested some responsibility for his death, so surely that's something."

"I'd suggest that such an investigation at this time wouldn't help you."

"Alright," Devlin thought for a moment. "I want to know about the guy from Angie's message. I expected to see his name somewhere in Tania's history." He edged himself closer to the keyboard and started keying in all of the names and details mentioned in Angie's message.

Glen nodded his concurrence with every detail he saw typed. He smiled as soon as he saw Devlin execute the search.

It was remarkable how the Research Interface charted Nebojsa's history. He'd managed to be granted asylum from the former Yugoslavia in what was later red flagged as an administrative error. Only after he'd been welcomed did new information come to light that he had more to fear from retribution than persecution in his homeland. Some bureaucrat had buried the truth rather than expose his department's mistake. In a stroke of pen, he'd been allowed to re-invent himself as an impoverished, wartime refugee ready to embrace a new country and a new start. Devlin recognised Tania's brother's name as the bureaucrat, surely localising the fallout from his sister's error.

The Research Interface was awash with pictures of Nebojsa with famous and less famous faces. Whether or not he was genuinely an orphan on coming to this country, it seemed that he now had no shortage of friends.

The guy was an animal too. Devlin waded through massed evidence, not just speculation which proved that Angie was only one of many to be victimised by the guy. He didn't bother counting them; that the list only started with his arrival in this country suggested that there were surely others, and he wondered what the guy had done beforehand.

It was obvious too that the guy was being closely followed, but less clear as to who or which organisation, or *organisations*, were keeping tabs on him. Devlin was comforted that it was more than likely Police, but that only spawned thoughts as to why he would be allowed to continue. Devlin also marvelled how appropriate his real name was. Nebojsa. It meant 'fearless'.

"Everyone's suggested that LastGasp' sees information being passed onto Police. So why's this guy still around?" Devlin asked with more than a little puzzlement. "Surely he should be locked up …or euthanized."

"Derrell thought the same thing. But what does this tell you?" Glen asked, watching Devlin closely, but he fell short of any attempt to make eye contact, as if he was looking more to gauge Devlin's reaction than engage him. "I'll tell you almost anything you want to know."

"I don't get it," Devlin began. "Maybe I should be looking at Angie and not this guy."

"Or maybe you're not looking hard enough."

Devlin looked over the Research Interface again, this time less pressured to read quickly. "I feel like I'm looking for something, and when I find it, it's not going to be good for me, you or LastGasp' either."

"I could care less what happens to LastGaspStore. Technically, it isn't even mine now, anyway."

"But …."

"I've never cared that LastGasp' persists for my own gains. I'm not so naïve as to think that you're not capable of the maths necessary to work out that you guys are all paid inordinately highly for what is essentially a free internet service. Clearly I'm paying you out of my own pocket rather than the proceeds of whatever sponsorship the site generates.

"As I said when we first met, I'm more interested in the service that LastGaspStore provides. I was sure that the world would see it the same way, and on the main, I've been right."

"But regardless of whether it's *yours* or not, it's still your baby."

"Bastard child is more accurate. I've been forced to see the good and bad, the best and the worst of people, and then I've seen it corrupted."

"So why don't you kill it? Terminate LastGasp' and just walk away. Surely the money that you'd be able to walk away with would buy a clear conscience."

"I've been trying to for years. The problem is that at inception I didn't realise that LastGaspStore was so corruptible. Of course I understood the attractiveness of the repository, but not the extent to which it could be exploited. I couldn't walk away, in much the same way that a nuclear power could hardly leave their weapons in the hands of some apes just because they'd grown weary of their responsibility. Whether I liked it or not, I was trapped by my creation."

Devlin picked up the semantics of what he'd heard. "You said, *was* trapped."

"Indeed I did. Initially I thought like Wonka and his chocolate factory. I couldn't walk away, but I could retire, leaving it in the hands of someone I trusted. And you'd think it would be simple.

"Where everyone before Derrell had issues about my vision to be a passive observer in the simple service of delivering a posthumous message, Derrell changed the rules. He was the one who suggested that my vision was flawed, and the one who suggested that I needed the means to do a little homework."

"The Research Interface?"

Glen nodded. "At the time I saw the merit in his suggestion, and while I had my suspicions, I tended to focus on the upside."

"So what did he do?"

"You know, different people, different readers more specifically, responded differently. I discovered that Derrell was doing the rounds of hospices. It seemed he was befriending masses of terminally ill patients, encouraging them to become LastGaspStore members no less.

"The guy was the embodiment of what I wanted for LastGasp'. I'd found the 'Charlie' for my chocolate factory."

"So what was the problem?"

"I called it an ideological misclose at the time, but I don't know what I'd call it now. The problem was that we basically wanted the same thing, except that we wanted to achieve it differently.

"So why aren't you trapped now?"

"I'm probably just as trapped as before but with acceptance comes comfort. Now I'm just more comfortable with what I've created, and you can thank your friend Malcolm for that."

"Why?"

"I know I explained that Derrell represented a 'changing of the guard', but I don't think I explained that this was more literal than cliché. My readers are effectively my guards, and before Derrell, their commitment was to the task at hand, to guard and protect LastGaspStore. But those who followed had their own agendas."

"Is that why they were killed?" Devlin risked the cheap shot as he re-scanned the list.

Glen didn't bite. "You know, Sampson Burbino had the same concerns as you. He joined me towards the end of Derrell's time."

"The Detective mentioned that he thinks that Malcolm is actually this Burbino guy."

"Quite," said Glen. "For a time after Derrell, there was only Carson, Sam and myself. It was hot on the heels of Derrell's departure and I was decidedly wary, but we settled into a rhythm and things went well."

"Sam's not on my list."

"Sam's not on any list and that was intentional. I knew I was on a winner with him. Some personal issues had forced him into isolation from when he was young, so he was denied a lot of corrupting influences, but of course he didn't live his entire life in a bubble, so he wasn't a saint by any means.

"I still remember when I interrupted Carson and Sam discussing the future of LastGaspStore. It didn't occur to me at the time because they weren't looking to breach my system, or otherwise bring it down. The status quo worked for me."

"So what did they want?"

"I know you've got your concerns about my protocols, all readers do, but Carson and Sam went even better. The fact is that there's always someone worthy of attention, the issue lies in what's done thereafter. Most want to punish someone, and I accept that. Readers are only human, and I wouldn't have it any other way.

"You know. The reason why I recruited Carson is that I understood the need for a woman's empathy at LastGaspStore. I don't like to generalise, but I figured that women would be better at this, and a lack of testosterone would reduce the potential for a liability like many of those who preceded her. Again, I say that different people have responded differently to the stresses of being a reader. Some change, some don't.

"Carson and Sam both made an effort to pull me to their side. Ordinarily readers have a nasty habit of feigning dumbfounded silence, but they both felt confident enough to argue their case. Carson suggested that the protocols were crap because they didn't see bad people go down. Sam, in a sense, agreed."

"So what was the problem?"

"Semantics arguably. Sam wanted the good to be protected, at whatever cost, personally, and to LastGasp'. Carson was less interested in protecting the good so long as those worthy go punished.

"It's all about the greater good, Devlin. It's always about the greater good."

"So what happened to Carson?"

"Carson lost sight of the greater good. Anything else that I could tell you about her wouldn't help."

"Wouldn't help you, or me?"

"Wouldn't help anyone," Glens face softened. "I'll tell you something about me, and I tell you this only because I think that you might understand this better than the others."

Devlin heard this and sub-consciously felt a little odd, as if he had achieved something the others had not. He wondered if this meant that he was any more, or less, at risk than he was previously.

"David and the others felt that their role was one of community service, and there's some element of truth in this."

"And what about Sam?"

"Sam moved on. We had a parting of ways, of sorts. We both understood how LastGaspStore was corruptible, and unlike others, we both weren't prepared to see it further corrupted."

"So why would Malcolm, Sam, change his name? If he's hiding from you and you know his new identity ..."

"He's not hiding from me. If I ever wanted to, I guess I could track him down, but that's beside the point. I don't want to find him, just as I don't really want him found."

"Why, if you're friends?"

"We *are* friends, but ideologically opposed and now distant. When last we spoke, he accused me of being just as bad as some of the people that we read about every day, and I'm not just talking about LastGaspStore messages here either. If I knew someone was at risk or at harm and I do nothing, am I guilty? Perhaps.

"It was then that we parted. If the Police and others could be so content to sit on information and do nothing, then I didn't want to facilitate any further corruption."

"So what did Sam, Malcolm, want?"

"Malcolm wanted to use the guilty."

"How can you use guilt?"

Glen scratched his head and sat forward in his seat. "What would you do if you met or even discovered the person who outed you?"

"Not only is he already dead …"

"So you maintain, and thanks to you," Glen interrupted. "But humour me."

Devlin thought about the confident way that Glen had raised the point and the doubt that it left in him was emptying. "Are you saying that he's not the one who outed me?"

"How should I know? My point is that you clearly aren't certain, even in hindsight. And look at what happened."

Devlin raised his eyebrows and made to defend himself from the accusation, but Glen held up his hand as if to retract the comment. "Whether you had cause or not is irrelevant. He's dead, you're not and when the media loses interest you'll be able to continue with your life."

"But if he's innocent then …"

"He's still dead. What you are grappling with is the question of whether or not he deserved it.

"Until now you've defended yourself with passion that you did what you did for the right reasons. In so doing you killed a family man over what amounted to a personal grudge. Now tell me what you'd do if you learnt, without question, that he was *not* the one who made the accusations."

"I'd …" Devlin couldn't even begin to frame a response. The thought ate away at him. He remembered that when his nightmare began, he was naïvely confident that the world, or at least a jury, would see the provocation that led to the whole incident.

"You don't really need to tell me, but consider this. What if you learned, before or after, that the world was better off without him. Wife beater, rapist, serial killer, income tax evader. It doesn't matter. How would that change how you feel now?"

"I'd sleep better."

"What if only you knew the truth?"

"I'd live with it."

"So you'd live out your life knowing that what you did served a greater purpose, regardless of whether anyone else knew?"

Devlin finally gathered where this was heading. "The greater good?"

Glen nodded. "I'll bet you're itching to use the Research Interface at this point. It won't change anything of course."

"But I have to know."

"Just make sure that you can handle each of the possibilities. That he's *not* the one, that he *is* the one and you're now public enemy number one for what amounts to a community service, and that he is the one but not the monster that you'd hoped."

"I can handle it."

"Alright then," Glen offered. "Because others couldn't."

Chapter - 80.

Devlin pushed himself away from the keyboard until the wheels of his chair stopped at the wall. He remained fixated on the screen, but he wasn't able to read anything but the largest type from that range. It didn't matter. He was finished.

"Was it worth it?" Glen asked sincerely.

"Probably not."

"You see Devlin, in the wrong hands, all the remorse or anger in the world won't change anything. But in the right hands, there is opportunity.

"You've got two, at least two, choices here. You could keep on with your anger at the world, but that won't get you anywhere. The world doesn't care, and neither do I. I see enough regret every day, as have you. Missed opportunities, lost moments. Regret and loss is everywhere and I don't want to see you waste your life on something that will be old news before the dust settles on your grave or you make your first parole review.

"Or you could get on with your life. Move on. That's why I recruited you."

"So your employing me is … what exactly?"

"Just like I've said, I just don't want you to head down a dead end path."

Devlin was incredulous. "Bullshit! Look me in the eyes and tell me that this is all to protect my interests."

"I sincerely do have your best interests at heart, but I won't look you in the eyes. It's not you, it's me. I do it, or more correctly *don't* do it with anyone."

"So why's that?"

"Years of conditioning!" Glen struggled a smile. "Others too have confronted me on the subject. They'd argue that they could never tell if I was telling them the truth unless I looked them in the face. *'The truth is in your eyes'*, they'd say."

"I tend to share that opinion."

"The fact is that I don't look at people because I don't want to know whether they are telling me the truth."

For arguably the first time, Devlin understood something of what Glen was saying. "So if you're looking out for me, why didn't you look out for David and the others?"

"You have to understand that until Derrell, my readers were there for me, but after Derrell and Sam, I changed my focus." Disappointment was obvious on Glen's face. "I've felt for each and every one of those who died because I wanted to help them. I figured that exposed to other people's secrets, they might learn something and save themselves.

"Most recently, David, perhaps found it too confronting to have his bias for forgiveness challenged. Maybe he could tolerate it particularly on account of his professional past, but not when immersed in guilt all day, every day. Whether that guilt was his or someone else's is no longer important.

"And Ikel. I thought I could change him by showing him how he and others like him have affected people. The problem with him was that he was so fickle that he was oblivious to my efforts and came to see LastGaspStore as a cash-cow and a means to meet bereaved women. Before you ask, I'm not above sadness that he died, but you saw the way he drove. It was just a matter of time. Perhaps the LastGaspStore message that he received from his uncle gave way to some great epiphany.

"So why then would Whitely feel the need to warn me?"

"Whitely's heart's in the right place. I trust that you know of his history, his shared history with your friend the Detective. You might know that he was arguably the least corruptible of my readers and I was appreciative for that. I thought I could drag him from his shell and get his mind off revenge. In that sense I was partially successful; Whitely's still alive and out of jail."

"And Malcolm?"

Glen took a look at his watch after first shaking his wrist and holding it to his ear. "Can I ask you to hold that thought, your question, for a few hours."

"Fine," Devlin reluctantly accepted the request with a sigh.

Glen stood and stretched his arms high such that his palms approached the ceiling. He gave Devlin a heart-felt but gentle pat on the shoulder. "Relax. You'll understand more before too long."

Devlin shrugged as if accepting the suggestion, but with reservation. He tried for an answer to a different but he presumed related question. "So why tolerate the Police here at all?"

"I'm sorry?"

"Why allow Police on staff in the first place?"

"For so long as they are trying to get in, then I know that LastGaspStore is secure. When they stop trying, then theoretically I should be worried."

"I think you've been breached."

"I doubt that."

"Don't you think that it is amazingly co-incidental that Malcolm would meet Angie, and that Malcolm would tell her about me."

"It's not co-incidental, but not important, just the same."

Chapter - 81.

Tania woke in unfamiliar surroundings but in a familiar place. It was daylight, early morning judging by the lack of any traffic hum, and her memory of the preceding night was patchy.

She knew the drill. She first allowed her body to check for any significant injuries before she even moved, and only after she was satisfied that nothing was broken did she make any effort to roll off her stomach onto her back. As soon as she moved her legs she felt the constriction at her knees, her underwear for sure, and she knew the rest instantly. She began her ordered injury assessment, first face, then limb by limb. She anticipated the pains and damage, but still checked them off in a mental 'top to toe' checklist just the same. Her hair was sure to be a mess, even as short as it was, but at least it didn't smell. Her face felt like orange peel, even after scratching off a little gravel, but at least there was no bruising and no grazes, so nothing that wouldn't be fixed with a long shower and adequate hydration, water not alcohol. Her jaw was stiff, but that would pass, as would the taste of rubber. She still had most of her clothes, though she wouldn't be considered presentable in any forum. Getting home and changed, dressed, would be a priority, but not before checking the rest of her body. Sore breasts? Check. Sore, sticky, wet loins? Double check. Sore ass? You betcha. She hoped she still had some haemorrhoid cream at home.

She reached for her handbag that was, gratefully, within reach, but didn't bother to check its contents. There was nothing in it yesterday, and there was sure to be nothing of any value in there now. Tampons and cheap makeup were never the subject of any

357

robbery, and if she had any money to begin with she wouldn't be feeling the after effects of god knows how many penetrations now. She was not up to seeing if any or all of the condoms that she always kept at hand had been used, but judging by the squelching in her loins she was not hopeful.

She rose to her feet, grabbing the adjacent dumpster bin for support. Once upright, she was happy that her mobility was not impeded. Being off the ground allowed her to get a better grasp on where she was, and she recognised the back-side of the bar across the road from her flat. Even in her still clouded mental state she could smile that at least she didn't have far to go home.

Chapter - 82.

True to his word, Devlin kept his mouth shut and mind open for the drive. He had no idea where he was going, and Glen seemed content to keep him in the dark. Glen seemed generally contented, even bordering on being exuberant as he drove.

"Are you going to talk to me at all?" Devlin asked.

"There's not a great deal to say. You'll know more soon enough."

"But if I want to understand now. What harm could it do for me to know more."

"Knowledge is a powerful thing."

"Whitely said knowledge isn't truth."

"Very true," Glen replied succinctly.

Chapter - 83.

Once again Tania exercised her oft repeated plan to wash away the past, hopeful. Standing under the shower, her face pressed against the perpetually cool tiles and her back to the soothing heat of the water, memories flooded into her now sobering state. If only the memories would disappear down the drain like the residue of a cheap hair colour. As ever, she knew she'd run out of hot water long before that happened.

She was thankful that her memory of last night was lost forever, more than likely blacked out in a wash of spirits and never to return, rather than just suppressed. The body would heal, it always did, but her mind's wounds were accumulating faster than she could expect to recover. Each painful memory just made those before it worse, and no matter how much she drank, she would always sober up eventually.

In some ways, she figured that Tim understood to some extent. No matter what happened, no matter how many times she'd fallen off the wagon, he'd always stayed as close as she'd allow. Unlike the rest, her so called 'friends' who'd distanced themselves gradually or ritually broken contact.

Family was another matter entirely. That Tim had been her sole surviving relative was an isolating thought, but in retrospect, as each of her other family members had passed she'd grown progressively ambivalent to how they each had actually died. Whether they'd died before their time, like the question of 'how', was largely irrelevant. They were dead now and nothing would bring them back. Even just thinking about it, she felt the usual anger that her family never understood her pain, so whether they were alive or dead was of no great benefit to her. In any case, she knew that she'd long since used up all the favours and goodwill on offer from friends and family.

No matter how much she expected it, Tania was always surprised when the hot water did eventually run out. The jolt of cold and the subsequent frantic rush to extricate herself from the freezing water had a tendency to awaken her from her delirium. She'd be aroused in the middle of a memory, and with the randomness of a roulette wheel she'd hope that the house would show some pity and some luck would come her way. The reality, however, was that the wheel was loaded and she didn't even have a bet on the table. There was no upside to her memories.

She marvelled too that it was high time for her to be given a break. For what seemed an eternity now her life had been going from bad to worse. Friends were long gone, family were gone, career was gone. If there was any justice in this life, she was sure that she'd more than paid for anything and everything that she'd done.

Chapter - 84.

Devlin was surprised to arrive at the café near Tania's house. While Glen had taken a completely different route and even parked in a back laneway several streets away, Devlin recognised the smell of bad coffee before he could even see the café. Even more surprising was the fact that both Whitely and the Detective were waiting for them.

There was no sense of reunion from either Whitely or the Detective, and barely any acknowledgement other than for them each to check their watches simultaneously. Instead, they just edged around their table, as if to allow Glen to occupy a position of seniority between them.

Devlin remained standing for a time, but eventually seated himself at the opposite side of the table facing the others.

Glen beckoned the waitress, who reacted at first as if such customer service was significantly outside her job description. She looked as if she was prepared to stare down Glen while she made some obscene gestures under the counter, out of sight of any of the customers. It was unclear whether she responded to Glen's reciprocated stare, or if she just felt an odd need to interact with a customer, but in any case she sauntered to the table. Glen placed an order for himself and deferred to the others for anything that they too might like. Devlin steered clear of the coffees, but didn't feel like sharing any warning. He smiled, somewhat relaxed by the fact that he knew something that Glen didn't. Glen thanked the attendant cum waitress cynically for her 'above and beyond commitment to customer service' and paid up front for the table's order and included a sizeable tip. She trudged her way back to her domain at the counter, either oblivious or ignorant to Glen's comment. Devlin was all the more appreciative that his order, a simple can of coke, couldn't be tampered with, if she suddenly understood what Glen had said.

By the time that the order arrived, Devlin was comfortable in his seat, but unsettled by the fact that no-one was talking to him. There was an easy, bordering on jovial mood between the Detective, Glen and Whitely, but they seemed content to continue their banter between themselves without making any effort to include him in their discussion. He put up with it for a few minutes, but eventually he felt an overwhelming need for his subtle isolation to end. "I've kept an open mind for long enough, Glen. It's about to snap shut."

"Relax Devlin. Just a little longer," Glen appeased.

"Haven't I waited long enough?"

Whitely laughed heartily, much to the amusement of the Detective before turning serious as the laughter subsided. "What the fuck do you know about waiting?"

"So what am I waiting for?"

"You're waiting to round out your understanding," offered Glen as he rested a placative, calming hand on Whitely's shoulder. "What Whitely and Alan here could have said was that they've waited substantially longer than you."

"So we're here to see Tania?"

"Of sorts," replied Glen. "I'll let them answer more fully." He slid his chair backwards away from the table, as if to leave centre stage.

"You know Devlin, I've spent years loathing that woman on a personal level, and until relatively recently I've had little to do with her professionally," Detective Reymond began. "Of course, with the death of her brother, I'd be lying if there wasn't something bittersweet in seeing her in pain. But it's an abstract kind of feeling, just sitting back and effectively revelling in someone else's misfortune. There's nothing *legally* wrong with it, and probably nothing *morally* wrong with it. So should I feel bad that the bitch who took away my life should experience a little loss?"

Pending silence suggested that the Detective actually wanted a reply. "Probably not," said Devlin. "I'm assuming of course that you weren't directly implicated in what happened to her brother, but on the surface at least I see what you're saying."

"The question is whether I'm an active or a passive observer. How close do I have to be to causing that misfortune before I hit your moral speed-bump? Before I've done the wrong thing?"

"I don't suppose you'd care to be more specific," suggested Devlin.

"Fair enough." Reymond drank from his coffee, his face shrivelling up like a prune at the bitterness of the brew. He looked to Whitely, as if warning of disclosure. "You know over the years I've sat back and waited, appalled at my own inaction, but too gutless, or possibly smart, to do something about it. Unlike some of us, I couldn't act on my own suppressed want for revenge for fear of the implications, which in itself is comical given that I had, have, nothing left. Unlike some of us, I couldn't bring myself to partake of petty, or more serious, acts of revenge. I couldn't leave the contents of sharps or other biohazard containers in soap. I couldn't break into her home only to stick toothbrushes in my ass and leave without any indication that I'd even been there. Unlike others." Whitely took a protracted drink from his mug.

"You haven't explained why we're here," Devlin said dismissively. "And Glen, you still owe me where Malcolm fits into this."

"Relax Devlin. It won't be too long now."

Glen's comment did nothing to settle Devlin's anxiety, but it was apparent after looking at the others that he was the only one who was not relaxed. Whitely was struggling a smile in between long periods where he appeared to observe the other café patrons. The Detective was similarly settled as he rhythmically and continually stirred his cup. Glen himself seemed more interested in checking his watch. Periodically, someone would look to the street or scan the other patrons of the café, and doing so seemed to alert the others to something. In a weird kind of way, Devlin felt like he was watching a wildlife documentary where one animal's heightened anxiety alerted all those around. The thought made Devlin look at Reymond's ears the next time his eyes drifted from his cup, as if they would be furry and erect, listening for an approaching lion.

Chapter - 85.

Devlin's wait dragged on, but he seemed to be the only one in any way perturbed. Eventually, he asked, "Can we talk about Malcolm then?"

At first, Devlin assumed that it was his question that made Glen, Whitely and the Detective sit up and take notice. They stopped what they were doing, and Devlin hoped that at last his question hit a chord such that he'd finally get the answers he craved. When a reply did not come immediately, he wasn't too surprised. Being seated across the table from the others, Devlin felt the heat of their stares. He saw the Detective's tired eyes brighten and Whitely even removed his sunglasses to reveal his battered face made moderately presentable by probably a hint of makeup. Even Glen was breaking his own golden rule, staring right through him so brazenly that his eyes could not have been focussed. It was then that it occurred to Devlin that no-one was actually looking at him.

Devlin turned to see a lone male at the counter. The guy was well dressed; good cut of a suit and re-soled expensive looking black leather shoes, but Devlin couldn't tell much more about him until he turned around. He figured that it was Malcolm, and the quiet fixation from the others was paramount to a *'he's here, ask him yourself'*. But then as he watched, the guy pivoted a turn away from the counter and left. It wasn't Malcolm. In the few steps it took him to cross from the counter to the entry the guy had managed to look down on everyone present with disdain, which at least gave Devlin the opportunity to see the guy's face for a fraction of a second. The electronic chime of the door sensor marked his exit.

As if hearing the chime was a cue to continue any pending conversation, Devlin turned again to the front, expecting that someone would recover from the distraction of the visitor. Assuming of course that Malcolm's arrival had been anticipated, he expected to see perhaps a little disappointment or even inconvenience at having their wait extended. Instead, he saw and felt smiles. The Detective wore a warm glow, and even his eyes being closed couldn't hide the contentment that he obviously felt. Whitely was beaming such that a few of his wounds were starting to weep, if not bleed outright. Glen himself was more subdued, sitting with a knowing grin and his arms folded.

Devlin was about to re-ask his question about Malcolm, or possibly to ask about the change in the mood at the table when Whitely stood and put on his jacket from the back of his chair. It was only then that Devlin noticed that Whitely had clearly gone to some effort for the morning and was out of his dressing gown, and the smell of his house had not followed him. Devlin wondered how much showering that took. Whitely rested his hand on Glen's shoulder while he walked to the Detective. The Detective too stood and received Whitely's protracted embrace. Whitely then nodded in passing to Devlin as he headed for the door. The Detective was more formal, opting to shake Glen's hand before he too sauntered from the table into daylight.

"Where are they going?" Devlin asked of Glen incredulously. "I'm no wiser now, and they're not going to help now that they're gone, are they?"

Glen beckoned the waitress over again. "Whitely and the Detective are every bit the reason why you needed to be here, to learn. You didn't need to speak to Malcolm." He ordered more coffees, knowing full well that Devlin was drinking Coke. "I want you to figure it out and understand."

Devlin kept his mouth shut for no other reason than he didn't know what to say.

Chapter - 86.

Sun on his face, Malcolm sat in a child's swing in the playground looking at the bank of windows, one of which was surely Tania's living room. Exactly which window was Tania's was not important. He knew she was inside and he didn't need to see her face at the window to confirm the fact.

Malcolm smiled and sighed for a job well done. Thereafter, the culmination of this particular project was something of an anti-climax, much like the rest. He couldn't share in any celebratory drinks, he wouldn't receive any pats on the back, and he knew he'd never hear an appreciative word from anyone. His efforts would go un-rewarded, but they would not go un-noticed. Not that he undertook this project for anyone but himself, but selected people would sleep better for his efforts, regardless of whether they understood or cared for the role that he had played. It didn't matter. He could look at himself in the mirror with pride for what he did, but it was just unfortunate that others couldn't share his pride and were on the main oblivious to what he did.

There were few regrets in Malcolm's memory. His mother never had any time for thoughts or emotions that weren't implicitly positive. Just as he didn't allow his bad days to interfere with his good, he didn't let bad thoughts drag down his plans. He focussed on a greater good. Doing so allowed him to feel pride, even if he couldn't share it.

There was one notable exception. To make a point to Glen he had done one thing of which he was not proud. Admittedly, there were actions which he recalled with ambivalence, neither positively nor negatively, but only one thing that made him feel what others would describe as 'regret'.

His mood on the turn, he wasn't thinking clearly when he felt backed into a corner after an ongoing discussion with Glen. The mistake was his and his alone; he couldn't blame anyone but himself. For what he'd deemed naive arrogance, Glen was not prepared to listen to his concerns and so Malcolm decided to show him. With the impetuousness of a child, he stormed out of LastGasp' and into the first internet café. There he'd watched a live news feed, waiting for someone to die, like the angel of death himself.

It was the middle of the night, and Malcolm waited for many hours before it happened. Sirens and fire engines coincided with a flurry of news traffic; the media alerted to a fire at a little known suburban chemical facility. Two Police officers working out of hours to legally supplement their incomes were injured and the first news crews couldn't help themselves in a rush to identify them.

Malcolm did not play any odds to make his point. He prepared two messages. He knew what to do, it just required a little homework to get right.

For the officer with family, '*his*' message was a simple, heartfelt stream of words much as he imagined his own mother would have said on her last night. Perhaps she did say them, but he never heard them. His brief research indicated that while the officer, Robert Duffton, and his wife were having more than their share of marital issues, '*his*' message focussed only on the upside and potential for a complete reconciliation. He didn't think there was anything to be gained in any mention of any of the negatives. He included an anecdote for each of his children and an earnest request that they grow to live and love and know that they were loved. It seemed appropriate, particularly when he was already a LastGasp' member.

The other police officer, sadly, was known to him. Malcolm understood their history following long discussions on the matter with Glen. Albert Fenton. Glen owed him a debt for the role that he'd played in the Leon Newman debacle, but Glen's persistent scepticism with police interest forced him to keep Albert largely at arm's length. When Malcolm thought about what message was necessary or appropriate for Albert, he struggled. The guy was alone and with a dubious sexual orientation it was unlikely that he'd ever father any children to justify the need to pass on any endearing message. It struck him that most of Albert's adult life had been spent with his friend, right down to the fact that they were both now injured together. Malcolm decided it was time that Alert was outed.

It was a spiteful thing to do. Malcolm knew it at the time but he did it anyway. He now understood that some things can't be undone and some secrets are better kept. Albert's determination proved it. Not one to fear, he did sometimes worry if Albert himself would eventually be able to see the greater good of *this* episode.

In the meantime, Malcolm looked forward and focussed on the future, his next project. Nebojsa's time had come.

Chapter - 87.

The coffee had not improved in the 24 hours since Devlin last sampled some from the café. Yesterday, he was oblivious to how bad it would be, but today even though he was expecting it, he was too distracted to brace himself fully. Glen appeared to be content to flit through any of a pile of magazines and Devlin found the guy's smugness intolerable. Between the coffee and the look on Glen's face, he found it hard to even think coherently.

"Are you comfortable with things yet?" asked Glen.

"Not really. Perhaps if it was Malcolm who appeared before Whitely and the Detective left, then maybe I might have put it together by now."

"But it wasn't," Glen said nonchalantly.

Devlin continued thinking, but there was nothing logical in the manner that he thought. As confused as he was, his thoughts darted randomly and spasmodically between what he'd heard, what he'd seen, what he'd read, and who he'd met over the preceding days. He thought about the list of names, as apparently incomplete as it was, and how Glen had been so disinterested himself in what it represented, but how he'd been so supportive for related discovery. He thought about Tania and how his initial sadness for her recent loss had evolved through suspicion when David's message entered the mix. When he learnt of her role in the death of Whitely's wife, Alan's daughter, he couldn't help but soften his sadness, as if her loss was offset, even lessened, by the loss that she'd caused to someone else. He didn't allow himself to dwell on whether she deserved it, but that made him ponder David's references to 'karma'. If karma was really at play, or divine intervention as he might have described it, then it did beg the question as to how some degree of balance might be achieved.

Devlin tried not to think about David's death. He didn't really know David, and if he was honest, he didn't like him either. With enough time, the simple fact that he was gone would not rate a mention in his memory, except for the way that he'd been found, or more importantly that Devlin himself had found him. He could have done without *that* picture on his mind. A mass of pallid skin spinning centrally around the room on a fast cycle above a suite full of blood covered furniture. He avoided any consideration as to why David might have done it to himself, primarily because he wasn't certain that he had actually done it to himself. That the Police or the coroner would inevitably make their decision on that front was justification enough for him to think about 'why' rather than 'who'. Perhaps David was carrying a volume of baggage and stress from his past that caught up with him or wouldn't leave him. Perhaps the guy found the stress at LastGasp' too much. Perhaps these stresses were one and the same. Devlin felt as if he had made progress.

That David would join LastGasp' with some stresses, regardless of his background or history was a reasonable assumption. The guy was human. Everyone has a history. Glen and all his disciples had told him that. The hotel manager had even said that all of Glen's employees attracted media attention which was sure to be a sign that they came to LastGasp' with at least some history. Thereafter surely media attention would have to be directed squarely at LastGasp' itself, rather than individual employees … and that couldn't happen. So David joined and LastGasp' didn't make his problems go away. Maybe LastGasp' even made his problems worse or wouldn't allow him to move on.

"If you won't answer my question of why David died, can you at least tell me why he joined?"

"You're the first to ask that. I put up with no end of innuendo about why people leave and perhaps what they do afterwards, but no-one ever gives me credit for why people join."

"So his joining wasn't a result of some *random* meeting on a train?"

"Well yes. There was nothing *co-incidental* that led to him joining LastGaspStore, just like the rest of my employees. You included, but you'd worked that out obviously."

Devlin shrugged, a little wary of the fact that he'd needed Whitely's assistance to understand even that detail. Looking back it was probably blatantly obvious, but at the time he was so prepared to accept that an opportunity would have to appear from out of the blue that when it actually came, he didn't question it.

"I extended the opportunity to David, just as to you, for largely the same reason. He wanted to reclaim his life, just like you."

"So where does Malcolm fit in then?"

"He doesn't."

"Others disagree."

"Others are wrong. I'm trying to show you something."

"So this *is* about Malcolm?"

"No," Glen replied, sloshing the last of his coffee in his cup before pushing it aside. "When I told you about Malcolm, Sampson, I said we had a parting of ways. But in reality I do keep loose tabs on what he's doing."

"So what are we doing here then, right now?"

"We could be here for the coffee, but clearly that's a lie. Or we could be here, now, because at *this* time, in *this* place, because this is the single best place to understand."

"You think a little Devlin. I sense you are close."

Devlin did not have the heart to quash Glen's confidence. He felt no closer to any epiphany. Minutes passed while he retraced his thoughts, hoping that perhaps he might identify something that he'd missed the last time, but nothing revealed itself. He tried something else. "So who was that guy?"

"What guy?" Glen replied teasingly.

"The guy who made you all sit up and take notice, and then when he left you all had a group hug.

"He's no-one particularly special. You'll read about him, or those like him, every day."

"In the papers or at LastGasp'?"

"Both."

"So what protocol would apply to him then?" Devlin asked. "Would I know him from a LastGasp' message?"

"All of the bastard protocols have applied to him at some time."

"So you knew and you did nothing?"

"Not at all. We're here aren't we."

"Based on what you said the other day about that woman at the café getting dragged into the taxi, I wouldn't have thought that would be enough."

"When *you* lie in bed at night, *you* can contemplate whether this is enough."

"Does that mean that you sleep well at night?"

"Not particularly, but that doesn't mean that *you* can't, Devlin."

"And Malcolm? Does he make it harder or easier to have a clear conscience?"

"He does. For me. And he should for you too."

"So Malcolm does your dirty work?" Devlin asked without any confidence. "His abstraction protects LastGasp', I guess."

"Malcolm's hands are clean. He's just an observer."

Devlin picked up on a similarity with what the Detective had said before he left. "So does this mean that Malcolm is an *active observer?*"

Glen only smiled.

"So why didn't he help Angie then?"

"He did, or he will."

"You know she accused me of attacking her."

"She'll get over it, just give her time. I'm sure Malcolm put in a good word for you." Glen tried his best to sound reassuring.

"But who is she?"

"Angie? She's just some victim that Malcolm found. They're everywhere if you care to look."

"And you're not going to do anything to help her?"

"Her life is about to significantly improve. Chances are I'll offer her job and give her the same opportunity that I gave you."

Devlin thought a little, content that he'd scored a minor victory. "So what about Tania?"

"Alright. Based on what you know, are you likely to be more compassionate for the Detective or Tania, or Whitely for that matter?"

"If I had to choose, I'd say the Detective, though it's a line call with Whitely."

"You've read Tania's history. You don't think that she's been through enough?" Glen allowed Devlin a little time to think.

"But did she deserve all she's got?"

"I try to distance myself from such debate, but it's interesting that *you'd* ask that question. *You* think someone deserved to die just because of some groundless innuendo about you."

Devlin accepted the comment.

"As difficult as it may be for you to understand at the moment, you've already proven your worth for the greater good."

"What's that supposed to mean?" Devlin asked aggressively, but his mood was immediately subdued by his own thought process. In particular, he dwelled on what he'd learnt in the research interface.

Glen continued only after he saw some acceptance on Devlin's face. "You should be able to raise your head high for your part."

"But what I read in the research interface told me ..."

"The greater good is not all about you, Devlin. That's why we're here, so you understand that much."

"So why did we need to come here?"

"If you hadn't come here you might never have understood the greater good.

"I still don't."

"Think about it," said Glen. "One thing you should now know from the messages is that bad people exist, possibly hidden under a thin veneer of good, just as good people can exist largely hidden by what others choose to see. Far be it for me to suggest that there is good in everyone, but everyone can contribute to a greater good."

Devlin searched for the poignancy in what Glen was saying. "I don't see how this affects me."

"I just want you to see what Malcolm is doing."

"If Malcolm is doing anything then maybe LastGasp' isn't as secure as you think."

"How do you think that may be then?"

"Alright. I figure Albert gets told stuff, maybe everything, by your readers when they need a little headspace. Doesn't that constitute a leak?"

"Albert is indirectly harmless. He's only interested in finding Malcolm, which isn't a concern. If you look into their common history you'll work that much out for yourself without any effort at all."

"The fire?"

Glen shook his head. "Malcolm, Sam, taught me a lot, but to do so, he needed to make a point. I would have preferred that he did this differently, but that isn't what happened. Albert is concerned that *his* legacy might have been compromised, just like most people would do, if they were at all aware. For this, he's desperate to find Malcolm.

"It's unfortunate, but Malcolm's actions represented a significant change for LastGaspStore. He forced a serious system rethink."

"What about the use of laptops in the bunker? Surely one could be taken out of the building and in the right hands *something* could be gleaned from it."

"You're assuming that others want what is in LastGaspStore. I thought you'd understand by now that it's not about what's *in* LastGaspStore, but rather what comes *from* LastGaspStore."

"If LastGasp' is secure then surely they are one and the same thing."

"So did I," Glen said morosely. "Getting at a single machine wouldn't help anyone because the real power is not in the premature release of secrets, but rather in what secrets dead men, people, tell."

"The difference being what exactly?"

"You can't challenge a dead man," said Glen. "Do you ever wonder what the guy you killed might have said in a LastGaspStore message, if in fact he was a member?"

"No. What?"

"I have no idea. The point is that he could have said anything, about anyone."

"So?"

"So, what he said is out there. It can't be withdrawn or retracted. Even more important than that is that it can't be refuted or challenged. Libel and slander don't apply and there's no going back. Think about what can happen when such a message is received."

Devlin did as Glen had suggested. Would his life have been different if the guy's message, if there was one, had said something in his defence? What if such a message had existed but never been brought to public attention, particularly to the attention of either the police or the media? The thought was both inviting and angering. Devlin then had another thought; that the corollary was also true. What if such a message had implicated him? Devlin felt a rising gulp of bile, this time not caused by the coffee.

Sensing a degree of realisation in the expression on Devlin's face, Glen continued. "The trouble is that things stay said. Sam worked it out, and I didn't believe him until I saw it for myself. No protocol could help and no algorithm I could envisage could prevent it. For all my vision I'd inadvertently created a tool of social engineering. Real people armed with untruths and devoid of any recourse could change the world.

"Your situation, what happened to you, was a classic example. If you can be comfortable that the family of the guy you killed is better off for what you did, then that's a good thing. That he wasn't who you thought he was is not important."

"But why? Why me?"

"I can't say for your case. I never claimed to have all the answers. That your family, your father in particular, shared in your fall is possibly significant. I can't say.

"My penance for what I created is to try to make amends, as much as possible, where I could see obvious abuses of the truth. It was the least I could do to try to show people, like yourself, why.

"When I realised what Sam did I closed that particular avenue for abuse and prevented anyone from creating a message on behalf of someone else."

"So what's Malcolm, or whatever his name is, doing now?"

"Nothing as far as LastGaspStore is concerned," said Glen smiling subtly. "What's more, on account of the system privacy and security I can't even be sure if he's a member."

"Does that mean that you feed him information on the sly?"

"He's not getting anything from me."

"But the protocols? Who gets the information?"

"An incessant reminder of the scope of my creation, nothing more. I certainly don't do anything with them anymore, though they do serve to focus the attention of my readers."

"So why still have them?"

"That would raise more questions. It's better that I just keep up the façade."

"So how do you explain what Malcolm knows? If he's not getting it from you, then how would Malcolm know about Angie, or me for that matter?"

"Malcolm sees what you see, reads what you read and hears what you hear. Admittedly not at LastGaspStore, but that's irrelevant. He just knows where to look and he's alert to it. Who he helps is purely the domain of his own conscience."

"So why are we here now?"

"The fact that we are here right now is only to show you that social change can be engineered by good people, not just bad people. And that bad people can do their part."

"For the greater good?"

"Indeed," said Glen. "For the greater good."

Devlin was unconvinced, but quiet.

Chapter - 88.

On return to Glen's car, Devlin finally felt an inclination to ask more questions. He'd been content to walk silently beside Glen the entire walk from the café, just as Glen had appeared satisfied that he'd explained enough to render Devlin silent. He finally felt that he understood enough of LastGasp', and possibly even of Malcolm to put his mind to rest. Tania however, remained, like an extra piece left over after completing a jigsaw. "How well did Malcolm know Whitely?"

"Well enough."

"And Malcolm knows Tania?"

"Not that I know of. Certainly not in the biblical sense, but he knows about her."

"None of this explains David's involvement in the death of Tania's brother."

"I didn't think that was a particular concern of yours. If it's any consolation, Tim, Tania's brother, was killed by the very person who the police identified. Case closed. That much has nothing to do with David."

"But why?"

"Who's to say. Tim happened to be in the right place at the right time with a mentally unstable, paranoid schizophrenic."

Glen's choice of words caught Devlin's attention. "Not wrong place and wrong time?"

"The greater good, Devlin. Perhaps you should ask that question of Whitely when next you see him."

"Is it worth asking how Tim came to be in this right place at the right time then?"

"That might be a question for Malcolm. When next you meet with him you might want to ask how he's doing it."

"So what is it about Malcolm?"

"You have to understand that until Malcolm, I'd seen my vision corrupted despite good intentions. I never meant it to be a tool for others to settle a score without retribution, be that for personal, professional or even cultural gain. My solution of having Readers largely backfired, and who am I to have the final say as to whether a message gets sent.

"For all my corrupted legacy, Malcolm helped me see that there could be an upside. He wasn't like other readers. There was nothing in it for him then, just as now."

"I still don't understand what he's doing," Devlin said.

"I hope you learned in the messages that there are good and bad people. I was focused on serving the good and denying the bad, while Malcolm is effectively serving the good by using the bad."

"So you let it happen?"

"If Malcolm wants to help align those in need with those wanting to provide, is that so wrong?"

"But the guy in the café. That was the guy from the Research Interface and Angie's LastGasp' message."

Glen smiled. "He's just someone that Malcolm, Sam, knows. They met long before he met Angie."

"But why? Why him? Why don't you just let the authorities know about him?"

"What's to tell," Glen explained. "There's nothing that couldn't be known by anyone who wanted to learn for themselves. You yourself marvelled that he wasn't in jail. Interpret that as you will, but maybe they don't want him touched. In the meantime, Malcolm's clearly got him working for a greater good."

"And me. What about where I fit into this?"

"If it makes you feel any better, the world is better off without the man you killed. I know that in my heart, but whether you or anyone else sees it is irrelevant." Glen sighed, mindful he had Devlin's full attention. "As sad as it is, Devlin, you are inconsequential. Your demise served a greater good, so get over it. Think bigger, move on and don't waste your life. It's not just the bad people who can do something positive for others."

Devlin returned a smile for his understanding of the greater good. "Thank-you."

For the first time, Glen did not reject Devlin's appreciation.

Chapter - 89.

Tania was not in a door answering mood. She was feeling the familiar twangs of post binge regret, and the last thing she wanted was to have to interact with people. Instead, she would have preferred to have continued her internal struggle until she found familiar middle ground somewhere between anger and disinterest. Anger at the mess that was her life, and disinterest that she was so far beyond caring that if confronted she'd just as soon as say that she didn't give a shit. By chance, in the pendulum of emotions, she was swinging very much towards hate fuelled anger when the doorbell rang, but a moment on either side and she might well have been suicidal or contemplating another trip to the bar, any bar.

She knew it was sure to be her new landlord. Her brave call to just blow off his scheduled visit yesterday only delayed the inevitable, and his phone call this morning was not the best way to start an otherwise bad day. At least he wasn't so much angry for his wasted visit, but only disappointed that their meeting had been delayed. That would have been a bad way to start their relationship. He sounded nice enough on the phone, foreign of course, but that he also knew 'Cat' helped break the ice. She braced herself for the need to impress him and be polite, but that couldn't suppress her immediate need to vent her frustration.

She headed for the door, still cursing a list of people under her breath. Her oblivious father, her well-intentioned but naïve brother, her past employers, the larger of her suitors from last night. This. All of this. Her life was not her fault. Perhaps this was the 'rock bottom' that her brother had encouraged her to embrace, the upside being that her life would surely improve from here.

*   *   *

Nebojsa always enjoyed meeting new people when not at work; it was like foreplay. It was fun, and with it would come the anticipation of what would follow and what he would learn about himself.

The woman answered the door and he recognised her immediately, even if it was clearly not reciprocated. The 'pijan'. Others might consider this priceless, but Nebojsa was confident that he'd find the right value.

She was fired up and angry, and he could sense it even through the security screen. He liked that. He was expected obviously, but still he liked that she would open the door willingly, already mindful that she couldn't deny him. Nebojsa liked that too. This one had a fire that even Angie had taken a lot of encouragement to share.

The landlord's inspection was a formality and for the most part, he took it for the ruse that it really was. The legitimacy of the meeting was intoxicating. It was probably important for her too, but he didn't care. He decided to call her 'Seed'. This was the start of a relationship for sure.

He asked to see the bedroom. He asked once.

The End.

ABOUT THE AUTHOR

Garrett is a forty something Australian novelist, and also a geek, husband, father, cub scout leader and struggling marathon runner. He grew up in Perth, Western Australia, and has been lucky enough to live in or visit most of Australia and much of the world. He now lives in Melbourne with his family. Not averse to change, thus far, he has been an Army officer, software consultant and author. But this is just the beginning. 'Minions' is his first novel.

BY THE SAME AUTHOR

The Traveller.

Enter the world of an unnamed family man struggling in his pursuit of a work/life balance. Too much travel at the whims of his tyrannical boss, known variously as Stalin and 'the Anti-Christ', has left him failing at work and at home, but after his wife prophetically warns that his next trip will be different, he is suddenly a world apart from his usual self. Confident, capable and unafraid of his manager, opportunities abound as he embraces his altered state away from home.

What begins as a quest to reclaim his career and satisfy his ego and soon descends into the pursuit for revenge on his boss. With nothing but success in his wake and seemingly limitless potential at his disposal, it's only fitting when he is coerced to work with his nemesis in a remote corner of the world. It's more than just a chance to get even after years of abuse, more than the opportunity for a confrontation; a final solution to what he sees as the bane of his life is on offer. What could possibly go wrong when he's in his prime? Succeed or fail, either way this trip will be the making of him or the end of him.

Sometimes to get the measure of your life you just need a break from being yourself... because nothing lasts forever.

Garrett Addison